CAROLE ENAHORO

DOING DANGEROUSLY WELL

RANDOM HOUSE CANADA

 Published in 2010 by Random House Canada, a division of Random House of Canada Limited, Toronto. Distributed in Canada by Random House of Canada Limited.

www.randomhouse.ca

This book is a work of fiction. Names, characters, places and incidents either are the product of the author's imagination or are used fictitiously. Any resemblance to actual persons, living or dead, events or locales is entirely coincidental.

Library and Archives Canada Cataloguing in Publication

Enahoro, Carole
Doing dangerously well / Carole Enahoro.

ISBN 978-0-307-35690-1

I. Title.

PS8609.N33D64 2010   C813'.6   C2009-905233-4

Design by CS Richardson

Printed in the United States of America

2 4 6 8 9 7 5 3 1

To the memory of Arthur Campeau, environmentalist
Finally at peace
And doing dangerously well

Prologue

Kainji Dam was the pride of Nigeria in the 1960s, one of the largest dams in Africa, providing electricity to the richest, most powerful black nation on the continent. From miles around, from cities nationwide, people would make the pilgrimage to the dam to bear witness to man's power. And greeting them would be a monumental structure of forbidding concrete, its arms spanning the entire Niger River, pushing back that which nature intended to flow on and inspiring awe in all who beheld it. It was worshipped for its power and providence: not as mistress of humanity but rather as its handmaiden.

The dam was more powerful than the mighty river goddess, Osun. It held her in its shackles, even though it was built of the very materials it was constructed to contain: mere sand and water.

Over time, however, the dam began to deteriorate. Its firm sluices started to silt up with the precious red earth of the land.

Small cracks appeared in its facade, but no one was willing to buy the powder to hide its wrinkles. There was little reason. Younger and more beautiful dams had been built, and its courtiers–the government, the World Bank, the IMF–turned away, neglecting a goddess whose jealousy grew by the hour. Some knew of its growing infirmity, as it had already failed to protect villages downstream during heavy rains, though few would whisper of such things. Certainly those who could help were not willing to let nature's whim rule over profits.

The day Kainji Dam vented the full force of its fury was a day that will be remembered for centuries to come. The lesson of neglect, greed and nature's wrath would take longer to learn.

ONE

Kainji Dam

Striding like a panther, but with greater self-assurance, Amos parted the crowds at the market in Ndadu. His threads were making visual contact with the General Public and, not surprisingly, jaws dropped, flies entered. It is true that the GeePee had seen his sort before–local boys who had made good in Lagos or Port Harcourt–but Amos had added a lemon twist of *indiv* to the mango juice. From his snakeskin boots to his sheepskin jacket, all was as it should be.

Yes. I'm looking fine. Continue to check. No payment necessary, he thought, with a grin that made his toothpick stand out the more.

Blustering gusts of wind that heralded the season of sandstorms only added to the drama. His bell-bottoms (or "Keep Nigeria Cleans" as his friends called them) flapped at his ankles while his jacket ballooned behind him to create a framing effect that pleased him greatly. As boards banged around him and tin roofs rattled, he fought against the blasting currents of torrid air, head down. Yes, the wind was strong, the air stifling, but what breeze could stop a proper whappasnippa from broadcasting his whereabouts?

He had rolled up his left sleeve to display a watch the size of a coconut, with dials informing everyone of the time in Lagos, London and Lima.

As every Nigerian knows, sunglasses maketh the man, and variety was not the spice; uniquatiousness was. Amos was well satisfied that no pilot on earth would be able to find shades like his own. At the top they were mirrored; at the bottom they were almost transparent. In the middle the mirrors formed droplets, while the transparent parts looked like waves. Yet, as shades, they performed their duty. No squinting was necessary. The wearer could walk down the street with pupils the size of cocoa beans and still never blink. Try as you might, there was no street in Lagos that could sell you this one particular pair.

This was Amos's week off from a dry job in cellphone sales in the big city, so he had decided to surprise his parents with a visit. He had taken the bus north (motto scrawled across its windscreen: "We Are In God's Hands"). Where strictly necessary, the bus veered onto the wrong side of the two-way highway until the route became clear enough to swerve back onto the right side. As for oncoming traffic, who would be idiot enough to drive into a fully laden bus?

After his arrival, Amos headed towards the food stalls with two large, empty flour bags to help with his load.

"Yepa! Amos!" Amos heard a thunderous roar to his left as he jumped across an open drain. "Am I seeing correctly? Amosquito! Ah-ah!" He turned towards the source of the commotion. Momentarily distracted, he bumped into a crowd of haggling women, who pushed him away towards the drain.

"Yes–walking like a Titan!" Straining to see over the tops of people's heads, he spotted Gambo, a boyhood friend. "Why are you limping?" Gambo shouted over the heads of a group of men. "What is the matter with your leg? Has it grown shorter? Amos with your Lagos Limp!"

"Gambo!" Amos yelled, shoving aside knots of shoppers to reach his friend. "Gambo–still walking as if a snake is in your trouser! Long time! How body-now?"

He elbowed a man refusing to move and sidestepped the rubbish, threw down his shopping bags and hugged Gambo ferociously. They exchanged an intricate handshake of five distinct phases, ending in a snapping of each other's fingers.

"Amos! Worraps? We no see your brake light for long-long time. How your parents? Ah-ah! Look how your trouser rhyme your shirt. Don't jealous me-oh!" He looked at Amos's sunglasses with approval. "Everywhere tinted!"

Amos opened his mouth but was suddenly shoved sideways by the brute force of a market woman.

"Oga, sir! Oranges. I beg-oh! Oranges. Come and see my oranges."

He was turning to look at the future victim of his tongue-whipping when he was body-slammed from behind and a voice piercing the very drum of his ear screamed, "Eh? You are taking my customer? He was standing here! Oga, please take a look at theses fruits. Look at my oranges here. I have melon, banana, grapefruit–"

"Please, sir . . ." The first woman took Amos by his arm, yanked him sideways and dislodged his beret.

"Ah-ah!" Amos exploded. "Am I dreaming?" He stared at the two women. "Have I fallen asleep? Did you just touch my hat? Gambo, I beg-oh, wake me up. Is this my own hat that she touched?"

"Who . . . who . . ." An enraged Gambo kissed his teeth, hardly able to form his words. "Who are you touching? Is this man a customer? Is he not a customer?"

As could only be expected, other women joined the altercation, expressing the fierce contempt granted to all those who had travelled far from home.

"Who is this Been To?"

"Who is causing this wahala? Eh–do you think this is Lagos?"

"I am trying–" Amos exploded.

He immediately checked himself, noting Mama Tela's bulk heading his way. "I am trying . . ." Amos talked slowly and calmly. "I am trying . . ." As more women gathered, he realized the rabble could kill them both like cockroaches. He lowered his voice further still. "I am trying to buy some food, ONLY I cannot buy anything if I am squeezed into paw-paw juice before–"

"It's Amos. Amos Jegede!" Mama Tela announced.

"Amos? Is that you? What is the matter with you? What are you wearing? Ah-ah. Is it not hot enough?" The market women broke into hysterical laughter.

"Amos! Always different. Separate-Amos! What are you wearing on your head?"

"Mama Tela!" one of the women shrieked. "Let me bring scarf and gloves. Amos is catching a cold!"

"I beg, bring some Vicks VapoRub as well!" another screeched.

"So–you are back, Amos?" Mama Tela called, walking towards the knot of market people. "I can hardly recognize you. Where did you get these fine shades?"

"That's a trade secret. Go and find out the recipe for Coca-Cola, then come and ask me where I get my shades," Amos replied, not impressed at all. "So, Mama Tela, I just came to buy food and water for my parents. I don't need more wahala–just give me a good price."

With Gambo at his side, Amos fought his way to Mama Tela's stall, where he was able, through much commotion, to buy fruit, vegetables and twelve bottles of water. He haggled over the water for a good ten minutes, yet it still cost him the equivalent of two weeks' wages, although it was locally produced–tapped from the regional aquifer by a national conglomerate owned by the minister for natural resources, Chief Ogbe Kolo.

His parents would cherish this gift, placing the bottles in a display cabinet under lock and key, dusting them off regularly and offering the water to only the most honoured guests. Other visitors would receive ordinary brown tap water, boiled for fifteen minutes and filtered twice to rid it of some of its impurities.

Mama Tela carefully wrapped the bottles, then Amos, accompanied by Gambo, walked towards the small house occupied by his parents, flour sacks slung over his back.

The red earth, parched and fine, fringed the bottom of his trousers. As Amos struggled on against a shearing wind, the sun beat down upon him, its throb playing time with his pulse. The scorching air seared into his lungs, its steam offering no relief from the heat. He could hardly breathe. He panted as he laboured upwards towards the house, struggling to keep a foothold on the path. The wind tried to push him back, force him away, using its full might to block his onward journey.

Amos, chatting and complaining to Gambo, turned past an outbreak of dying bougainvillea towards a boulevard of umbrella trees, trunks painted white.

Then it hit him. A smell, an overpowering stench, a punchy stew of putrid gases that almost knocked him to the ground. Amos's eyes watered as he tried to suck in breath. He choked. He tried again. He could feel no oxygen. He began to panic.

"Breathe through your mouth-oh!" warned Gambo. "You can't breathe through your nose here."

Amos opened his mouth to breathe, but not willingly. It did not seem an adequate enough filter to shield him from the noxious fumes.

"What is that smell now?" asked Amos. "Gambo! Wetin? What has happened to the creek?" Amos gasped as he looked at the bed of clay, in which lay a thick black gunge. Fetid refuse, raw sewage, foul chemicals, all humanity's waste and business's excess, pooled into a narrow river that had been drained to almost a trickle.

"No water," Gambo replied. "The IMF will not authorize any loan to Nigeria until we pay for water. All the rights have been sold."

"Sold? To who?" Amos kept staring at the riverbed.

"Sold to Kolo's companies, of course."

"What does he want with our water? How are we to bathe or drink? Even, how are we to plant seeds or fish?"

"You didn't get gist about the sale?"

"Lagos rumour. Village complaints. Dry season. I thought that was all. Can any man believe a sight like this?"

Amos looked from the river to Gambo and then back to the river, as if refreshing his view might take away the terrible sight. Its banks were parched and cracked, littered with plastic bags, rusted mufflers and excrement. This place of idyll, where Amos and his brother, Femi, would scramble and giggle, jumping off ropes or tires tied to trees, somersaulting and water-bombing into the cool, playful water. This place of history and ancestry, where the local priests would hold rituals and ceremonies in honour of the spirits; this place of worship, where the evangelical churches would baptise their fervent newcomers; this place of passage and fruit, where boats and fishermen could ply their trade, was now nothing but a stinking vessel, witness to man's defiance of nature and the basest evidence of his existence.

"Anyway," Gambo cut into his reveries, "we have to pay."

"Pay for what? Pay for water? Pay for our own water? For a loan? Yaaay! That President Mu'azu."

"No, not the president. Kolo! White Mercedes-Benz himself. He told that idiot president that Nigeria needs another World Bank loan. Then the IMF said we have to pay for our own water as part of its restructure this and redevelopment that before we can get any loan or grant. While the president is talking to the World Bank, Kolo is already running to write up the contracts so his companies can receive the financing, buy our water and then sell it back to us."

Amos was flabberwhelmed. "So Kolo is going to the World Bank for extra aid to buy water that we already have? Doesn't that man already have enough money? How much can one man want?"

"Kolo?" Gambo cut in. "Greed can never quench for that man. He will just institute another National Frugality Year. Do you think he's going to reach into his own pocket to finance his own ventures? His hand couldn't even find his pocket. His hand has never seen the inside of that place. Never! He's just living with his nice helicopter pad, wearing his gold agbada, driving his white Mercedes-Benz and his this and that."

"Can you imagine?" Amos raised his voice a few notches. "The World Bank. Can you see how the World Bank's hands will shake when they write the cheque to 'Government of Nigeria'? They know they will never see the money again. They know it!"

"The oga writing the cheque, he knows he will never write another cheque again in life. That is his last day at the World Bank. What can he do? Joh, nothing. He can just take his pen and go. Finish."

They walked past the river as quickly as they could.

"Don't worry." Amos's voice filled with confidence. "Femi will go to Abuja to protest." He smiled, a feeling of pride banishing his gloomy thoughts. Femi, his elder brother, could inspire confidence in the most hopeless of causes.

"He's already on seat there."

"What? About this small village?" Amos's eyes twinkled with admiration. "Is he trying to kill us all? What's the problem with him?" Fierce in defence of his idol, he waited for Gambo to contradict him.

"He won't rest until the river is flowing. Even if he has to pump it back himself," Gambo exclaimed, indignant.

"Femiiiii . . ." Amos chuckled and shook his head, smiling as he visualized the reaction of his parents. Femi the Activist. Femi, the bane of his village, who thought he had wasted his hard-won education on such fruitless quests. Although he had become one of Nigeria's most prominent activists–a legend to other humanitarians–he had wasted his legal education on protecting others, rather than enriching himself and his clan. But to Amos, Femi was the man who would meet his death throwing off his blindfold, grinning like a lion eyeing an antelope.

They made their way past palm trees to a short road, at the end of which sat a small house. Initially white, it was like all other houses in these parts, covered almost entirely in the red sand whipped up by the wind. That fine silt seemed to creep into every corner of life–inside the leaves of every book, the holes of every transistor radio and the straws of every mat.

Amos could tell his parents were in–oblivious to the heat, goats were sitting on the car, so the hood must still be warm. He opened the back gate, making sure not to grip too tightly lest the rust crumble into splinters in his hand. Passing the smell of pepper soup, he rounded the house to the front steps and shouted his welcome through the open windows. His skin prickled in excitement as he heard feet running.

As his anticipation reached its height, as the door opened, as Gambo turned to him with a smile of encouragement, as his mother's kind eyes opened wide with surprise and her lips parted to mouth the word "Amos," it happened.

First, the sound of the sky exploding, the ground quaking past its point of integrity, then, arching over them, a huge darkness. And finally, as high as the horizon of the human eye, a wall of water. Not a cleansing, sharing, pure water, but water of rage, of greed, of death.

Kainji had burst.

The water dammed up for over fifty years had exploded. It travelled, blundering at first and then with greater assurance and intent, smashing everything in its path, destroying lives within seconds. Almost half a million lives. Lives of texture and flavour, lives of promise and purpose, lives of caretakers and listeners, advice-givers and guides, scoundrels and thugs, emotional, volatile lives as well as lives of those most given to contemplation and quiet tenure. In one instant, all was gone. Amos, his parents, Gambo, Mama Tela, the market, the oranges, the village. All gone.

Waves punched through waves, the swells growing even more immense, throwing a monstrous night upon the landscape. The quaking ground exploded, flinging trees upwards like tiny twigs, leaving them spinning in the air before plunging back into the rushing currents. Houses and factories cartwheeled alongside them. Humans, too, shot up and out of the torrent, small specks spiralling in erratic arcs, and then flopped downwards like thousands of fish. Others, spared the indignity of such an end, were merely slammed into the surge, flattened and crushed. Everything in the water's path was razed.

Once the turbines burst, the country was plunged into darkness.

The river stormed right down to the Niger Delta on the coast. News of the catastrophe surged into every village, each city, through words, through images, through touch. Nigerians went into deep mourning. The boisterous fell into silence. Those who walked stopped, swaying in place as if rocking their own cradles. Hands became numb to all sensations, unable to distinguish between one object and another. Eyes lost focus and vision turned inwards to the past. Some grieved over the death of family or friends. Others wept over the loss of homes, businesses or farms.

There were others, however, hidden like the sand in the darkest corners and crevices of Nigerian society, who felt not only grief but passion.

Loss can always be transformed into profit for those able to envision reconstruction. Indeed, the greater the calamity, the more seductive the prospects. Old arrangements are washed away and new opportunities surface. To direct the flow of such blessings, it takes not only a thirst for acquisitions but a certain gift for deal-making. And in areas of contract and negotiation, Chief Ogbe Kolo, minister for natural resources, was not just a master craftsman; he was the pre-eminent artist of Africa's greatest nation.

TWO

The Qualitative Guy

Unaware of Kainji's struggle to hold back the waters of the Niger, a group of concerned activists from around the country congregated in Abuja, the titular capital of Nigeria. This important but isolated hub had been placed in the alleged wilderness of the country's geographical centre, an act that had made billionaires of many government ministers.

The group met in a crowded municipal conference room, trying to make headway with the issue of water provision in their hometowns. The heat lay heavy in the room, with one aging fan struggling to provide air for over two hundred bodies.

Femi Jegede sat in the middle of the room, listening as one person after another tried to explain to a particularly never-plussed official the absurdity of taking water and then selling it back to the communities that originally owned it. One woman, who had spoken with the sequential logic of an elementary schoolteacher, finally sat down in defeat.

Then Femi's comrade Ubaldous, a robust and brilliant lawyer, took the floor for the fourth time. His voice sounded weary from debating. "Why should taxpayers subsidize big business in order to privatize our own water? We will be making these companies richer and ourselves poorer. We will not only pay higher taxes to support this initiative, but the cost of water will triple, so who will be able to afford your precious water?"

The official, wearing shoes with the backs trodden down so that the soles of his feet could be better aired, fidgeted in his chair poised on top of a small dais. He restated his position: "Em, it costs money to make good water."

"But we cannot afford the water you're selling us!"

"Em, the government is concerned that all Nigerians can drink good water."

"Good water!" Ubaldous exploded. "How do you know it will be good water? Every disease you can think of sits in American water yet which idiot is going to try and sue a multinational?"

The official giggled. "They drink water from the tap, my friend." He shook his head, as if speaking to an imbecile.

"And where do they get E. coli from?"

The official tilted his head in bewilderment. "What kind of cola?"

Ubaldous kissed his teeth for a good ten seconds. He attempted to compose himself, then inched his argument along at a more restrained pace. "The government will drain away all we have to sell to the highest bidder–and it is guaranteed," he pointed at the official, "guaranteed that Nigeria will not be among that select group, my friend." His hands trembled as he held on to the chair in front of him, a tactic he often used to evoke sympathy in a jury.

"How can you move water from one country to another?"

The official chuckled again, nodding with mirth into his crotch.

Ubaldous's eyebrows shot into their highest position, unable to believe the man's idiocy. He stumbled onto the person seated next to him to attract the official's attention once more. His voice grew hoarse and cracked, sounding as if he had crossed a desert free of all liquid. "Water is traded already. Have you not read of environmental degradation?"

"No, no. That is global warming."

The group issued a long groan. After an hour of circular debate, they had made no progress with this coconut-for-brain official. An irate and weary Ubaldous collapsed back down onto a wooden seat.

Femi Jegede stood up, scraping his chair so loudly that all eyes rotated to him. He waited in position for a few moments for the full effect of his presence to be felt. The official's eyes turned to him and bulged. His left heel started to jiggle up and down.

Here was one of the great orators in Nigeria, who could make the ears and eyes of even his most radical opponents prick up like an antelope's. Femi possessed wit and style, backed by strong legal training, and so could make pounded yam out of the most logical argument. Added to this, his exchanges had an air of theatricality to them, his greatest prop being his ever-present agbada–a voluminous tunic that expanded his physical presence and gave weight to his authority–though certainly no item was too minor to employ.

However, more than this, he had that one gift that makes even the listless adjust their clothing in anticipation. He was a beautiful man, with skin as soft as Guinness beer and gentle, transcendent eyes. All in all, he was a very qualitative guy.

Femi started as usual, slowly, shuffling papers in his hands. "Does a man whose house is on fire worry whether his floor is clean?" His eyebrows raised in question.

The official looked at him in total and unconditional incomprehension. Femi let the effect of these words sink in and then bob up again. Silence. He waited for an answer.

"Em . . ."

Femi continued, louder this time. "If our throats are on fire, can we afford to worry about whether the water is clean?" He turned to the other delegates, astonishment on his face. He hitched his agbada onto his shoulders.

They erupted in raucous response. "Of course not!" "We would be crazy!"

After some time, the official replied, "No man can quench his thirst with poison, sir." Satisfaction was positioned on his face. He was barely heard above the din.

"Does a river flow with snake venom?" Femi roared. "Do we wash our faces with hornet poison? Are we drinking scorpion stings today? Does a river not flow with water?"

"It flows with water, of course, but this water is not clean."

"Exactly. So, if a man does pee-pee in my beer, why should I have to pay for another bottle? It is not for me to pay! Is it not for the man with the bladder of a field mouse to come and pay me?"

"You are downy-stream, my friend." The official drew out the words "downy-stream" as if no one would understand their import.

Femi slapped his papers onto his chair with irritation. "Are you a polar bear?" Femi asked suddenly.

"Pardon?"

"Are. You. A. Polar. Bear?" Femi said, enunciating each word.

"Of course not!" the official responded, perplexed once more.

"Is anyone in this room," Femi turned to face his audience, "a polar bear?"

"No!" "Of course not." "Not today, anyway." They answered in an incoherent babble.

"Well, that is a relief. I was mistaken in thinking we had a polar bear in this room. So I can assume that none of us is currently living at the North Pole, correct?"

"Correct!" they shouted.

"Thus, is it not true that we all live downstream?"

"Correct!" they screamed, applauding.

Having used his first weapons–an assault of Nigerian proverbs–he made his way towards the realm of legal jargon.

"Given that we have now agreed on this point," he adjusted his agbada to the left, "are you of the opinion that access to fresh water is a human right?"

His body thrust itself off his heels to emphasize the point.

"That is to say, an inalienable human right . . ."

He left a giant pause, looking around the room to observe the effect of this legalese.

"Or . . .

"that water is . . .

"simply a commodity?" These last words shot out like air expelled from a balloon. Femi had sat down by the time the last syllables had been uttered. He busily aired his agbada and crossed his arms, frowning at the municipal official.

The crowd glared at the bureaucrat, some adjusting their seating to indicate a need for greater self-control. All mouths were fanning the air in noisy accord.

With visible discomfort, the official leaned forward, closer to the microphone. It screeched. "Em. Yes, of course."

He leaned back and sat on his hands, eyes darting around the room.

A few voices from the audience shouted at him, "Of course, what?" "What are you trying to say?" "Who is this idiot?"

The official released his hands, shuffled his chair forward a bit and cleared his throat. He grasped his elbows and bent towards the microphone once more. "Em. We are all aware of the government's position."

Femi shot up again, hiking his agbada back on his shoulders. The room fell silent. "May I beg to differ, honourable sir."

Femi stepped back in a bow.

The official seemed puzzled, but relief quickly washed over his face–this bow, a symbol of respect, could mean only one thing. He smiled at Femi.

"Thank you very much," he interjected, unknowingly. "And I, on my side, also agree to differ."

The room looked at the helpless official in silence. Jaws dropped. Flies entered. This man was so incompetent, so idiotic, he must be a government minister's son.

Femi prepared to sweep away this last speck of dust. "It seems we have reached a juncture of the highest consequence. In conclusion, for the record, let me restate the government's position." He cleared his throat. "The government agrees, according to your good self," another bow, "that access to fresh water is an inalienable human right and is pathologically consolidated," his finger stabbing the air, "in its position against water privatization, while, on our side, we claim," hands circling back, "that water should be provided for free and not bought and sold like Coca-Cola. Is that the point we have now reached, in so many words?"

"Em, correct. In very many words," said the official.

Femi paused to regroup, then continued. "It is sad to see that we can come no closer than that in our debate." A note of defeat. "Are you of the highest certitude," he thundered, "that you are unwilling to move from the statement I have just provided?"

"I am afraid the government cannot and will not move from that position."

"Am I correct in stating that the government stands irrevocably and immutably in its position and we, on our side, support our own contention?"

"Em, you are correct."

"Are there no other arguments we can bring to bear on this matter of serious national import?"

"You have brought many debates to this meeting, but no one can be swimming against the tide of change and live to tell the tale."

Femi shook his head with a look of shrivelling dismay worthy of the most austere schoolmaster at his moment of greatest shock. "My friend," he breathed in a soft voice that the back row had no trouble hearing, "a lion can eat a man, but can't a mosquito bite a lion?" He raised his eyebrows in enquiry.

The official twitched in discomfort.

Femi shook his head sadly and sat down again, while journalists quickly tapped at their laptops at the front of the room. The official looked at the fan, knowing that the mosquito/lion/man cluster had a point of weakness that, for the moment, eluded him.

The room tingled with victory.

The great man, the human colossus, who held wisdom, craft and, most importantly, the full breadth of the English language at his fingertips, had achieved a critical victory in the debate. Within the click of one Send button, news of the government's new position against the purchase of water would be received by stations as far as clocks tell time.

The assembly gathered up their belongings. Femi avoided all eyes in the room, and the crowd knew that any tittering would alert the official to his blunder. The next meeting would now have to be with a more senior official, perhaps even Chief Ogbe Kolo, minister for natural resources.

As Femi walked out, the creaking fan slowly stopped. The room tutted. Electricity was so erratic, the only constant was that blackouts were the norm.

"Ah-ah. Light done quench."

The back door opened and a man quickly scuttled to the official's side. They scurried out together, but not before Femi noted the terror now written over the face of the official.

As the crowd bustled out of the hall and into the courtyard, Ubaldous called to Femi, "And?"

"Aaah! Ubiquitous Ubaldous!"

"Femi, you were vibrating today-oh!" Ubaldous smiled. "Why use shorter words when longer ones can provide better climate control? The poor official. He was too cold-oh! When you were blowing your rhetoric, he was sitting on his own hands!"

"Me? And your own good self, nko? Were your own lips not fanning the air? Did they hire you as an air conditioner?"

"Potato in ear," replied Ubaldous. "I can't hear you, my friend. Isn't your own tongue tired? Can you swallow food today?"

"I was just warming up. Bring me a pot of egusi and I'll show you if I can swallow. If you don't have egusi, just bring your potato."

Both men chuckled.

"Well, I must blow. Will you branch by the office later?" Ubaldous shouted as he passed the gate.

Femi's eyes filled with pretend confusion. "Em, correct."

The two men exploded into laughter.

"Please keep the air conditioner on." Femi, turning to head out into the street, threw his head back in another eruption of laughter. As he came up for air, he heard a piercing scream from far away. The assembly stopped. Two people with tears streaming down their faces came running up to a woman.

They spoke urgently to her. She listened and pushed out "No!" in a loud hush. They gave her more information. She put her hands over her ears, looked up to the sky and screamed. Her friends tried to pull her arms back down, but she was rigidly in position, save for a trembling of all her limbs.

As the crowd watched in bewilderment, another scream pierced the air. Then another.

"Na waa oh! What is the matter? Wetin?" Femi asked.

Someone tapped him on the shoulder. He swivelled around to see his beloved companion, Igwe, looking at him. His eyes were hidden behind his large brown glasses, but the horror in them was unmistakable. His thin frame, usually so lively, appeared to be weighed down by some unknown trouble. "Please," he said to Femi. "Come home now. There is some news."

Femi looked at Igwe, frightened and puzzled. He had often seen in his partner's eyes a flash of alarm, a stiffening of the body. It was his habit. Yet this time his body was charged with an insistence and foreboding Femi had never before seen.

Igwe took Femi's arm and pulled him away, struggling to talk. "A tragedy. Terrible tra–"

As they rushed through the streets, they heard more screams. They saw one woman running without her wrapper, frantic as if she were on fire, followed by friends trying to grab her.

"Kainji!" Igwe gasped for air. "It's Kainji!"

"Enh?"

Igwe ran faster, struggling to catch two motorbike taxis while the frenzy in the streets grew. As they hopped onto the bikes, Femi hunted for clues, searching Abuja's sterile boulevards and forbidding concrete for hints of trouble. The quiet avenues, planned before the city had even been inhabited, had become chaotic. Cars moved in all directions, at erratic speeds, their drivers frantic.

Femi tried to push away troubling thoughts. Giant trees with flame-coloured flowers shimmered in the region's tender heat. Blood canna lilies, towering over the heads of men, swayed in the gentle breezes. Even the elephant ears, with their emerald leaves, waggled in the sun.

When they arrived at a dilapidated apartment building, Igwe tugged him upstairs.

"Amos's cell." Igwe's disjointed utterances continued. "No answer."

"It's okay. He went to the village."

Igwe's sandal slapped a concrete step as he stumbled. "No!" This hushed sound, voiced almost as a question, was followed by short vowels as if he was trying to build a sentence for which no words existed.

He pushed Femi into the darkened room they shared. A low, unbroken wail–a thin echo, carried from an upper floor, that laced through the building–unsettled Femi.

Without waiting for the question, Igwe said, "Kainji Dam has burst."

Femi slammed his papers on the desk. "Did I not tell you that a catastrophe of this enormity would befall our people?"

"Femi, I beg . . ." Igwe looked down, pushing his glasses back to the bridge of his nose.

"Does the government care about the plight of the people?" Femi came closer to Igwe's face. "No one listens in this country unless the business community has been affected, and then," he leaned over Igwe's small frame, "oh, then suddenly everyone's ears become ultrasonic like a bat's."

"Light don go for the whole country," Igwe said meekly.

Femi stared at him, for once unable to utter a word. Finally he said, "So the whole dam has burst?"

"Yes." Igwe started to weep.

Femi lurched forward, threw his arms around him and cradled him. "Which villages has it hit? Have people been killed?"

"All the villages downstream have been wiped out. Ndadu has been wiped out. From Kainji past Jebba, it's all gone." Igwe started to sob and put a hand on Femi's shoulder. "I'm so sorry-oh! Your family is gone."

"Ndadu?" Femi sprang up again and stared at him. "That can't be. It's nowhere near Kainji. Where did you get this . . ." He started to shout. "Why can't we Nigerians provide accurate information? Ah-ah! Everything in this ridiculous place is rumour and gossip!"

"Hundreds of thousands have been killed. The government has declared a state of emergency."

"The government is always declaring . . . pardon?"

"Half a million killed."

"Igwe, you are my friend-oh! Why are you telling me this?" An image of the latest fashions in Congo clothing punched into Femi's mind. Amos!

Igwe held his head in his hands, helpless. Femi stood staring at Igwe's limp body, a toy doll folded over itself. Slowly, very slowly, tears started to well in Femi's eyes. He pressed his thumb and forefinger to them, pushing the sockets to keep the tears at bay, pushing to force pain into his body, pushing to keep the information away. It was becoming increasingly difficult for him to avoid the truth. Screams were piercing the streets around them.

Femi slowly moved his hands down to Igwe's head, pulling his face to him, cradling the back of his head. He pushed his cheek onto his companion's face, burying his nose into the crook of Igwe's neck, eyes screwing into fierce knots. He cried, small choking sounds. His tears ran down his friend's neck, pooling on his shirt at the shoulder. One arm moved around

Igwe's back, pulling him closer and closer, gripping furiously. His arms clasped tighter, drawing his friend in even more, as if hanging on to history, onto a present now denied him. He snatched at visions of Amos lost in a permanent childhood, unable to reclaim images of him as an adult. Femi started to tremble, his whole body convulsing with a quiet violence. His thoughts raced to his beloved parents, to the grandfather who had hidden kola nuts for him, to the grandmother who had sung to him about his ancestors as he lay in her lap. He could no longer control his weeping.

THREE

Turkey with Stuffing

On the outskirts of the world's most powerful political centre sat a large house with fake porticos and a strong sweep of crescent driveway cutting through the front garden. Protected by wealth and fortified by social superiority, the house rigorously deflected the onslaught of chaos that nature tried to impose. Two or three large trees stood to verify the legitimacy of old tenure, while bearing silent testament to the neighbourhood's mastery over Creation. Alexandria, Virginia, was bedded in verdant grass, shorn with legally specified precision. Its November leaves–now dismantled for winter and classified as "yard waste"–had been swept up and carted away for compost.

Within the house, an overburdened taxpayer flipped through his newspaper and glanced at an item hidden on the seventh page. His outline was that of a bulrush: thin, with a pale stem and greying brown hair frizzing at the top. Hair also protruded from his ears and nose, but most startlingly from his eyebrows, almost as a visor.

He scanned the item and smiled to himself, nodding in approval. He had a special interest in dams, having had the privilege of serving as an engineer on some of the giant projects of the 1960s, most notably the Inga Dams in the Congo–his most cherished project.

"Aha!" He flicked his finger onto the newsprint in triumph. "Another of my predictions comes true."

"Ernest!" A deep boom from the kitchen, clipped tones with strong dental fricatives. "Put that down now and help me with the clearing up."

"Chalk another one up for Ernest, my dear." He licked his finger and marked an imaginary blackboard in the air, waggling his crossed leg in self-approval.

Catherine entered the drawing room, detective eyes darting back and forth, following a trail. She stopped. Then exploded: "Have you brought mud into the house?" She fell back two or three steps in shock.

"If you'd given me the weather patterns for the last five years . . ." he continued in a conversational pattern woven from forty years of married bliss.

"What the hell have you done to my carpets?" she snapped.

(A conversational pattern woven like chain mail, that is.)

" . . . I could have told you the dam would break," he pointed at her, "and the exact month and year of rupture," waving his victorious finger in a final flourish.

"Ernest! Get your feet off that table now!"

Ernest held his feet up in the air, letting them hover above the table. " . . . With a month or two of leeway, of course."

Catherine's box-shaped hands roughly unburdened her

husband of his shoes, staring at him with a depth of loathing that only intimacy allows.

"Wonder if you can bet on these things. I'd make a fortune, you know."

She rushed to the hall closet, chucked in his shoes, liberated the vacuum and handed it to Ernest. "Mary and Barbie are due today," she snapped, "and you've decided to open a greenhouse in our front room–don't respond!"

Ernest stood up and looked out the window towards the sprinklers. "Always die in droves, don't they?" he mused in his wife's general direction. "They'll no doubt harass us for foreign aid. Arrange a few pop concerts and so on. As if we don't pay high enough taxes already!" He sighed. "Still, far, far less than if we'd stayed in England." He turned to his wife for a congratulatory nod.

Catherine stood in front of him, blood collecting around her throat and chins, anger mounting.

Ernest turned on the vacuum. "Looks good for Mary's company, I must say," he reflected, as he pushed mud to the farthest corners of the carpet.

As this deeply connected pair continued their interchange, another pair of eyes alighted on this innocuous snippet of information. Unlike most reading the piece, these did not scan quickly and move on. Mary's eyes rested carefully on the words and then slowly crinkled up at the corners.

Spider fingers darted to the first memory button on her cellphone. "Hello, Janet. Sorry to disturb you. I want information on all the major players in Nigeria on my desk by Tuesday."

"But it's Thanksgiving!"

"Don't worry. They don't celebrate it. See you Tuesday. I'm available on my cell all day." She was about to hang up when she remembered a small point of etiquette. "Best wishes to your family, by the way."

Mary rang off and sat back in the limousine sailing past lunar landscapes and ragged bush on her way from Santa Fe to the airport in Albuquerque. A hairless replica of her father, Mary was all angles, points and corners, with a plumb line for a body, a mercilessly rectangular chin and a gash on her lower face that served as a mouth.

She caught a first-class flight to Washington DC. There she hopped into another limo, which coasted into Alexandria and cruised up the crescent driveway, coming to a smooth but forceful stop. She set her cellphone's ring to loud, hoping that an emergency would arise, and chucked it into her bag, almost as a basketball trick. As she walked to the front door, she inadvertently trampled the meticulous row of small, tight, fairly ugly flowers that led up to it. She checked her watch. It was 1200h. She rang the bell.

"Hello, darling!" It was her father, already slightly sloshed. "You look like an enchantress, darling, doesn't she, Mum? Do come in!"

"Thank you, Daddy. You look spectacular yourself. How's the golf? Mom, what a wonderful dress you have on. Where did you manage to buy such a thing? It matches your skin colour so wonderfully!" Mary didn't bother to listen for responses. No interest. "I've brought you presents. Hope you like them."

Her assistant had purchased and exquisitely wrapped the presents in TransAqua International's gift paper, and written and signed the cards as well.

"G and T, darling?" Father said, taking her burnished brown cashmere to hang but turning away before the coat gained any purchase on the hanger.

"Thank you, Daddy." Mary headed to rescue her coat. "So, Mom, how's the garden?"

Mary's sister, Barbara, charged into the Center for Beatific Light, which remained open on Thanksgiving Day to promote the serenity its clients required to endure family occasions. She ripped off her coat to reveal a purple leotard a couple of sizes too small and bounded into the yoga room, reared slightly and coughed. Some over-eager yogi had lit a bit too much Nag Champa–it must be Dayisha–despite her submission of a written complaint on the matter only one week ago. As she ran to the props, she threw the teacher a glance of black contempt.

Ignoring the odium emanating back at her from Dayisha's half-closed eyes, Barbara busily rifled through the yoga mats until she found her favourite purple–the colour of the spirit–and tiptoed hurriedly and loudly to the front of the class. She unfurled her mat with a flourish and lay down in corpse pose, panting like a dog.

To slow her breathing, she started taking in prana breaths, whistling through a pinched "o" for the uptake and exhaling loudly in a slow groan for the exhale. After a few seconds, she tapped the shoulder of a strange creature to her left. She could not tell whether it was male or female, nor did it seem to be of any fixed race. However, she had noticed it in class over the last few months. It always arrived early and sat in its front/centre spot.

"Could you move your mat over?" she wheezed. "I can hardly fit here."

It turned its head and opened its eyes. Barbara smiled and blinked a greeting.

"No." It closed its eyes again, rolled its head back to centre and silently linked its thumb and forefinger for added concentration.

"Well, I can't fit in," Barbara continued, displeased that the creature had ignored such a blatant overture.

"There's no room." Its eyes remained closed. "Go to the back."

"I can't see what–"

"Sshh!" the teacher interrupted. "No conversation, please. Keep focusing on your breathing."

"I can't see what she's doing unless I'm at the front," Barbara whispered.

"Go to another class, then. I'm sure they'll let you back in Beginners."

"I don't think this is terrific for your karma, you know," Barbara barked. She stared at the ridiculous object–neither male nor female–lying on its blue mat, hair twisted in the manner of a Dutch milkmaid.

"Who put you in charge of my karma?" it asked, opening yellow-green eyes and talking to the ceiling in irritation.

"You'll pay for this in your next life," she said. "You'll come back as a virus. Or maybe worse. You'll come–"

"Ssssh!" Dayisha again. "Please. Keep quiet!"

"You'll come back as yourself." She could see that life had already played the creature a cruel joke, with its female face on its stringy male body. Barbara stared at the hermaphrodite, battling with her deeply held Taoist beliefs. On the one hand, he/she/it represented a pulling together of all of nature's threads; on the other hand, the object represented the frayed edges where reason disintegrates into chaos.

Moving her mat, she opted to stay in the here and now, as one of her Buddhist gurus had so wisely instructed. Filled with vexation, Barbara pledged to enlighten the creature as to the spiritual dangers of its unreasonable behaviour.

As the other students attempted to push their thousand thoughts away from their busy minds, Barbara lay–as if entombed–with that single thought heralding her in-breath and trailing her out-breath.

Fifty minutes after her sister, Barbara arrived in a rattling and rusting hybrid, late as usual. Spotting the limo, she hid her car behind the house, where it stalled to a halt, sputtering for many moments afterwards. She stormed up the front path with a tut and veered off towards the side of the house to turn off the tap that supplied the sprinkler system, disgusted at her parents' open violation of municipal guidelines on water use. Then, shaking her head in reproach, she clinked up to the door, her Papuan trinkets clattering against her chest, and rang the bell.

She checked her reflection in the brass-plated keyhole, jabbing the antique barrettes lurking in the ink splash atop her head into new positions. She knew her appearance would cause comment of a disparaging nature. However she tried, and despite her parents' constant advocacy on behalf of the family aesthetic, she could not create "willowy." Slender, slim, even thin was good. Anorexia would have made them proud, but Rubenesque was simply unacceptable.

She looked down at her Tibetan skirt. "Of course," she muttered to herself, "patriarchal hegemony will always repress those elements that threaten the status qu . . ." She adjusted the skirt to look more slimming. "I, for one, refuse to subordinate myself to such an obvious form of tyra . . ." She reached into her bra and flattened her breasts into her armpits. " . . . nny which performs the same role in 2020 as foot binding did in whenever."

And so this robust item of seventeenth-century splendour stood staring at the door, trying to persuade herself that five hours behind it could do her little harm, as long as she said as little as possible of any depth or consequence. Her beliefs differed from her family's to such an extent that they considered her slow-witted: slightly more intelligent than a rock, but certainly less gifted than any creature that might live underneath one.

As there was still no answer, she rapped on the door.

"Ernie, tell her not to bother. We've almost finished," her mother instructed on the other side of the door.

Barbara could feel the anxiety rising in her and the blood rushing through her veins, but was able to release the tension by acknowledging it (her Gestalt therapy had been well worth the money). As a safety measure, she also popped 2 milligrams of clonazepam.

This time, she vowed to unleash all her expertise on her family–her listening skills ("What I'm hearing from you is . . ."), her conflict resolution training ("I feel x when you do y"), therapy techniques ("And what makes you think that?"; "How does that make you feel?"; etc.)–and, if all failed, she would simply remain in a deep meditative state.

"Hello, darling!" Her father finally opened the door, a beaming smile on his face. "You look like an enchantress, darling, doesn't she, Mother? Gained some weight? Do come in! What's happened to your face? Let me take your coat, sweetheart."

"Ernie!" A screaming voice. Mother was not far behind it. "In! Don't keep that door open. Barbie, darling, it's so wonderful to see . . . You seem to have put on a lot of . . . Jesus Christ! What the hell have you done to my . . ."

"Like a drink, luv? Vodka tonic, isn't it?"

"No. I'm Scotch."

"Who cares what she drinks, Ernie? Look what she's done to my flowers!"

"No, you're not!" Father added.

Barbara was already confused. "I'm not what?"

"You're not Scotch."

"Yes, I am!"

"It's never passed your lips. You're vodka."

"I hate vodka. I'm Scotch. Always have been. Since I was thirteen, for god's sake."

Temporarily distracted by the sight of her sister slithering into the hallway, Barbara turned to catch her mother crouching deeply behind her, legs wide apart, hands on knees, surveying her daughter's shoes.

"Mom, I am at one with the flowers. I respect nature's bounty! Besides, my car is parked over there! That was Mary."

Mother stood up, crossing her arms, her lips pressed and indignant chins thrust so deeply into her neck that blood collected within the creases. Her eyes stared dead ahead, fixated on their target–the small frame of Mary.

Barbara unknowingly mirrored her mother's body language, staring down at Mary in profound disbelief, arms crossed, slicing her body in half. Mother pivoted slowly from one hip to the other while the room echoed her silence. Barbara also switched her weight to her left hip. Mary shot a look of loathing at her sister.

"Such a pity," Barbara said. "They were such beautiful flowers too."

She spotted panic in Mary's bat-like eyes–as the elder sister, perfection was Mary's watchword, and anything less could destroy her. A wash of empathy swept through Barbara: her sister was only adopting the role the family demanded of her. Even she expected this unwittingly fragile creature, placed at a precarious height, to represent the bastion of the family's ideals. If Mary fell, Barbara would feel the bruise just as keenly.

"I'll get some more flowers," Barbara said.

Mary strained a smile. "Don't bother. I'll get them. Cost really isn't an issue." Then the stab. "For me, anyway. Another G and T, please, Dad."

Stung into silence, Barbara vowed to rein in her compassion.

"G and T? Of course, darling." He turned to Barbara. "I'll just be a sec with your vodka, pumpkin."

"Scotch!"

"Scotch? Coming up. Always good to try out new things."

With that intervention over, it was now time for the family to focus fully on Barbara.

"What in heaven's name has happened to your face?" Mother was a foot away from Barbara's nose. She could feel the hot air from her mother's nostrils on her cheeks and see the beams of disgust radiating from her eyes. "Don't you care about your appearance? Did anyone see you come up the road like that?"

"How should I know?"

"Can't you just comb your hair?" Her mother touched Barbara's hair, as one would pat a flea-infested dog.

"Barbie, you certainly seem to have put on the pounds. How much do you weigh? Mother, how much would you guess she weighs?" Father always had a scientific interest in weight-bearing objects such as Barbara. From the corner of her eye, Barbara spotted the slit that represented Mary's mouth widening across her sparse features in what was unmistakeably a smirk.

The family sat down at the table almost immediately. As Barbara had suspected, they had not yet started eating. This year, as always, Mother had ignored Barbara's pleas for a vegetarian alternative. Instead, there sat the sad victim on an oval platter, a turkey violated by bread crumbs and parsley, with its own blood splashed over its body. Around it, nestled into its skin, were the vegetables, snuggling up to its warmth. Barbara felt her stomach heave.

Mother dished out the day's massacre, loading Barbara's plate—an act of silent disapproval from an otherwise non-silent mother.

"So, Mary," said Father, a glass of red wine twinkling in his hands, "did you hear about the African dam?"

"Africa's a continent, Dad, not a country," Barbara cautioned, to a pair of deaf and hairy ears. "What country specifically are you–"

"Yes, Daddy." The gash opened up into a smile. "I want that project. I'll go for the hydroelectric deal, but my main goal is water rights. I had a flash of inspiration on the way here."

"Quite natural, my dear," Father offered, nodding in agreement with himself. "You'd be in your alpha state on the plane. Best time to think. Quite simplistically . . ."

At this phrase, her father's favourite, Barbara shut down her communication system. She watched his mouth yaw and lunge, and then scanned around to her sister. Scotch-taped across Mary's face were admiration and awe–but who knew what lay underneath.

" . . . on a basic level . . ." the tap continued.

Then Barbara remembered one minor missing item. "By the way, Mom, where's Grandma?"

"Kicking up her heels at the home, I think," her mother answered. "Cavorting, as usual, with her chums."

"Unless she's run away again," Father added.

"It may sound far-fetched," Mary leaned forward to give her fat-free body more presence, "but I'm going to buy . . ." she halted.

"Yes?" Mother paused, her eyes on her daughter, though her fork continued its circuit from plate to mouth.

Father put down his glass–an indication of deep interest.

"I'm going to buy," Mary continued, "the Niger River."

Both parents gasped, one with crimson teeth, the other with a mouth full of food.

"Oh, spirits of nature!" Barbara exploded. "Does this ego know no bounds?"

The hair on Mary's forearms stood on end, making her skin look like plucked chicken. "TransAqua will be the pioneers of this type of deal. It's a perfect time to negotiate, now that the country's in such a weak position. Once one country accepts it, it'll be much easier to replicate the deal with other developing markets."

"Well, well!" A smile danced upon Father's lips. "My own daughter buying the Niger River. Who knows? Maybe one day it'll be known as the Glass River. Certainly has a ring to it, doesn't it, dear?" He looked at his wife for signs of interest. None forthcoming. He turned back to Mary. "Glass River. Very appropriate. Very appropriate indeed."

"You're planning to own the Niger River?" Barbara folded her arms over her outrage. "Look at you!–some minor functionary who thinks she's David Livingstone!"

Mary's face turned ashen. Barbara noticed her sister's body rise and fall ever so slightly as she engaged and released the muscles of her rectum, a habit she had picked up in childhood. It calmed her in the most stressful situations. Barbara's system tingled with victory, and she set to eating again.

Mary's pellet eyes stared unflinchingly into Barbara's. "A minor functionary?"

"You're just a salesguy. So what?" Barbara ran a turnip through her gravy, thrilled to have unbalanced Mary's equilibrium with such ease. She threw the turnip into her mouth and chewed philosophically.

"You consider the Associate Director of Sales a 'minor functionary'?"

"How can you get excited about making money from so many deaths?"

"Oh dear! It takes all types, doesn't it? Every family has one," said Mother, in obvious reference to Barbara.

"Whoever gets this project," Mary slowed down the tempo of her voice, "will be a shoe-in for VP." She stared at Barbara for confirmation that she had understood.

"VP? Oh, how wonderful!" Mother beamed at Mary. "That's my girl. Keep it to yourself and don't let anyone get in your way." She tucked into the bloodbath once again.

"Have you actually bothered to read any newspapers at all?" Barbara exploded. "You've got civil war in over twenty countries, all fighting over rising water prices . . ."

"Civil war?" Mary tinkled. "That's hilarious. Everyone else calls it terrorism, Barbie calls it civil war." Mary snickered out some small sneezes, her knife-edge shoulders shaking with mirth as she looked with pity at her parents. "Where, Barbie? What civil wars?"

"It's all over the place," Barbara replied, her mind crowded with a hundred instances, but no particular one rising to the surface. "Africa. The Middle East. South America."

"Really?" Mary collapsed into pinprick titters. "Just a few spots, then? Glad to see it's pretty localized. I'm impressed. We've got a world war on our hands and no one told me."

Father exploded into a laugh, dribbling some wine onto his tie. Mother's face crinkled up into her eyes as she set forth on a high *tremuloso* screech, passed to a grating vibrato in random notes and ended on prolonged retches.

Barbara rolled her eyes and whispered to herself, wanting to smash into her sister's brittle body and fracture each calcium-deficient bone. She felt outrage for herself, as a victim of Mary's contempt, as well as for those other victims, the people of the Niger River.

"As usual," Mother pointed at Barbara with her fork, "you're talking absolute nonsense. Don't be ridiculous. It's terrorism, plain and simple. They're lucky to get water. So," she picked more peas off her skirt, "let's have none of your ridiculous political posturing in this house, young lady." She turned to her husband. "Bit of skin with that, dear? Lovely bit of skin?"

"Here we are, helping the rest of humanity, with not a word of thanks in return," Father sighed to himself, then nodded for skin.

The sky grew overcast, and obstreperous grey clouds unfurled their black cloaks over a submissive sun. Mother turned the lights on. A simple chandelier, with many years of silent service, hung over their heads. It had presided over moments of heartache and indifference, treachery and damnation, retribution and ruin, shining brightly through all the seasons of the family's relations.

"Lucky to have companies like TransAqua," Father continued. "Remember Thailand, dear? One week on the toilet. One week, absolute minimum." He heaped some carbs onto his protein.

"I told you not to have ice," Mother sang. "But would you listen?" She smiled to herself. "I'm only your wife, after all. What do I know?"

For the next ten minutes, the family focused on feeding, mixing its carbs, proteins and trans fatty acids with reckless abandon. All that could be heard was the clatter of cutlery on crockery.

"Well, Barbie," Father said at last, trying to steer the conversation into calmer waters. "How is your uh–what is it exactly that you do again?"

Three pairs of eyes triangulated on Barbara.

"Conflict management."

"Aaaah! Ah-ha. Conflict management. Sounds very important, doesn't it, Mother?"

"'Conflict management'?" Mary butted in, unwilling to relinquish the bright lights. "Oh, they think up words for everything these days. Do you know what they call garbage collectors? 'Refuse management.' Can you believe it?" She smirked and shook her head in disbelief.

Barbara's temper started to flare, but something held her back, a small tool learnt through four years of teaching. "I hear what you're saying," she said through clenched teeth. "However, I feel denigrated and invalidated when you belittle my chosen profession. I'd welcome your support in this matter. How does that sound to you?" Small smile.

All three looked up again from their food. The clock ticked a few seconds off the day.

"Well-well-well-well-well," said Father. "They certainly have taught you some long words, haven't they? Very, veeeery impressive."

"I feel . . . de-validated, was it?" It was Mary again, bringing the attention back to its centre.

"No, *in*-validated, my dear," said Mother, chucking a piece of corpse into her mouth. "She feels *in*-validated."

"And de-what?" asked Father, truly perplexed.

"You still haven't told us what conflict management is, Barbie."

"Is the pay any good?" asked Mary.

"Yes," Barbara replied, looking down at her plate.

"Yes? Really? Aren't you self-employed?"

Mother and Father froze in horror.

"Yes. No. So what? I get a base rate."

"Well, you don't get health benefits, insurance, stocks."

"But I choose my own hours."

"What's your rate, by the way?" Mary was relentless.

Barbara's parents were unable to continue chewing until this question had been answered.

Barbara smiled. "A dollar. I get a dollar an hour. But I'm also collecting welfare on the side. I spend it all on crack."

Silence reigned. An unwelcome guest had arrived, a guest that seldom entered the flattened ionic columns that framed this austere structure. And Sarcasm was its name.

"Barbie," Father leaned forward on his elbows, attempting to prevail as the voice of reason. "Have you ever thought of asking Mary to get you a position in her company? I'm sure she would be able to find something a bit more stable for you– a secretary, anything!"

Mary coughed on some carrot as Barbara's soul shrank in humiliation. "The pace is pretty fast at TransAqua. I'm not sure Barbara could cope. It's very task-oriented."

"Ah, yes." Both parents nodded their heads. "Of course."

A bulb in the chandelier burnt out.

Barbara looked around the table, as if viewing her family in slow motion, a frame-by-frame report of their dynamics. Their beliefs flowed together in effortless constancy, a wellspring of certitude. She could not understand how she had drifted such a distance from it.

FOUR

The Quantitative Man

Two days after the disaster, a white Mercedes-Benz pulled up outside the house of General Abucha, the head of the Nigerian armed forces. Out stepped the short, plump form of Ogbe Kolo, enfolded in a gold agbada. He immediately opened his Chinese parasol for the twenty-yard trip to the front door. There, he waited for his driver to press the bell. After this formality, he handed his driver the parasol and exchanged it for his briefcase. They both stood at attention and looked straight ahead at the door.

A steward in a white uniform, small cap and bare feet answered the door and ushered them in. He left them in the cavernous sitting room. Soft white leather armchairs with gold accents surrounded a glass table encased in gold tubing. To the side stood two gold and pink flamingo lamp stands atop a pink carpet peppered with orange flowers. Presiding over this splendour was the rainbow delight of a multi-layered chandelier hanging low over the table like a wedding cake turned upside down. Its heady clusters of bulbs were kept alight by one of the few operating generators in the capital, Abuja.

A few minutes later, a jovial General Abucha appeared, wearing a casual Malaysian cotton shirt and trousers.

"Minister Kolo," he beamed. "An honour."

"General," Kolo bowed. "Always a pleasure."

Kolo waved away his driver, who backed out of the room, and the two sat down.

"Something to drink?" the general asked.

"Well–maybe some Scotch."

"On ice?"

"Dry."

The general called out for his steward and asked for two Scotches.

"How is your daughter?" Kolo asked.

"She's doing well, thank you."

"What a girl! Does she still want to be president?"

"Yes, but now she wants dual nationality," the general sighed with feigned indifference, "so she can be president of Nigeria and prime minister of Britain at the same time."

"Oh well." A smile lit behind Kolo's rash, caused by an excess of skin whitener. "How hard can it be to govern the UK? It's a rich country. They all have food to eat and water to drink. They have hospitals, schools. What more could they want? It would be more of a hobby for her."

"After Nigeria–true."

Both men chuckled.

The steward brought in a tray, poured the Scotch into two European crystal glasses and padded away again. Kolo stole a glance at the general. They had known each other since childhood, but not closely: Kolo had been shunned by other children, whose parents had considered him cursed. Nevertheless, ties of heritage were strong, so they had offered each other clandestine support as they rose in the corridors of power. He had always found the general unusually difficult to read, and the general was a cautious man. As the minister for natural resources, Kolo had to distance himself from the Kainji ordeal. He wondered if he could rely on the general's support over the coming months.

"Well," Kolo ventured, "I fear for the government. There is so much unrest in the country. I hear the president has as much as barricaded himself at Aso Rock. Which is a pity. I love neoclassical buildings." He grew bolder. "I pray they don't get damaged."

The general halted the progress of the crystal to his mouth. He peered at Kolo through heavy eyelids, remaining silent. One thing Kolo had learned in his journey through life was to wait for a reaction, no matter how long that wait took. With the general, this could represent a formidable length of time.

Kolo eased forward for his Scotch, swirled it around, sniffed it, held it to the light and very slowly took a tentative sip. He closed his eyes as if he were in a trance, lulled into that sweet state by the gentle wonder of the "water of life." Finally, he opened them.

The general leaned towards him. "So–you have heard news?" he asked.

Kolo was not one to be outwitted by a question. He pondered awhile, then gave a noncommittal shrug and reached for the Scotch again.

The general finally buckled. "There have been rumblings in the army."

"Rumblings?"

"Perhaps looking for a change in leadership."

Kolo's eyes flickered in anticipation.

"I have ensured, of course," the general rushed to explain, "that all dissidence, any hint of discontent, is quashed at its onset."

"Of course!" replied a shocked Kolo. "The government needs the full support of its armed forces at this tragic juncture."

"Which I am in every way committed to providing on an ongoing basis in this hour of our country's greatest need."

They both sipped their Scotch.

"Yet," the general proposed, "the people are suffering."

"There's no doubt that that is so."

"And I wonder . . ." The general paused, eyes boring into Kolo's.

Kolo stopped blinking. He now knew that he had the general's support for any change that might make his position more secure. He lay back in the pampering leather and closed his eyes again. "You still have the best Scotch in Abuja." A smile surfaced behind Kolo's yellow skin.

"Reserved only for the best company."

Both men paused, lost in their separate thoughts.

"Tell me–how can I help my countryman?" Kolo asked at last.

"Maybe some information. Are there any new . . ." the general paused, " . . . initiatives, any changes, perhaps changes of personnel, that I should be aware of?"

The general swallowed the rest of his Scotch. Kolo recognized that the general must be under considerable strain and chided himself for not having approached him sooner.

"The British and the Americans want to see a new . . ." Kolo flicked a small silk thread from his agbada, "grid of power–by power," he hastened to add, "I am referring, of course, to electricity–"

"Of course," the general quickly rejoined.

"And it is about that initiative that I wish to talk to you today. Can I count on your support for such an enterprise?"

"So you're in touch with the Americans and the British?"

"On an informal level." Kolo stared directly at the general.

"Aha." The general considered for a moment, then responded. "The army will provide whatever support is necessary for the good of the country." He looked at his glass. "More Scotch?"

"Thank you." Kolo drained his drink. The general refilled their glasses.

Kolo raised his. "Cheers!"

Kolo was accompanied to his car by his driver, who carried his parasol aloft. Once enveloped in the leather seating, Kolo lay back, exhausted. He took out a small pot of Oil of Olay and applied it to his face.

"So, Innocent," he asked. "What news of the general?" The car passed crowds of people carrying jerry cans on their heads, water spilling from some of them.

"The general's driver said the president has visited him twice this week at home."

"Well, that's to be expected. Anyone else?"

"Yes–the minister for the environment two days ago. The general's driver had to drive the minister back to his office." Innocent scowled in disapproval.

Kolo looked at him through the rear-view mirror and smiled in appreciation of the relative importance of resource consumption over protection. "Well, the minister has no driver of his own."

"Yes, sir," the driver replied, still irate.

"Anything else?"

"Yes, sir. Madam is no longer in town. She left with the general's mother."

"Really? And where is she?"

"His driver took them to the airport last night."

"International?"

"Domestic."

"How much luggage did they have?"

"Five big suitcases, television, new oven."

Kolo smiled, the rash making the expression quite painful. "Back to the village. Ah well, at least they'll be safe there."

Kolo saw that whatever the minister for the environment had proposed, it had not allayed the general's fears.

"Good work, Innocent."

They arrived at the residence of the British High Commissioner. The flag flew at half-mast. Kolo wondered whether flags in the rest of the former empire also lay at half-mast, or whether this was merely a local courtesy.

The architecture was colonial, but the entrance door bore the imprint of the Nigerian artisan. The great sculpting lineage of the Fakeye family had carved the history of contact between Nigeria and Britain on the door, panels that chronicled the benefits of trade, minus the delicate issue of exploitation. They depicted the arrival of the queen, skirting the thorny issue of British rule; they celebrated the bucolic idyll, without reference to rural unemployment. The door had been a bold commission by an adventurous and self-confident High Commissioner, His Excellency the Honourable Sir Peter Wigglesworth-Lyle.

A steward in a white uniform with shiny brass buttons and white plimsolls ushered Kolo in. The High Commissioner, an icon of punctuality, was waiting for him under a portrait of an aging queen.

"Ogbe, how do you do?"

"Peter, how *are* you?"

As per tradition, neither question needed answering and Kolo had slipped easily into his British public school accent. They were old school chums; formalities could be discarded.

"Pray, do sit down. Beastly weather today, isn't it? So very hot."

Not, however, the formality of the weather exchange.

"Abso-bloody-lutely. Thank Christ for air conditioning."

"Ah–your generator's still working, is it?"

"On its last legs," Kolo said apologetically. "*Forsan miseros meliora sequentur.*"*

"Bloody right," the HC sighed. "Can't argue with that. Now–can I get you something? Dry Scotch, isn't it?"

"Tremendous."

Kolo was offered a silk armchair in muted gold to rest his weary frame. He scrutinized the painting of the queen, slightly envious that he had not been born into a safe haven like Peter. Who could a Nigerian hang in his parlour? The president, that representative of folly and greed? No. The oba of Lagos? The sultan of Sokoto? They could hardly be considered a uniting force for an Islamic north and a Christian south. Where was the Nelson Mandela, the Mahatma Gandhi, of Nigeria? None existed–the country had been collated out of too many nation groups. No one had yet managed to integrate the interests of the Hausa north, Igbo east and Yoruba west.

Still, did the British royal family represent the British people? Were they also not a divisive force between the English and the Welsh, Scottish and Irish, between south and north, between the ruling elite and the working classes? No, few countries had figureheads truly representative of the country's struggle for identity.

Kolo, reflecting, suspected he would have to fulfil that role in Nigeria, that his was the face that would grace the walls of

* "For those in misery perhaps better things will follow."

Nigerian embassies for forthcoming centuries, even though others might note his great reluctance at receiving such attentions.

"So, how can I help?" Peter asked, always one to get straight to the point.

Kolo was not to be rushed. "Very little, actually. I merely thought I'd avail myself of the benefits of one of the few active generators in Abuja."

The HC smiled briefly.

"Any news of Henry?" Kolo asked.

"Left the Foreign Office. Joined UNHCR. Deputy Executive Director."

Kolo's skin crawled. Peter's bullet points had always irked him. He spoke as if his innate superiority released him from the momentous effort of replying in whole sentences.

"UN?"

"Apparently so."

"My god."

They both shook their heads in disbelief. The HC sipped his Scotch with a grimace and a shiver. "Bloody strong stuff, must say."

The generator shut off.

"Blast!" exclaimed Kolo. "Time to visit the French ambassador."

The HC laughed, displaying a row of crowded and yellowing teeth. "Kolo, old boy, you're hiding something." He ushered his guest to the privacy of the veranda. "What's up your sleeve? Always so obtuse. Something's up."

Kolo felt he should reward Peter for the exertion of having formed a couple of almost complete sentences. He looked down the compound to the blood red hibiscus, a luscious flower with no inhibitions, petals splayed wide, opening its most private parts to the sun. Now was not the time for discretion. "I thought you should know that General Abucha doesn't know how much longer he can hold the army together. Major unrest. He approached me today to ask if I would be willing to assume leadership should anything happen to the president." He rotated his face to witness the HC's reaction.

"General Abucha? Really?"

"He already has the support of the Americans."

"The Americans?"

"The Americans."

"Interesting." Peter's mouth tightened. "Profits, of course, with them. Self-interest only. After the oil, no doubt." His lips threatened to disappear altogether. "And the water. Worship of the almighty dollar."

"Utmost discretion is necessary, of course, for the safety of all involved."

"Absolutely," the HC hurried to respond.

After a few casual courtesies, Kolo called his driver and walked back to his car under the parasol. A guard opened the geometric gates and Kolo's Mercedes slid away.

"So, Innocent, did you get any petrol?"

"The driver sold me five gallons, that's all. The embassy is watching petrol too closely." He looked in the rear-view mirror with apology. "Where now, sir?"

"American Embassy."

Kolo had a natural disdain for Americans, whom he considered politically naive, socially dislocated and self-idolizing. He disliked these people with no history and no culture who had, nonetheless, exported their desultory offerings–fast food, simplistic films and evangelical economics–erasing the history, culture and identity of others. More tragic still, they had succeeded.

The embassy compound was designed and built by American architects and landscape gardeners. The grass was razed, the garden clear, so that the windows looked out onto a magnificent view of the compound's concrete walls.

The car parked next to an eggshell white Cadillac SUV with tinted windows–the ambassador's official car–and a van carrying water from Nevada Springs.

Treated like a market trader, Kolo negotiated passage through a series of security stations before gaining entry to the ambassador's office, a vast monstrosity of rectilinear rigour sporting three giant American flags.

"Your Excellency," Kolo adopted his deepest Nigerian accent, "thank you so much for seeing me, sir."

The ambassador put down his dumbbells. "Mr. Cole. C'mon in! Have a seat. Can I get you a drink?"

"Thank you, Your Excellency. Some whiskey, perhaps."

The ambassador poured himself and Kolo a glass, then drained his in one gulp. Kolo's sip looked prim in comparison.

The ambassador stood up to get another shot. "We've been worried about the oil supply. Is there any way to get it pumping again?" He wandered over to stand underneath a large painting of a rodeo.

"We will be producing again by Thursday. However, I thought you would like to know," Kolo took a larger sip of whiskey, "it appears there might be a change in leadership. Had you heard?"

"I've had no intelligence of that nature." The ambassador looked like a child who had not been invited to a party.

"There has been an uprising in the army."

"A military coup?"

"Almost, sir, almost. But I have managed to persuade General Abucha to maintain civilian rule." Kolo thought he could detect some disappointment in the ambassador's eyes. "It appears the president is planning to adopt protectionist measures during the period of reconstruction." Kolo deliberately reverted to his British accent.

"What?" The ambassador sounded alarmed. "He's never mentioned that!"

"It came up behind closed doors."

"Closed doors? What closed doors?" There was the childhood look again.

"Of government, I'm afraid," replied Kolo, bemused by the ease at which he was able to deploy quite rudimentary tactics to accomplish his goals. "The British have approached me to assume leadership during this interim period."

"The British have backed this?" The tips of His Excellency's ears went pink. "So they're allowed behind closed doors, right? Goddam colonial rulers. Haven't let go of the reins, I see."

"Please don't misunderstand me," Kolo added, enjoying every moment of the interchange. "They have very specifically insisted that I gain the sanction of the US government in the first instance. They simply could not make any decision without it."

"Ah, sanction–yes, I see."

"It may cause some embarrassment for them if you mention it. A bit humiliating for a former colonial power. You know how it is."

"Yes, yes, of course. Well," the ambassador finally grunted, "thanks for keeping me updated." He patted Kolo on the back, happy that he had now been invited to the party.

Having laid the groundwork for a change of government, Kolo dropped in at the glittering offices that housed his numerous business enterprises, built in the shape of four droplets of water– an unfortunate choice, as these contours could only be seen in aerial view. Otherwise, the building looked like so many others in Abuja: large and mirrored.

Kolo visualized how the financial jigsaw would fit together, but kept each transaction separate, his commercial interests managed in discrete entities independent of each other.

"Sir! This is a great privilege." The vice-president of Northwest Water came to attention immediately, knocking over his coffee in his haste to rise from his chair.

Kolo puffed with fatigue and collapsed into a leather couch. "I need you to acquire rights to the northern Benue River in case it is needed for fresh water. It is of prime national interest. We cannot afford for Nigerian water to fall into the hands of foreign powers."

"Foreign?"

"TransAqua International, along with the French and British, will bid for the rights. We need to be in a position to . . ." he paused to consider phrasing, " . . . to decide if the country should sell them."

The vice-president bowed. "Of course, sir!"

"Obviously you will be entitled to a percentage." He surveyed his subordinate. "However, I expect you to keep this highly confidential, because you don't want other businesses," he slowed down to let the implication of internal rivalry sink in, "to get hold of this information. Someone else might decide to take over the portfolio."

The vice-president gripped the side of his desk to steady himself. "You can put your full trust in me, sir," he whispered. He took Kolo's hand and shook it in both of his, not stopping for a full minute.

After this ordeal, Kolo flicked his wrist with concern and, as he did so, caught sight of his fingernails. The stresses of his life were exhibited there, despite his fastidious nature. His nails had been chewed into uneven lengths, their cuticles frayed, their beds miniature. In disgust, he hid his hands underneath his agbada.

Next, he wended his way around the serpentine corridors of the curved edifice to visit the team headed by the vice-president of Mideast Water. This ritual continued, albeit with hands firmly in his pockets, as he visited the head of each geographical division.

Finally he got to the centre that connected all four droplets of his personal panopticon. There, he kicked closed the door to his own office, he settled back in a chair of emerald velvet and applied moisturizer to his fingernails. He wondered if a manicurist would be able to help him. Picking up the phone, he ordered his stockbroker to buy shares in TransAqua International, the company he had already decided would partner with him in reconstruction. He planned not only to profit from TransAqua's future stranglehold on water supply via the Niger River in the west–which would be contaminated with bodies and bacteria from the flood–but also to compete with his own supplies, which would come from uninfected groundwater, aquifers and other fresh-water sources near the mighty Benue River in the east. In this way, he would own almost all of the fresh water in Nigeria.

After securing military and diplomatic support, as well as his own business interests, it was time for Kolo to address the formalities expected by a grieving populace. He toured the devastated areas with the eyes of a politician and the sight of a man of commerce. As he drove west to the banks of the Niger in his Mercedes, now soiled by mud, he heard the screams of horror through his bulletproof windows. He could sense the panic of those who had witnessed the hunger of the water, devouring all that stood in its path. He knew no aid would reach them, that they would rot with their kin in the stinking mire.

Everything around him was razed–factories, farms, drains, village centres, even cities. Electricity poles lay like fallen giants, telephone lines like broken matchsticks, mighty buildings like sand castles after the tide. Lead clouds, black sky, metal sun, heavy with mist and dust.

Kolo saw one man hanging upside down, with his leg caught on a window grille, the other leg like a third arm flopping over his head, a human tripod. The aerial on a roof displayed human remains like a clothesline, a banner testifying to the horror of the dam's wrath. More images from the darkest realms of human imagining: bodies like torn plastic, slung high on tree-tops, dead and rotting; others folded over balconies in garish poses or washed up into piles around the corners of buildings.

Most areas were inaccessible by road, so he toured the banks of the Niger by helicopter. Always fearful of that which he could not control, he would look out of the helicopter, every muscle straining in fear.

"Don't bank so far," he commanded the pilot. "Are you in an air show?"

The pilot gently levelled out. Kolo's short nails continued to grip the handles of his white leather seat.

"Okay. We need to go round this area," he instructed. "But my drink must remain level. Circle gently. You're not a Hollywood stunt man today-oh."

Kolo looked down and saw that which no human should ever behold–horizons of horror, as far as the eye could see. Where buildings once stood, a raging river thundered; what once contained the to and fro of human activity now held the current of an almighty sea, its waters flowing with human flesh.

Where the flood allowed, the tops of houses could be seen. Occasionally, Kolo would spot someone waving a shirt from a roof or tree, begging for him to save them. He left them there, knowing that they would die before any help could reach them. He would be the last witness to their existence, his eyes the last to turn away from their despair.

With these damning images as bait, he then made his way through meetings across the country, consoling the lost and forlorn, expressing his heartfelt sympathies to community leaders and pronouncing his disgust and shock to the international press.

In the north, he quoted the Qur'an; in the south, the Bible. In rural areas, he invoked the spirits. With ordinary people, he listened to stories, shook his head, shed some tears; with politicians, he discussed how best to save their jobs; with analysts, he offered statistical details of the tragedy; with journalists, he painted colourful pictures of horrific deaths; with the international community, he pointed the finger of blame; with his voters, he promoted restitution; with the business community, he talked about reconstruction.

Kolo read the papers daily as he flew from meeting to meeting. The news delighted him. Many politicians could plead, beg and cajole. Very few could weep. But Kolo enjoyed performing; it challenged him. He had collapsed on the arm of a local leader. All the papers ran the story. On the inside pages, in smaller print, they reported on the president's meeting with European ministers.

After an exhausting fortnight spent with community leaders, politicians and the international community, Kolo finally went home. He was sitting in the back of his famed white Mercedes-Benz, deep in thought, airing himself softly with an exquisitely decorated Spanish fan.

"Joh. Turn left here. There's too much traffic ahead," he said wearily to Innocent. He lay back on plump seats and stroked the rare wood. His hands–as always, too dry–made swishing sounds on the surfaces. He turned the air conditioner to high. As others believe in gods or sons of gods, Kolo believed in consumption, and he practised his belief.

The car came to a halt outside a bright white compound protected by wrought-iron gates in beautiful filigree shapes: on the left, "O"; on the right, "K." Ogbe Kolo. O.K. The tops of the surrounding walls were studded with broken glass.

A guard peered into the car and immediately set to opening the gates. Kolo looked at him from the corner of his eye. As a night guard, he was above average. However, Kolo knew that, if any harm were to come to him, any threat to his person, any potential for violence or mischief, the guard would disappear as quickly into the night as he had appeared from its depths.

And Kolo had reason to fear. He was now on the verge of his boldest move.

FIVE

It Takes a Corporation . . .

On a hill within the moonscape that overlooked Santa Fe's warren of adobe houses rose a mighty building, out of harmony with its surroundings, an oasis within a thirsty desert. Its mirrored facade assumed the features of a mirage, a veil to hide the extent of its dominion. While obscuring the activity behind its walls, it offered unobstructed views for those within of that which lay outside. Despite the implied transparency of this glassed giant, the outside world would not be let in, nor the corporate world out.

Mary Glass sat in her crystal office, looping a pen through her fingers, afloat one of the largest multinational corporations on the planet, TransAqua International. Its subdivision, Sparklex, was the foremost American provider of bottled and fresh water. Monstrous fortunes were made through corporate control of this finite natural resource, once considered, like air, as "commons." A trillion-dollar industry had emerged almost overnight, profiting from a recent global obsession for water privatization.

However, the most profitable sector of TransAqua, the division that hired those with the most robust ambitions ("bold, creative, energetic people"), that is to say the leviathan to which Mary had tethered her future, focused on the acquisition of water rights in a highly competitive market. To own water was to own life.

Except for those in close proximity, colleagues considered Mary one-dimensional. The character was her own creation. She ensured that no hint of her competitive, ambitious personality rose to the surface–and she often succeeded. Her desk was almost bare; her room devoid of any personal touches; her face expressionless. She rarely referred to her personal life. She wished to provide only a mirror to those who interacted with her, so that no threat presented itself to them.

The rapid competition for water rights in Nigeria had intensified pressure within TransAqua, and Mary had to work quickly. Thus, this silent, camouflaged creature had slipped through the corridors to her office. She clicked her door closed, sat down and speed-dialled her father. Days had passed since the dam broke, and she had not been able to contact the government complex at Aso Rock.

"Hello, Dadsie. How are you?" she said, scrolling through her emails.

"Spectacular. And you, petal?"

"Wonderful." She started typing a response. "Your little girl needs your help."

"Anything for my . . . It's Mary!" he screamed, a hand over the receiver. "No, Mary–your daughter!" He took his hand away. "Your mother says hello. She hasn't got those flowers yet."

"Oh, yes. I forgot." Mary scribbled a note. "I'll send them. Now–can you help me?"

"Of course, darl–. . . No!" he screamed again. "She's sending them!" He turned back to the receiver. "When?"

"Today." Mary buzzed for her assistant and cracked open a bottle of water.

"Today!" he shouted, then turned back to their conversation. She could hear her mother yelling in the background.

Mary swallowed some water.

"Now," Father continued, "how can I help? By the way, have you found Barbie a job yet? Something slow-paced? Mailroom? Delivery, perhaps?"

Mary almost spewed out her water. "Uh, nothing yet." She could just imagine Barbara, with her purple harem pants, booming voice and jangling earrings, jeopardizing her reputation and status on a minute-by-minute basis.

"Too bad," Father sighed. "Ah well, keep trying. It's such a huge organiz–"

"Will do. Anyway, Dadsie, I'm working on the Nigerian contract. Any advice? Do you know anyone?" She pressed Send and continued through her email.

"Well, I haven't been following it closely . . . No! Peas will do . . ."

Mary's assistant entered. Devoid of facial expression, Mary handed her a piece of paper with a list of plants on it, handwriting neat. Her assistant looked at the list, glowered and shut the door.

"Who should I contact? Do you know anyone? We've got an article in *West Africa,* but no calls. The Nigerian presi–. . . Just a moment." She put her father on hold and answered the other line in an insipid voice. "Mary Glass. Yes. I'll find out. Please hold." She returned to her father.

" . . . that would be a good idea." He was in mid-sentence.

"Pardon?" She rifled through some papers.

"I said, I don't think the president would be a good idea. He won't last . . . No, just two potatoes, love. No, just two . . . He won't . . . I'm trying to watch my weight, darling. Now, please put those potatoes back, Catherine. Put–"

Mary put her father on hold. "Lebanon? James Stiffner has the contracts. You can get the number from my assistant." She switched back to her father.

" . . . know I never mix proteins and carbohydrates, love. Please, put those back . . . Now–what was I saying?"

"Not to contact the president." Mary took another drink of water.

"Ah, yes. He won't last long. Keep an eye on whoever heads the military. They'll be in contact . . . No, I said no carbohydrates. Turnips are carbohydrates . . . In contact with the next . . . Yes, they are. Look it up, dear . . . See who's meeting with him."

"How do I get in touch with any of his visitors? Aso Rock isn't answering."

Her father replied with surprise at her naivety. "All their children are educated abroad, darling. They'll have the home numbers."

"Yes, I knew that." She cleared her throat. "Just checking other avenues."

After she hung up, she waved her assistant, Janet, back in for some more chores, making sure not to mention this new approach.

"To the representative of the World Bank dealing with Nigeria. Start with the usual formalities." Mary retrieved an intonation of indifference. "Ask if they are providing a loan on Nigeria's behalf–purely confidential. End with the usuals."

"Uh, Mary. I thought Sinclair was going to deal with Nigeria." Janet sat facing her, legs slightly apart, as advised by her Alexander Technique Training, a habit that greatly irritated Mary.

"Well, Africa's my remit too," Mary replied with the innocence of a lamb. Mary's little lamb. "Can't just sit here twiddling my thumbs, can I?"

A row of contoured teeth (a benefit of the dental plan) gleamed back at Mary. "You'd better watch out. You Type A's are prone to all kinds of illness. Bet you clean your teeth, read the newspaper, eat your breakfast and walk your dog in the shower every morning."

A personal note, of threatening accuracy, had been introduced–Janet's usual tactic in defence of Mary's colleague and rival Sinclair. Mary kept a cold eye on her assistant, then transformed to exaggerate the warmth of their relationship. "You overestimate me, I'm afraid," she said, attempting dry humour. "I get my cook to eat my breakfast, you to read my newspaper, my dog to take my shower and my maid to clean my teeth."

"That would explain all the cuts on her hands," Janet shot back as she headed towards the door.

"Saucer of milk for the woman in the ill-fitting suit." Mary scratched the air, her thin lips sliced right across her face. Her smile was known widely in the company as The Slash.

As Janet shut the door, Mary watched her through the plate glass, her smile fading in an instant. She wondered whether Janet knelt in a position endorsed by the Alexander Technique as Sinclair thrust his semi-flaccid penis down her throat. She had to get rid of her rival; he infringed on her territory in a reckless manner. She considered him in the same way a gardener armed with salt would look at a slug. It was something that had to go, not just because it was destroying the garden, but also because it was slimy and distasteful.

And, of course, nixing it was not a difficult thing to do.

Janet power-walked down the corridor to her meticulous cubicle, then power-typed Glass's letter. She was dying to make a phone call but had to finish the dispatch first.

Finally, she dialled 5646 (no one knew whether Sinclair had deliberately requested an extension that spelled his name). Goosebumps appeared on her forearms. She repositioned one of the plastic plants surrounding her desk for more privacy.

"John Sinclair," a voice as smooth as massage oil answered.

"Hello, lollipop." She was tingling with excitement. Power was an aphrodisiac, and John Sinclair, Director of Acquisitions, Middle East/Africa, occupied a corner office with its own water cooler.

"Jane! Well, this is unexpected! What a wonderful surprise! Great to hear from you!"

"How're you doing?" she asked, juicing up.

"Dangerously well. And you?"

"Couldn't be better." She crossed her legs, trying to minimize the leakage to her thong. She pictured him: headphone clipped to his gelled hair. As a salesman, he was magnificent, and as a specimen of humankind, he was dazzling. He shone. He was handsome, clean, with fiercely manicured hands and a smile that would drive a dentist out of business.

"Well, great to hear your voice. What can I do you for?"

"Nothing. Just wanted to keep you abreast–"

"Ooh! That sounds yummy . . ."

"Self-control. The key to a higher state of being." Janet lowered her voice and cupped her hand over her mouth. "Look, I'm trying to warn you that Glass is working on rights to the Niger River."

"Oh, don't you worry, my little sweet. Uncle John's got it all under control." After a pause, he threw out an off-hand question. "What's she working on?"

Janet mouthed "Bingo!" to herself. "A letter to the World Bank."

"Look, Jeanie, great work. Wonderful to hear from you. Tell me, are you free Tuesday?"

"Karate. And my name's Janet."

"Well, how about Wednesday?"

"Therapist. I'll cancel."

"Great. Wonderful. See you then. Bye."

Janet put down the phone, looking forward to seeing Sinclair again. He was beautiful to look at, in contrast to his nickname, The Slug. Still, if only he had a slug's propensity for sexual prowess. The great grey garden slug, she had been told, has a penis nearly twice its body length and engages in an elaborate courtship ritual lasting hours, covering its partner almost completely in sticky mucus. Janet could not see herself attaining this in the few short ten- or fifteen-minute spurts offered by Sinclair.

Sinclair stood in shock. How the hell did Glass have the balls–no, the flaps, he corrected himself–to take him on? The women he associated with were passive organisms, wallpaper, background items. Women were supposed to excel at the emotional side of office life, offering supportive leadership, doing performance reviews, helping people to "communicate" and other human resource issues. How could Glass behave with such vicious self-interest? What was her problem? He swivelled his chair around to look at the early winter frost covering the trees. Was she frigid?

He had no particular enmity towards women–he loved them, in fact. He simply did not trust them. They gossiped. They made decisions based on emotion rather than fact. And as human resources had become the province of women, they had managed to hijack the workplace and make it fit their twisted logic. He had no intention of allowing Glass to threaten or supplant him in the industry.

The water business had its frustrations, but it was also the most profitable business on the planet, eclipsing the dying oil business. The value of the water market already sat in the trillions; however, with corporations supplying only 6 percent of the world's population with water, the profit potential was limitless. You could pick up the rights for the cost of a paper cup and then set the price at any ceiling you liked. If he could hold on to his position within TransAqua for a few more years, he could retire in his mid-forties a multi-millionaire. But only if he could get hold of the Nigerian president before Mary's monotonous life form tricked the tribal leader into signing something after sending him into a light doze.

Sinclair grabbed his water bottle and downed half a litre to ensure his minimum daily intake of eight litres as he looked out over the snow-littered landscape. Winter had come a bit early. He considered his strategies as he studied the snow. If winter could be premature, he could also herald in the winds of change ahead of schedule.

He dialled his buddy Beano Bates, who currently worked in TransAqua's Sewage division. Sinclair had greater plans for him. He intended to mentor Beano in Water Acquisitions and, if all went according to plan, move him into Glass's role. Although his floppy-haired disciple had little ability and less intelligence, he had the secondary advantage of being the youngest son of the American Ambassador to Nigeria.

"Hey, Beano! What've you been doing with yourself?"

"Sinclair! Just back. One word: Thailand!"

"Ha ha ha. Cultural trip, I presume?"

Beano snorted a laugh. Sinclair snickered too, but really did not wish to know what manner of pleasure Beano had encountered there.

"Could you do me a fave and drop by for a moment?"

"Of course. As long as you don't mind the shit on my shoes," Beano snickered.

Sinclair bellowed back a laugh. "Touché, Beano, touché." He had heard the joke a thousand times. It was part of the stock-in-trade of Sewage.

Sinclair could see Beano coming towards him down the glass hallway, scraping his hair off his face. He knew Beano was as desperate for status as the rest of the employees at TransAqua. No one, most particularly Beano, with a family seat in Connecticut and a dynasty biting at his heels, wanted to admit to working for Sewage. Beano could chase the current Nigerian president while Sinclair covered other bases.

Beano arrived, his taut body a tight bundle of boyish charm. "Sinclair! You look fantastic!"

"Right back at you, Beanz!" Sinclair applied ChapStick to his lips and waved him to a chair. "Look, it'd be great to have talent like yours on the team. Skiing with Cheeseman on Friday. Maybe a personal intro then?"

"Really? You think that's poss?" Beano flicked back an errant flop of hair off his forehead. He sounded like a schoolboy being asked to a dance. "What about Glass?"

"She's great, but . . . To be honest, she's all over me, like cling film. Once you're on board, we can get you straight to work on the Nigerian president. She's so distracted, every time she sits down, she sticks to her chair, know what I mean?" Sinclair laughed.

Beano flushed crimson and giggled like a child.

"Makes her own Post-it notes. Ha ha ha ha!" Sinclair issued a flashbulb smile. "So I like to keep her at arm's length. And in her case," he pointed a finger gun at Beano, "I make sure they're fully loaded." He eased out another chuckle.

"Arms loaded." Beano's dimples deepened. "You have such a way with words."

"You know, I feel sorry for her. She wears those air hostess suits, and I keep expecting her to ask me if I want peanuts with my martini." Glass had never given him the type of eye contact he expected from women. It occurred to him that she was most probably a lesbian.

"Peanuts would be her first choice, I'm sure," Beano chuckled. "She'd pay mucho dinero to see you in anaphylactic shock."

The little joke sent a shiver up Sinclair, and he continued on a graver note. "Probably why she dresses like she's flying United," he smirked. "Anyhoo, to be honest, we need someone with more technical knowledge. Not sure she's up to it." Sinclair did not like lesbians who dressed in skirts, like they were available.

"I'd really welcome the opportunity, Sinclair. And as you know, you can't get more technical than sewage." Beano wrung every last drop of gratitude from his shallow depths.

"As it happens," Sinclair added, "I'm going to be in touch with your father, so I'll take it as a *fait accompli* and pass on the good news. We'll celebrate. I'll get my girl to call your girl. Okay?"

"I'll bring some peanuts. Ha ha ha."

"I'll write that down on my Post-its," Sinclair rebutted.

Beano spluttered back into laughter.

After Beano had bounced out of his office, Sinclair leaned back in his generous, ergonomically correct chair and put his flawlessly shined shoes on his perfectly polished desk.

The phone rang. Mary bounded from the water cooler outside her office and picked it up on the second ring. "Y'ello?" she drawled. "Mary Glass."

"Yes, madam," the line crackled. "Good evening."

Mary realized how late it must be in Nigeria. "Good evening," she said slowly and loudly, as if her caller did not speak English. "Do you have any news for me?"

"Yes, madam." The voice was now shouting into the phone. "The general has had many visitors. The president has come eight times, Mr. Kolo three times–"

"The minister for natural resources?"

"Yes, madam." The voice grew excited at its own resourcefulness. "Also minister for the environment, five times; minister for foreign affairs, two times."

"Do you know why they visited?" Mary articulated each word.

"To discuss, madam," the voice replied with a note of self-importance.

"Did you hear anything?"

"No, madam."

"Okay. Thank you. We'll send your pay today."

With this information, Mary quickly discounted dealing with the president and the minister for foreign affairs–the latter was strongly allied to the president, from his hometown, and making speeches in his favour. Her father considered the president destined for the mortuary. That left the other two. She'd have to wait until 3 a.m. Santa Fe time to get them, so left work early.

In the small hours, she marched back up to the building, now reflecting a clouded moon, and noticed other offices with lights on. Her eyes immediately darted to Sinclair's corner. Only a faint glimmer–a lamp, perhaps? She quickened her pace.

Her first call, to the minister for the environment, was not successful. He was too circumspect–he did not have the mind, the soul, of a businessman. He was so fearful, so nervous, it made her skin crawl. Mary put down the phone in disgust.

Ogbe Kolo would have to do. Another call.

"The residence of the minister for natural resources," a voice answered.

"Hello. Could I please speak to the minister?"

"Who may I say is speaking?"

"Mary Glass, from TransAqua International in Santa Fe, New Mexico."

"Mexico? Just a minute."

"No," Mary snapped. "Not Mexico. United States."

"You are calling from the United States?" the voice asked in panic.

"Yes."

"Just a minute. Just a minute." The receiver was put down, though she could hear the voice–"Just a minute . . . Just a minute . . ."–still with the note of panic.

Mary stood up, placed her foot on her chair and leaned towards it, stretching her hamstring. Classical music crackled through the receiver.

"Ms. Glass, is it?" Mellifluous tones flooded the phone.

Mary stopped in mid-stretch, astounded. "Yes," she said, almost rudely.

"How may I be of assistance, Ms. Glass?"

This did not sound like a simple tribesman.

"Minister Kolo, I am phoning from TransAqua. We have heard about the terrible events."

"Tragedy. Absolute tragedy. Terrible, terrible tragedy." She could swear he was sucking on something.

"I can't tell you how sorry I was to read about it." She did not sound convincing, but that was not her job. She had not been trained as a therapist. They must have relatives they could cry to. "I think there are ways in which our company can help."

"Oh! How kind of you to offer," the notes slid out. "Now, please refresh my memory. Your company is involved in water rights and licensing, hydroelectric power, desalination, water supply, sewage–"

"Uh, waste management, yes," she corrected.

" . . . bottled water and filtration technologies, is that correct?"

"Yes." Mary adopted a tone of greater formality to cover her growing unease. "That is correct." Had Sinclair already called?

"What a fortuitous call! You are interested in rights acquisitions? To the Niger River?"

"We're interested," she corrected, "in assisting with the supply of uncontaminated fresh water, waste management systems and, of course, hydroelectric–" She stopped herself. "Minister Kolo, have you received a call from the company already?"

"No. Indeed, no."

She could not tell from his tone whether he had or not.

"Now, are you planning to provide this for free?" More sucking.

"Well, of course we'd only expect nominal repayment as you rebuild your–"

"A country in such a sad state of disrepair rarely receives calls from such eminent prospectors as TransAqua. Allow me to let you in on a secret, Ms. Glass. I have a plan–a bold plan for this great country." More sucking. "I wish to build the biggest dam in the world at Kainji and to rename the Niger River."

Mary hardly dared to breathe. She had struck the mother lode. With such a grand scheme, he would have to relinquish any rights to the river, and TransAqua would control their electricity as well. The corporation would effectively own the country.

"If you and your company wish to be involved, we will need to come to an agreement."

"Yes?"

"For this plan to come to fruition, it would be in your best interests to advise the American ambassador firstly that I have your full support, and secondly that you wish the American government to provide equally strong support in my forthcoming ventures." The sucking grew louder. "If, for example, that leads to the presidency."

"That's certainly a bold plan, Minister Kolo." Mary hesitated. "I'll do all I can to–"

Kolo stopped sucking. "Please." His entreaty had an undertone of mockery. "Please don't make me call the French. I do so detest their long-winded conferencing, although I must say they certainly love grand plans."

Mary pondered. She had no directive to negotiate this kind of deal, but she could always retract later. "TransAqua is interested in purchasing the Niger River. And if we invest in the dam, we would, of course, need sole control over electricity pricing and distribution," she said.

Silence.

Then Kolo's voice, unperturbed, slid back through the receiver. "As I thought. You're a daring woman, Ms. Glass." The sucking began again. Kolo swallowed whatever he was eating before embarking on the next phase of negotiation. "In general, we have agreement. Obviously, we'll have to work on the nuts and bolts, minor details, the renaming of the river, that kind of thing. We might need your help on that."

"Do you have any ideas as to its new name?" Mary asked.

"Oh–no, no, no. Certainly not. We Africans are always renaming something. It's in our blood. I haven't had time to think about it. So," he added, "I will leave a week for you to think this over. You'll need to get the support of your executive, no doubt." Mary flushed at his insight. "Naturally I expect the strictest confidence. Perhaps you could be so good as to phone me–say, a week Tuesday? As you doubtless know, I have a lot to do. Then we can meet in the new year."

"Yes, sir. Tuesday the 15th." Mary suddenly realized an important item that had been left out of the conversation, "By the way, I am the Associ–"

"Yes, Ms. Glass. I know. The Associate Director of Acquisitions for the Sub-Sahara. I have your contact details."

Mary put down the phone with a clear feeling of having been outmanoeuvred. This did not sit well. Nevertheless, she quickly foresaw that this character–whoever he was–would be the most likely candidate to assume the presidency.

A full twelve hours later, Mary sat in the boardroom, watching the team as they prepared for the arrival of Cheeseman, the president of acquisitions. Her chestnut orbs surveyed the acquisitions directors, who all perched in terrified silence. Finally, her eyes rested on her own team, the associate directors, hired to compete with the directors, raise the pressure, tread on toes and dethrone. They chatted on the opposite side of the conference table, more relaxed.

Sinclair lounged as he flirted with Rachel, Cheeseman's executive assistant. He had the hots for her. He actually had the hots for Cheeseman's job, but he could barely distinguish between the two. "Your eyes are such a beautiful colour. Are those contact lenses?"

Cheeseman finally appeared ten minutes late, his high-heeled cowboy boots clacking a warning to his entry. He sat down, placing his boots on the table, hands folded across a denim shirt stretched tightly across his lower belly. Jeans one size too small and a belt with an ornate buckle squeezed in some of the excess flesh like a girdle. Mary could make out his penis, tucked to the left of his fly. He surveyed the table like a shark picking out a surfer.

Mary felt her stomach twist.

"Sinclair," he moved in for the first kill, "where are you with Nigeria?"

"Well, um, I've had very good news with the World Bank, uh, as you know–"

"I din'ask where you'd like to be with Nigeria." Cheeseman spoke in a low hush, so that Sinclair had to lean towards him. "I din'ask what leads you've got in Nigeria. I din'ask what kind of wet dreams you have regarding Nigeria. I asked where you are with Nigeria." His face turned red, the colour internationally understood to signal danger. "It's not a difficult question, Mr. Sinclair." He began yelling. "I want numbers, not a personal chronicle!"

A searing electric thrill shot through Mary's body.

"Sorr . . . sorry. The World Bank will support reconstruction. They plan to introduce me to the president."

Cheeseman stared at the table, smiling faintly. "Really? You got a date?" His eyes shot to the heavens. "Well, don't forget to invite us to the wedding."

Mary's lips trembled as she fought to hold in a volley of laughter. Sinclair looked mortified.

"Glass?"

Her stomach almost emptied its minimal contents on the table.

"Yes, sir?"

"Update."

"I am in regular contact with Chief Ogbe Kolo. He's the current minister for natural resources but is rumoured to be the next president. He's interested . . ." she paused, " . . . in selling rights to the Niger River." Mary turned to Sinclair, whose handsome eyes burned with loathing.

"The Niger River?" Cheeseman asked, his face relaxing from its red alert.

"Yes, sir. Not only pricing but outright ownership."

"Rights *and* licences?"

"Yes, sir. And, if we invest in dam reconstruction, he'll give us exclusive rights to power pricing and allocation. He'll want his own percentage of profits, no doubt, but that's to be expected in Nigeria."

"Full control over their electricity supply, huh? Impressive!"

"With your guidance, sir, I am hoping this deal will become a, uh, blueprint for future deals with the developing world."

"Whoa!" Goosebumps appeared on Cheeseman's hairy forearms. "Now, that's brilliant, Glass. I am in awe. I stand here in total awe. Great work, Mrs. Glass!" Mary was not married, but she was not about to correct him. "Round of applause."

Mary's lips pinched a repressed smile of acknowledgement. She shallow-breathed through her elation.

"Mrs. Glass, see me in my office. Sinclair," Cheeseman added, "you'd better watch yer ass."

SIX

Baa-Baa Black Sheep

Barbara sat in the Library of Congress and pinched her left nostril with her fourth finger, wheezing in a deep breath. She grunted out through the other nostril, then swapped nostrils and repeated the process ten times, eyes closed.

All around her she could feel the power of the universe, the electricity of nature, urging her onwards towards her future. It had rained overnight, washing summer's bird droppings from her car, a portent of great things to come. Next, she had accidentally splashed a bothersome neighbour with icy water while driving through a puddle–another rare and unique omen. Then, beyond all odds, she had secured her favourite desk at the library, narrowly beating an aging academic to the spot. All signs pointed to success.

She flipped open *West Africa Magazine* to review recent events in Nigeria. Flicking through the panoramas of horror, she pored over scenes of rioting, images of starvation, pitiful shots of people drinking from the same rivers in which dead bodies floated. Increasing numbers of people, from all walks of life, now suffered from water blindness.

She took a pink pen out of a capacious handbag made in Morocco. With care, she wrote down in her circular scribble the names of the politicians who graced the magazine's pages: President Mu'azu, denying all previous knowledge of the dam's defects, and Chief Ogbe Kolo, minister for natural resources, plump face in tears as he commiserated with those in mourning, wishing only that his warnings had been heeded.

After a while, bored with facts and figures, Barbara rifled to Employment Opportunities. She punched the page open, flapped it straight a few times to steady her nerves and scanned down the page for a position.

Nothing.

Despite the multitude of premonitions, she could find no positions suitable for her. She sat there in disbelief, shocked that the universe had played such a cruel hoax on one of its most ardent supporters.

She had already applied to all agencies specializing in water politics–numbering almost fifty–both within and outside the United States. None had responded with any interest. It appeared her skills had imprisoned her in a life for which she had no more passion. Daily, she struggled to get to work, to find the strength to pull off yet one more team-building session, to present a cheerful face to the world. For Barbara, such stress was not easily borne.

A mood of black despair engulfed her. She looked at the others seated near her. They appeared fulfilled and focused. Why had it taken thirty-seven long years for her to find purpose? Why couldn't she be like Joan of Arc, who always knew what she was destined for? Her parents were right. She would never succeed at anything.

Barbara flicked back to the pages on Nigeria. More trauma awaited her there. TransAqua, her sister's company, had announced that it would submit a bid to reconstruct the dam. Barbara knew that her sister would be front and centre of that proposal.

"Goddess Kali!" Barbara barked, her words echoing around the library's silent walls. "If Batwoman gets the contract, I'll never hear the end of it."

She threw the newspaper down with a whack, making some of the more fragile readers jump, and stormed out to buy a cup of fair trade hot chocolate made with soya milk.

Scandalously early–i.e., at 8:20 a.m.–Barbara struggled to a three-day end-of-year team-building session with the Association of Rare Heritage Stock and Poultry. She had facilitated an exercise with them twice before, and the only difference her efforts had produced was the addition of "and Poultry" to their title by non-unanimous vote. For some members, any animal that did not eat hay was considered more pet than livestock.

Though a committed vegetarian whenever possible, Barbara had a soft spot for Rare Heritage, a well-meaning group who preserved breeds that farming giants had made almost extinct. As humane farmers, she supported them philosophically and therefore continued to slog along with them, despite their lack of solidarity.

She bundled into a small room at the back of a deserted local library in the Virginia farmlands and set up her white-boards and papers. She was not looking forward to the session; she knew it would signal yet another professional defeat with a group whose mutual distrust merited sociological enquiry.

She sighed and swirled a Taoist quote on the board.

Nothing wears away hard, strong rocks
As well as soft, weak water.
From this anyone can see that softness is harder than hardness
And weakness is stronger than strength.

–Lao Tzu

A full five minutes passed before she noticed that the first arrival, who cleared his throat to get her attention, was already in his chair, sitting upright and perfectly still. Ned represented the equine contingent. He was a small and efficient man who lived alone and exchanged pictures of horses on the Internet. He gave her chest a curt nod.

At 8:45 a.m., a woman with large, assertive breasts entered the room. She looked over her half-moon glasses at Barbara. A second pair of glasses was slung around her neck by a chain. She surveyed Barbara, then introduced herself with a firm handshake. "Dahlia. Poultry." Barbara was impressed. She had a fine, operatic voice.

Then Jack arrived to head up cows. According to him, the bovine contingent represented the only "real farmers" in the group, and he thus insisted on being called "Farmer Jack." He looked Barbara up and down as if he had never met her before, sat down on the opposite side of the room from Dahlia and started to flick through some livestock journals.

Raymond and Florencia traipsed in together fifteen minutes late, adding to the variety of manure laced with snow on the library carpets. The distinctive odour was now beginning to waft to Barbara's sensitive nasal passages. Raymond, a jolly, round man with pink cheeks who smelled of the farm, was Barbara's favourite. He spearheaded pigs. Ovines were managed by Florencia, a failed artist, musician and dancer who favoured shawls, headdresses and bright lipstick that bled to her teeth. Her remit included sheep, goats and exotic ruminants such as llamas and vicuna.

The last to arrive was the least powerful of the group: the Director of Rare Breeds and Poultry. Norm Blacksmith was a drained individual with the pallor of dried grass. He had given up farming to take up the directorship, since which time, Barbara noticed, his weight had fallen dramatically.

She surveyed her trainees with an audible sigh, wondering how to calm the waters of hostility and prove to herself that her life had some worth, even if in small measure.

Throwing caution to the wind, she started with a bold exercise. "Write down on the strip of paper in front of you something shocking that you feel others do not know about you. It should have nothing to do with farming or animals."

"Or birds," added Farmer Jack, arms crossed.

"Jack," Dahlia trilled, looking over her half-moons, "simmer down!" The omission of his honorific was not lost on him.

"Do not add your name to the paper," Barbara continued, staring at Farmer Jack. "When you are finished, pass the paper to me. And remember, as always, nothing that takes place or is said here leaves this room. This must be a safe environment for all."

As the six members began to ruminate, Barbara drifted into a reverie in which she was wearing African clothes, throwing herself in front of large bulldozers, demanding that dam building be stopped. Photographers were using long-range lenses to catch the action.

Ten minutes later, a hesitant Norm finally handed the last slip in.

Barbara scanned through the responses, shocked that her flock had taken her so literally. Nonetheless, she carried on, hoping the exercise would draw the group closer together. She wrote the responses on the board.

- *I enjoy the switch of the lash on my bare buttocks.*
- *I had sex with a contortionist.*
- *I went to Mexico for a holiday–viva México!*
- *I once had sex with my brother for a dare.*
- *I suffer from paranoid schizophrenia and once tried to kill my teacher.*
- *I am a vegan.*

As her magic marker screeched each bullet point onto the whiteboard, the participants grew increasingly pale. At the last sentence, the entire group gasped in horror.

"A vegan? Thath's ridiculouth!" Florencia lisped, her lipstick collecting in the corners of her mouth.

"What kind of aberrant behaviour is this?" Farmer Jack shouted. "A vegan? I demand to know who it is!"

"A deviant in our ranks?" Ned reared.

Pleased that the group had shown such openness, Barbara clapped her hands for silence. "Now I would like you to match up each phrase on the board with the person who wrote it. The person who gets most correct answers wins a pen inscri–"

"What?" Norm struggled for breath. "You didn't say anything about guessing who said what."

"There is no way," Ned added, his miniature hand held up in a stop sign, "that I will participate in this exer–"

"This is highly invasive," Dahlia's voice soared above them all.

"Please." Barbara's lips stretched out into a small smile, head tilted to one side. "I think I know what I'm doing." She looked down on them as a missionary might. "It's vitally important that we continue our work here. Now, let's get going." She whispered out the last sentence.

The no-brainer for everyone was Ned. Steadfastly single, known to proudly stroke the flanks and buttocks of his horses, he was pinpointed as Raw Hide.

Only Raymond guessed that Dahlia had had sex with anything, let alone a contortionist. She had to explain in twenty minutes of painful, tearful detail over three octaves before anyone was even halfway convinced.

And Florencia, the failed free spirit of the ovine world, had nothing more interesting to offer than Mexico. Her erotic paintings and lusty voice hadn't even got her into an orgy.

Raymond, Dahlia and Ned plumped for Farmer Jack and the incest. Correct. It was "a long while ago" after a "drunken night" and a "dare." Doubtful. He still lived with his brother.

A fight broke out as person after person guessed Dahlia as the vegan. In fact, it was Norm.

The biggest surprise for Barbara was that Raymond won the competition. As a paranoid schizophrenic (medicated), he was the most highly observant of the bunch.

After a shattering two hours of "bonding," Barbara suggested they take a break. She worried about the prospects for Norm's meatless directorship and, most particularly, about the weapons she had unwittingly put in the hands of the other participants. She was also somewhat desperate, since she calculated that her own prospects of future employment stretched to a maximum of twenty hours.

She needed to shift her focus to an area of obvious strength–i.e., conflict creation rather than conflict resolution–and so Barbara approached Dahlia. As a woman interested in the welfare of birds, although more on the eating side, Dahlia might be involved in wetland preservation.

"Dahlia," Barbara adopted a more operatic voice without being aware of this shift, "I'd really love to work as a water activist. Can you help?"

"Well, although we'd be sad to see you go," Dahlia's voice trickled up and down the scales in a mournful minor key, though her eyes betrayed relief at this news, "I certainly have some contacts. Is there a field you're particularly interested in?"

"TransAqua is going after rights to the Niger River. They need to be stopped."

At this statement, the entire room erupted into an explosion of loud commentary. How could it have escaped her that every farmer would be intimately involved in water privatization?

"You need to try Drop of Life in Ottawa," Ned piped up, nasal voice struggling with the n's. "Now there's an effective group. Small but effici–"

"What about that group in Santiago?" Raymond asked, eyes halfway to the ceiling.

"My dear, she'd have to learn Spanish. Do you know any Spanish?" Dahlia looked down her half-moons and over her bosom.

"*Sì. Un poco,*" Barbara said, with a flourish of Italian.

"Oh, very good. Is there anywhere else?" Dahlia asked herself. "Ah, yes. I know the exact spot. United Nations Environment Programme in Nairobi. How about that?"

Barbara pictured herself in khaki, being fanned by beautiful men in chunky jewellery. On safari. "That would be perfect. Can you help?"

"I'll certainly try either UNEP or any organization that requires your particular . . ." Dahlia lingered on a single note and then dipped into the last two words, " . . . skill set."

"That would probably be UNEP, then," Barbara replied. "I love Kenya."

After a whispering manager fired her for her efforts three hours earlier than she had anticipated, Barbara crawled to the Center for Beatific Light, ready to rip apart the first breathing biped that crossed her path.

She was well pleased with the array of delights twinkling behind the glass cases in the vegetarian whole food delicatessen. Fruit curries, salads with leaves of the darkest green, exotic foods from forgotten regions, breads made of spelt, amaranth and rape seed–the last of which Barbara refused to buy on principle.

She edged in front of a woman dressed too brightly, with loud bangles, smelling of patchouli. Next to her stood an annoying cherub with no shoes on her blackened feet and little stars in her hair. They were taking a long time to choose the flavour of that night's doubtless Ayurvedic cuisine.

"But Twilight," the mother reasoned, "you liked this when we bought it last time."

As Twilight screamed that she would refuse to eat any tofu with green bits in it, Barbara stared in shock as the child called her mother by her first name–something sounding like "nipples."

Barbara edged in front of them towards a young woman wearing a nose ring, black lipstick and a blob of red, which Barbara supposed was a dot, on her forehead. "Excuse me, darling!" She commanded the full width of the bread counter with her spread-eagled arms. "Was that couscous salad made today?"

"Pardon me." Bangles tapped her on the shoulder, clinking. "I was here before you."

"Congratulations!" said Barbara. "When you and Nite-lite here . . ." she stared pointedly at the soiled cherub, " . . . have made up your minds, you'll doubtless be served."

Barbara turned back to the Dot. "The couscous needs to be fresh. And tap water please." She emphasized "tap" with some satisfaction.

"Hey!" Bangles tried to ease herself in front of Barbara, who stared at her as though she were a thug.

"You really need to get to a meditation class, sweetheart. This is not appropriate behaviour for a child to witness." After getting her salad directly from the chef, Barbara surreptitiously tucked the number for ChildLine into Twilight's sticky hand, then turned on her heel. She slammed straight into the hermaphrodite from yoga class, yellow irises staring in disbelief, hands on hips, nodding in firm disapproval.

"What is it with you purplicious people?" it asked in disgust.

"We've got schedules," Barbara snapped and bustled to claim a table near the window. She opened the blinds to give her retinas more sunlight to ward off seasonal affective disorder. In the process, she flooded two other tables with unwanted light and heat, oblivious to the loud tutting sounds around her.

A few minutes later, she noticed the hermaphrodite looking for a spot. Barbara's table now had the only free chair in the room. She put her coat on it as The Thing approached.

"Is this taken?" it asked.

"Yes. 'Fraid so." She wished to be left in peace.

The hermaphrodite raised its eyebrows and placed itself between Barbara and the sun. It stood there looking down at her, daring her to meet its eyes. Finally, it slammed its tray on her table. "I'll get up if your guest shows up," it said.

The two sat in sullen silence, chomping on their organic dinners.

Soon the mysterious spices in the salad wafted their calm through Barbara's mind, and after a short while, her mood lifted. She broke the ice. "What's your name?" she ventured.

"What's my name? It's Astroturf."

Barbara's eyebrows shot up. As she suspected, it had adopted a genderless name.

"Got a problem with that?" it asked.

"No. I was just wondering whether your parents were also named after garden implements."

"Turf isn't an implement. It's a substitute."

"Garden substitutes or plastics of any kind," Barbara continued, crunching more of her couscous salad.

"Yours?" It drained a bottle of water with loud gurgling sounds as it looked at her. It had flawless skin, cheekbones from the Cherokees and the ease and grace of an African. Apart from the gurgling.

"Barbara."

"Barbie." It came up for air. "Great name!"

"No, not the great name of Barbie, but the wholly commonplace name of Barbara. I'd like it to remain that way."

Yellow irises shot to the sky and a pouty mouth formed a pretty grimace. "Aw, man! You take the gateau, Bar-bar-a. You take all eight layers, man, icing and all." It opened its second bottle of water.

Barbara sighed a note of invalidation. "So, what do you do?"

"I work with plants."

"Plastic?"

"Oh-ho. Very funny. No, real." It had olive skin, large piercing yellow eyes and long, curly hair–a mixture of corn blond and tawny brown–reaching its lower back. It was hard to define how many races had been brewed and bubbled to thrust it into earthly existence. Perhaps this ridiculous specimen represented all people, bound within a timeless geography and a placeless history.

"So, do you talk to your plants?" Barbara sipped some green tea, staring at the creature.

"Yes, we discuss the history of the Congo, Barbunkle. Do you also talk to plants? You look like the type."

"No. I tried but found they were too argumentative."

It stared at her for a nanosecond, then cackled, a sudden look of delight on its face.

"You're very unusual-looking," Barbara observed. "If I had to categorize you, I would say you're beautiful–like a painting."

Astro almost choked on its guava. "Aw, Jesus Christ!" It looked at the café plants for support. "I don't believe she just said that." Looking back at Barbara, "I hope I don't have to respond in kind, 'cause I don't want to keep you waiting here all night."

"I don't need to wait. I've seen you looking at my sun salutation."

"Aw, please! You've got to be–what–ten, twenty years older than me?"

Barbara gave it a look of withering contempt. "Well," she replied with some heat, "when you find someone in their twenties," her voice carried through the café, "who can have multiple orgasms–both clitoral and vaginal–then please write and inform me."

Astro glanced around at the other customers, horrified. "I can't believe you just said that. Do you think I'm interested? Anyway, I won't need to write. Know why?"

"No, not interested."

"Because I can orgasm without ejaculation."

Barbara noted that it must have a male organ for this task. "Congratulations. And why would you want to do that?" she asked, maintaining a pretence of boredom.

"Because firstly," it added on its fingers, "ejaculate is very rich in nutrients and it's best to keep it in your system." It waited a moment for her to digest this information, along with her couscous. "Secondly, I don't need a partner and thirdly," it lowered its voice, "I too can have multiple orgasms."

"Glory, thy name be AstroSeed. Well, I hope you have many happy moments with yourself." Barbara wiped her mouth and stood up, grabbing her bottle of tap water. "I must take my leave. I have to get my walking frame upstairs."

"You don't need to, Mom. They have a handicapped elevator."

"That's not funny. Handicapped people shouldn't be the butt of your jokes."

"Then plastics people shouldn't be the butt of yours."

Barbara climbed up to the yoga studio, one hour early, hid the incense box and turned off the fountain that sounded like a flushing toilet.

Twelve minutes of quiet meditation later, someone turned the fountain back on and tapped her on her shoulder. "Hey, man! Could you like move over, please? That's my usual spot."

Barbara opened her eyes, looked up and frowned. It was The Thing. "En Oh. No."

It huffed, "Aw, no, man." Reasoning initially with the stack of mats, "She knows this is always my place." Looking down at Barbara, "Did you, like, take some police car over here to get my spot? Eee-ooo, eee-ooo! Get me to the yoga studio, man. I need this guy's spot!"

"Are you done yet?"

"Hey, don't worry about that old lady crossing the street, man. The ambulance can get to her later." It slapped its mat down next to hers. It waited a full minute, then said, "I can't concentrate if I'm not in that spot. What are you trying to do to me here?"

"Why don't you go back to Beginners, then?"

"What's your problem? Is it that time of the month?"

"No. It's that time of the decade. And . . ." she whistled in another in-breath, " . . . I never forget a favour." She groaned out the exhalation.

"Oh, man. Are you listening to this?" Now reasoning with the fan, "Can you hear this?" Looking down at Barbara, "I mean, okay. Look, I'm sorry. There's no way I should have talked to you like that. Okay? Are we okay now?"

Barbara waited for a counterattack. Nothing. She could not believe it. "What did you say?"

"Nothing. I just apologized. What? You want more? Are you fundamentalist or something? Do we have to cut off some body part now?"

"I didn't mention amputation per se, although that would be a nice sight. Keep your eyes on me. I'm moving over, okay?" Barbara ceded the front/centre spot to the hermaphrodite, who had doubtless suffered untold abuse and thus had to sit in the back row at school. "I hope this small act of kindness has been seared into your memory. Sssssss! I want to hear this memory burning itself in." She moved over, a small tear collecting at the side of her eye.

"Aw, jeez. What have we got here? Some daytime soap? Look, if you really want that spot," it said, "take it. Just take it."

"Don't worry. That's not the problem."

"So what is?" it said, wriggling into a comfortable position.

"No one's ever said that to me. Just said sorry."

It looked at her for a plump moment, then reached out and smoothed down the hair at the top of her forehead. It turned around and they both went into meditation.

However, that small touch had ignited a violent yearning.

A desperate desire to have sex with a hermaphrodite.

Barbara bundled out of the yoga studio. She heard a jaunty whistle behind her. It was The Thing.

"Hey, Bra-Bra," it shouted. "Have any orgasms during class?" It was chuckling to itself, emitting puffs of cold air.

"If I had, I'd still be having them." Something about it irritated her–perhaps its cavalier attitude towards her. "You must feel very proud of yourself, preserving your fluids while standing on your head."

"Don't take this personally, but there was nothing in the class to prime my pump–"

"There was a mirror–"

"–no disrespect to you, of course, Blah-Blah."

"–which I noticed you never took your eyes off."

"That means you never took your eyes off . . ." it pointed both fingers at its face, " . . . this. Compliments accepted, man."

She slipped through the slush in regal silence, chased by snorts of laughter. Finally they reached The Thing's car. It was an old, rusting Volvo station wagon. On the roof, Astro had planted hardy grasses and multicoloured heather.

"Why the flowerbed?" Barbara punched her fists onto her hips.

"Well, Car-bra, this is technically a car roof–not a garden or flowerbed, as it is mobile. Thus, it is not covered by municipal law. I took it to municipal court."

"Why did you bother?"

"They tried to stop me watering my plants. Some bureaucrat with a brand-new pen his gran gave him or something. No offence to grannies there, Bing-Bang. Those municipal guidelines on water, man, they really tick me off!"

"Well," said Barbara in her most self-righteous tone, "if we all wasted water as you're so recklessly proposing, there'd be none left. That's the problem with being so young. You don't know such things. If you spent more time reading and less time stalking–"

"If you don't green the planet, you have what is known as a 'desert.'" It quote-marked the air. "If you have a 'desert,'" air quotes, "you have no more water."

"Oh, please. Do you even know what you're talking about?"

It looked at a hydrant for confirmation. "Do I know what I'm talking about?" Back to Barbara. "I think so. Do you?"

"I'm not willing to continue with this conversation. I have to go."

"In a hurry, huh? Leo, right? Fire sign. I'm Aquarius–air." It made a quick calculation. "Yep. Good enough. You could come for dinner one day, I guess."

"I *am* a Leo!" Barbara was impressed with this deduction, but quickly retreated back into indignation. "But we fire signs don't have time to watch air signs talking to themselves." She swivelled around.

"What can I entice you with? Hey, I know! I've got a few pictures of myself you can pore over. Maybe that'll stop you staring at me during yoga. Yeah–we could go in my car, man. You could tell the police you don't need a drive home this time. Save the taxpayers some money."

"I thought," Barbara said, turning a dismissive eye to it, "I was 'too old' for you. I wouldn't want to be accused of child molestation."

"It's okay, Bar-Bell. I've got protection." It stopped and looked her in the face.

She stopped walking.

"ChildLine," it said. It raised its eyebrows in disbelief and exploded into hysterical laughter.

Her face flushed with a wash of pink. "Stalker," she spat.

Tears came into its eyes as the tempo of its laugh grew more erratic.

"Have you finished yet?"

It couldn't stop.

"Done yet?"

It breathed in heavily but broke out again into a high giggle. "Fine, man. Next week Thursday, dinner. Seven o'clock. Don't be late, okay? And don't bring anything, alright? I only eat stuff that's been cooked in my kitchen. Then we know it's hygienic."

"So what were you doing eating at the delica–?"

"And don't eat before you come."

"Oh, all right," Barbara huffed. She reckoned that, perhaps, if she could get it to shut up, the sex would at least be noteworthy. "That'll give you time to take my photos off your walls, stash your long-range lenses into some closet and dismantle the shrine."

"That'd take more than a week, but I'll see what I can do for Thursday, Baa-Baa." It bleated out the last word as it wrote its address neatly on a precisely cut piece of paper.

"Can't wait!" Barbara said under her breath in her most sarcastic tone. She headed for Tribal Treasures to buy four sarongs for her move to Kenya.

SEVEN

Peekin' Ducks

Lifting herself from the Oaxacan blankets that covered her couch, Barbara began to dress for her date with Astro. She threw on a purple skirt from Afghanistan and a plunging V-neck top, then added a series of provocative amber necklaces and clinking Indian earrings. After snaking globules of aromatic oil through her generous cleavage, she wrapped herself in a Norwegian cloak and grabbed a voluminous bag made of mud-cloth from Mali.

She arrived on the outskirts of the city, assaulted by the sound of a saxophone played off pitch at full volume. A neighbour one floor below the sax player poked his head and net-vested chest out the window. "Turn your fucking flute off or I shove it up your ass."

Barbara, on the verge of joining the protest, followed the man's gaze. There, serenading her into the building, stood Astro with its saxophone. Barbara took pity on the hermaphrodite.

Poor kid, she thought. *Trying so hard to cope with its disability. Such a lesson in courage.*

Astro played even louder. The neighbour leaned farther out his window. "Better to put grease on flute. I coming up now. I shove it up your ass."

"Hey, Bra-Bra! I'm up here." Astro stopped mid-note. "You're late, man. How do you expect me to time the meal?" It sounded annoyed.

Barbara, displeased, bundled upstairs.

The creature was wearing a loose-hanging cotton summer dress that reached to the top of her knees. A female hermaphrodite. A female hermaphrodite with very little taste in clothing.

Barbara entered the apartment, kicking off her shoes. She could hardly believe her eyes–the carpet was made entirely from Astroturf. Deck chairs had been placed on real sand, which surrounded a large piece of glass. On the ceiling, Astro had painted a blazing blue sky with crystal clouds, creating a sense of elation and exultation. Barbara felt like she had floated into a dream.

Offered a beach chair, Barbara sat down. Astro headed for the kitchen, but not before straightening Barbara's shoes at the doorway. Barbara harrumphed. She looked towards the glass at her feet and saw something move. She budged forward and peered down to see a collection of tropical fish. This outlaw–wearing little more than an unflattering flowery sheet–had circumvented another important municipal law on water use and had built an aquarium into its floor!

"Why did you put this in here?" she shouted.

"What? The fish?"

"No. Not the fish. The aquarium."

"Boo-Boo, that is technically a floor rather than a fish tank and therefore is not covered by laws on water use in aquariums.

In fact, there are no laws about how much water you can use in floors."

"Potential droughts mean nothing to you, do they?" Barbara chided.

"There wouldn't be any if the corporations hadn't got control of our water, Blah-Blah."

Barbara grew worried about consorting with such a sociopath, yet at the same time, she felt protective of a creature who could be thrown into neither male nor female prison.

Astro appeared, balancing plates laden with purple food in her honour. She realized that, despite the creature's disorder, she was doing the best she could. *Poor kid,* Barbara thought. *She's running as fast as she can.*

Barbara sat down at table, smiling with gracious acceptance of Astro's imperfections.

"You're beautiful when you smile, you know," Astro said, pupils widening through the yellow. "You look like Ava Gardner, man."

A female hermaphrodite who was also a lesbian.

Astro leaned towards her in a confidential manner, and Barbara tilted her head to receive whatever confession the creature wished to whisper.

"You probably don't know, but . . ." Astro hesitated, " . . . Ava Gardner was an actress in the–"

"I know who Ava Gardner was. I'm older than you are, you know." She flapped open her serviette in irritation.

"You can say that again, man," Astro whispered to herself–Barbara could read the lip movements. "So, why are you in such a bad mood, bud?"

"I'm not in a bad mood, Estro," Barbara snapped. "However, since you're so interested in my life, I'll tell you what my biggest problem is. Have you been watching the situation in Nigeria?"

"I don't have a TV. I don't have any electronic gadgets, man. They mess with your mind. Those electromagnetic–"

"Anyway," Barbara cut in, having had years of experience guiding a conversation back to base, "there's been a flood in Nigeria. It's killed half a million people, with more expected to die. They're afflicted with water blindness–"

"I know."

"You know? How?"

"I watch my neighbour's TV."

Barbara put her head in her hands, exasperated. "Well, I'm trying to find work there, but I can't." She spoke in muffled tones as she massaged her face. "Water companies are trying to buy up water rights now that Nigeria is in no position to negotiate. And they'll control all power generation."

"Really?" Astro popped a grape into her mouth, her face a picture of uninterest. "Why don't you find some contacts to help you?"

"I have." Barbara gritted her teeth. "They haven't led anywhere."

"Well, they didn't do a very good job, did they? Try the raspberry sauce. Who's your contact?" She swirled raspberry sauce on Barbara's salad.

"A woman called Dahlia." Barbara crunched some cabbage, her misfortunes creating a sense of listlessness.

"What–are you kidding? Aw, man!" Yellow eyes rolled heavenwards. "See how the cosmos works? She's named after a flower. We can't go wrong here. We should visit her this week."

"We? What have you got to do with this?"

"She. Is. Named. Af. Ter. A. Flow-er." Astro shook her head in disbelief. "Thus, she is my territory. Without me, what are the chances you'll know how to cultivate your most important contact?"

As Astro had instructed, Barbara phoned Dahlia and arranged a trip on the weekend to her farm, deep in the hilly Virginia countryside.

When they arrived at the farmhouse, Astro sniffed the air in appreciation, then repeated her earlier instructions: "Do not leave this place until you have a promise, a timeline and an action plan." She stared at Barbara, standing only a foot away. "Okey-dokey?" She continued staring, oblivious of the needs of personal space. "Three things. That's all. What are they?"

Barbara huffed, "Promise, timeline, action plan," then added a passive-aggressive "Quite simplistically."

"Good job, Bimble." Astro scrunched her mouth in pride. "And if she hesitates, don't forget to mention the Nigerian name. I know it's difficult. But see if you can remember it." She searched Barbara's face.

Immobilized by fury, Barbara did not answer.

"Didn't think so. Here you go." She handed Barbara a piece of paper, then ambled towards the turkeys.

Barbara swivelled on her heel and rang the bell. The farmyard smelled of country air–bursting with vigour and virtue–with a hint of the sulphur of chicken manure.

Dahlia opened the door. "Barbara!" Almost a high C. "Wonderful to see you. How are you? Do come in."

Barbara was caught in mid-smile as she breathed in a smell that did not belong indoors and then glimpsed two chickens darting down the hall. Dahlia led her to a large wooden kitchen full of chicken teapots, goose-shaped mugs and duck coasters.

"Norm has resigned as director." Dahlia cleared some papers from the kitchen table. "I don't know if you heard."

"No, I hadn't."

"Great pity. Anyway, did you hear back from the water groups?"

"Just rejections." A chicken pecked at Barbara's toes. "Which is a great pity, as this water damage is affecting key nesting sites." She tilted her head.

Dahlia gasped, "Oh no."

Barbara had never heard such a low note from a woman.

Annoyed by the nibbling, she dug her toes into the chicken's belly, hoping to shove it away.

"Who is heading up the groups in Nigeria?"

Barbara quickly scanned for a name. Her memory failed. She secreted Astro's paper onto her lap. "Well, um . . . Femi Jegede?" Regretting the note of query in her voice, she discreetly punted the chicken clear across the room. It flapped in distress.

Dahlia scooped up her charge. "Oh, darling!" She nibbled the chicken's warlike beak. The chicken stared at Barbara through violent orange irises.

"So, as long as Femi manages to stay alive . . ." Barbara emphasized the last word.

"Alive? Oh dear."

"We just need three things, Dahlia." Barbara cleared her throat. "An action plan, a timeline and a guarantee."

Dahlia put down the stunned chicken, sat at the table and began writing. "Tomorrow, contact eight water advocacy programs; send list to Barbara. Follow up three days, one week, fortnight, month. Deadline–Barbara at work by April, protecting Nigerian nesting sites."

"That's key," Barbara added.

"Absolutely. Now, the guarantee. I can only get that with a threat. What's the threat?" She tapped a pencil to her lips. "Ah, yes. The contortionist I told you about–do you remember?"

Barbara's eyebrows moved involuntarily. "Vaguely."

"He's now chair of the Global Environment Facility. He can make a few calls." She paused, bosom rising and falling, lost in reminiscence.

"Jumping through hoops for you again, hey?" Barbara suggested.

Dahlia turned a stern eye on her.

Barbara left the farmhouse, feeling more confident than ever. She searched for Astro and found her past rickety fences, near some large barns. She noticed that the tops of the silos had been hewn off, doubtless to collect rainwater, an illegality sited away from prying eyes.

The clouds–whipped cream white–hung low, heavy with moisture to replenish the earth. Icy drops began to fall as Barbara and Astro approached ducks of bronze and iridescent blue, quacking in excitement, running in circles and flapping their wings as if welcoming the rain.

Astro looked up at the sky with the glee of a five-year-old child. "Woo-hoo! Look at this, man!" Astro cried, closing her eyes, face heavenwards. "There's nothing like the taste of rain, Babu."

The ducks unfolded their wings, stretching their little necks to the sky, eyes closed, in a state of apparent bliss.

"Can you feel it on your face? It stings."

Barbara looked at her, a spirit of nature freed from all of society's constraints, the universe in its most joyful guise. Astro's T-shirt was now soaked, but Barbara could distinguish no nipples of note.

There was a flash of lightning in the far distance, and the ducks ran into a barn. Astro and Barbara followed them to shelter from the rain.

"Uh-oh. I don't think they like us being here, man. We'd better go," Astro said.

"What do you mean?"

"Well, Ber-Ber, look into their eyes. We're not supposed to be here."

Barbara looked down into the ducks' eyes. Into ten pairs of disapproving eyes. A tingle of excitement fanned out from her groin. She buttered up. Defenceless against such primal forces, she unbuttoned her shirt.

"What the hell are you doing, man?" Astro asked, shivering.

"We're having sex." She threw off her shirt. "Won't take long."

"Who's having sex? I'm not having sex!"

"Look, Astro," Barbara put her hands on Astro's shoulders, eyes flooded with pity, underpants flooded with nutrients, "I know you're worried what I'll think." She looked down at Astro in a gracious manner. "It can't have been easy to grow up with . . . you know . . ."

"No. I don't. What?" Astro crossed her arms.

"I realize you may not have fully developed organs." She chucked Astro's chin, an indulgent look posting itself on her face. "And I know they may not function fully." Her voice was therapy-soft. She tilted her head to one side. "But there are ways of getting around–"

"What?" Astro screeched. The ducks quacked in fright. "I may not have what?" She looked at a pitchfork–shock, horror, fury all fused into one facial expression. "Are you listening to this? Can you believe this woman?"

"Don't panic, Astro." Barbara's voice was soothing and empathetic. She loosened her greying bra. "I've been to a number of workshops, and I feel I have the experience to–"

"My organs are not only fully developed . . ." yellow eyes stared directly into Barbara's as Astro tugged at her zipper, " . . . they're overdeveloped. And as for functioning . . ." Astro snapped, ripping off her trousers.

Barbara surveyed an unrestricted length of penis. No stub. "Where's the rest?" she queried. Barbara's bra pinged off, catapulting away from its great burden, and her breasts slapped onto her chest.

"What?"

"That's all there is?"

"What?"

"You're a man?"

"Of course I'm a man!" Astro shrieked. "What the hell did you think I was?"

"A hermaphrodite." Barbara tried to compute. She screwed up her eyes to concentrate. "What were you doing wearing a dress?" Her breasts wobbled as she spoke.

"Well, Barbunkle, in case you didn't know, it's important to keep the scrotum well aerated," Astro said, his penis jiggling, "for health reasons."

"Oh. I see." She tried to hide her disappointment. With the heaviest of sighs, she turned around and wearily put on her bra. "By the way," she said, "I don't know why you think that's overdeveloped. Looks pretty average to me."

"It extends." Astro had a strange note in his voice.

She turned around and there, greeting her beneath a sprig of tawny pubic hair, an erect penis. Mechanically amazing. Aesthetically perfect. Her favourite sight.

"You're looking pretty excited."

"Oh, sorry. I didn't see you there. Ducks turn me on, that's all." Astro gazed down at his penis with a fatherly pride. "What did I tell you, Skippy?" He pointed at it with two victorious index fingers. "Fully functioning."

Barbara released her bra like a slingshot, and within minutes her waist-high, oversized flannel underpants plopped beside it in the hay.

She tried to focus on all she had learned at a Dutch workshop on prolonging the orgasmic state, but despite her rigorous training, she could feel herself near climax. So they both took a short break, lay back and exchanged the details of some of the finer sex workshops they had attended.

"I had a multiple orgasm with sixteen separate peaks," Barbara bragged. "The facilitator said it was the longest series he'd ever–"

"Multiples are for amateurs, bud," Astro cut in. "Best to go for an Extreme Massive Orgasm. Now, if you've ever been to 'Tantric Sexperience'" he quote-marked the air, "in Arizona–"

"T.S.?" Barbara tutted. "Too mainstream. For weekenders. The masturbation workshop in Costa Rica is for more advanced practitioners."

"You've. Been. Abroad?" Astro almost choked in admiration, staring at her with wonder.

Barbara stretched her toes. "We fire signs are risk-takers." She wiggled them.

The ducks came nearer. Barbara looked into ten pairs of shocked eyes. She pounced on Astro. As he thrust into her, she contracted her vaginal muscles, a technique she had trained in for many years. He sucked in his breath, looking as if he were about to faint. A high-intensity single orgasm rifled through her body, sending her flexing and flailing. Seconds later, Astro lost his vital nutrients.

She knew the frenzied teenage foreplay they had engaged in was beneath both of them and certainly negated the time and expense they had dedicated to attending various workshops on the subject of sexual arousal.

They both lay back, calculating how the session could have been improved, considering their proper responsibilities in the matter, thinking through their vast and separate training, wondering how to avoid a catastrophe of this nature again. After proper deliberation, they resumed their activities, in greater control, aiming for orgasms lasting more than just a paltry few seconds.

After five hours, they collapsed into each other's arms as freezing rain continued to pelt down on the barn's tin roof. For a while, they lay there, the passion of nature and the hunger of culture, admiring each other's singular qualities.

"Hey, Babu. Promise you won't leave me, man, okay?" Astro nestled between her breasts. "I don't like change." He looked up at her for confirmation.

She realized that she could depend on his consistency as much as he could draw energy from her unpredictability. "I promise." She smiled.

She had given her word of honour. She had promised to provide the constancy he craved. Despite the fear it induced in her, she would stick to that promise. She made a mental note to place a picture of him on her shrine as a daily reminder.

EIGHT

Happy New Coup

The general was a man ruled by fear. He had every reason to be. Many men of ambition could be found within the ranks of the military: a few men of strategy, but a greater number of brutality. Kolo was working on the general's fears, kneading them like clay until he created a vessel he could use. He had to keep the general on the move, so that he could not consolidate power. A military coup could not be allowed to bungle his plans.

"Joseph." He used the general's first name whenever he wished to promote intimacy. "You need to make sure you have the endorsement of the great majority of the people. You don't want some upstart to . . ." he placed his hands together in a steeple; the general blinked, " . . . to get any ideas."

As usual, the general reverted to questions, deliberately unhurried. "Have you heard anything? Any rumours?"

"Nothing of substance. Nothing that could be verified at this stage."

The general remained immobile, eyelids at half-mast, revealing no trace of his inner thoughts–with the exception of this immobility. Given Kolo's greater ability to sink into an endless meditation, the general finally had to break the silence. "And you suggest securing support?"

"No, no, no, absolutely not!" Kolo appeared scandalized. "I am merely suggesting strengthening the backing you already have."

A gentle wash of suspicion overlaid the general's temperate expression. It was now time for Kolo to deploy tactics familiar to any politician, but alien to a military man. The general, used to strict hierarchy and discipline, would naturally consider the principal leader as his main contact. Kolo understood that support could most effectively be built in the form of a pyramid, by approaching less powerful parties before moving to those at the peak. He appreciated that it was important to consult with those under siege first, then advance on those comfortable with their unqualified dominance. This prevented the alienation and resentment that inevitably led to the formation of allied opposition.

Kolo was aware of the growing rivalry between the sultan of Sokoto, who favoured the continuance of Islamic Sharia law, and the newly appointed emir of Kano, a more moderate Muslim who favoured international commerce, human rights and the advancement of women. The emir had gained an immense power base in one of Nigeria's giant commercial hubs, overwhelming the sultan's waning influence.

"My friend," Kolo's belly creased as he leaned in confidentially, "I strongly suggest you visit the emir of Kano as quickly as possible. The north needs to be reassured that the nation is stable, that Muslim and Christian will work together and that there will be no political backlash." He leaned back in his armchair to rest his tautened belly.

"You think so?" Anxiety trounced suspicion. "Maybe so. Maybe so."

Kolo nodded. He issued a few compliments as a parting gesture, then left the general's compound with soft steps, as if eggshells surrounded his colleague, signifying the fragility of his continued survival.

Kolo then flew to the fringes of the Sahara for an end run around his ally, having preplanned a visit to the less powerful sultan of Sokoto first, in the Islamic north. The sultan was the president of the Supreme Council for Islamic Affairs, reigning head of the legendary Sokoto Caliphate and one of the most powerful paramount traditional leaders in Nigeria. Radar did not assist Kolo's flight nor landing lights his descent. The airport itself was deserted and no taxis stood outside, save for the sultan's Rolls-Royce waiting for him.

Even here Kolo could not escape the terrible sounds of mourning–people screaming and praying, broken souls, spirits that would never again find rest. He drove through streets devoid of traffic. In the absence of petrol, the resourceful people of the north had bought donkeys, horses and camels for transportation. Wells had opened, charging exorbitant fees for small canisters of water, while farmers offered their goods at five times ordinary prices.

The Rolls entered the palace gates and parked next to the three others in the courtyard. A member of the sultan's retinue led Kolo to a chamber. Here, the paramount leader sat on a golden throne, and had discarded his usual Western attire, Kolo noted, to underscore the historical significance of his role. He wore a white turban wound around his head, one end of which was secured from one ear to the other under his chin and over his chest, and ceremonial robes of sparkling white embroidered with gold. Together, the sultan and Kolo looked like the figure 10, the sultan the long, straight form of the 1, Kolo the round, plump shape of the 0.

Kolo looked into the sultan's eyes, an act that few of his subjects were allowed. Betrayed there were genuine distress, real grief. Kolo wondered how such events could touch this man—one of the most venerated in Nigeria.

"Minister," the sultan said with rolling r's and clipped tones, "welcome."

Kolo creased into his lowest bow. "I have come here personally to ensure that the caliphate is safe in these troubled times."

"Allah is merciful."

With a Christian mother, Muslim father and pagan grandparents, Kolo ensured that any individual would consider him a dedicated adherent of whichever religion they practised. He had completed the Hajj to Mecca, stating, according to Muslim precepts, that Jesus was a prophet of Islam, and, within the south's many churches, he had claimed that this prophet was God's Son, in capital letters. Whether other sons existed, he left to the imagination. The Old Testament kept him free of problems. He occasionally worshipped the spirits of nature, as animists represented just 10 percent of the population. In this way, he had managed to sidestep the divisions of north and south.

The sultan gestured towards Kolo and the contrasting silhouettes of the duo walked towards an inner courtyard.

"How is the general?" the sultan asked.

"Very busy. Very tired. Very worried."

"Ah. No doubt too busy to visit Sokoto."

Kolo looked embarrassed.

"But not too busy to visit Kano, I see," the sultan continued.

Kolo stood, head hung in shame, eyes buried in apparent humiliation at the military's lapse, but internally ecstatic, floating. "Perhaps he is more liberal than expected?" he opined.

"Maybe he believes one day we will all worship at the feet of the dollar. I am happy to welcome you."

The sultan posed with Kolo outside his walled palace, intricately carved and painted with arabesques. They were surrounded by brightly adorned aides, attendants and retainers. A reporter snapped a picture of a new figure, a much higher figure than a mere 10: 1107111. The 7 held the ceremonial umbrella over the sultan's head.

Kolo was even able to read a little speech he had prepared: "Our ancestors are calling us to move forward. We will not let this mire engulf us. The great River Niger–which stretches from our north to our south, our east to our west–will be our friend once more."

The next day, Kolo flew to see His Royal Highness, the emir of Kano. The general's meeting there the day before would have had the added benefit of implying support for Kolo.

Each time he called on the general, Kolo donned more daring attire, a subtle message of mounting supremacy. His latest visit warranted an audacious yellow agbada, made of heavy brocade silk, a recent purchase that had to be sent abroad for dry cleaning.

"Did the meeting go well?" Kolo asked.

"Very well. The emir was very appreciative." The general visibly relaxed in Kolo's company.

"Ah, you had better luck than me." Kolo brooded in mock self-recrimination. "A tactical mistake to visit the sultan first."

"You live and learn, my friend." The general slid down in his armchair to a more comfortable position.

"Unfortunately, if you don't learn fast enough, you don't live long." A wistful thought followed this, seemingly unconnected. "Perhaps it's time to go to Kainji. The people cannot think you might be avoiding it. You must portray yourself as a man of integrity and authority."

The general pondered a while. "Agreed."

"A man who cares about their fate, even while the president runs away from them."

This emotion–caring–did not fit the general's repertoire, and he shook his head. "The area is too dangerous to visit at the moment. There's armed rebellion."

"Well, some of your junior officers are taking that risk, I note." Kolo left the thought to hang in the air.

The general softly scratched his cheek, a vehement gesture from such a discreet man.

"Meanwhile," Kolo sighed, "I'll visit the less affected spots downstream–just a few farmsteads. Hardly worth going to those bush areas." He took a last few strokes of the armchair. "Call me if you need political backup."

The general shrugged. Kolo understood the gesture. According to the general's logic, armed force trumped diplomacy on any occasion. Kolo suppressed a grin.

"I would keep a low profile in Kainji over the next few weeks, Joseph." Kolo stood up and moved around in silence, as one would in a funeral parlour. "The situation could become combustible. You don't want to be associated with that. Don't let reporters anywhere near the area."

Thus, he sent the general to the region where rage was about to erupt into organized protest, while Kolo visited settlements too far apart for any movement of solidarity to have formed. Getting Kainji under control would take weeks, if not months.

Kolo flew from Abuja to Lagos, the bustling commercial hub of Nigeria, unharmed by the catastrophe; a city built on islands criss-crossed by lagoons and creeks, named after the Portuguese word for "lakes."

While the general was away, Kolo courted the forgotten but powerful Christian groups, who represented almost half the population. The people flooded back to the centres of worship, as their belief in man's primacy over nature had been thrown into serious question. Kolo made sure to visit the leader of the newest Christian sect, funded by evangelicals in the United States. These churches were an increasingly popular form of entertainment.

He left the reporters outside as he entered a crystal temple to meet its spiritual leader. The bishop was dressed immaculately in a Nehru jacket and a thick golden cross encrusted with diamonds, which matched the fine baubles on his fingers and the large ruby and sapphire watch on his wrist.

"Minister!" the preacher sparkled. "You are the answer to my prayers!"

"Your eminence. Please tell me how I can assist your people."

The bishop's glittering eyes lifted up to the dull ceiling and walls of his glorious oasis in the filth and squalor of Lagos. They were constructed of glass, built high, soaring into the sky, in imitation of California's great monument–the Crystal Cathedral. Unfortunately, as with most ideas transplanted directly into Nigeria, the bishop had been unaware that no window cleaners existed to wipe their higher reaches. So the ceiling and upper walls were now covered in red dust, tree sap and bird droppings. The pride and joy of the bishop lay in a sullied state.

"Look–look at this foul dirt," he frothed. "It is not a fitting monument to the Lord. People come here to have their spirits raised, and all we can offer them is a glass hovel."

"Ah! You need water."

"Yes, clean water."

"I would be honoured to provide it."

"Oh, Minister Kolo," crystal tears glistened down the bishop's translucent face, "you are truly one of the Lord's chosen."

Outside the cathedral, bright flashbulbs caught Kolo and the bishop, gleaming smiles, sparkling teeth, shaking hands.

After this interlude, Kolo set about touring the seats of power: the members-only Yacht Club, the Polo Club and finally Ikoyi Club.

Built during the colonial era, Ikoyi Club stood in lush gardens, its facade white, paint-chipped and airy. It now teemed with people seeking information, all in pursuit of the benefits of its water supply and generator. Kolo had made a point of ensuring that the club was fully provisioned during these dark times. He did not wish his colleagues to go without the benefit of a swimming pool, or for its golf courses to become parched.

He donned a dashiki made of the finest Dutch lace for his meeting with his closest and most loyal business associate, the famed newspaper tycoon Alhaji Dr. Monday Ikene, LL.B., M.B.A., Ph.D. (incomplete). They sat at the nineteenth hole, fondling drinks while Kolo watched his friend's daughter play with some of the other mixed-race children–or "oyinbo pepper"–who had sprouted after the return of Nigeria's businessmen, intellectuals and diplomats from abroad. Their white wives sat in a huddle, trading horror stories of life in Nigeria and exchanging news of the best places to buy supplies. Some wore Western dress with flounces and flowers; others, with more adventurous spirits, sat there in bubas and wrappers, headdresses sliding down their silken hair to their eyes.

Ikene's oyinbo pepper came to greet him and settled to play with her doll at Kolo's feet.

"So, Dawn," Kolo asked, wondering why her father–who called her Don–had given her a name he could not pronounce, "what do you want to be when you grow up? A businessman like your father?"

"No," Dawn answered. "They don't make enough money."

"Oh really?" Kolo interlaced his fingers across his round belly. "So what do you want to be?"

"A politician."

Her father almost swallowed his toothpick. "Don!" he shouted. "Go and play with your friends!"

The child scurried off, carrying her anatomically impressive doll with her, leaving the doll's executive briefcase and pink SUV by Kolo's feet.

"So, Ogbe," Ikene rebounded quickly, "how's life?" His long, curved fingernails scratched white lines onto his skin.

"Good, very good." Kolo quickly checked himself. "Lucky to be alive."

"Oh God. This country will kill us all." Ikene snapped his fingers for some more Fanta orange with ice. "How can I run my businesses without banks, transportation, personnel? Even the newspapers–"

"The newspapers have to run," Kolo interjected. "It's very important that they continue to run." He attempted to recuperate from such a rash outburst. "Tell me what else you need, my friend. I'm sure this has taken a toll on your finances. News can wait."

Ikene turned an eye to Kolo–a vulture surveying the landscape. He stood up–perhaps the only Nigerian with hunched shoulders–and hooked his long fingers under Kolo's arm. They glided towards the veranda.

"You do me a great favour." Ikene could sniff out a plot years before it had hatched. He had followed the trail of Kolo's bold imaginings and had found his breakfast there. "Is there anything I can do in return?"

"I feel it is my role, as a public servant," Kolo sounded nonchalant, "to ensure that the people remain calm. They must be informed of the steps the government is taking to secure their future."

"What if I sent a reporter to follow you over the next few months? Would we find this," Ikene paused, claws digging into Kolo's arm, "newsworthy?" Ikene's eyes were fixated on the centre of Kolo's dark pupils.

"I should think so," Kolo said cautiously, knowing full well that in exchange for coverage essential to raising his profile he would be followed day and night by Ikene's spy. "And, of course, you realize General Abucha is deploying troops in Kainji."

"Yes, we will need a bit of, em, financial assistance." Ikene smiled, revealing a row of long teeth. "But it will be a privilege to provide coverage of both you and the general. May I make a suggestion? Perhaps you could start with a letter to the editor. Then it would be natural for us to follow your activities."

"I'll write one tonight."

Kolo left with a shiver. The "inducements" Ikene expected would only increase over time. Although one of his dearest friends, Kolo disliked the man intensely. He patted his pockets. Surely he had not left his antacid at home?

His chauffeur drove Kolo through empty streets to his Lagos home, the car's gentle suspension rocking him into a light trance.

For the average citizen, there was no petrol for transportation; the city had ground to a halt. Litter decomposed on the roadsides and people drifted as if in a dream, dazed and without purpose. Thrown across the skies, a veil of neon brown haze turned day into permanent dusk, erasing all colour. Even through the air conditioning, Kolo could hear the screams and wails of those who had lost more than everything–their history, their heritage, their people. He asked Innocent to put on some classical music and lay back in his seat, closing his eyes, shutting out the nightmare.

At home he settled down in a comfortable chair and started to compose his letter. He dipped into a box of specially imported Quality Street chocolate and, for inspiration, selected a rosy strawberry cream–his favourite.

Letter to the Editor:
It is my privilege to serve in government, at the behest of the people, to represent their interests and protect their well-being. I have failed in this august duty. And for this,

He sucked loudly on his chocolate, adding an orange crème to the mélange.

I pray almighty God

He immediately crossed out "God." Too explosive in a country with an Islamic north and a Christian south. His fat digits dived into the box for some nut centres.

the all-compassionate creator for forgiveness.

Kolo shook his hand, swearing under his breath. It ached from writing. He looked at it with concern, twisted it to the left and right. Did it look swollen? Yes, it did. It most certainly did. And it was aching. What could it be? Could it be cancer? Could he have cancer of the wrist? He reached for his high-potency multivitamins. Holding his pen at a new angle, one that made his elbow stick out across the entire width of the desk, Kolo continued writing.

> The country is in mourning. We yearn for the enfolding arms of our families, the welcoming hugs of homestead, the protective caress of history, the firm embrace of heritage. But all that greets us is the cold grip of despair.

He sat back and admired his words. "This is pure poetry," he said out loud. He envisaged his text under glass in a museum. The vision pleased him greatly.

> One voice could have saved a million lives.

He scratched out the latter half of the sentence; the initial count had been lower–he would stick with that.

> 500,000 lives. But no voice sounded loud enough to be heard. As long as I have a tongue to speak, I will commit to ensuring that such disasters never again occur.

Perfect. Another letter in which forgiveness had been sought but little blame assumed. And the implication that duties can be resumed locked right there into the heart of the text. Beautiful.

The next day, Kolo started on a northbound reconnaissance by military plane while Innocent struggled past potholes and flooded roads in Kolo's Mercedes, the passenger seats and trunk full of gasoline canisters. The car had to be ferried over raging rivers on makeshift bamboo rafts while a journalist followed on an aging scooter. All three met at a small airport. Kolo hopped into his car to visit a number of downstream villages, his mind filled not only with political strategy but also with future commercial ventures that would affect the region. Once again, he drew on his prodigious acting skills to garner local support, sobbing at stories too horrific to pay attention to.

While the general's name had become unaccountably sullied by the press, associated with brutal acts of violence against an already devastated people, a more diplomatic, soothing Kolo quickly seized upon this unfortunate fact to increase his popularity. He travelled widely, spreading his word like the harmattan's dust.

At the peak of Kolo's unassailable self-confidence, the white Mercedes stopped in a small town to meet with the chief. Although plagued by contaminated water, villages had fared better in the disaster than larger settlements, having little need for electricity, petrol or oil.

Kolo's reporter followed him as they trekked through the mud. The retainers pointed at the hut in which the chief sat.

"Where is the door?" Kolo asked in alarm.

"There, sir." The chief's retainer indicated a low opening barely large enough to crawl through.

"What? You can't expect me to go through there." Kolo's aversion to germs competed with his horror at any form of debasement. He had no intention of entering on his knees, in submission to a mere village chief. "I'm not going in there!" he shouted, his chin a-tremble.

"Yes, sir," an aide said. "But if you want to see the chief, he's sitting inside."

Kolo understood. There were few ways in which the village could protest recent events. In order to win a greater victory, Kolo had to submit to this defeat. But he had no intention of going down without a fight. "Innocent!" he called. "Handkerchiefs. Antiseptic."

His driver saluted, charged off and ran back with six newly ironed white linen handkerchiefs and a bottle of antiseptic.

"Lay them on the ground through there." Kolo pointed at the hole.

Innocent glowered at him until Kolo raised the back of his hand in threat. He heard the discreet click of a camera and dismissed the reporter with harsh words. Innocent started laying the handkerchiefs on the ground, crawling through the hole.

"Go in backwards," Kolo demanded.

The driver gaped at him, stunned at his employer's audacity, then turned around in the dust and backed into the chief's hut, bottom first, laying the handkerchiefs sequentially in a neat row. The first sight to greet the chief would therefore be the buttocks of the driver of the minister for natural resources.

The driver remained kneeling inside while Kolo dropped his rotund figure to its knees and crawled in over the handkerchiefs. As Kolo appeared, a photographer within the hut took a series of quick snapshots of the minister kneeling before the chief. The chief beamed in approval.

"Ah! Minister Kolo. A privilege to see you. Welcome. Please no formalities–I beg you to stand up."

Kolo stood, his face a picture of serenity as small atoms of rage exploded in every cell of his being. "The privilege is mine. I am so grateful, sir," he shook muddy hands with the chief, "for this opportunity." He then opened the bottle of antiseptic and splashed it liberally over his hands, wiping them on another handkerchief and ostentatiously handing the debris to the chief's aide.

A quiet smile played on the chief's lips–the smile of a snake in a henhouse.

"I have come," Kolo pronounced, "to listen, not to talk."

"Please sit down," the chief said. He smiled again.

"As I was saying," Kolo repeated, disconcerted by the chief's enigmatic behaviour, "I have come to listen, not to talk."

"Oh, I see!" The chief's eyes twinkled. "What would you like to listen to?"

Kolo shifted in discomfort. The smell of antiseptic was overpowering. "I have come to consult with you. You are a wise man. In order to move forward, I have to assess where we currently lie."

"In case the ministry has not informed you, we currently lie with one million dead. Are you not aware of this, sir?"

"Yes, yes, of course, Chief. Of course. However, I need your assistance to move forward from this terrible tragedy."

"You are a great man," the chief said with a pleasant demeanour. "You do not need our help. We are only a village."

Kolo understood what the chief wanted. "Is there any help you need from me?"

"Of course," the chief smiled. "And for many years we have been asking for it."

Silence again.

"How much?"

The chief smiled gently. "Minister, I am sure you are not offering me a bribe–you who so strongly oppose corruption!" The chief flicked some flies away with a cow-tail whip.

One of the flies landed on Kolo's cheek. He shooed it away with his hand, irate, uncomfortable.

"How is your father?" the chief asked after a while.

"He's fine. Still very active." Kolo cheered up at this question–he was proud of his father, a former minister of finance.

"Your wife? Your children?"

Kolo stiffened. This question had plagued him throughout his adult life, and it was one for which he could find no "political" response.

They waited. He could not escape an answer. "I have neither."

Those in the room stared at him as if he had sprouted a crocodile's tail.

"That is a great pity." The chief stared at Kolo, flicking the flies. "And your mother?"

Kolo sucked in his breath. No one ever mentioned his mother; few had ever seen her. Kolo could hardly believe the insolence of this uneducated, inconsequential scrap of bush meat. "Better," he answered, warily.

"Such a pity about your mother," the chief said, studying Kolo's shrinking frame.

How did the chief know anything about this most hidden of family secrets? "Do you know my family, sir?" Kolo asked in a voice and manner more of a child than a man.

"Yes, of course. Victoria is from our village. Do you remember her?"

Kolo's eyes widened, like those of a child seeing a ghost. Victoria had been serving as nanny in his father's household on the day when the flame in Kolo's life had been extinguished. "Yes, I remember her." Kolo trembled. He began to pick his nails. He wanted to leave, to be released from memory's shackles, yet something about the chief kept him rooted to his seat. "Is she here?"

"Yes, she's still here," the chief answered. "Do you want to see her?"

"No," Kolo replied quickly, panic in his voice. "However," he remembered his manners, "please give her my good wishes."

"That is very kind," the chief smiled.

Kolo left the hut feeling sick, weary, depressed, and with an increasingly desperate hunger for power.

In low spirits, he spent the next few hours on the flight south ruminating. He could picture the face of his beloved twin brother, smiling, at play. He remembered the moment that changed his life, as he and his twin played tag near the swimming pool on a sunny day, with the sweet smell of the mango tree mingling with the water's stiff chlorine. Kolo pushed his brother from behind, his brother looked back at him with a smile–he could remember the smile–eyes bright with laughter. Then a sequence of random instants of which Kolo had little memory, a series of frozen moments ending in a face distorted by terror. The piercing scream at its highest pitch as his soul's double tumbled into the water.

The brothers had not been encouraged to learn to swim, as a witch doctor had warned their father that this would bring misfortune.

The sight of his brother, his mirror image, struggling for air, screaming and panicking, had been etched on Kolo's mind for its eternity.

He remembered his father pulling the body from the water, looking at Kolo in fear, in disbelief. He recalled his mother shrieking as his father gave her the news. She screamed for four days. After that, every time he tried to enter her room, Victoria would gently lead him away, promising him food or toys. He tried to peek in at his mother through her window, but the curtains were always drawn. Eventually, Victoria stopped taking care of him in order to take care of his mother, and he lost the last gentle touch of his childhood. He never saw his mother again.

He thought again of Victoria. Despite her tender care, after the accident he had the impression that she despised him, a feeling that had grown stronger with every passing day. Her furtive glances in his direction implied blame. But how had she managed to escape all condemnation? Where had she been during this tragedy? Was it not her job to watch over them?

He ran to the toilet, knelt down on the floor and vomited.

The plane flew over flooded areas and Kolo saw people still sitting on rooftops, hands extended to him for help. Yet he could picture only his brother, that reflection of himself, begging for rescue, trapped in the all-engulfing water.

By the time he returned to Abuja, it was nearing Christmas–a critical time for his next move. He now concentrated solely on his ascent to the presidency.

The phone rang: Mary Glass, exactly on time.

"Ah, Ms. Glass." He ensured that his words slipped out with a tone of utter nonchalance. "I thought it only fair to mention that the French are making a bid–their speed vastly exceeds that of TransAqua. And of course, so does the verbosity of their contract." In-jokes would keep her loyal. "Unless you can assist in . . ." a judicious cough, " . . . other matters, we really have no use for you."

"But we have no contract! How could we make such a commitment without one?"

He spoke slowly, with meaning. "There can be no contract before the act itself."

"Pardon, sir?"

"Think about who signs the contract. At the moment, I can't."

Finally the woman understood. "I will call the ambassador."

"And what influence does he have?" Kolo drawled. "He's only a go-between, after all."

"He'll call the president."

"Timeline?"

"This week."

"Bonne chance, Mademoiselle Glass!"

On the 30th of December, exactly one week after that phone call, Kolo sat chewing his nails in his office at the Ministry for Natural Resources, a small wire leading from a radio on his desk to an earpiece in his ear. At 5:10 p.m., he stopped chewing and jerked into an upright position. His bleached skin brightened, a small flush of pink accentuating the rash on his cheeks.

An hour later, the general marched in, his immovable facial muscles finally allowing him to form an expression that could be widely interpreted–and Kolo had no doubt that it signalled a final comprehension, myriad recollections, a raw awareness nearing shock.

"A cunning man!" The general's voice carried admiration, if not a little fear.

"Political life!" Kolo shrugged with apology, as he hid his nails under his agbada. "Will you be able to, ehm, to manage the situation henceforth?"

The general stood rigid and saluted. There was no question that he had to support a man from his own ethnic group.

The next day, the entire nation heard the news that the president's helicopter had crashed as it carried his entourage back from a meeting with the emir of Kano. Kolo entered the government offices in an agbada in muted green–to reflect the colours of the Nigerian flag–head hung low in mourning. In the corridors of power, colleagues expressed outrage that their president had not left office voluntarily instead of being "forced out."

"Does the man have to pull the country down with him?" Kolo tutted. "Why couldn't he have left office gracefully instead of creating this wahala? Every man should know when his time is up."

On the preferred date for coups in Nigeria, that is to say the first day of January, Ogbe Kolo acceded to the presidency. Citizens greeted each other with the customary salutation for the New Year: "Happy New Coup."

Kolo's yellow face was placed in Nigerian embassies and high commissions worldwide. For Kolo, however, this represented a minor achievement compared to his greater ambitions.

NINE

Cocoon

Igwe and his sister Ekwii had stayed with Femi since November, through nights of ghostly screams. One morning they heard a commotion at the top of the apartment building, heard people begging with a woman to come off the roof and heard the thud as her body hit the pavement. The body lay outside the building for a week, tucked into an alleyway, waiting for medical staff diverted to the flooded areas to attend to it, waiting for family killed in the flood to claim her, waiting for space in an overcrowded morgue. As the smell of rotting flesh encased the building, Femi was sheltered and guarded by his two friends. They soon moved him from the sterility of a bureaucratic, preplanned capital to the peaceful, hilly paradise of nearby Jos.

Three months passed, yet he still lay in mourning, cognizant of events yet caring little of their import. He was sealed in the past, living through memories like an epic told backwards. His friends worried that the tales that had taken thirty years to tell might take another thirty to retell and Femi's spirit would grow younger and younger until he died at the story of his birth. And thus they feared he would walk his first steps, speak his first words, see the first pair of astonished eyes as he slipped back into the eternal peace of the womb.

Femi's system shut down to a baseline of survival, of near existence–a life of atoms, molecules and cells, of organs and tissue, of mere mechanics. The life of energy, of soul and spirit, of will and whim, of a unique character and its interaction with the world, these vanished as quickly as if death had taken him too. His days no longer contained the joy of living, or even the combat of survival. They were simply existence: the in-breath and out-breath, the feeding of the body and the expelling of that nourishment.

Femi wandered through the vast panoramas of his desolation, unable to find comfort. He pictured his mother feeding the chickens, could even hear the tick-tick-tick of the corn feed as it skipped across the earth, unable to stay put, and the feeling of the ground quaking under her feet. He heard the screeching of the hens, which caused her to look around in panic. He imagined her screams of recognition as the sky turned black, the deafening roar that obliterated everything. He saw his father flung above the water into the air, looking down and seeing the surging swell, tumbling back towards the horror, plummeting towards the chasm. He felt his brother's anguish as the water crashed down on him, realizing that his days of dreaming had come to an end. He imagined Amos struggling to live, closing his eyes and holding his breath in the hope that he would surface above the waves. He wondered how the water tasted, whether of living things or of death.

He pictured his brother lying with legs splayed, naked, in a final humiliation. He pictured his father's corpse hundreds of miles from the place that had nurtured him, wrenched away from his ancestors, lying alone in some foreign land. He imagined unearthing his mother and witnessing the bewilderment in her eyes.

Time slowed, moments condensed, squeezing ferocious despair from each articulation, as one instant crept onwards to the next.

Femi began to detest his very being. He could not understand why he alone had been spared, of his entire village the most worthless of all. He wondered why his friends continued to take care of him. He was certain that, in the dark corners of the rooms they shared, they whispered his name with loathing, detesting a character afflicted with such a selfish lethargy. He abhorred the fact of his presence.

Femi did not have the energy to bathe. He could hardly stand up to go to the bathroom. His friends tried to feed him, but he found it tiring to sit up. He felt no hunger, and the small amounts of food he ate made him feel sick. The sensation lingered for hours as he lay on his mat, too tired to vomit, too exhausted to digest. He lost weight. His strength drained away. He felt close to death–it festered within all his thoughts and its cadence invaded his body.

Sometimes he woke up, nauseated by an odour, rancid and putrid. He felt certain it was his body, emanating a vile stench that wafted through the entire room. He was convinced that his friends wished to rid themselves of this burden, yet to his face they would smile and soothe him like the useless animal he was.

He noticed that, when he lay in a certain corner, a nail stuck up out of the wooden floor beneath the linoleum. He felt it on his back, on his arm. He would grind against it, causing it to pierce his skin. For hours, he would rub against it, small movements against its sharp surface, bringing pain to his body, causing wounds that baffled his friends. The pain brought much relief to him–a brief but insistent connection with his body–but unlike the intense, biting pain of happier days.

Once, some fleeting words managed to drift through the miasma of bewilderment.

"Femi," Ekwii tapped him on his shoulder. "Kolo has been elected president."

He searched for an appropriate response, but her words echoed around the hollow that should have been his presence. He thought of his mother swallowing great gulps of water, thrashing about in the flood's raging torrent. "That's terrible," he finally replied, but in truth, he could not remember who Kolo was.

He thought he had said the right words, but the concern in Ekwii's face indicated that something troubled her. He shut his eyes again and lay back down on the mat.

As the weeks passed, he achieved small victories. At his friends' insistence, he would swallow more food, pretend to listen to the radio or hold his head up from its slump when they talked. He could not wrest himself from an overwhelming despair, knowing how vast a distance lay between his dreams and the bleak terrain of his reality. His friend Ubaldous paced in erratic circles, scolding himself–Femi wondered why his mentor did not direct his words at him instead.

"Did you hear that?" Igwe asked, squatting down by Femi. "One hundred thousand have now died of water-borne illness. Can you believe it?"

Femi looked into his friend's eyes. How Igwe must detest him. "Really?" he answered. "That's a lot of people."

Igwe frowned at him–not with anger, but with query. "It is a lot of people," Igwe said softly, putting a gentle hand on his friend's head. "Do you want some orange drink?"

Femi stared at Igwe and remembered Amos looking up at him as they walked through the fields to school, how he often touched his brother's head in the same way. Though these dear memories had not been fiercely imprinted during the routine of life, now that all was gone he could not escape them. Tears sprang to his eyes. He lay back down on his mat and cried.

TEN

Flower Power

Buoyed by her career prospects, Barbara decided to pamper herself. She ran a bath. Despite the astronomical cost, the water would calm her down.

The water stopped before it filled the tub. She had forgotten to pay her water bill. Irritated, Barbara sat in the bath, feeling it lap across her body, watching her breasts bob above the water line. They looked young again. She wondered if Archimedes had chanced on this same phenomenon.

After her bath, she wrapped herself in a robe made partially of hemp and called her parents.

"Hello," her mother answered. "Glass household. Hello? Who's speak–. . . Oh heavens, Ernie! Get the other phone! Quick! It's Barbara. No, upstairs. Barbara, we thought you'd been killed!" Her mother sounded almost disappointed. "We phoned all the local hospitals."

"No, I'm alive." She hunted for her water bill.

"Has Mary been in contact?" her father asked.

"I don't want to work for a corporate oppressor!"

"See what you get for letting her study English at university?" her mother whispered to her father.

He attempted to be the voice of reason. "Look, your sister has agreed to find you some work with her company, but first you'll have to apologize to her for your comments–"

"What? At Thanksgiving? What's her prob–"

"Don't you dare raise your voice in this house," her mother snapped. "We are your parents, after all. We will not tolerate anger, do you understand?" Barbara heard a click on the other end of the phone.

"Do you see what you've done now?" her father asked. "Is it too much to ask you to keep your temper in check?"

"But, Dad–"

"Now just phone your sister and apologize. She's very upset. Barbie, pride comes before a fall." The monk put down the phone.

Barbara lit her Himalayan salt candles, sat in lotus position and meditated in front of her shrine for a few minutes, her temples throbbing. She spotted a photograph she had placed there of the two sisters as children.

Barbara fingered the picture, wiped the dust away from it and unfurled its edges. The girls looked so sombre. The perfect Mary, with her socks sitting regimentally at her knees, hair glistening in a bob that always retained its shape, and dress freshly ironed, as crisp as the day of its purchase. Next to her, Barbara–box-like, stern, no socks, hair in a ball, staring at Mary. Her timing was off as always, gaping just as the shutter opened.

Barbara moved closer to the lamp. She studied the eyes in the photograph. Mary's expression shimmered with self-confidence, shooting little sparkles of admiration and self-respect. But what was in Barbara's eyes? Was it idolatry, awe? Bringing the photograph closer to the light, Barbara saw more in there. Was it jealousy, envy? No, she could not make sense of it. She moved closer to the light and the idea finally came to her: she was staring at her sister with disdain!

Barbara gasped at this notion–a younger sister looking with contempt at that which the angels cherish and exalt?

But there was no denying it; there it was, plain as a pixel, displayed for the entire family, recorded for the ages and for all eyes to see. Memory now had little role to play. The cold evidence was before her eyes, and Barbara's heart froze at the sight.

She now remembered what the years had buried. She had always grasped new concepts and abstractions too quickly, had always been able to create new worlds and visualize bizarre realities. She had not been an easy fit in a family that worshipped facts, that only believed in things they could touch and visions they could see. Her rebel label had arisen as a result of her questioning given wisdom and drawing on her imagination.

Barbara was the only person who could challenge Mary's fragile world view, who could see past the glistening facade to the imperfections beyond; the only one who knew it had taken Mary twenty minutes to prepare for that photo. Was this how Mary–so outwardly confident–had developed such an antipathy towards her?

This must be the secret. Barbara turned to her icon of Saraswathi, Goddess of Wisdom, and lit two joss sticks.

She had to change the territory on which the two sisters connected, leaving behind the minefield of facts and data and moving to the grassy meadows of human relations. She realized how she could provoke Mary by forcing her to plumb depths she did not possess and thus bewilder her. She could blindside her sister at whim. Here, in this revelation, lay her power.

Trembling with excitement, Barbara placed a call to the dreaded 505 area code.

"Mary Glass."

"Hey! It's Barbara. How's everything going?"

"Look, I don't have much time. What do you want?"

Barbara adopted a therapy-soft voice that she knew would throw every filament of her sister's razor-sharp nervous system on edge. "I understand you were upset at Thanksgiving by my comments on your job."

"No," Mary corrected. "Not upset–"

"Well, hurt."

"Not hurt, Barbie." Mary's prim voice was like sandpaper on Barbara's ears. "Angry. I'm furious."

"Well, anger's just a mask for something deeper." Barbara adopted an even softer tone, which she knew would send flesh crawling down her sister's back. "Look, I honestly didn't mean to make you feel ashamed of your job or to demean you in any way. I am sure you find your work very fulfilling. I'm sure you're good at whatever it is you do."

"I'm not distressed, Barbie." Mary's voice was rising. "I'm furious."

"I hear what you're saying. It can be painful to be considered inconsequential, but believe me that wasn't my intent. To me," Barbara continued, dispensing a key tenet of Taoist wisdom, "I am you and you are me. There is no separation. We are as one in the great flow of the universe. So," more brightly, as she had found her water bill, "how's life generally?"

"Apart from being angry, I'm fine. Have you found a job yet?"

"I already have a job, Mary." The bill amounted to $500.

"Conflict resolution? That's a joke. With your temper?"

The secret is not to judge her, Barbara thought. *She's doing the best she can with what she knows.* "Well, you might be right. I guess I don't think I could ever settle for the solitary, I should say the, uh . . . singular devotion to a job." She sat back to enjoy the jab.

The line went dead. Barbara thought she had lost signal. Then she heard a wisp of Mary's breath, doubtless struggling to find a fitting response. The attributes that propelled Mary so far in business–lack of emotion, cold calculation, superficial interactions–did not bode well for her personal life.

Mary started to speak. Too late. Barbara changed the subject. "By the way, I've found a new job."

"Oh, really?" Barbara could hear the tightness around Mary's mouth. "What?"

Barbara panicked. Why had she said that? Why had she run back to the minefield of facts again? Now she had no option but to lie. "With the United Nations."

"I don't believe you. Which agency?"

Barbara scrambled for a reply. Well, all she could do was bring forward the future. "UNEP."

"The Environment Programme? No way. What's your role?"

Barbara frantically searched for a name, but could think of only one agency from the back pages of *West Africa Magazine*. "It's with the Dam Commission, I think." She had to get back on safe ground. "Not sure, though. Maybe it's gorillas." She paused. "Hmmm." She paused again, since Type A's could not bear a dawdling pace. "No, I remember now. It *is* the Dam Commission. They're into conflict resolution."

Mary's tone changed. "The Dam Commission? Who do you report to?"

Was that concern in Mary's voice? After all, Barbara would have diplomatic immunity–which would pretty much make her a diplomat. She could not produce a name, so instead she relied on her reputation as a simpleton. "Can't remember."

"Oh, come on. You know who it is. Is it Herman Meyer?"

Herman Meyer. Barbara picked up a purple pen and scribbled the name on a corner of the Yellow Pages. She needed to know more, so she played the ingenue. "Don't know. Sounds like a hot dog. Who's he?"

"Of course you do. Executive Director. C'mon, who do you report to? What the hell is wrong with you? Don't you realize that with TransAqua's help you could be one of the most important people over there?"

"No. But I do realize that with my help you could be one of the most important people at TransAqua." Barbara said this in a carefree, indifferent tone that she knew would send Mary into one of her legendary rages.

"Hope they don't fire you," Mary snapped.

"No one gets fired in the UN. You just get reassigned, that's all." Barbara yawned slightly.

"I've called Mary and apologized," she announced to her father.

"What took so long?" Father asked.

"Oh, we talked about–"

"Well done, darling. Now, apologize to your mother."

He handed the phone over.

"Well?"

Barbara could tell her mother was about to explode. "Sorry to make you so angry. I didn't realize how furious you were getting." Barbara adopted her therapy voice.

"I'm not angry." Her mother tried to keep her voice level. "I'm upset."

"Of course you are. Mom, you shouldn't feel embarrassed about expressing your emotions–even rage."

"Rage? What the hell do you mean, rage?" Catherine's voice cracked. "I was in tears."

Father came on the phone. "What have you done now?"

"Well, if you would just listen, you'd hear the great news. I've got a new job with the UN."

"Really? What division?"

"UNEP."

"UNEP?" He sounded relieved and disappointed at the same time. These dualities were his special gift. "Oh well, we can't all start with UNICEF, can we? Well done, darling. How did you get it?"

"I just applied. They need people with conflict manage–"

"Do you get any benefits?"

Mother picked up the other phone: "Is it full-time?"

"It's in the UN. Full benefits."

"Oh, finally!" Father expelled a breath he had been holding for twenty years. "What a relief! It's with UNEP, my dear." He opted for enthusiasm this time. Brave enthusiasm.

"UNEP?" Mother asked. "What's UNEP? Why didn't you apply to UNICEF?"

"It's the Environment Programme. I have to leave for Kenya in the next month or so."

"Kenya!" they both exclaimed simultaneously. "How exotic!"

Once she had put down the phone, Barbara went to her window. She decided to sit in appreciation and awe of winter's amethyst sunset. After a few minutes, she got bored, grabbed her Norwegian cloak and rushed through the stripped trees and sullen landscape of mid-January to the local library. On entering, she put her hands together in a Namaste greeting and bowed to the librarian, who shuddered down into his patterned sweater. She headed directly to the travel section and rifled through books on Kenya and Nigeria.

After plopping into a chair and wedging herself into its soft arms, she jotted down a number of safari companies in Kenya, then turned her attention to Nigeria. Her square fingers flicked through the pages of a coffee table book until she found a few pictures of the Tuareg. *Stunning,* she thought. *Amazing turbans.* She pictured herself in the Sahara, wearing an elaborate indigo turban, surrounded by camels with saddles of carved leather, as the endless sands stretched before her.

She flicked the page. Here, even greater bounty lay, as she scrutinized the jewellery worn by the women. She laid her head back on the chair, imagining herself in a tent with multicoloured carpets, wearing a host of bangles and necklaces, drinking yak milk, sorting bombs into different piles.

She caught the eye of a fellow reader and smiled. "Travelling to the Sahara," she said in a loud whisper that could be heard throughout the entire reference section.

As winter's chill deepened, Dahlia finally called. "Success, my dear!"

"UNEP answered? I knew it. I just had this feeling about Kenya. I have some psychic ability, you know. People have often mentioned–"

"Kenya?" Almost an octave for one word. "No, not Kenya. Ottawa!"

"Ottawa?" Stupefied. "Ottawa in Norway? Not UNEP?" Barbara panicked. No sarongs needed in Norway.

"Ottawa's in Canada, and that's where Drop of Life is. It's a much more radical group than the UN. You'd be bored. No," Dahlia was firm, "this is most definitely the group for you."

Barbara panicked. "And Kenya?"

"Oh, I wouldn't even try. The UN takes over a year to hire anyone."

Barbara's heart was thumping. She wondered how she would get herself out of this mess. She could not admit her failure to her parents, nor could she let her noxious sister realize she had never even been in contact with UNEP. No, she would simply have to pretend she was leaving for Kenya to embark on a fact-finding mission. This would put her out of contact until she could sort this mess out.

Barbara prepared for her interview with Ottawa. She revised her strongest and weakest points. She decided not to mention punctuality as a weakness. In the end, she plumped for timidity. "My weakest point? I lack assertiveness, but I have taken classes to overcome this."

After protracted interviews over two months, Barbara was accepted at Drop of Life. Arrangements were made to transfer her to Ottawa at the beginning of March. She looked up Ottawa on the Internet–six months of winter, with temperatures well under freezing. This was followed by three months of summer with temperatures over 100°F. Even Ulan Bator sounded more appealing: at least she could live in a yurt.

To honour a promise made in a barn under freezing conditions, Barbara knew she had to get Astro to come with her. She addressed him as gently as she could as they walked into the yoga studio.

"Astro, I've been accepted by Drop of Life in Ottawa."

He stopped in his tracks in front of a woman with unshaven armpits who was lying down, stretching her back. He turned to look at Barbara, pupils dilating through bright yellow irises until it seemed his eyes had turned brown. He stood fixed in position, not moving, his face expressing no particular emotion, just contemplating, perhaps.

Or panicking.

"What?" he asked, a tremble in his voice. "I thought you weren't going to leave me. You promised!"

"Of course I'm not leaving you." Barbara walked towards the

centre of the studio. "I love you." The yoga students opened their eyes and looked up at the pair. "Why don't you come with me?"

"How?" Astro's bottom lip began to quiver. "I don't have a work permit."

Barbara picked up a purple yoga mat. "I'll support you," she called over a woman in lotus pose. She walked to the front and unfurled her mat.

He started sobbing violently. "Leave home?"

A large woman in shorts and dangly earrings looked up at him and then back at Barbara, concern etched on her face.

"Don't worry, Astro." Barbara hopped past a couple of yoga students in relaxation pose, both with eyes wide open, and she encased him in a hug. "We'll work something out. It's not that far."

"No!" A strangled sob. "You're leaving me. I can't believe it."

Barbara could do nothing to help; it appeared as if the blue fingers of panic had grabbed his soul. He fell to the floor, sobbing, barely able to breathe, next to a woman in a pink leotard and matching headband.

Dayisha and the other students looked on as he wailed. Even Barbara knew it would be quite heartless to ask for silence at a moment like this.

ELEVEN

8-011-234

John Sinclair sat in his office, squeezing a stress ball, his mind flooded with images of Mary. Mary being pushed off the top floor of TransAqua, her body falling in fractured reflections past the building's mirrored panes. Something had to be done to put her in her place.

He hit speed-dial. "Hey, Beano!"

"Johnno! If you want to ask me for a date, just come right out with it!"

"Too shy. That's my problem. I prefer stalking. Anyhoos, just wanted to be the first to congratulate you. The Big Cheese has agreed to hire you. As usual, he's made sure duties overlap–you're dangerously close to Glass's region in the sub-Sahara because, as you know, sands do tend to shift." An easy chuckle slid out. "Got time to come to my place, as they say?'

"I'll check my little black book. Hmm. Gotta bit of time right now. I could slip you in." A snort.

Sinclair could hear the dimples. He stood up to survey the landscape he detested, bleak scrubland hostile to human dominance, now plastered with snow. Downwards, towards the city, dreary, desiccated bushes poked through the cluster of adobe houses. The buildings' dried clay architecture only reminded him of the region's lack of moisture–his head swirled with dreams of an oceanside villa, the reassuring lull of waves on the shore.

Beano vaulted into the office as if his sneakers had coils in them. He looked like he had just come off a skateboard–younger by the day.

Sinclair affected an avuncular tone. "This is the big one. So don't underestimate Glass. Behind that bland facade lurk hormones from the very depths of hell."

"Really? Could hell be that drab?"

"Playing insipid puts her under the radar–great strategy. And she's placed the mantle on a king of her choosing, in whatever they wear over there."

"I think it's leopard skin, John."

Why were the second generation of the world's achievers always the idiots? Two worries surfaced simultaneously in Sinclair's mind: that they had kept Beano back in Sewage for a reason, and that he would have to wipe up after the boy. "A mediocrity like her has helped oust an entire government," he explained.

"Yeah, but I hear they're all but illiterate."

"Well, let's put it this way, Beano, someone apparently downright incompetent has persuaded TransAqua to part with unheard-of levels of kickbacks."

Beano scraped a flop of hair and held it in place, thinking. "That's not very savvy. She'll have to keep paying. Does she know that?" He looked neat, yet he wore jeans and no tie.

What was Beano's secret? His uncommonly straight legs? His artless protegé continued. "Is it sex appeal? I mean, she's got none, right? Am I mistaken? Is the great ship Mary, uh, docking onto Cheeseman, so to speak?"

Sinclair perched on his desk and gestured for Beano to sit. "Listen, she's got the Niger River project all but signed. It's the most powerful country in Africa! It's got a consumer base of almost 180 million."

"Hey, they're in desperate need. All she'd have to do is remember their phone number. How difficult is that?"

Displeased, Sinclair cleared his throat. "These deals are more difficult than you might appreciate. Despite her hysteria-induced achievements, Beano, you may have noticed that Mary has yet to meet Kolo. You have to be in this game for a while to realize something's up. Two months since she first contacted him, one month since he became president. It never takes that long to arrange a meeting that his presidency depends on. Is she going to go straight from phone calls to signing a contract?"

"Can the guy write?"

With escalating irritation, Sinclair skidded into sarcasm. "An X or a thumbprint would still meet requirements." This elicited some juvenile tittering, and Sinclair realized Beano had been kidding. Perhaps joking all along? "I don't know why Cheeseman's swallowing it. Must have other things on his mind."

"What d'you think's going wrong?"

"Competitive offers from the French. No backup from his own government. Staving off another coup. Who knows?"

"I don't know if it'll help," Beano offered a shrug of impotence, "but I can ring Dad and see how the land lies. He'd tell you the best people to deal with."

A quick worker, Beano had already proved useful. After the ambassador called, an idea popped into Sinclair's mind. Interesting. Perhaps it might work. What harm could there be in trying?

He dialled 8 for an outside line, plus 011 for international, then 234 for Nigeria.

Following a long, enlightening conversation, he shut down his password-protected files, locked his cabinet, then headed to the weekly meeting with Cheeseman, settling into a chair opposite Mary so that he could keep an eye on her. Beano entered with a wink. Everyone cracked open their bottles of water–something to suck on during the forthcoming ordeal.

After an uncomfortable ten-minute wait, Cheeseman appeared, tufts of unruly chest hair poking out of his denim shirt. Why did the man not have the dignity to wax? And his pants were hitched so high, it looked as if his balls had been sliced in half. Sinclair shuddered as a dense concentration of fear punched the pit of his stomach–an emotion only Cheeseman could prompt, despite the fact that Sinclair knew that even Cheeseman was expendable. No one quite knew who maintained the tank; it appeared to be a self-generating system.

The boss sat down and spread his legs wide. "First of all, I wanna welcome Mr. Bates to the team. He'll be working on Acquisitions Sahara and Sub-Sahara."

A round of applause. Mary paled, an act that accentuated her blue veins. She forced out The Slash, then whipped it back into its impassive shelter, challenging anyone to identify the underlying panic.

"Now, Mr. Bates, water is a diminishing, finite resource–most people don't know that. They look at the oceans and think, "That's water." Well, it's not. It's brine. We don't deal in brine. No one drinks brine. Taking salt out of brine is very expensive, and then you have to figure where to dump the salt, right?"

"Right." Hair fell into Beano's eyes, but he did not even blink. He simply sent forth a boyish smile in Cheeseman's direction.

"But it's pretty useful for us that yer average Joe thinks he can drink it."

"Sure is."

Mary could tell that the hair was stinging Beano's eyeballs. Still he did not blink. A mere boy. An adolescent simpleton. Why would Sinclair want him?

Cheeseman leaned back in his chair. "We deal in water–stuff you find in aquifers, in the mountains, in streams and rivers. Water, Mr. Bates, is the oil of the twenty-first century. Wars will be fought over it. What the hell, the world is already fighting over it. TransAqua plans to own it. And I mean own. Licences and rights. We're gonna be the ones controlling it and how much money it's sold for."

"Blue gold, as they say, Mr. Cheeseman, blue gold."

"Exactly. You get my point. So we're making sure that international trade agreements define water as a commodity, not as a human right as some tie-dyed Y-front-wearing hippies are demanding."

"You mean the Senate and Congress?" Beano blushed into another smile.

Sinclair cackled.

Cheeseman rocked back and punched out a concession of laughter. "That's great–gotta tell the boys that one."

Beano finally managed to whip the hair out of his eyes.

"Okay," Cheeseman slapped a hand on the table. "Glass–update."

"All going well," Mary replied with a strained smile, her thin lips disappearing entirely. "Kolo has agreed to sell the entire length of the Niger, but in exchange he wants us to insist he rename it. And he's after the biggest dam in the world."

"What?" Sinclair blurted. "Is he crazy?"

"He's looking for over twenty thousand megawatts." She flicked her pen in circles on her index finger as she talked. A neat trick. Sinclair stared at it, wondering whether there were any hit men for hire in Santa Fe.

"What's the cost?" Beano asked.

"Over $30 billion," she replied, looking at Cheeseman rather than Beano. "They'd get World Bank financing, but we'd need to pitch in. We'd own most of the power supply to West Africa."

Sinclair felt his chest constrict, as if he had swallowed an entire handful of peanuts and triggered full-blown anaphylactic shock. His life expectancy at TransAqua had probably just been reduced to hours. Beano whistled through his teeth, making Sinclair unaccountably jealous. He had recruited him; it was to him that Beano's adulation should be directed.

Cheeseman tried to shove his hands in his pockets. Only the tips of his fingers made it. "Okay. We need a dedicated meeting. Two o'clock tomorrow?"

"Yes, sir," Mary replied, two miniscule circles of blush on her angled cheekbones.

"Good girl. Round of applause fer Glass."

The whole room clapped, but only the associates smiled.

"Now, Sinclair. What've y'all been up to?"

There was nothing to lose at this point in the game, and he had an inexperienced devotee to impress. Sinclair lounged back in his chair. "Just been getting inside information on Kolo.

He won't last long, I'm afraid. General Abucha is planning a coup. He's willing to talk about rights to the Niger too, but plans to build a much smaller dam. Less outlay for us. I think he's worth pursuing. Cost us less in the end."

Mary accidentally flicked the pen off her finger.

"Who told you this?" Cheeseman asked.

"I've been speaking to Abucha himself."

"Well, that kinda shit's gonna block the drain, don'cha think?" Cheeseman fingered the eagle on his sterling silver bolo tie.

"Not really. A bird in the hand is worth two . . ." he winked at Beano, " . . . in the bush. I'm happy for Ms. Glass to pursue the Kolo angle. I'll follow Abucha. Either way, we get the rights."

"Excellent! Excellent, Sinclair. Well done."

He started to clap and the rest of the directors followed in thunderous acclaim.

Cheeseman then turned to the numbers. "This chart shows our projections for this month."

Details, details. Sinclair's attention drifted to the pinpricks that represented Mary's breasts.

Cheeseman spoke softly. "Maybe one day Mr. Sinclair will pay less attention to his colleague's projections and more attention to *these*! " Cheeseman banged the chart.

Sinclair's scrotum shrivelled in fright.

A wash of pink fanned around the angles of Mary's face.

After the meeting, Mary sped from the boardroom, cold rage freezing her blood as it pulsed through her fat-free body. She slammed her door and hit the tenth memory button on her phone. She had no intention of letting the slug Sinclair put her future in jeopardy.

"Good evening. Residence of the president."

"Hi. It's Mary Glass, TransAqua."

"Yes. Just a minute," the voice trailed off, "just a minute, just a minute" until it diminished into silence.

Five minutes later, another voice answered the phone. "Hello, Ms. Glass. I meant to thank you for the box of chocolates. How can I help you?" Kolo was sucking again.

"I've just heard some bad news. Abucha is planning a coup."

"What?" he coughed. "That's not possible."

"It is. He's been speaking to a colleague about rebuilding Kainji."

"Who did he speak to?"

"John Sinclair. This morning." She bit some skin off her thin lip.

"This is very serious."

"Mr. President, with all due respect, I would highly recommend that you deal with Abucha."

"I'll do no such thing, Ms. Glass." Kolo put down the phone.

A cold, venomous rage froze the blood in every vein of her Type A constitution. After all she had suffered at TransAqua, with twice the barriers he faced, and this so-called politician could not even rouse himself to action!

For Africa, this was the deal of the century. And if TransAqua managed to obtain rights to such a prime piece of fluid real estate, the rewards would be immediate. They would, to all intents and purposes, own Nigeria, as they would proceed to own India through the Ganges and Egypt via the Nile. For Mary, there would be the final and lasting approbation. And this deal was about to slip through Mary's spider fingers.

Two agonizing days passed with Mary fossilized into inaction. Then she noticed an interruption to the looped broadcast on TV Afrique that played constantly in her office. Reports were flooding in of the unfortunate death of General Abucha in a car accident. The car had exploded after impact, leaving little trace of his or his driver's remains. Kolo, in tears and wearing a black armband on his golden dashiki, declared a national day of mourning for his dear friend. He looked heartbroken, his rash flaring red from sorrow.

Watching the lucent images felt unsettling, as if she were diving into her own psyche. This man had adopted a veneer of composure, a glossy coating. Like her, he had to construct an outer shell that, to others, seemed believable. Mary knew much more lay underneath. She did not know, however, what experiences had driven him to such highly polished performances.

Sinclair smiled as he read about Abucha's death on the Internet. Glass had fallen for the bait. The president would no longer have the general's vital military support, leaving him vulnerable. He dialled 8 on his personal cellphone, then 011, followed by 234 for Nigeria.

"Office of the minister for the environment," a female voice announced with pride.

"Hello. Nkemba, isn't it? What a pretty name. How are you? I bet all the men love that name."

"Oh, Mr. Sinclair. I'm fine, sir. Thank you, sir. Fine. And you? How are you also?"

"Couldn't be better."

"You want speak to the minister, sir?"

"That would be fantastic. Thank you, Nkemba."

After a couple of minutes, the minister was put through. "Mr. Sinclair. How are you?" A broad accent in a baritone growl.

"Dangerously well, sir, dangerously well. And yourself?"

"Feeling as dangerous as yourself, my friend." He issued a hearty hee-haw.

"Well, as you see, I was as good as my promise. Now–do we have a deal?"

The minister hesitated for a second. "Yes, sir. We have a deal. Can I ask how you managed to deal with the, em, situation?"

"I didn't have to lift a finger. A colleague told our man in mourning that his best friend was planning a coup against him. Your path should be pretty clear now. Without the army behind him, you-know-who will soon be too weak to continue. Time for you to make a deal with the military."

"Walahi!" the baritone croaked.

"Don't you worry. There's no risk here. Absolutely nothing to worry about. You've got our government behind you."

They exchanged a few pleasantries, then Sinclair signed off, relieved.

Only a few minutes after he had put down the phone, it rang again.

"Hello? Please may I speak to John Sinclair?"

"Speaking." Sinclair clipped on his headset and leaned back in his adjustable chair.

"This is President Ogbe Kolo speaking."

Sinclair jerked to attention, cricking his back. "Yessir. A privilege."

"The privilege is mine, sir."

"To what do I owe this honour?" With the tips of his toes, Sinclair rotated to face the window, away from inquisitive eyes outside his plate glass office.

"I understand you are interested in water rights near Kainji." Kolo sounded as though he were sucking on something. "And that you have been discussing such rights with some of my colleagues."

"Yessir. TransAqua is interested–"

"I would be most honoured if you would in future address your concerns to me directly." The voice had a musical quality to it, behind the sucking.

"Yessir."

"Perhaps we could meet in London?"

"I would be honoured." Sinclair was in excruciating pain.

"No, please. The privilege is mine." The phone clicked off.

A bold man, Sinclair thought. *He must have balls of titanium. Well, let's jack him off too and see who spurts first. If it's not Kolo, then back to Plan A.* He swivelled his chair around towards his desk so that he could lever himself into an upright position.

Early morning free-riding eased Beano into his day. He sprang up the stairs to his new enclosure and leaned his snowboard on the wall, then pulled up the sleeves of his black polo neck and ruffled his hair. Its blond extravagance had been too long hidden in Sewage. He planned to grow it.

From his tiny glass office down the Africa Acquisitions corridor, Beano could glimpse Sinclair's corner tank situated on a dais. His relationship with it felt more than visual, it was carnal: an incorporation, an embodiment, a union. Four doors down stood Mary's office, also on a plinth. It had little effect on him.

An artist friend had designed a phone that contained bubbling water. On this gadget, he called Nigeria. "Hey, Dad! It's Beano. Howzit going?"

"Don'ask. I hate this damned country. The Brits get knighted once they've served over here. All we get is high blood pressure." After a groan of self pity, he asked, "So, have you finally wiped the shit off your ass?"

Although he resented the disparagement of his previous role, Beano's dimples deepened with determined good cheer. "Yeup. Still, everything's a bit precarious. I don't know how you cope, Dad."

"You're dealing with Nigeria, son! Whaddaya expect? It's stormy seas from here on in. And if you think you've spotted land, you can be sure you're hallucinating."

"I hear Kolo–"

"Don't mention that upstart's name! Arrogant prick with that damned aristocratic accent. Why doesn't this place just go back to military rule? It's easier to deal with."

Beano adjusted a picture of the Sewage division at karaoke, which he'd propped on his desk to remind everyone of his humble origins. "That's actually what I was calling about, Dad. Did you tell Sinclair about the minister for the environment?"

"As instructed. When did you suddenly become so efficient?"

"Gotta get dirty sometime. My body might be in water, but my mind is still in the gutter."

His father groaned. "D'ya have to keep mentioning it?"

"So, who do you think's gonna replace General Abucha? I told Sinclair I'd get him a name. Can you try for Major General Wosu P. Wosu?"

"Wosu? Almost impossible! Why?"

"It'd be a real help. I mean, if you're looking for a military coup, he's a Muslim who's migrated to the Middle Belt, Dad. So the army will accept him. But he's not originally from Benue State, so in the meantime Kolo won't feel too threatened by him, right?"

"By an Igbo? No, 'course not." He paused. "But you want an easterner? Why?"

After two months of negotiation, Mary had finally managed to secure a meeting with Kolo on the 8th of March; at the weekly meeting, she had announced a much later date to build in time for delay. She purchased some wax earplugs, which she placed securely in each ear for her first-class flight to London so that the pressure change would not topple her physical or mental equilibrium.

The flight was without complication. But in line at Immigration, she heard a familiar, unctuous snigger that sent the skin crawling up every rib. Her freeze-dried frame ducked behind another passenger and scouted out the territory.

Sinclair.

What was he doing here in London? There were only two possibilities. He was either following her or he had his own meeting with Kolo. She tracked him for a while. Easy. Like a slug, he left trails wherever he went, this time to a giggling flight attendant.

There was only one conclusion to draw. He had come to meet Kolo.

Mary jumped into a limousine in the madness of London's traffic, heading towards the city's core. She tried to figure out if Kolo had contacted Sinclair or vice versa. In the final analysis, it was unimportant. Either way, Kolo was double-dealing.

Mary had agreed to meet Kolo for tea in the marbled halls of the promenade within the elegant, old-world splendour of the Dorchester Hotel. London disoriented her with its complicated array of architectural styles, its twisting, crowded streets and dishevelled population. However, the Dorchester, harking back to an era of opulence and defined status, provoked a sense of calm and relaxation.

Kolo was shorter than she had expected, and sported a rash across his face that did not match the colour of his hands.

"Thank you so much for this opportunity," Mary began as they sat down together at a small table, her small, blunt teeth appearing behind a wide smile. "I appreciate that this is a difficult time for your country and for you personally." She sounded harsher than she would have wished.

"The pleasure is all mine, Ms. Glass." Kolo smiled, the rash cracking somewhat as his facial muscles pulled. "Perhaps we can get down to business." He clicked his fingers to order tea.

Mary opened with a lateral move. "I would certainly be relieved to get our terms down on paper, Mr. President." She crossed her legs to display a bony kneecap. "My colleague, John Sinclair, has been dealing with so many different parties in Nigeria, I think it would be best to bring this to some closure under your leadership."

Kolo froze.

Mary took a bite out of a crust-free cucumber sandwich.

"Mr. Sinclair is dealing with whom?"

"Unfortunately, that's confidential. That's always been his strategy. Negotiate with everyone. See who ends up on top." She shrugged with a remorseful smirk.

"Really? Many separate parties?"

"Well, that's how he got to where he is. He's our best negotiator." She flipped a sprig of parsley into her mouth. Check. "I personally prefer to deal with one person at a time." Mate.

"Indeed."

Kolo looked distinctly out of sorts, out of depth and out of choices. She pulled a folder from her briefcase and opened it.

Two days later they had signed the deal. He had guaranteed TransAqua a 70-percent annual return on its investment, tax incentives, shipping rights and exclusive rights to all water in the district.

With men, Mary mused, *all you have to do is throw them some meat and they think it's dinnertime.*

She was hardly to know, however, that Kolo's tastes were strictly vegetarian.

TWELVE

Abundance

Another of the planet's vegetarians stood at a door, but there was no answer to her persistent knocking. She went downstairs to the one neighbour she knew would be home: the meat-necked bully who had attempted to stamp out Astro's musical serenade during her first visit.

She found him talking to a tramp dressed in layers of sweaters with a blanket draped over him, carrying assorted plastic bags.

"Do you know where Astro is?" she butted in.

"Hey, Bra-Bra." Yellow eyes peered in her direction from under a fake fur hat with earflaps. "I thought you were supposed to be here at seven. It's seven thirty already. Where were you? I thought . . ." Barbara waited for the words of her parents to assume their position on the tip of his tongue. " . . . you'd died!"

She looked at Astro in silent disbelief. "What the hell are you wearing?"

Astro to the neighbour: "I thought she'd died, man. I called all the hospitals."

"Where do you think we're going? Antarctica?"

A bobble on his hat jiggled as he spoke. "I was listening to the traffic reports and everything."

Barbara also turned to the neighbour for assistance. "We're driving, for god's sake! What's he wearing? What in Shakti's name is he wearing?"

They both looked at the neighbour, who stood mute.

"Just get ready," Barbara turned to Astro, "because we're leaving. What's this?" Barbara snatched some sheets of paper from the neighbour's hand.

"None of your business." Astro whipped the sheets back. "Just instructions on taking care of the place."

"You'll be back by the time he's finished reading it."

"Ho, ho, ho, so." Astro turned back to his neighbour. "If you have any trouble," he spoke slowly and deliberately, "any trouble at all, call me at this number, okay?"

"Okey-dokey." The man scratched his armpit.

Astro looked up, obviously unsettled. "So, what number do you call?"

"That one there." The neighbour stabbed at a large number in red letters.

"Good."

They looked at each other.

"So," Astro raised his eyebrows expectantly, "are we okay here?"

"Solid gold." The man leaned in his doorway and folded his arms.

Barbara could tell that Astro was about to change his mind, that the puncture in his routine might be too great to bear, so she grabbed some of his bags and stole downstairs. "I'm leaving in one minute, Astro," she called back tartly.

After a minute, she started honking, waiting for Astro to appear. He finally managed to pry himself out of the building and ran across the street with a few plastic bags and a picnic cooler.

Barbara leaned over and opened the door. "What's that?"

"Food and water, Babu." Astro's eyes were on the window to his apartment.

"Food and water? Why?"

"Look, man," he said, struggling into the car, "I don't know what the hell they eat in Canada. I'm not taking any chances."

"They eat the same crap we eat here." Barbara reached over, slammed the door and secured Astro's seat belt.

"Oh, really? And when were you last in Canada?"

"What–you think I have to go somewhere to know about it? Oh, please!" Barbara accelerated out of her parking spot, then released the hand brake.

"Well, let's just find out who's right, okay, man?" he snapped. "In the meantime, don't ask me for any food, okay? If you want to eat whale blubber and boil some snow, whatever, man, be my guest."

"I do not believe this." She swerved into the fast lane and proceeded to drive at a crawl, carefully scanning the signs. "Don't ask to borrow my clothes when we get there."

"Ditto, man." Astro grabbed the dash. "Turn left here."

"I know where I'm going."

"Could you change lanes, please?"

"I'm fine in this lane."

"I know, but look at that car, man. It's too ugly. I don't want to follow it for the rest of the journey."

She hovered on the line between two lanes, and swerved into another lane.

Then she checked her rear-view mirror.

The next day, they arrived at a piece of land that divided two discordant nations of almost identical history, language, religion, culture and heritage.

A Canadian Immigration and Customs agent greeted them. "Hey. How are you? Great to meet you. Where are you going?"

"Ottawa."

"Great! Beautiful city."

Barbara and Astro looked at each other. This guy must be on drugs. Privilege of working in Customs.

"Anything to declare?"

"No." Barbara kept her answers short. She feared the unlimited, unchecked power of the world's most unfettered authorities.

"Awesome. Okay. You're through!" He waved at them as they left his post.

"There was something weird about that guy," Astro said. "Are all Canadians like that? That's just scary. Are we officially in Canada?" Yellow eyes searched the landscape.

"Yep." An utterance pregnant with meaning. "Wonder where our dogsleds are."

"This is it?" Astro looked disappointed. "It's just like the States!"

"I don't have a map to the igloo. Perhaps the dogs can sniff it out."

"How come they're a separate country? This looks just like the States, man!"

"Hope they have some whale blubber sandwiches. Don't want to go hungry . . ."

"They speak like Americans. They act American. They look American," Astro's bobble was jiggling again as he looked out of the window, "but they're a separate country? How stupid is that?"

If everything in Bethesda was green, then Ottawa could only be considered blue. Here was a jewel perched over blue, flowing with blue, shielded under blue, melting into blue. Azure dawn, aquamarine day, cyan evening, sapphire night. Its buildings bordered three merry rivers, bubbling and chattering, tumbling and rolling marine, cobalt, indigo. The Gothic towers of Parliament stood like a bastion protecting the riverbanks on a promontory. Its copper roofs had turned turquoise from the effects of moisture.

They drove past Ottawa's Christmas card scenery, admiring the beauty of a city cloaked in water's chameleon white, muffled in winter's hush. The strict lines and severe angles of human habitation were radically altered by gentle undulations of snow, the piercing noises and shrill ubiquity of industry tamped down into a soothing quiescence. Barbara liked winter's quiet despotism.

It was a city that worshipped beauty, where form, space and contour, art and nature, were as important as food and water. The crystal spires of the National Gallery winked at the water's transparency, while across the river the sinuous curves of the Museum of Civilization paid homage to its flow. Yet no building had been allowed to obstruct the view of water. It could be seen from most parts of the city.

People strolled silently and peacefully in their liquid paradise, unaware that any other relationship with water could exist except that of abundance.

"This is the capital city?" Astro asked, yellow eyes wide with wonder.

"I guess so."

"Looks like a town, man. It's a village. Look at this place! It's beautiful. Does anything ever go wrong here?"

"I doubt it. They're all liberals."

"Like democrats?"

"Oh, no, no," Barbara said with some authority. "Quite simplistically, that would be their right wing."

They stopped to eat at a mill on the water's edge, their eyes bulging with alarm as they watched a waiter run the tap, waiting for cooler water without a care in the world.

"No wonder the US is forcing Canada to sell its water," Barbara whispered. "I mean, this kind of waste is criminal!"

Astro checked around the room. "Not a municipal officer in sight."

THIRTEEN

Just Kidding

Having taken a few days to settle into a Victorian apartment featuring ornamental flourishes and cracked paintwork, Barbara crunched her way over the snow and salted pavements to the Drop of Life headquarters. Her teeth chattered, as she had refused to concede that Astro had been better informed about the city's weather conditions. She skidded past a man on the street, who was begging for money.

"Spare a dollar?" he asked.

"No," she replied gruffly.

"Okay, have a nice day."

Barbara stared back at this man, the prototype of the Canadian beggar, sitting on a street corner, and almost tripped over an uneven flagstone.

At last she paused before a turreted house with no identifying signs. Surveying the building, she wondered if she had the right address and then made the decision to enter. As she crept through its corridors, she passed a design made of broken glass, ceramic and lead grout. She inspected it closely and saw that each piece of glass was layered with colour, so that an entire world was captured in the smallest fragment. Just like life. She had expected harsh slogans to confront her but quickly understood that an organization involved in clandestine activities could only hint at its purpose. Instead, she found the curative embrace of art.

Barbara approached a woman whose smile extended to her gums.

"Hi. You must be Barbie! It's great to meet you. How are you?" This woman did not look like she would know how to light a stick of dynamite, let alone organize a revolution.

"Um, fine, thanks," Barbara replied, baffled.

"Awesome! What a great day, eh?" She gummed another smile.

Barbara was getting worried about these Canadians. They had a pathological cheeriness that certainly had no place in the world of international intrigue.

"You must find it very congested here," the gums said.

Barbara considered. This woman must be very sheltered.

"Just kidding," the gums quickly added. "I hope you'll feel comfortable in Ottawa. Some people find it a bit small."

"Actually, I drove right through it straight to Montreal. I had to turn back." Barbara guffawed.

"No way!" the gums gasped.

"Uh, just kidding," Barbara added. With these two magic words, the gums burst into a tinkle of pleasant laughter.

"Oh, awesome! You Americans have such a great sense of humour."

Barbara considered her parents, but she was not about to correct her new colleague on her first day of work.

"So, Barbie–"

"Barbara," Barbara corrected.

"Oh, gosh–I'm so sorry. Barbara. Great to have you here! My name's Krystal." She stretched into another smile. "I'm computers. I'll introduce you to the others on your team."

Barbara breathed a sigh of relief. The woman worked in support services, not activism.

Along the corridor, Gums peeked around a door. Framed beyond its entrance sat a woman with brittle, over-bleached hair, wearing a shirt cut into a low V that displayed over-tanned, dry cleavage. Barbara stood in shock. No matter how hard she tried, she could not picture this entity smearing black goop over her tangerine tan.

"Mimi. This is Barbara Glass. Barbie, Mimi will be working with you on the Niger River project."

Barbara gasped. "Working with me?"

"Hey, hon!" Mimi smiled tightly and patted a chair. "Park your little bum-bum over here, dear." Her nails had been artificially extended so that their whites looked like boiled egg shavings.

Barbara sat down and folded her arms across a belligerent bosom. She could not understand how the life of a fireball insurgent and that of an over-fried tanning extremist could cross in any meaningful way.

"I work in corporate liaison," Scorched Earth offered, as Barbara fiddled with the tassels on her Peruvian skirt. "If you have any problems at all," her bleached teeth flashed, "you just come and see me. Okay, sweetie?"

"Yep." Barbara scowled as she stood, annoyed at being patronized by an organism at least ten years her junior. As she left, Mimi flicked back the hair on her shoulder, centred a paper on her desk and waved at her with her fingernails.

Gums took Barbara's arm and accompanied her through

the corridors and up the stairs leading to the executive director's office. In mid-stride, Gums suddenly stopped.

"Oh, by the way, this is Brad," she said.

Barbara looked around in confusion. Then she spotted a man slouching against the corridor wall, blinking at her in apology. This item gave the impression of bland non-existence. She surveyed him up and down with disapproval. He wore a grey suit, white shirt and some unmemorable tie, his face a blank canvas waiting for its artist, his movements and expressions anticipating their stage direction. It was as if he had been condensed to mankind's most inoffensive essence–like meat that has been boiled for hours, losing its flavour, texture and structural integrity.

"Good morning," a voice tinged from the minor chamber of his mouth. "Nice to meet you." The voice had almost no bass: the entire range was carried only in the trebles. "Great to have you here." Barbara's pulse rate slowed down as if readying her body for sleep. "My name is Brad." Redundant information. "I'm the accountant." Ditto.

Barbara bowed a Namaste, her necklaces clattering with authority.

Having suffered three setbacks, Barbara prepared to meet the ringleader. She hitched up her bra to cover any fleshy overflow.

The door to the executive director's office opened.

Barbara gasped and clutched Gums. Far from the handsome young man of South American origin wearing a lopsided beret she had expected, the spearhead of this extremist organization was none other than a retiree hardly able to stand unaided.

Behind the desk, a primeval woman sat like an ancient tree, her imposing features made noble through age. She wore a sari in emerald green and mustard yellow, as though she were the empress of a forest kingdom. On her forehead, a crimson dot like a succulent berry hinting of further fruit. She sat perfectly still, but the craggy face moved into a mischievous smile, deep furrows carving into the muscles. Wrinkles entirely encased her eyes.

"Wonderful to meet you." She grabbed a cane of, Barbara guessed, hardwood (endangered) and ivory (banned) and stood up. "Name's Jane Singh." She sounded like a British colonial during the dying days of the Raj. Yet she was of Indian descent. "Such a privilege to have you here." She smiled a whorl of wrinkles. "We've been hoping to work with Femi Jegede for some time."

Barbara's heart sank. This artefact must date back eighty years, if not more. Although Barbara had supported the theory of later retirement, she had never imagined she would have to work for such a relic.

"We'll meet at the end of this week. That'll give you time to settle in. Friday, 3 p.m. If you could suggest a strategy for Nigeria, we'll see how we can help the activist groups. How's Dahlia, by the way?"

"She's just been promoted to Director of Rare Heritage Stock."

"Wonderful! About time!"

The office set aside for Barbara occupied a turret on the third floor. Whichever way she turned, she could see the sky and powder-puff clouds. She twirled around a few times in her mesh chair, thinking through the dilemma she now faced. As the sun flashed past her in circles, she became a child once more, delighting in a sense of freedom, growing dizzy and giggling. She realized that her new colleagues' ineptitude offered her a bonus that a more effective organization never could. Here at Drop of Life, she did not have to be shackled by the foibles of a consensus-based system.

With only three hours to go before the all-important Friday meeting, Barbara began to panic. She knew far less than they would about Nigeria, water politics, TransAqua, activism or any other question she might have to field. Plus, she had never met Femi Jegede–never even seen a picture of him. A sense of impending disaster hung over her.

With no one else to turn to, she called Astro–he who lived at the shimmering periphery of existence, far from the complexities and intrigues of life at its epicentre.

She dialled her new number. "Hi. It's Barbara."

"Yeah. I know it's you, man. You think I don't know your voice?"

"Well, yes, but this is a typical phone greeting." She tried to keep her temper in check. "I have a problem."

"Ooh!" He sounded pleased. "Okay, Skippy, let me get a pen and notebook."

Barbara sketched out the big picture, leaving Astro in utter confusion. His tendency was to work from fact and detail outwards towards the visions of others, whereas Barbara worked from the big picture down to its unnecessary details. It took almost forty minutes for Astro to get the specifics in correct order, by which time Barbara had almost depleted the shallow pool of her tolerance.

"Well, it's pretty obvious what you've got here, Bibble. You've got no facts."

"I've just given you the facts!" she shrieked.

"Those aren't facts, Babs. That's what is called 'train of thought.'" She could hear the quote marks. "Just get three facts. For example, where was Femi when the dam broke? You only need to be one step ahead. Know why?"

She let a disapproving silence hang between them.

"Because, Bibs, to them, you're the big cheese. And why?" He waited for an answer, then cued himself back in. "Because you lied to them . . ."

"Okay, I can do that. What else?"

" . . . which I don't think will get you very far."

"Next?"

"Well, what's your sister been up to? I'm sure she'd love to hear from you. Let's see. Facts. What's the president like? Is he an approachable guy? You just need three–"

Barbara's body tingled. Astro had found the answer. She slammed down the phone and clicked back on to the Internet. It took her very little time to find out that Femi's last meeting had taken place in Abuja; therefore, he must still be alive. Barbara decided face-to-face contact was called for. Perhaps she could take a train across Nigeria. She had always wanted to pat a zebra.

She emailed one of the journalists who had reported on Femi's successes in Abuja, then turned her attention to President Ogbe Kolo. After much searching in the hidden bowels of the virtual vault that tenaciously hoarded histories, she struck gold. Here is where the tragedy of Kolo's early life was laid bare. Barbara tilted back in her chair, sensitive to the prevailing winds of providence and the momentum gifted to her through this information. Kolo must have an indelible impression of the devastation wrought by the power of water. It had accidentally killed his twin. His relationship with it would doubtless be defined by reverence. This could only work in her favour.

Barbara flipped her cellphone open to get information on the last remaining item.

"Mary Glass."

"Hi. It's Barbara."

"What do you want?"

Barbara waited a moment before responding. "Just phoning to see how you are. You asked me to call you when I found out who I report to."

"Uh-huh. Really, Barbie? I can hardly remember, since it was so long ago."

"Well, I had to tour key sites, of course. I can hardly do my job sitting at a desk! Just a moment. Someone's at the door." She put Mary on hold for a minute, then casually resumed the conversation. "You were right: it's . . . hold on." She put Mary back on hold. After looking at her nails for a further minute, she picked up the receiver again. "Mary? Oh, are you still there? What was I saying again?"

"You were telling me," Mary's voice resonated with restraint, "who your new boss is at UNEP."

"Ah, yes. Yes, yes, yes. That's right. My new boss. At UNEP. His name is, um . . ." Barbara checked her notes, " . . . Herman Meyer. Does that sound familiar to you?"

Mary took Barbara off speakerphone. "You're kidding!"

"No–is that such a big deal?"

"With his support, the World Bank will spring for funds needed by the Nigerian government for dam construction."

Barbara had a sense that even more was at stake. Her sister sounded too excited. She spoke as slowly as she could. "Surely," she dragged out the word, "surely the World Bank will approve of anything Nigeria needs right n–"

"Not necessarily. The World Bank hardly funds any large dam projects anymore."

Barbara yawned. "How big is the dam?"

"It's going to be the biggest in the world. Over twenty thousand megawatts. And it's got support from the top."

The pride in Mary's voice forced Barbara to deploy even more aggressive tactics. Such as indifference. "Twenty thousand megawatts? I think they've built a bigger one in Brazil, haven't they?" Then, before Mary could respond, "So you say you have support from the president?"

"Yep. And in return, we get rights to the Niger River. Actually, you're lucky you caught me. Contract's just been signed. I've literally just returned. By limo."

"Well, I'll see what we can do to help speed things up. Oooh. Sandwiches are here. Must go." She hung up.

Barbara now had her three pieces of information. Astro had been right–build from the ground up. With this information, she could draw others to her cause.

At 4 p.m., or to be exact, at ten minutes past, Barbara entered the boardroom.

"Welcome!" Not one muscle on the monolith's face moved. "I hope you've all been introduced."

Barbara had no idea why Jane had invited support staff to such a critical meeting, nor why Dahlia had considered this ramshackle group of outcasts radical.

"So, Barbara," Jane continued, "tell us your ideas."

Barbara shuffled some papers into a pile and launched into a powerful introduction. "TransAqua is a psychopathic monster, a rampant egomaniac, in the most florid stages of its madness. To date, no individual, no organization, no government, has challenged its ascendancy."

The room plunged into an immobilized awe.

Her voice assumed a perilously muted tone. "A no-doubt beleaguered President Kolo just signed a contract yesterday with TransAqua to build a twenty-thousand-megawatt dam, and they have forced him to relinquish the rights to the Niger River."

A collective intake of breath as her audience plummeted into hideous regions of disbelief.

"We need to expose culpability at all levels within the corporate structure. Not just the CEO, but every VP, every sales guy, every secretary; it's time for each member of the corporate family to be called to account. Whether corner office or cubicle, no one should be afforded protection. Drop of Life needs to combat a monster at the height of its lunatic powers. With such disclosures, Kolo's regime will topple."

Gums was awestruck by the new note of adventure that had landed there. Mimi looked outclassed, her overly white teeth gleaming like a plaster cast embedded in her face. Barbara could not discern Brad's reaction.

Jane's wrinkles shifted in approval. "Sounds innovative. How do you propose to do this?"

"Facts! Details!" Barbara slapped the table twice, inadvertently stinging her hand. "That's all I deal in. We need someone in the organization to record the route of one piece of paper. From mailroom to manager to meeting to media to . . ." she couldn't think of another "m" word, " . . . to recycl–," then found one, "to mulch."

"Do companies use paper anymore?" Mimi battled with a nail.

Barbara lifted a stern index finger into the air. "It's only those obscure scraps of paper that contain the truth. The first jottings of a to-do list. For example, a list of villages to be evacuated. As it moves around and outside the corporation, it goes, as they say, from prose to poetry."

"What an awesome saying!" Gums twinkled.

"Let's not be seduced, Krystal. It's our job to put a stop to all poetry. If any crumpled bit of paper mentions anything covert, any financials, anything that would implicate the people who process it, we need to follow it."

They all turned to Mimi, who straightened in her chair. "Can do, hon."

Brad may have added something. Whatever it was, Barbara cut in. "I'll fly to Abuja to meet Femi Jegee-dee. I'll explain how to organize a resistance movement. And I'll arrange a meeting with President Kolo; given how he is being taken advantage of, he should be very sympathetic to our cause." She dropped to a tone of deepest empathy. "You may not know, but his identical twin accidentally drowned in the family's swimming pool, and that's why he, and he alone, continually tried to warn the former government about the dangers of Kainji Dam. But no one would listen. Well, I intend to listen to everything his heart wishes to pour out."

Jane nodded, took her cane and swayed to a standing position. Her gravitational pull stirred the energies of the others, and they swirled up in gentle eddies as she dcparted.

FOURTEEN

Lube Job

Slowly creeping its way to the team meeting was the creak of sneakers. Not boots. Sneakers, in the depths of winter. Cheeseman must have had to cut short a golf trip to Hawaii for this. He would be at his most unforgiving. Mary's leg doubled the tempo of its jittering. The entire team cracked open their water bottles.

"So, what have you fuckers been up to now?" Cheeseman had brought his putting iron.

"Good morning, Mr. Cheeseman." Sinclair displayed his house of marble. "I hope your game–"

"Sinclair, wipe that idiotic grin off yer face." Cheeseman leaned over and put an ashtray and golf ball on the carpet.

Sinclair's smile snapped shut. Mary's spirits rose for a nanosecond.

"Glass?"

"Yes."

"Report." He wiggled his ass as he readied for the putt.

"Well, Kolo has signed the agreement–"

"What?" Sinclair jumped, his gelled hair glinting in the glare of halogen lamps.

Cheeseman beamed. "Good work, Glass."

"Signed, Glass?" Sinclair asked. "I doubt it. I've got the *signed* agreement." Sinclair drew a file out of his briefcase; his manicured hand slid it towards Cheeseman. "Here it is." Sinclair dispatched a sparkling flossed smile.

Mary almost vomited the tiny morsels to which her system clung so desperately.

"Check mine if you want." Mary placed her own papers in a neat pile in front of Cheeseman.

He grabbed both piles. "Let's see the signatures."

He checked them both over and then broke out in a smile. Mary could feel a vein pulsing in her neck.

"What is it, Mr. Cheeseman?" Sinclair ventured.

"Same signature. And on the 8th of March. In London." He chuckled as he tightened his grip on the putter. He looked as if he intended to swing it at both their skulls. "You each signed a different contract with the same guy?" His merriment morphed into fury. "What the hell have you been doing, Sinclair? First you back some dust-kissing loser with the lifespan of a cicada, then you sign a contract with some hobo–don't interrupt. I won't even *ask* what you were doing, Glass, but I sure hope it felt good, 'cause it's gonna cost you your job if you don't get something on my desk by 8 a.m. Monday. Do you understand?"

He scanned the documents more closely. "Okay, Glass, you've managed a 70 percent return on investment . . . Whoa, Sinclair–well done!" A burning sensation ripped through Mary's lower abdomen, joining a network of other internal spasms that riddled her panicking body. "It seems you've actually managed

30 percent!" The pains subsided. "P'raps one day," he addressed Sinclair as if telling a nursery story, "you can ask Glass how to negotiate." He kept scanning down. "Glass–cut the construction burden down. It seems Kolo's willing to assume 80 percent of the burden. You've got him at 40 percent. He'll get the money from the World Bank. If you don't know how to do this," he peered up from the paper, "ask Sinclair. Glass, get to it. Report on my desk Monday. As for you, Sinclair–"

"Sir, please." Sinclair's bronze tan could not hide his deathly pallor. "I have another plan."

"Another plan?" Cheeseman turned away from Sinclair to include his audience. "I can't believe the creativity of this guy."

"I would need to discuss the full details with you in private. Please, sir. Kolo is hardly someone we can do business with."

Mary's heart thumped so hard, she could swear the others could see her ribs twitch. She wanted to wipe the drip off her nose, but like an animal whose only defence is camouflage, she dared not make a move.

Cheeseman continued staring, not allowing a single blink to soften his features.

Then he looked down at his fingers.

"Phone me tomorrow at 6 a.m.," he finally said to Sinclair. He turned to the rest of them. "I don't want one word–nothing–about this disaster to leave this room, unnerstand? If anything leaks out, you're fired. Hell, we're all fired."

He slammed the door as he left.

Sinclair polished off an entire litre of water without coming up for air.

As Cheeseman's footsteps faded down the corridor, Sinclair stalked towards the door. Beano just managed to catch up with him. "Anything I can do to help? I may have friends in Sewage–"

"That bitch. I'd ask her to go to hell, but I know she'd just grab a pair of sunglasses and a bottle of suntan lotion."

"What happened?"

"Can't you remember anything, Beano? She said she was signing at the end of the month, not the 8th."

"You're kidding! She lied?" Beano flushed with shock.

On the subject of complexions, Sinclair's tan aged him, not in terms of wrinkles, just in style. It gave Beano the psychological advantage he needed. "If it helps, and it probably doesn't, Dad said he's met with Brigadier . . . hold on . . ." Beano felt inside a pocket of his unironed jeans for a scrap of paper, smoothed out the crumples, then flipped it right side up. "No, Major General Wosu, who fully supports the minister for the environment. He said our government's willing to do so as well, if I . . . uh . . . if we need his support, when the time's right."

Mary rushed to her office and with trembling spider fingers dialled Kolo's residence. She had dangerously underestimated him. He had taken their operating principles–firm, robust, made of steel–and twisted them like rubber bands. She had heard of forged signatures, corrupt accounting methods, ruthless lawyers. But she had never even conceived of the president of a country signing two different contracts with the same company on the same day. Kolo had sniffed out the company's ethos of internal rivalry, sensed that her department hid information from itself and gambled on his intuition. It had been four months since she had boasted to her parents about her plans for Nigerian water rights, and she had come no closer to completion.

After a great fertility of dead ends, she finally tracked Kolo down to the Mandela compound in South Africa, where he was staying as a guest.

"Ah, good evening, Ms. Glass." Kolo's voice revealed no unease. "How may I help you?"

Mary kept her cool. Control and composure were her watchwords. Irritable bowel syndrome was her most pressing medical condition.

She straightened the items on her desk to calm herself down. "Good evening, President Kolo," Mary began tartly. "Something very odd has occurred. You appear to have signed two contracts with us for the construction of the dam."

"Oh, my Lord!" Kolo was sucking again, a tone of deep concern overlaid with a soupçon of utter indifference. "Is this true?"

She remained silent.

"That is a serious concern," he continued, unperturbed by her lack of participation in the charade. "How did it happen? I signed two separate contracts with TransAqua? That's impossible! Does your company not communicate internally?"

"With respect, sir, it's a complex situation. Perhaps we could arrange to nullify the contracts and re-sign."

"I have heard a most disturbing rumour," Kolo replied, off topic. "I understand that Mr. Sinclair has been dealing with other parties. Before I sign, I would obviously need the names of his contacts."

"Pardon?"

"Who else has been dealing with Mr. Sinclair, Ms. Glass?"

Mary picked up a pen and began to doodle, lines drawn on top of other lines, straight and unforgiving. No circles, no curves or arcs.

"Ms. Glass?" Kolo prodded.

She looked down at her doodle. She had unwittingly drawn an organogram. It triggered a thought. Who in TransAqua would have leaked this information to Kolo? Who was the spy? Her mind flitted through the alternatives until she rested on one name.

Her own.

She remembered the words she had uttered in London: *My colleague has been dealing with so many different parties in Nigeria.*

Mary felt her chest implode. She knew if she provided the information Kolo wanted, all those listed would die; yet if she did not supply the names, she would lose her job. He had given her no budge room. With IT's help, she would have to log on to Sinclair's computer to find the names. She considered the dangers of politics in a country as complex as Nigeria. It must be like playing three-dimensional chess blindfolded while sitting in a pit of snakes.

"If you agree to sign a new contract, without delay, I'll get the names," she said.

"Of course I'll sign. By the end of April. On my word of honour."

Aso Rock surged out of the landscape–a mighty granite mound, hard and worthless–as surprising a sight as a vast verruca overlaying a field. This oversized boulder loomed over Abuja, a conceit that claimed ownership of the capital. Tourists visited it; locals praised it; politicians posed in front of it. Even the presidential palace nestled underneath it.

Kolo loved the permanence of the fossilized wart. No matter the political changes the capital faced, whether the city spread to cover the whole of West Africa or was annihilated by some terrible tragedy, it would always have to contend with this monstrous hump. It was, as local journalists liked to point out, the Ayres Rock of Nigeria.

Kolo snorted to himself. Who would even want to visit Ayres Rock?

Yet Aso Rock had a hidden purpose. To his fellow Nigerians it symbolized victory conferred by gods, which is why they had built the presidential complex underneath this pagan site, despite the pleading of its Modernist architect.

The giant pebble reminded him of the farce within all things; the fact that you could get away with anything in Nigeria. Eventually even an obstruction like Aso Rock could become a site of pilgrimage. Kolo had no doubt that over time the site would draw disciples to worship quite another deity–one that took human form.

He loved the grandeur of the presidential villa, its colossal rooms and European elegance, the crème soufflé feel of it and the surrounding fortifications that offered so much protection; it fit him like his own skin. He was loath to give it up and had no plans so to do. Yet Kolo had served as president for a mere three months and had accomplished very little, although on a personal level he had profited handsomely from the catastrophe at Kainji.

He buzzed his intercom.

"Yes, sir?" The voice of the minister of information crackled through.

"Here. Bring pictures."

The minister arrived, carrying bundles of photographs, canvases and designs, looking disgruntled.

"How goes it?" Kolo surveyed him.

"Well. And yourself?"

"As well as can be expected."

"Things will change."

Kolo studied the minister more intently, trying to excavate any meaning behind that remark, his unease increasing as his confidant plopped the designs on Kolo's desk from a fair height. Annoyed by this breach of etiquette, Kolo flicked an upward-pointing finger at a chandelier.

The minister of information slowly strutted to the light switch, which gave Kolo time to note the expression of disdain on his haughty features. He flicked his finger again, indicating a chair. "Sit."

"Sir." The minister lingered on his way to the chair, sat, crossed his legs, and watched his president through arrogant eyelids.

"We need some decoration in this place. It's a bit drab."

The minister merely nodded.

Increasingly irritated by the minister's lack of enthusiasm for such a monumental project, Kolo sorted through the many portraits of himself–paintings, sculptures and large ceramic murals–that he had commissioned from Nigeria's most prominent artists. He beckoned his advisor with two fingers, and the minister dutifully laid out the architectural plans of the entire governmental complex.

"Now, what should go where? This is the question." Grabbing a pencil, Kolo waited for a response.

Designed in neoclassical style to signify democratic intent, the legislative, executive and judiciary buildings huddled together beneath the protective posture of Aso Rock.

"Sir, in view of the fact that the three branches of government have been unfortunately co-sited, I think that perhaps it might be best to confine these splendid works of art to the executive branch. This would assist in symbolically indicating a separation of powers between your office and those of the legislature and judiciary."

"Really? Perhaps we should also symbolically indicate a separation between the executive coffers and your paycheque."

The minister shifted in his chair, his discomfort finally palpable.

"Personally, I find the arrangement quite snug," Kolo continued.

The minister of information reluctantly replied, "It makes communication much faster."

"Indeed." Kolo waited for more contrition.

"And, em, who can deny the therapeutic properties of art."

"They use it in hospitals."

They both pored over the plans, placing objects throughout the entire complex in pencil. Thereafter, Kolo personally oversaw their positioning. It took less than a week for the implied surveillance of Kolo's virtual presence to be felt in all sectors of the administration.

After a successful meeting with Cheeseman the next morning, Sinclair placed a series of red-flagged email herrings to three Nigerian ministers for the unwitting Mary to hook and offer to Kolo as fodder. Then he picked up his handset and dialled 011, followed by 234.

"Office of the minister for the environment. How can I help you?"

"Nkemba! Lovely to hear your voice. How are you?"

"Fine, thank you, Mr. Sinclair. And you yourself, sir?"

"Dangerously well, Nkemba. I'm a menace to the world today."

"You want speak to the minister, sir?"

"I'd be infinitely grateful, Nkemba. A million thanks."

Sinclair sat tapping his desk, attempting to contain his anger. Kolo had screwed him over. It would be the first and last time. He'd let Glass try to cope with that maniac, while he would throw his full support behind the minister for the environment. He might not be the brightest of the bunch, but at least he knew how to bend over and enjoy the ride.

After a few moments, the phone clicked.

"Mr. Sinclair, sir!" The baritone had less energy than usual. "How are you?"

"Dangerously well, sir, dangerously well." Sinclair smiled as he spoke. "And yourself?"

"Not so dangerous, maybe, but alive, praise to God. You-know-who is still too strong."

"The last tree felled didn't help, sir?" Sinclair was all sympathy, though his patience had almost run out.

"My friend, you live in a forest. I live in a jungle. As you're cutting bush in front of you, the bush grows behind you. It's very difficult."

"Wonderful analogy, sir. Wonderful! And if I might use the same analogy, I'm here to clear the way, in front and behind. Three trees will be cut down very soon–they are old, with many roots. Your path will be clear, but make sure you take it at the right time."

"Three trees? Same method?"

"Same method. Don't you worry, sir. I'm still working in your best interests. I think you'll provide some exciting leadership for the country." Sinclair applied the necessary lubrication to his words. "You're a man of great vision, Minister. Your country needs a man like you."

"Oh, thank you, thank you. So, Mr. Sinclair," the minister offered himself up, "can I do anything for you in return?"

"Can I make another small suggestion, sir?" He eased himself in.

"Anything." The minister's voice quivered.

"Perhaps you could make contact with Major General Wosu P. Wosu. He's on board. And if there's anything else you need, just call. I'm behind you all the way." Sinclair could feel them both moving in the same direction, thrusting forward together. It felt great. "I think you'll find, in the next few weeks, that OK will be KO'd."

"Ah-ah! OK will be KO'd!" The minister neighed a laugh. "You're a poet, my friend. A true poet!"

"And you will be crowned king, sir."

The minister whinnied in approval. "Ah-ah, Sinclair!" His excitement grew to fever pitch. "You have the mind of a businessman but the heart of a politician." He screamed out the last words. "You're a true Nigerian-oh! Yes, oh yes! Oh, Sinclair." The excitement of the news overcame him at last. He let out a groan. "If only I could depend on others as I can depend on you." He sighed and bid his friend farewell.

When he put down the phone, Sinclair was exhausted. He had to take a few minutes to catch his breath.

FIFTEEN

Oyinbo

Ottawa's cotton wool blossoms flurried past Barbara's window, a festive confetti of blushing white, flamingo pink and daring fuchsia carried by the breezes of an unseasonably early spring. The petals tripped over people's feet in giddy circles, revelling in the last few moments of their short lives. High above, the pines looked down on this uncouth display of nature at its most intoxicated, appalled by its unbridled sense of elation. The pines stood tall through all seasons, sober and staid, but this annual carousal made them question the substance of an existence based on certainty rather than celebration.

Mary–bland, unchanging Mary–she was the powerful pine. And Barbara, tumbling and capricious, was the blossom. She knew Mary despised the blossom as much as Barbara scorned the pine. She nodded to herself, ingesting this wisdom.

Barbara moved away from the window, catching sight of

Astro packing his plastic bags for his trip back home. Astro–neither pine nor blossom, more constant, yet ethereal.

The wind. Astro was the wind.

She flipped open her cellphone and dialled a number. "Hello. It's Barbara."

"Barbara, darling," her father shouted. "How are you? Can you hear me?"

"Yes. The line's pretty clear."

"Can you hear me?" he repeated. "Speak louder. The phone . . ." Then, to his wife, "The phone lines are appalling."

Barbara rustled some paper in front of the mouthpiece and tapped it a couple of times. Yellow eyes shot heavenwards.

"How's Kenya?" her father shouted.

"Pretty hot. I've been on safari. Did you get the carvings?"

"Ah, that's much better," her father said to her mother. "Yes," he yelled. "We got them. Why did it have Canadian stamps?"

"UNEP ships everything to Canada," Barbara yelled back. "For security reasons."

"Very wise," her father commented to himself.

"I'm just phoning to say they're flying me to Nigeria today, so I'll be gone for a week."

"Be careful," her father shouted. "I've been in those kinds of places. Have you got a pen?"

"Yes."

"Right. Take this down. Don't, I repeat, do *not* eat the food. Got that? And for god's sake, don't drink anything. Even bottled drinks." He raised his voice half an octave. "Never, I repeat, *never* ask for ice–that's made with local water too. Don't talk to anyone you don't know. Don't take local transport. And most importantly, if you're in an accident, and I'm only saying *if,* don't, I repeat, do *not* under any circumstances get a blood transfusion. It's probably infected."

"Okay. Got it."

"Now, read it back to me. Let's make sure you've got it."

"No eating, no drinking, no transportation, don't talk to anyone, no transfusions."

"And no ice. Well done. Don't forget they still have AIDS there."

"No sex. Got that. Okay, gotta go. Bye."

Barbara snapped her cellphone shut. She dodged and bobbed around the apartment, throwing her most valuable items into a suitcase, cramming in numerous boxes of condoms around the sides, as these would doubtless be in short supply.

Astro watched her pack. "Bobble, what are you planning to do over there?"

"They're just presents, Astro. For my friends."

"What friends? You don't know anyone!"

Barbara adjusted her sarong. "Yes, I do. There's Femi."

"You've never met the guy! You don't even know if he's alive!"

"And I have an important contact I'm seeing in Lagos. She's a journalist called . . ." she scanned her memory, " . . . some local name."

"Oh, okay, then. What was I thinking? I can see you're right on top of things." He marched out of the room with his plastic bags.

At the airport check-in, Astro knotted the tops of his plastic bags with sharp tugs and wrote "A" on them in felt tip pen. He chucked them onto the scales, sniffling.

"Take care, Bimble." His voicc wobbled. "Send me a postca–"

"Passport?" the woman at check-in reached for his documentation.

"Yeah, I've got one," Disoriented, Astro sniffed. "Bib, why–"

"Can I have it, then, please? And your ticket?"

"Sure! Take it! Take everything! What do I care?"

"Just need the passport and ticket, sir." She tapped into her computer.

Barbara traced the outline of Astro's lips with her finger, then fell on him in a passionate embrace in which time/space and all material existence disappeared. After protracted complaints from check-out and other passengers, she abandoned him at the US Immigration checkpoint, making her way to the Air Nigeria counter, bound for Lagos. A vast array of people stood in a haphazard queue, all jostling, arguing, bidding noisy, tearful good-byes, some screaming recognition of long-lost friends. They carried oversized boxes of electronics, suitcases wrapped with duct tape and overstuffed bags, some of which emitted a pungent odour of meaty food. Almost every passenger carried crates of fresh water, water filters and the like; some rushed to airport washrooms, returning with dozens of filled water bottles.

The women wore enormous headdresses and voluminous wrappers of vivid colour, while the men, in billowing tunics with elaborate embroidery, gesticulated their way past the airport's officialdom. Other passengers leaned on their luggage, slumped, their despairing eyes conveying the mark of death. Perhaps they had discovered yet another dead relative or had to attend yet another funeral.

The plane was two hours late. Barbara, anxious to secure a seat and having heard horror stories about overbooking, stormed her way to the front through the crowds at the gate. After a brief sprint to elbow out any last competitors, she finally made it onto the aircraft and sat between a large, boisterous woman with a cooler on her lap and a businessman on his cellphone.

"Is Wole on seat?" he boomed.

"Excuse me." Barbara tapped him on his shoulder. "You can't use the phone while we're taxiing. It's totally against IATA regulations."

"Wole?" the man shouted. "Hey, Wole! Worraps? I'm on the plane. Yes. We're just leaving the terminal now."

The woman slammed down the tray in front of her, opened a dish and spooned out some hot food smelling of rotting flesh. She then started to slurp it up.

Barbara fumed to herself. "Okay. Just keep centred. Stay in the ever-present now. Find joy in this moment."

"777," the progress report continued. "Pretty full. The stewardess is now walking down the aisle . . . Twenty litres only . . . I have an oyinbo sitting next to me." He paused, and then discreetly, at the top of his voice: "Forty-five, maybe fifty."

Barbara butted in. "Thirty-seven, actually." When she heard no correction, she snatched the phone from him and yelled into it. "I'm thirty-seven, though I can't see how it's any of your business."

He snatched his phone back. He kissed his teeth and threw her a long look of deep contempt. He lingered in this censorious scrutiny before gathering himself, turning his shoulder away from her and resuming the conversation. "Oh. The stewardess is starting her instructions. No, I'm not scared. We all have to die sometime. But I'd prefer to die first class."

Barbara pressed her buzzer.

After a minute, a flight attendant appeared. "Yes, ma'am?"

Barbara looked knowingly at her fellow passenger. The flight attendant looked at her, query in her eyes. Barbara nodded again at the cellphone and the tray. Finally, the attendant understood.

"Sir, sir."

He waved her to hold. "The stewardess is trying to speak to me."

"She's called a flight attendant," Barbara pronounced at full volume.

"Yes. No, she's standing next to me. Ah-ah! Wole! How am I supposed to know?" More discussion. "Just a minute." He turned to the flight attendant. "Yes?"

"Please put the cellphone away, sir. We're getting ready for takeoff."

He turned back to his cellphone. "She says we're getting ready for takeoff. She wants me to put the cellphone away." More discussion. "Well, those are the regulations. Otherwise the pilot cannot hear what the control tower is saying." A pause. "Yes, but the plane could crash . . ." Barbara tried to grab the cellphone again. He held his hand in an imperious stop sign. " . . . if people use their cellphones."

The woman next to Barbara unbuckled her seat belt. "Where is the toilet?" she barked in enquiry.

"Please," the flight attendant said. "Sit down. You can't move until the seat belt light–"

The woman shifted her cooler onto Barbara's lap and stood up. "I need to go now." She bumped past Barbara and the businessman.

The flight attendant lurched after her. Barbara, seizing the opportunity, stormed to the front to deposit the foul-smelling cooler on the flight attendant's seat. She had specifically requested a seat next to vegetarians.

"No," the man was saying when she got back. "I said it could *crash* . . ." he shouted the last word, " . . . if the pilot cannot hear the control tower." He settled back, legs wide, and laid his arm across the back of Barbara's seat. "That Russian plane crashed because some idiot didn't close his cellphone-oh." He took his shoes off. "Oh–now we're taking off."

"Please, sir, turn your cellphone off," the flight attendant called from the back of the aircraft, where she was busy rattling the toilet door.

"Of course," he yelled back at her. He stretched out his toes. "Well, the pilot thought he was cleared for takeoff, but no, there was another plane landing. Anyway, *sha,* you know these backward countries like Russia. You would think people died quickly. But no–in a crash like that, people burn. It takes time."

Barbara popped 6 milligrams of tranquillizer into her mouth and looked down at the newspaper on his lap. Laid out in florid colour–a shocking report of another dam rupture.

She grabbed the paper and scanned the news, breathless: a dam downstream from Kainji had broken. Young, proud and strong, Jebba Dam had been heroically carrying the extra load its older sister had abandoned. Now, buckled in pain and screaming for help, it could hold no more and had broken, killing another hundred thousand people.

Discouraged, she laid her drugged head on the welcoming bosom of gentle slumber, eventually slumping onto the businessman's outraged breast, and only awoke, with a jolt, after the plane had executed a bumpy landing. She could already smell the humidity through the air conditioning system.

She grabbed her bags as passengers started jamming the corridors to the exits.

"Please sit down!" a voice urgently warned. "Stay in your seats until the plane has come to a complete halt and the warning lights have been turned off."

Women dragged bulky objects into the aisle and blocked the exits.

Finally, after an interminable taxi, the plane stopped and the doors were opened by the flight attendants with vexed scowls, looking as if their nerves were frayed to one or two gossamer threads that linked them to continued sanity. The boil of passengers burst and the plane emptied. Barbara followed as people ran across the tarmac of Lagos's Murtala Muhammed International

Airport towards the terminal. Small women assumed Herculean strength as they carried bags twice their size on heads, shoulders, hips, streeling children.

It was nighttime and, though Barbara could see very little, the humid air punched into her and she could smell the odours that signalled a shift of culture–smells that carried more weight, stronger presence, greater purpose. Voices shouted from all directions, workers lolled in doorways or strolled to their posts, and the stars could be seen through the haze of humidity, as there were few lights to erase the night sky.

Inside the terminal she followed the crowd as they rounded a corner and dashed into customs and immigration, joining a vast sea of people in a cavernous hall with no working fans. Only four or five officers were on duty. The heat was oppressive. There were no seats.

Barbara spotted the man who had sat next to her. He had managed to bulldoze his way close to the front–within thirty people he would be served. She could see him on his cellphone. He was no doubt relaying his good news to his friend. Barbara sat down on her suitcase.

Over two hours later, Barbara reached the immigration counter.

"Name?" The immigration officer fanned himself with some papers.

"Barbara Glass."

He flicked open her passport. "Glass? That's your name?" He leaned on his podium. "Are you sure?"

"Yes. Of course I'm sure."

"Why?"

"Pardon?"

"Why Glass?"

Barbara, sensing danger, decided to mirror his body language. She leaned on his podium. "Don't know."

"Oh–really?" He looked at her as if he had caught her in a lie. "Very interesting . . . And where are you from?"

"The United States."

Then another trick question.

"Is this your passport?"

"Yes."

The officer beckoned to a comrade, who was in the middle of a long-winded anecdote to two other colleagues that eventually met with generous laughter. Barbara sighed loudly. Her officer did not notice. She closed her eyes, breathed deeply and emitted a long, resonant "ohm." She meditated on the word that appeared to cause such confusion. "I am as the glass," she intoned. "I am here, yet I am not here. Absence is my presence. My presence is absence. Viewers lie behind, the viewed in front. Where is behind and where is in front? Light flows through. I am the glass."

She opened her eyes. The officer's face betrayed a look of deep concern. He scribbled on her landing card in red pen. Some minutes later his colleague strolled over in slow motion. The two conferred.

"She says her name is Glass."

They turned their backs to her, checked the passport again, then turned round.

"Is your name Glass?" the second officer inquired.

"Yes," she nodded to herself. "Oh yes, very much so."

They were confounded.

"Are you married?" the second officer asked.

"No."

"Enh?" They looked perplexed. "A pretty girl like you! That's too bad. What happened?"

"Is there something the matter with you?"

Both pairs of eyes peered at her, compassionate.

"No." Barbara catapulted out of her gentle musings. "You see, this is a typical example of the obsolete notions of patriarchal hegemony in which–"

"Look at this woman vibrate!" The first officer kissed his teeth in disgust.

"You should get married-oh!" the other instructed. "What are you waiting for?"

They examined her passport further and called a third officer. He was the most astute of the bunch, and he conducted an interrogation worthy of Solomon.

"Is your father's name Glass?"

"Yes."

"Are you sure?"

"Yes."

Outclassed, the first officer stamped her passport, then sent her on through customs, where three officers stopped her. "Anything to declare?"

"No."

"Please come this way."

Barbara knew much of her cargo might be hijacked at this point. She readied herself for the battle.

They flicked through her passport.

"Glass? Is that your name?"

"Yep."

"Are you sure?"

"Uh-huh."

Confused, they put the passport to one side and opened her bags. A large, black vibrator popped out. Two officers looked at each other, the whites of their eyes turning pink. The third officer, obviously less a man of the world, took it out.

"What is this item?"

"A vibrator."

"What is it used for?" he asked in dictatorial fashion.

The other officers tried to stop the further interrogation.

"Masturbation, of course," Barbara said, turning it on for a demonstration on her knuckles. She gave it back to him.

He dropped it in fright. She bent down to pick it up. "I hope you haven't broken it," she said petulantly, "or you'll have to replace it." She turned it back on, trying it out on the palm of her hand. It still worked. "Thank god. We're in luck."

Looking fragile, the officers continued a gingerly search. After a layer of sarongs, they came across the condoms, which sprang out and fell on the floor. The officers gawked at Barbara. One rifled through her passport for a last time.

"Where are you staying?" the third officer asked.

"Ikoyi Hotel."

She picked the condoms up from the floor and separated them into neat piles on the table, according to flavour. "I hope," she said with irritation, "that you plan to repack this bag, because I had a hell of a time closing it. Christ, the embassy didn't say it would be this bad."

"Oh, so you know the American ambassador well?" the second officer asked, looking at the condoms.

They helped her repack her bag and led her to the exit. According to the legendary tales she had been told, she knew she was perhaps the first person in history to emerge out of customs and immigration in Nigeria without paying even a dollar. Indeed, she mentioned this fact as she left.

"Wow! I was told I'd have to bribe you."

The officers responded with outrage. "We do not accept bribes!" "Are you serious?" "We are officials of the Federal Government of Nigeria!"

In the hotel lobby, acquaintances yelled with an excitement that rioters would envy, crashed into each other and then smothered each other with asphyxiating hugs. Others announced their recognition of friends or relatives from opposite ends of the lobby with screams that, at first, appeared to be cries for help. More exchanged raucous jokes that met with laughter, making beer bottles rattle on the glass tables. Some, who had obviously lost relatives far away near Kainji, wailed their greetings, throwing hands up to the skies, begging for pity.

Barbara forded the chaos of the lobby to check in, then carried her bags up to her room and collapsed.

The next morning, she scurried back down to the lobby, which was just as crowded, her pulse racing with delight at the energy and boisterousness of these people. She stood and eavesdropped on the conversations around her, spoken in a form of English with widened vowels and heightened drama. One story flowed into another, one joke built on the momentum of the last, one tragedy led to the next. Language was as pliable as clay, as plentiful and precious as water. She had entered a realm where oral expression reigned in flamboyant splendour.

Barbara at last approached the front desk. "Have I received any visitors?" she asked the receptionist.

As if he had not heard her, he finished reading an article of interest. He shook his head. "Oh, these Nigerians," he said to the paper. "They will bury this country." Then, turning to Barbara, in a lazy voice he said, "Yes, ma?"

"Have I received any visitors?"

"Em," he said, leaning on the front desk, deciding. "Yes."

"Who was it?"

"Maybe a friend, ma?" He slouched onto his other foot.

"What?"

"Maybe someone you know?"

She decided to ask another clerk. "Excuse me, excuse me . . ."

The other receptionist was talking to the porter while sipping a soft drink. She turned a surly eye to Barbara. Without listening to Barbara's request, she yawned. "Not my job, ma."

Barbara retreated to a lobby chair to wait for her contact to arrive, where she was interrogated by passersby.

"Are you married?"

"No."

"A pretty girl like you! Why not?"

"I'm independent. Since the advent of feminis . . ."

"Ah-ah! Listen to this overgraduate blowing big grammar!"

A small crowd circled around her as she expounded on her beliefs, growing steadily into a throng. Hours later, a voice boomed from the other side of the lobby and an exhausted Barbara looked in its direction, as did the entire reception area. Behind the voice stood a woman of vast girth, exuberant and mighty, festooned with a wrapper of kaleidoscopic colour.

"Welcome, Miss Glass!" Aminah bellowed. "Welcome to Nigeria!" Her voice atomized all other sounds in the reception area.

SIXTEEN

Cracking the Chrysalis

Instead of taking her to Femi, Aminah gave the taxi driver directions to a bar. The driver crunched the gears. The springs squeaked as they took off. Barbara could see the road through a hole in the floor. There were no mirrors in the taxi.

"So–where are you from? Unirred States?" The driver looked back at her.

"Yes. Please look at the road."

"My wife's cousin's son lives there. In Texas. His name is Dayo." He swerved into the left lane, then gestured with a floppy, lazy left hand. "Do you know him?"

"No."

The driver eased himself around to face front again.

"Why are we going to a bar?" Barbara asked as she adjusted the African map across her T-shirt, her breasts distorting the continent's eastern and western extremities. "Is Femi an alcoholic?" She tilted her head as a social worker might.

Aminah opened her mouth and issued a scream. Barbara opened her eyes, ready to jump out of danger's way. The scream mutated into a vomit of laughter. "No, no," Aminah cried, sputtering out the last few giggles. "Just to get information. He must be somewhere in Abuja."

Seeing a traffic jam ahead, the driver turned abruptly into the oncoming lane. Cars sped directly towards them. Barbara shrieked and pointed to the road.

The driver cackled. "Ah! These oyinbo!"

Aminah screamed, plunging into a long howl that ended in a cascade of chuckles.

The driver continued in the opposite lane for a while, until he was satisfied that the traffic had thinned out, then veered back into the right lane, now moving at exponential speeds.

Satisfied that proper attention was now being paid to their survival, Barbara leaned towards Aminah, eyes still on the road. "What exactly is an oyinbo?" she whispered, hoping not to incite the driver's attention.

"Oyinbo means 'peeled,'" Aminah announced, as if speaking to a convocation of thousands. "That's what we call white people. They look as if their skin has been peeled."

"Hmph! That's not very complimentary, is it?" Barbara huffed.

She settled back to look out the window, struck by the quality of light. While Ottawa's light was on the blue end of the spectrum, Lagos's light had a more golden hue and shone with a great intensity. Whereas Ottawa's blue hue appeared regal, Lagos's dazzling light seemed raucous. It toyed with surfaces, bouncing off them, twisting around them, wrestling with them. No matter how vivid the paint, how graphic the design or how textured the surface, the light erased all with a blinding white glare. Even the sullen shadows and moody niches could not escape its pranks. It lit up the darkness and exposed the hidden.

Indeed, where the shadows lurked, delicate tones and subtle hues prospered most.

The radiant heat made pavements shimmer and people glisten. There were children everywhere–some with their mothers, others begging in gangs, yet others asleep on the pavement. Lagos seemed to be a city of children.

Everywhere she looked, she saw food stalls, most offering mere scraps of cooked meats and rotting fruit sold in neat piles. Chickens and goats shared the pavement with their predators, innocently believing in their own exclusion from the fate of their kin. The unending smell of a carnivorous culture assaulted Barbara's nasal passages. Emaciated dogs and cats, teetering on the edge of existence, walked among the crowds, lost in their own thoughts.

Lagos was charged with an overpowering sense of unending and frenetic activity, yet everybody walked in an exhausted stroll, as if loitering. In the same way, although her taxi careened through the streets in a quest for oblivion, it also seemed to crawl towards its destination. Barbara could not reconcile these two conflicting sensations. It was as if society ran at a much greater intensity than the world she came from, but at a slower pace. Existence was a flash of moments, spinning like a top so that it only just maintained equilibrium–any slower or any faster and it would topple. To an outsider looking at the city, the spinning top appeared almost stationary, but the evidence of blurred colours hinted at another reality.

The taxi rattled, its springs puncturing Barbara's buttocks, as the driver charged at a car trying to get in front of him. Suddenly, he slammed on the brakes. Barbara's neck snapped forward. He greeted another driver. They stopped for a minute to chat, bringing traffic to a complete halt. After a few minutes of friendly repartee, her driver took off again with a jerk. Her neck snapped back.

After a three-hour death drive in the city's traffic, through its unpaved streets and around its potholes, the duo finally arrived at the bar, a small concrete building with a low, corrugated iron roof. Inside, the locals conversed at the top of their voices over the sounds of the generator. Aminah tried to buy Barbara some water, but the bartender informed her that stocks had run out. Instead, she bought colas. They loitered for an hour, until, finally, the bartender mentioned that most of his clientele would arrive in the evening.

"What a stroke of luck!" Barbara exclaimed, pulling Aminah away to shop for fabrics. They hailed another taxi, imprisoned in gridlock, and meandered past a dozen cars to grab it. After a shopping spree, they returned in the late evening through another of the city's notorious go-slows, Barbara in a Nigerian wrapper and self-fashioned turban.

An exhausted Aminah spotted a contact. "Kunle!" she yelled over the music, making the man jump somewhat. "Do you know where Femi Jegede is?"

"Femi Jegede? He died-oh!"

Barbara spilled her drink.

"In the flood?" Aminah barked.

"No, no. He died after. Didn't you read about his funeral?"

Barbara could hardly believe her ears. Her entire mission rested on the fact of Femi's existence; without it, her web of lies would unravel. The air lay heavy upon her, the music set her nerves on edge, the presence of others now became oppressive. All around her the sickly smell of spilled beer and light smog drifted, carried by the humid air.

"How can this be true!" Her intense pitch attracted the attention that such a drama deserved. "We were such great friends." Barbara collapsed into a chair. She looked up in distress at Aminah and the occupants of the bar. "The forces of Tao had been manifesting so well for me until this point!" she said in a plaintive lament in their general direction.

They looked down at her, puzzled. "Forces?" "What forces?" "Juju?" "Is she a witch?"

"Femi died?" Aminah exclaimed, thunderstruck. "I never read about it!" She stood with hands on hips, her voice growing louder as her displeasure increased. "What happened to him? How did he die?" The men flinched as she spoke, trepidation in their eyes, unsure as to who should answer.

"He died of grief, *sha*." A man at the back lounged on one hip, sucking on a bottle of beer. "So," he said to Barbara, his eyes shining brightly as the drama increased, "you didn't know?"

"Didn't know? Of course I didn't know! I've flown from America to see him."

"Aaah!" the crowd exhaled in appreciation. "America!" Each one then took a sip of beer in collective sympathy.

Barbara closed her eyes to usher in calm. She linked her thumb and forefinger, groaning in inhales and moaning out exhales. Grounded, she opened her eyes again. Beer bottles stopped their progression to the lips of a now entranced bar room. Aminah sat down and almost obscured Barbara from their view.

"It's okay," Barbara informed the patrons as she peeked round Aminah's bulk. "I've managed to centre myself." The music stopped. This caesura allowed her to dispense a key tenet of Tao wisdom. "The universe is unfolding and I become part of its flow. I am part of the flow of being/not-being. I am the window. I am the door. Through not-being, I be."

A fly buzzed around a bare light bulb. The sound of its erratic orbit echoed off the cement walls. A soft breeze wafted over the tops of the beer bottles. No one moved.

Barbara looked around at the faces flickering in the light of kerosene lamps, eyes bright with query. She smoothed back an errant wisp of hair, embarrassed but proud. Her words had obviously ignited something deep in their souls.

Tentatively, they resumed their drinking.

Aminah raised her massive bulk off her chair again. "Who . . ." The men backed up a few paces. They raised their eyebrows in anticipation. Beer bottles once again froze in mid-air. "Who is the new leader of Wise Water Nigeria?" Her voice echoed off the silent walls. "I need a contact."

The bar took a collective sip of release, mixed, perhaps, with a tinge of disappointment.

Her initial informant proffered the information. "His closest confidant was Igwe, so he is now the interim leader, but . . ." He came closer to Aminah to whisper in her ear. The entire crowd craned their necks for this nugget of information: "Igwe's a drug addict."

A collective gasp as they shook their inebriated heads in censure.

"How does the man think drugs can help him?" a man asked in a philosophical vein. He shook his head mournfully, then tossed it back as he threw the last few drops of beer down his throat.

"Drugs?" Barbara stood up with conviction. "Well, who hasn't tried them at one time, right?" She searched in her bag as the crowd's unblinking eyes threatened to dry up altogether. The men held their breath, waiting for what would emerge from her handbag. They flinched as she took out a couple of bank notes and slapped them down on the bar.

"What zone does Igwe live in?" Aminah hunted through her own capacious handbag for a notebook.

"Zone? Ah-ah, a drug addict in Abuja? Where does he have the money for that city? No, they had to move him to Jos."

"Let's go, Aminah." Barbara fluttered out the door, leaving Ogbe Kolo's face to soak up the excess beer on the counter.

They packed and headed for the airport, following Igwe's trail. Their flight took them to Jos, within the picturesque plateau region–the cool, tranquil highlands sited a mere hundred miles from the capital city, Abuja, Nigeria's centre of political turmoil.

The taxi drove past small hamlets made of wattle and clay with grass roofs surrounded by farms divided by cacti. The earth, cracked in areas, was yellow, not red, and grasslands had given birth to boulders higher than buildings. They sputtered along at a majestic pace until the taxi reached the wide boulevards and tree-lined splendour of the city centre. Jos was bathed in a serene calm, its gentle vegetation easing across rolling hills, birds in trances as they floated overhead in the cool breezes of the plateau. Here she was, surrounded by excited flowers exploding with colour and matronly trees too wide to hug. She could hardly believe that this city and Lagos had any connection.

They stopped in front of a dilapidated building with hints of past glory, rusting filigree grillwork over the windows. Walls echoed the motif, engraved with gentle circles and other geometric designs.

Barbara hopped past chickens, goats, stray cats and skinny dogs at which the children threw stones. She issued a terse lecture on animal abuse. The children followed her, begging for money. Aminah shooed them away.

On the second floor of the building, they entered a small, dark, dank room where menacing faces peered at them through the gloom–faces that had lost all hope, all certitude of life, smothered by the drug's jealous embrace. Water-filled jerry cans, plastic buckets and canisters littered the room. A jumble of people sat on mats, a few staring wide-eyed at nothing, some mouthing silent words. Others slept. Several rambled around the room, muttering to themselves.

"Poor souls," Aminah whispered. "Everything they have is gone. What could possibly be encouraging them to survive?"

Barbara addressed the room. "Is Iggy here?"

"Who wants to know?" a surly addict mumbled from a corner.

"My name is Barbara Glass. I'm a good friend of Femi Jegeedee. We were very close. Like brother and sister."

"Who are you?" another asked, fighting to extricate himself from the drug's haze.

"I work for Drop of Life in Canada on water rights."

"Do any of you know," Aminah's voice echoed around the walls, slamming against delicate eardrums, "where Igwe is? We need to speak to him."

"I'm Igwebuike," a man slouched against a wall answered. He wore dark glasses, no doubt to protect bloodshot pupils from the intrusive daylight the duo had let in.

"Although to some you represent the dregs of society," Barbara said in a reverential hush, tilting her head to one side, "the lowest form of life on this planet," she looked at him with plaintive sympathy, "to me, I am you and you are me. There is no separation." She nodded to herself, then shook her head in empathetic sorrow.

"Who . . . ?" someone hissed from the corner of the room, making everyone jump. "Who is calling my friend Igwe the lowest form of human life?" He looked like a king, his throne a broken stool.

"Please." Aminah's voice shot through the room, reverberating across the windowpanes. "Please–we don't want to cause wahala. We are here on urgent business. We are looking for the leader of Wise Water."

"You can talk to me. I am Femi Jegede, although my 'sister' here should doubtless recognize me."

"You!" Aminah barked. "How can you be Jegede?" Everyone winced as she spoke. "He's dead."

Saddened faces erupted into rare laughter. A few who had lost their mental moorings became increasingly bewildered.

"I'm dead?" The king's handsome eyes screwed up as he laughed. "How did I die?"

"Of, em, of . . ." Aminah hesitated. She sat down. "Of grief, sir."

The room erupted once more into a fit of giggles.

"So . . ." Aminah talked a little more softly when the laughter died down, " . . . you're really Femi Jegede? And this is Igwe?"

"Himself." The man in dark glasses pointed at his own chest. "Am I dead too?"

"No, sir, no. You're . . . you're a drug addict."

For a moment silence reigned as people fought to maintain control over their composure, but then all was lost. A collective scream of appreciation ripened into chokes of laughter, chuckles retched out in long wails.

One man in ragged clothes, his eardrums plugged with mud, who paced in chaotic circles, began to mewl in a chilly ascending note.

"Ubaldous. Everything is okay!" Igwe quickly got up to comfort him, following him on his desolate journeys with a protective arm around him.

Barbara, bewildered and impatient, put her hands on her hips. "What's happening here?"

A sympathetic Aminah turned to her. "Naija gossip. If you're out of circulation, one person will say you must be ill, the next says you're very ill, the next says you're dead. Nigeria is like a small village."

"We had to move from Abuja," Igwe explained.

"So you're Femi?" Barbara asked the man on the stool. "You're alive? And your friends–they're not drug addicts?"

"We couldn't afford drugs if we wanted to," Igwe replied.

The room once more gasped with quiet laughter, as Igwe patted Ubaldous.

Barbara looked at Femi with fresh eyes, noting the aura that fanned out around him. He had a handsome face, with piercing, gentle eyes that told of recent tragedy. His demeanour suggested a weary strength, an exhausted fortitude. His voice resonated with a sad depth; even his laugh, a delightful snicker of descending notes, carried a melancholy charm.

She moved towards him. Eyes flitted to meet other eyes. The room's nervous tension increased with each step. "I was so sorry to hear about your family. You know, like leaves, we are born, we live, we die, and new life begins in our place." She put her hands on his shoulders. "None of us, in the great scheme of things, is more or less important than a leaf."

"Enh?" Igwe stopped walking, gold logos flashing with vexation. "Who is not important?"

"A leaf?" another protested, the words producing some spittle that glinted in a dusty shaft of light. "Who is she calling a leaf?"

Femi looked directly at Barbara. "Did this oyinbo call the lives of one million people unimportant?" His eyes shimmered with fury.

"Stop!" a voice boomed, making the panes of glass rattle. Aminah scraped her chair as she stood. "No one is a leaf. No one in this room is a leaf! No one in Nigeria is a leaf!"

"But," Barbara interrupted, "we're all part of–"

"No one," Aminah's loud voice obliterated all other sounds, "no one is a leaf."

Everyone looked at Femi in astonishment as he tried to stand. Several people rushed to help as if he might fall, gently admonishing him. Igwe ran most rapidly to his side. He held his friend under the elbow, gazing at him with worry, whispering softly to him with concern.

"What happened was not the work of nature," Femi said, "but the work of man."

"And/or woman," Barbara corrected him. "Which is not to say–"

"A leaf didn't fall. A tree was cut dow–"

"You see what your problem is? You may have *listened* to what I was saying," Barbara paused for Femi to assimilate this information, "but you didn't *hear*. This leads to miscommunication, which isn't going to help when we're working together."

"Working together? No! Oh no! Someone get this wom–"

"You interrupted again!" Barbara looked around the room for confirmation. A vein on Femi's forehead pulsed. "Have you ever read *The Dance of Anger*?" she asked.

"What?"

"*The Dance of Anger*. I'll send it to you. It'll really help you with the issues you have around rage."

Femi looked at Igwe, aghast. "Have I gone crazy? Or is it this woman?"

"–meant to say," she spoke over him, "was that what the caterpillar calls the end, the rest of the world calls a butterfly. That is my belief." Barbara bowed in Buddhist fashion.

Femi stared at Barbara. "Who told you we would be working together?"

"Well, that's why I'm here."

"Femi," Igwe interrupted. "Calm down. Don't worry about–"

"Who told you to come?"

Barbara searched her memory. "I can't remember." She pondered the question again and then shook her head in defeat. "Someone." She wandered off to her handbag. "By the way, I've brought some gifts. Probably in short supply over here." She distributed the condoms, addressing a woman who sat paralyzed in embarrassment. "Best not to leave them on the floor. They'll get dusty."

She turned back to Femi. "We have a revolution to organize. Kolo intends to sell rights to the Niger, as well as outright ownership of water resources through licensing, and full custody of Nigeria's electricity in exchange for the construction of the biggest dam in the world." The room erupted into noisy confusion. She could hardly be heard above the din. "So," she raised her voice, "we have to organize some riots, maybe target a few sites. Do you have any explosives, by the way? Obviously I couldn't bring–"

"What are you bombing?" Femi cut her off.

"Sites."

"What sites?"

"Important sites, of course." Barbara twiddled with her beads.

He stared at her, the twitches on his face becoming more violent.

"I've brought some dark clothing. It'll be good camouflage."

"You're not bombing anything."

"Well, we don't have to bomb. Dynamite will do."

"No! No bombing. No explosives. Not even a firecracker."

"Look, you can't stop me coming with you. Just because I'm a woman–"

"Coming with us? Where to? We're not going anywhere! Anyway," he shook his head as if to clear it, "what am I talking about? We're not working together."

"But–"

"No!"

Barbara looked around at the oddball assortment of activists lurking in the corners, realizing the futility of attempting to transform them into the efficient army she envisaged. Dejected but not defeated, she turned to leave. "Oh spirit of the trees," she murmured to herself. "I'll have to find the African Water Warriors–"

"Enh?" Femi grabbed her by the arm. "What do you mean, the Water Warriors? They're terrorists! Nigeria will fall into anarchy!"

Barbara turned to face him, chin up. "I must continue my work," she replied in a low, dangerous hush.

He paused as if taking in for the first time what she'd said about Kolo's plans. "So you want to enter trouble. Maybe, then, it's best if we work together."

His voice contained an edge of panic, Barbara could not help but notice. Still, she beamed, feeling once more that she was merely a conduit. "You know, there's a Taoist saying–"

"Please." Femi rubbed his face with his hands. "I beg-oh, no more Taoist sayings."

"It goes, 'Be wary of men who have nothing to lose.'"

"I know another saying," Femi replied. "It goes, 'Beware of women who quote Chinese sayings.'"

She sat down on a mat and clicked open her purple pen. "So, where can we find some armaments?"

"Have you ever seen a dead person?" Femi asked.

Barbara waited for a suitable lull in the conversation around them before making her pronouncement: "I have no fear of death." She gave a curt bow of her head.

"Ehen!" Femi gazed at her. "Let me show you some fallen leaves. Let me show you death. Then you can tell me if you fear it or not."

SEVENTEEN

Fearsome Farewell

Early the next morning, before the sun grew too hot, Barbara took her yoga mat out onto the grounds of the famed Hill Station Hotel and practised in her purple leotard. A sizeable assembly of people gathered to comment on each posture, tone wavering between outrage and fascination.

At noon, she flew with Aminah and Femi to the area surrounding the collapsed Jebba Dam. Leaning over Aminah's shoulder to look at her newspapers, Barbara stared at photographs of Kolo commiserating with local survivors. She shook her head in pity and tapped Aminah on the shoulder. "Your president seems touched by the tragedy."

"Really?" Aminah's eyebrows rose to meet a headwrap of architectural merit. "Then I wonder why his government didn't warn those downstream of Kainji to move before the next dam burst!" She kissed her teeth with a proficiency Barbara could only admire.

A driver picked them up in a jeep, and they set off on their tour. Brown mists of faint sickly smells hung over them as they stopped at a pretty village on the outskirts of the catastrophe. Children ran up to them, shouting an excited welcome.

Round huts made of clay blended seamlessly into the landscape, throwing into relief a scattering of low concrete buildings with corrugated iron roofs. As she looked to the periphery of the village, Barbara spotted conical granaries with doorways built halfway up, surrounded by a multitude of earthenware pots filled with water.

While the other three stopped at a roadside eatery that had been hastily erected for sightseers, Barbara unwrapped a vegetarian sandwich with a certain fanfare. An ancient and garrulous vendor stood as the eatery's proud proprietor. Femi gave him a bottle of water, which the vendor secreted away with pleasure, then brought some sticks of grilled meat with a glance of challenge at Barbara.

"So," the vendor croaked, "you come look village or you come play?"

"We come play," Femi replied, ripping apart the meat, eyes trained on the vegetation entering Barbara's mouth.

"Play?" Barbara put her hands on her hips, sandwich quivering with her indignation. "We're certainly not playing here, Femi!"

Femi spoke under his breath. "Play is Pidgin. We're touring. As opposed to visiting people in the village."

"Actually," Barbara corrected the vendor, "we're not tourists. We have important work to do. We've come to save people."

"Missionary?" He wobbled on rickety legs.

"No. I'm Buddhist," Barbara replied. The old man looked at her. "Well, a mix between Buddhist and Taoist."

"Okay. I see."

He clearly did not.

"I practice yoga. I meditate. I chant. I find it grounds me; it centres–"

Femi muttered something to the vendor in a local language. The vendor looked up at Femi, pity spreading across his shrivelled face.

"I respect the flow of nature," she carried on. "That's why I don't eat meat."

The vendor stared at her, chewing, though he had nothing in his mouth.

"We are worried about plans to build a new dam," Femi interjected, licking the animal fat off his fingers with undisguised hostility towards his vegetarian guest.

"A dam?"

"Yes. Kolo is planning to build a bigger dam."

"What! Is he mad? Why did no one tell us?"

"Does a hawk warn its prey?"

The vendor crossed his arms as he looked up at Femi, squinting, perhaps considering the separate qualities of the many hawks he had witnessed. Finally, he shook his head. "No, sir. No hawk like this exists in Nigeria," he announced with certainty. His voice then went up a notch. "So, you have come to talk with chief?"

"No," Femi replied. "Why?"

"He met Kolo long time ago. Yes, come and talk to him."

He creaked off to find the chief, beckoning them to follow him. They walked through the village, which was filled with the sounds of women pounding yam. At a distance, Barbara could see women hoeing the ground, babies on their backs, while others carried water. She was creeping towards the field to snap some pictures when she heard a harsh whistling sound, as if alerting her to some danger. She turned around to find

Femi snapping his fingers at the ground behind him, calling her back as if she were a disobedient dog. She obeyed with a disgusted huff.

The vendor led them inside a concrete building, where he introduced them to a group of men sitting in a semicircle. An unassuming figure with a cow-tail whip and a dirty agbada sat on a chair, higher than the others. He almost obscured a shrine on which a variety of objects sat, but through the flicker of candlelight Barbara spotted two identical dusty wooden carvings, bells and all manner of natural objects such as cowrie shells, bones and dried leaves. It all looked so exotic. She tried to elbow past Femi to get a closer look, but a strong hand yanked her back and pointed once more to the ground behind him. Barbara lingered in no man's land, then unwillingly returned to her designated position.

Femi, Aminah and the driver laid themselves on the ground in prostration. Barbara looked down at them, then took a closer look at the man in the chair. It was then that she noticed his aura–bright, luminous and crackling. She dived down, her breasts slapping the unforgiving clay.

The chief rose from his seat, then bent down to help her up, looking appalled. "Please, madam. Stand up. This is not necessary. Please, stand up. Welcome–welcome to our village."

Barbara refused to move, pleased to be involved in some ancient ritual. Only when Femi poked her with his toe, and she peeped up to find the other three already standing, did she struggle to her feet. Her eyes darted around the room, fascinated by its atmosphere of primordial wisdom. "You must be the village chief." She searched his face for clues to the mysteries of life. "How wise you must be! How very, very wise. What a magnificent aura!"

Femi glared at her for a long moment and then turned to the

chief. "Sir, we greet you. We have heard that President Kolo came to see you some time ago."

"Yes," the chief replied, peeking around Femi to stare at Barbara. "He only branched for a few hours."

"What was he doing in this area, sir?"

"Maybe the same reason a dog pisses on a tree. But Kolo does not waste his piss on small bushes."

"Wise words, wise words," Barbara agreed, imbibing the ancestral knowledge.

"What you say is true, sir." Femi dodged to hide Barbara, obliterating her view of the proceedings. "As you say, sir, Kolo is not a stupid man. Apparently, he is trying to build a bigger dam at Kainji. Even though your village lies so far downstream, you will lose your water."

"Aha! So that is why he was here. He just want parasite our water. We thought maybe he came to see Victoria. But it is not only to rest its belly that a snake hides in a tree."

"And a snake is not a stripper just because it sheds its skin," Barbara added.

"Pardon?" the chief asked.

"I said that just because a snake sheds its skin, that doesn't mean you can hire it as a stripper."

The sound of women pounding yam resonated through the village. A mangy dog walked past the doorway, caring little for the philosophical import of their discussions. Flies buzzed around its patches of bare skin.

The chief's retainers looked at each other, perplexed. Femi drew circles in the clay with his toe, avoiding lines of sight. Aminah put her hands on her immense hips, wondering what spirits she had offended to bring this woman to her.

Femi then embarked on a long whispered interchange with the chief in a local language. The chief seemed to grow more concerned as Femi spoke, glancing in Barbara's direction with a look of compassion, accompanied by a hint of alarm. She smiled back at him.

"I'm sorry," the chief replied in a muted voice to Femi. "May Allah take pity on her and her family."

"Thank you, sir," Femi bowed, his face rigid with sorrow.

"Please, sir." Aminah's voice rebounded off the walls of the concrete building as if it were made of rubber. "Who is Victoria, sir? Why would Kolo come to see Victoria?" Three aides flinched as her utterances detonated.

The chief waited for the walls to be free of all vibration before replying. "Victoria took care of Kolo when he was a child. But when I mentioned her name, he stood up and ran, as if he had heard of a ghost."

Aminah's eyebrows shot up in enquiry. "Why, sir?" Her voice blasted across these two syllables.

The chief waited for the echoes to end and silence to return to the room. "Victoria knows something about his childhood, some terrible secret that Kolo has hidden from everyone. We don't ask her, because it frightens her to speak of it. And it happened a long time ago. However, let me show you something that maybe you can use."

He turned to a retainer and murmured something. The man left the room, while the rest of them hung their heads, grinning, unable to contain their amusement.

After a few moments, the aide returned and handed a photo to Femi, whose eyes crinkled until he wept with laughter. Aminah peeked too, then set off on a journey through laughter's wild and varied landscape. All Barbara could see was Kolo kneeling before the village chief. She did not understand what was so amusing. In fact, she was surprised that the president still respected the traditions of yore.

"We took this photo of Kolo after his company put meters on our wells to charge us for water," the chief explained.

The jeep bumped along the road out of the village, swerving past potholes and chickens. As it jolted along, Barbara gripped the back of the seat in front of her to stay upright, using long forgotten muscles to counterbalance the swaying of the vehicle. After half an hour she grew quite exhausted with the effort.

They moved through the faint odour of decay, carried by winds held in brown clouds. She tried to fan the smell away, but it only grew stronger, more rancid, the entire sky a hazy brown. It seeped into her clothing, clung to her hair, leached into her skin. Its pungency was unlike anything she had ever smelled–a bitterness that she felt on her tongue and the roof of her mouth, right through to the back of her throat, as if she were being force-fed decaying meat.

The jeep struggled through the mud until it reached a village blanketed by the smell, a choking stench of putrefaction. Stinking mist with a biting sweetness brought tears to Barbara's eyes and stung her nasal passages. Though she tried to breathe through her mouth, she could not escape the noxious gases, the fetid stench of decomposing bodies.

The jeep turned a corner. All around, flung recklessly like clothes in a bedroom, were bodies swollen to the point of puncture, bodies disembowelled by that which once cleansed them. Birds pecked at them, throwing the crimson flesh up in the air and then catching it in their beaks.

Barbara spotted one man trying to move, his body writhing on the ground, twitching as he willed himself to live. As the jeep approached him, she saw his open wounds, through which maggots crawled, wriggling under his skin, squirming for dominance. Someone screamed–an ear-splitting, unending screech. After a few seconds Barbara realized that the voice was her own.

In the midst of the horror, she was transfixed by one sight: a hand sticking out of the mire. She could not embrace the logic of what had occurred. Why was it there? Had some wretched being struggled frantically to free itself from its muddy tomb? Or had the water, in a brief moment of mercy, allowed it to fashion its own bloody headstone?

She sat, rigid, in silence, staring at the hand–a hand that beckoned a gory greeting to all who saw it, a hand that bid a frightful farewell.

As the mud grew deeper, the group had to abandon the jeep. Each step they took, over pieces of flesh, fragments of bone and the remnants of people's lives, sucked them deeper into grief's belly. They reached the trunk of a baobab tree that had been snapped off in the flood; this mutilated landmark indicated that they now stood at the heart of the village.

Here, a few people engaged in a forlorn search for bodies, wandering as if in a dream. One or two had managed to find their dead relatives and were digging rectangles of differing sizes in the mud. Others nailed papers onto the tree–pictures of people still missing. Some just sat, stunned into inertia or keening with voices that had grown weak.

The stench that winds would not bear away suffocated her, causing her muscles to pull in hard like stone; wails that usually evaporated into the air vibrated on her skin and lodged in her spine; images of life that often flitted past without note now became etched as separate visions with their own individual power; thoughts that might have fluttered away were stamped into the permanence of memory. She hunted around for meaning, from the silence of mutilated body parts to the awful sounds of those left to grieve, from the rigidity of death to the limp torpor of the living. She searched and searched, but the annihilation of so many made no sense.

Barbara looked at Femi, hoping for some kind of guidance as to how to deal with these images of horror. But he stood as if rooted in the mud, disbelief on his face, terror in his eyes. It had not occurred to her that these sights would be as far from his experience as they were from hers. She wondered what appalling thoughts such grisly scenes produced in him and to what terrible landscape his imagination might lead him.

The foursome at last returned to the jeep in silence, their footsteps squelching in the mud. Even Aminah had nothing to say. She only dabbed at her eyes with a handkerchief.

Had she been alone, Barbara would have simply done things. But now she was trapped in the back seat, next to Femi. Their arms touched and she could feel his limbs trembling, his breathing erratic. She glanced at him. His eyes were glistening with tears, and he appeared to be mouthing words, as if reasoning with himself or urging himself on. She tracked her vision away from this sight.

Femi had been right. She had never been acquainted with even a small death at close quarters, let alone seen death on this scale. She wanted nothing to do with any of it and so coped the only way she knew how: by moving from reflection to action.

"Well." She flicked open a notebook with the words "Miracles Happen" emblazoned on its cover. "What do we do now?" She sniffled and then clicked open a pink pen.

Her words jolted Femi out of a hypnotic state, and he blinked rapidly to dry his eyes. "Our Mau Mau warrior wants to start her revolution." Barbara thought she could detect a hint of derision in his tone. "Our colonial master wants to take us to war." Yes, on closer inspection, his delivery did contain a nuance of sarcasm.

Barbara understood Femi's contempt. The mayhem of death had an appetite for the spirits of the living. It had not only reduced all mankind to one station, it had also released its wounds to those still animate. She felt this keenly; it found its seat within her.

Too embarrassed to admit to her former designs for heroic carnage, she retired into denial. "I am a pacifist." She put her hand up in an exonerating stop sign. "Thus, I do not support armed struggle. I follow the path of non-violence." She looked out the window in contemplation. "I'm sorry. It's part of my belief system."

Femi and Aminah actually broke into giggles.

"Is there nothing I can say to persuade you otherwise?" Femi finally asked, wiping away tears as he snickered. "I cannot see how we can work together if our views are so different."

"I am sorry," Barbara whispered, clicking her pen closed. "I cannot be persuaded to act against my conscience."

"That is a great pity. You have taught us so much. Is that not so, Aminah?"

Aminah's mighty form was positioned in the front seat. She turned around, her headdress deleting all view of the approaching landscape. "True-true, my friend. I have learnt more than I thought necessary in a few days alone."

"Something you said struck me particularly," Femi continued. "You taught me that I am you and you are me. Is that not so?"

"Yes. That is so."

"That is such an interesting idea." His voice assumed a tone that calmed Barbara's jangled nerves. "Sometimes I feel that I am one with others. For example, sometimes I feel like I died with my family in the flood and that I do not exist if I am not connected to them. I am dead. In that village, I felt like I had died there, too. But I also felt a deep sadness, like I had survived and was looking for my relatives there. And yet I also felt that I was me, looking at the people looking for their relatives, distant from them. We were all one, no be so?"

"Wise words, wise words." Barbara nodded, listening to Femi, this philosopher with links to a mystical past. Through him, she would find the strength to cope with images rooted too deeply to extract.

"Could you explain that idea once more to me?" Femi asked, as a boy to a schoolteacher.

It seemed the sage needed her guiding spirit as much as she needed his. Barbara cleared her throat, then looked around like a missionary at her flock. Meanwhile, Aminah flung a mistrustful glance at Femi.

"I am more than my physical body. I am energy. I am, I be, I flow. Thus, I am you and you," Barbara stressed one last time, "are me."

"Really?" Aminah barked with disdain. "You don't look like us at all."

"So," Femi intervened, "according to you, if I support violent struggle, because you are me, you can support it too–because I am just a different facet of you, *abi*?"

Barbara hesitated. "Well, uh, I wouldn't–"

"We are born, we live and we die," he continued, looking out his window, as if meditating. "We are like leaves–no more or less important in the great flow of history." He turned to face Barbara again. "Correct?"

"Yes. You've got it." She flushed with an embarrassed pleasure, patting Femi's hand.

"So what *you* think has little importance in the greater scheme, true?"

She realized how difficult missionary work might be. "It's a bit more complicated than that. I can send you some–"

"I'm glad we're in agreement. We must fight force with force.

So please, take this down." He snapped his fingers and pointed to Barbara's notebook.

"But . . ." Aminah's brows knitted across a wrinkle-free forehead.

"What other solution is there? This is worse than anything I imagined."

"Worse," Aminah agreed. "Much, much worse." She wiped her eyes with a rough rub of her handkerchief.

Their expressions reminded Barbara of many of the faces she had encountered in Nigeria. She now recognized the grief that lay behind the Nigerians' rambunctious behaviour, under all the laughter and beneath the banter. She could not understand how she had missed it in the first place.

"Our group will attack infrastructure only." Femi tapped Barbara's notepad imperiously. "We'll need explosives, detonators . . ."

Satisfied with this approach, Barbara clicked her pen open again. Her head wiggled as she scribbled down his instructions, her writing containing some swirls at the end. Once finished, she surveyed the list. "I've got the finances for you to start your activities right now. But Femi–your group," Barbara struggled to find the most tactful phrasing, "can barely even strike a match, let alone light a stick of dynamite." She blinked, waiting for Femi's solution to this dilemma.

Flicking his bottom lip with a forefinger, Femi kept quiet. Finally, his voice rigidly controlled, he replied, "They are in mourning. But this will give purpose to their lives. And we'll care for the ones who are not able to function."

"Ah, yes, it takes a village," Barbara nodded. "The African way. I should have remembered."

Femi sighed audibly.

And so the trio laid out a plan to sabotage the efforts of Kolo and TransAqua.

EIGHTEEN

Schemata

As April began its final bow, Barbara made her way to the airport a more prepared woman than the naive maiden who had first set foot on the rust-coloured soil of Nigeria. She started for the airport an hour late and on the way shouted in agreement with the taxi driver about the deplorable state of the country.

"*Na waa oh*," she yelled. "Who knows when things will improve, *sha*?"

In the terminal, she fought her way to the front of the queue and bribed the counter staff, flapping money above everyone's heads. In customs, she again "dashed" an officer with money. He waved her through. On the plane, she unpacked her food and spoke at full volume to her neighbour about the lamentable political environment and the sham election of Kolo. She scratched her crotch when it itched and widened out her personal space as she sat.

When she landed in Washington, DC, her spirits flagged and she began to suffer from a crushing sense of boredom. Shining through this gloom, one face–Astro, eyes radiant, limbs trembling with excitement, face infused with passion. Barbara sped through the crowds towards him, swift and light, and threw herself into his open arms.

After an hour of passionate kissing near Baggage Claims, Barbara delivered the bad news.

"I have to go to Santa Fe next week, *sha*." She hitched up her *adire* wrapper to prevent it from unfurling to the ground and exposing her. "Business before pleasure."

"But I thought you'd come back for good, Bing-Bong!"

"Soon, my friend." Her American vowels widened into their Nigerian counterparts. "A cheetah is not a spider."

"What?"

"A cheetah must sprint to stalk its prey-oh!"

"That's pretty obvious. You didn't know that? Are you sure you're the right person for–"

"It's metaphorical!" Barbara yelled in her usual East Coast drawl. "Jeez!"

Mary smoothed her blouse across the angles of her body and played with her cuffs as she waited for the president to come to the phone. In her innocuous passive-aggressive style, she had made him wait for the list of names that threatened his very life, as punishment for an act that could jeopardize her job: his delay in signing a fresh contract.

"President Kolo?"

"To whom do I have the pleasure of speaking?" Kolo oozed an unconvincing confidence.

She took heart from the fact that his apparent poise would be short-lived. "Glass. Mary Glass, sir. I have some bad news."

Kolo's breath grew louder and more erratic.

Suffused with pleasure, Mary recited the news in a neutral monotone. "I've got three names for you. The ministers of Information, Women's Affairs and Justice."

"These people are planning coups! But this can't be. These are my closest allies! They are all from my home state, Ms. Glass. The minister of information is my personal confidant!"

Kolo's voice edged into panic. However, Mary had no interest in soothing his fears. She needed the contract signed. Using another tool from childhood, she paid no attention to the rise in dramatic tension, communicating instead a bland indifference to his fate. "So, where do you wish to meet, sir, to sign the contract?" she asked.

"The contract? Ah, yes. Let's discuss the terms again. You want political control of this country through its water and energy resources, correct?"

The thin trickle of blood that coursed through Mary's tight veins almost ceased its pilgrimage around her body. "Well, Mr. President, I am just eager to get the original contract re-signed."

Kolo left a silence. A silence that he, without question, expected Mary to fill.

Knowing that rival bids offered the most logical explanation of his conduct, Mary had no choice: she suggested a 40-percent guaranteed return on profits from water rights.

"Interesting," he replied. The sucking started.

"President Kolo," Mary finally broke the silence, "what is it you want?"

"Fifty-five-percent return." He announced this without apology.

"But our initial outlay alone, the cost of the dam . . ."

"Ah, thank you for reminding me. The World Bank will only lend 60 percent of the financing requested. So, I'm afraid you will have to assume the extra burden."

"Pardon? But that's not poss–"

"You don't know this country," Kolo sighed. "It's a mathematician's paradise. One dollar earned is two dollars bribed. Consider them tariffs. As president, I am expected to offer enticements to my people–well, I suppose the anglo tribe would call it my ethnic group–and my political supporters. I am, if you like, the chief of the village, the head of the family."

Mary could hardly believe it. In one move, he had managed to transform his government's position from victim to victor, with a majority share in profits for less outlay. He had used the distorted mindset of the corporation to his full advantage. She studied the contours of this new deal. Finally, desperate to keep her job, Mary agreed.

"Thank you so much, Ms. Glass," Kolo rasped. "It's such a joy working with you."

After she hung up, Mary flopped back in her chair, wondering what else could go wrong with her week. It took only a few days for her to find out.

Astro had specially decorated his apartment for Barbara's return, dotting small sparkles of twinkling white lights on the living-room ceiling, like stars in the night sky.

After ten days of solo activity, Barbara could hardly wait to substitute the plastic and batteries for flesh and blood.

They stretched out on Astro's makeshift bed: Arabian rugs, on top of which lay odd-shaped cushions and clashing styles of bedding. He put his arms around her and kissed her forehead, looking down on her like a cherished child. She stroked his lips, now engorged. A quick image of a body bloated by the sun flashed into her mind. She pushed it away.

"I missed you, man," Astro said. "I couldn't stop thinking about you. It was as if you'd died, buddy."

An image of birds eating human flesh whizzed past.

"Oh, man, I was so worried."

"I missed you too, *sha*." She ran her finger down his cheekbone. "Sometimes I'd just touch your picture to make sure everything would be all right."

His penis, much more pleasing in appearance than her vibrator, more realistic, was erect, its purple tip welcoming her home. Barbara could feel her pelvis aching. He licked her belly button and then moved down, licking her clitoris.

Astro grasped her wrist with his hand.

She froze.

It reminded her of the hand in the mud. She shuddered.

"Already, man?" His head popped up.

She stared into his eyes–as bright, as huge, as yellow as sunflowers. She wondered how those eyes would darken as a wall of water crashed down. She pictured the innocence in them changing to horror.

"No, no, don't worry. I haven't come yet." Barbara settled back into the sheets. "Please continue," she instructed.

He frowned at her then dived back down to finish his work.

She squeezed her eyes together, trying hard to concentrate. She looked down at him. He reminded her of a bloated body lying face down in the mire. She began to weep. How could she enjoy herself like this in a world of such brutality?

"It's okay, bud. You've been through a lot. You need some sleep." He stroked her hair, cradled her in his arms and rocked her, as if she were a child awakened from a terrifying dream.

In their shared bed, the one space where all troubles were usually resolved, the blood of the nightmare soaked into their sheets.

The room that had become the effervescent epicentre of office fun, jokes and passing welcomes–Beano's tiny glass cabinet–

uncharacteristically featured a shut door.

Securing his shoulder-length hair behind his ears, Beano phoned his father. "Your Excellency? It's Your Inadequacy speaking."

"Hey there, Your Mediocrity! Howzit going?"

"Kolo's signed. If you want Wosu in, I think you'll need some kind of tactical–"

"He's signed? He didn't tell me!" His father sounded hurt. "And no press? What's he up to? Can't trust that guy. Can't trust him. He's as sly as they come."

"If you want to avoid any further civilian rule, Dad, you need something to destabilize public confidence in the whole, you know, system."

"Why Wosu?"

"While TransAqua is fighting over rights to the Niger, Kolo is picking up rights to the Benue River in the east. He can easily undercut our prices. Major General Wosu is from the Benue area. He'll care about Kolo owning their river."

"Listening."

Unlike others, Beano recognized the importance of pandering to his father's fragile self-esteem. "Not try'na tell you how to do your job. I've never even set foot there. But why don't you raise the profile of an insurgent? Then the people will demand a stronger response, like, you know, a non-constitutional system."

"Got anyone in mind?" His father's voice sounded sarcastic. "I'm not sure there's much of that about at the moment."

Beano held up an article featuring a recent explosion in the Kainji area. "I dunno. You're the Man, Dad. I mean, mentally, I'm still a Sewage guy."

Rumours had been circulating for weeks about Sinclair's impending dismissal, staved off only by an unexpected but minor success in Ghana. In his corner office, Sinclair paced like a shark in a tank, glued to his headset, trails of cologne wafting back and forth. Though intent on the conversation at hand, he was still able to watch his reflection in the plate glass as he paced.

"How are you, Mr. Sinclair?"

"Nnnot bad. Dangerously well. And yourself?"

"Tired. Weary, my friend. Things have turned very ugly."

"Well, Minister, the trees have been cleared for three weeks. Have you made any move at all?"

"How can I, my friend? The man will stop at nothing to stay in power."

"That must be very trying." Sinclair was at the furthermost point of his patience, the outermost thread of his tolerance, ready to sever all ties with this coward and deal with a more able man. It might be expedient to bring the minister for the environment's name up at the next meeting. Mary would doubtless tip off Kolo, who would, yet again, order an extermination. At least this time, for the first time, he would actually be targeting a potential threat to his power. "Is there anything more I can do to help?"

"It takes time, Mr. Sinclair. Everything takes time in Nigeria."

"Of course it does, Minister. Of course it does."

Yes, it was definitely time to cut the cord. He researched a list of alternates, finding one almost immediately. Like Kolo he'd been top of his class, not in the UK where a weak nation taught students to survive on guile, but in the US, which opted for a more straightforward approach based on presumption of dominance. No doubt as dangerous as Kolo, this minister had an impressive portfolio, both domestic and international. As Sinclair's relationship with Nigeria hit the rocks, he merely slipped this candidate into his mental back pocket.

Turning to Plan A, he opened his Day-timer and double-checked the maps. The Niger River flowed south into Nigeria. Perhaps it was time to negotiate with those who lived upstream in the adjoining desert nation of Niger.

Janet buzzed to inform Mary that an important visitor had arrived from Africa.

Mary felt on edge and close to physical collapse. Her mind, now hazy, found it difficult to tackle routine issues. She gazed over the cubicles.

A woman sporting a turban, an African wrapper and a riot of turquoise jewellery on her chest, arms and earlobes waved merrily in her direction. Her armpits had not been shaved. Pendulous breasts, unencumbered by the supportive structure of a bra, swayed with the movement.

Mary bounded from her seat in a rush to block the hideous sight.

"Mary!" Barbara threw her arms around her sister.

"Get off me!" Mary shuddered. The hair in Barbara's armpits had touched her white shirt at the shoulder. "What the hell are you doing here?"

Mary could see her co-workers standing up to peek above their cubicles, the bolder ones pretending to walk to the water cooler to get a better view.

"How are you, my sister?" Barbara asked, a Nigerian twang easing its way into her voice.

Mary propelled Barbara towards a glass-free meeting room, out of the sightlines of her colleagues.

"Mary!" Barbara yelled. "I beg, stop making *gra-gra*! What is your problem-oh?" More necks craned in their direction.

Barbara's stinking incense wafted past the cubicles as the mismatched duo marched by. Mary walked directly in front of

Barbara in an attempt to obscure her jangling, hirsute sister from widened eyes. Once she had found a suitable enclosure, she pushed her sister in and slammed the door. "What the hell are you doing here?"

"Herman Meyer needs to see the blueprints and plans, *sha*."

"Meyer? Jesus!" Mary kicked a chair. "What the hell is Kolo up to now?"

"Are you okay, my sister?" Barbara tilted her head.

"Fuck off! What does Meyer need the blueprints for?"

"Kolo has asked us to rush this through, *abi*." Barbara replied, confidently using the wrong Nigerian terminology.

"Finally! Why the hell does it take you guys so long to get your shit together?"

Barbara's Nigerian accent deepened. "Even a tortoise–"

"Fuck off!" Mary had to get this eyesore out of the building.

She bounded out of the meeting room to get a copy of the blueprints.

NINETEEN

Going Digital

Having dispatched the blueprints to Wise Water, with a complimentary copy to Drop of Life to keep them quiet, Barbara embarked on the next stage of her mission. She woke up early, after an uneasy sleep, plagued by an almost irrational sense of urgency. She slipped on her Turkish kaftan and crept to her laptop. She surfed the Internet, investigating sources, pricing and varieties of armaments so that she could put together a rough inventory for Femi. Occasionally she clicked over from this arduous task to search websites selling toe rings to match her new Nigerian sandals.

At 6 a.m., Astro, previously always the earlier riser, wandered out to the front room. "What's up, bud? Couldn't you sleep?"

"I have work to do, *sha,*" she replied.

"Oh, really?" He picked up a trail of her clothing, while kicking the sand to an even level. "What kind of work?" His summer dress floated behind him.

"Important work." Shades of a Nigerian accent crept into her voice.

"Ooooh!" He seemed impressed. "I guess you're a pretty big cheese over there now. I'm real proud of you, bud."

He left the room to dump her clothes, then returned to the dining table. He closed one eye and spent a few moments aligning her coffee mug with the edge of the table. After completing this critical work, he ambled behind her. She quickly clicked off the armaments page.

"So–you gonna help your friends?" He leaned over her. She could feel his excited breath on her neck. He straightened up. "Toe rings? Are you sure that's what they need, Bibble?"

"No, it's just–"

"I'd think they'd need flotation rings and life rafts. That's what they need."

The Nigerian accent disappeared. "How the hell would you–"

"I mean, if you wanna buy them jewellery, get them some waterproof watches. At least they'll be able to tell the time, like, how long have I been sitting on this roof? Oh, let's see, two weeks, seven hours and thirteen minutes. Thank god I was given this waterproof watch."

"What the hell would you know about it? You've never even set foot–"

"Towels. Now that's another idea. Did you think of towels?"

"Why don't you just stick to your damn flower arranging and let me do the real work, okay? You have no idea what you're talking–"

"What?" The colour drained from Astro's face and his eyes widened in disbelief.

"I'm saving lives here, not watering plants, so just leave me alone." She swivelled back around to her computer as Astro stalked out of the room. She heard no more noise, save for some muffled sniffing sounds from the bedroom.

When Barbara finished her work, she drifted into the bedroom to find a note on the bed.

i'm off to buy dinner. it's 8 a.m. according to my watch.
i'll be back in an hour.
your acquaintance, astro.

Barbara tutted, realizing the gulf that now existed between them. She had been thrust into the dizzying vortex of revolution, where he, sadly, had little role to play. She shook her head. She hoped this would not cause a problem in their relationship.

Astro returned just before nine, his eyes red and puffy. He rattled about in the kitchen, preparing breakfast, avoiding her company.

Barbara marched to the phone to call a travel agent. "Hello!" She spoke in staccato tones. "Name's Glass. Barbara Glass. I need a ticket to Ottawa, Canada, pronto."

Astro wandered into the front room to listen to her call. She leaned back in her chair, flinging a self-important elbow across its back.

"Oh, are we going to Ottawa again? I'd better pack my . . ." Astro looked at the ceiling, thinking. "Huh. With that place, who knows?"

"You're not going anywhere." Barbara's arm now dangled behind her. "I'm going. You're staying here."

"How come?" Astro looked at her, grief-stricken.

She stopped his complaints with a stern index finger, and he stormed into the bedroom. When she got off the phone, she followed him.

"Why are you treating me like this, Bee-Bee? I don't get it."

"Look, I'm on a top-secret mission." She put both hands on his shoulders and looked directly into his eyes. "I don't want you involved. This is very dangerous work."

"Dangerous? What do you mean dangerous?"

"I can't tell you." Barbara walked to the window and looked out, her arms spread-eagled, hands clutching the window frames. "The less you know, the better."

Astro forced her to face him. "What's up, Babble?"

"I can't tell you." She pushed some wisps of tawny hair behind his ears. "I wish I could."

"But we're a team, Babu. We're in this together."

"I have to do this alone, Astro." Barbara turned to look out the window again, wistful, pensive. "It's a lonely number–one–isn't it? But it's the only number 1 know." She paused. "Apart from . . ." she tried to stop the thought, but it expressed itself nonetheless, " . . . apart from zero." She looked back at Astro with solemn intent. "I've often wondered if God is digital too." She shook her head, rapped the windowsill with her knuckles twice and walked out the front door.

She returned a couple of moments later. She had forgotten the cash for flashlights and balaclavas.

After buying these indispensable items, Barbara had one more task to complete in Washington: a trip to a dynamite supplier with connections to the Nigerian construction and mining industries. This entrepreneur worked from a home office overlooking the amiable Virginia hills. He could supply Femi with explosives to continue the work his group had already started.

Barbara had to borrow Astro's car, but he refused to let her go alone. So she devised a plan.

She ripped off her Nigerian clothing and selected a maximum-support bra, a severe white shirt and a plain black skirt. She then bound her feet in her flat, Salvation Army–style lace-ups and flattened her hair with a centre part. She checked herself in the mirror. Something was missing. Though it did not suit her purposes, she could not stop herself from adding one small item to her outfit: a beret. She smiled in self-appreciation–she looked very much like a female Che Guevara.

She made Astro change from his formless, bland summer dress to more traditional garb, and they both hopped into his car. She swerved into traffic with a honk and swore at other drivers, a habit she had picked up in Nigeria.

Astro closed his eyes. "Where are we going, bud?"

"To see my family-oh." Barbara's Nigerian accent re-emerged.

"Oh, Babu, I can't believe you're finally introducing us! What a privilege! I guess I'm officially your significant other now, huh?" He scrunched up his mouth with pleasure.

"Look, my friend-oh, don't–"

"I thought you didn't get on with your family." He looked out the window, taking in the sights.

"Family is important. Even lions must live in a pride."

"A what?"

"A pride."

"A pride?" He turned to face her. "Are you sure? I've never heard of a pride. I thought it was a herd."

"It's a herd of elephants. But it's a pride," she pronounced the "d" with a blunt emphasis and a slight "uh" at the end, "of lions. I know. I've been there. You haven't."

"With all due respect there, Bob, I think it's a herd of lions. All cats live in a herd. I mean, have you ever heard of a pride of leopards?"

"Yes, I think so."

"Then you would think wrong, man, totally wrong." He edged into her face. "It's actually a leap." He articulated the last word with great care. "A leap," his mouth stretched to form the word, "of leopards. And I suggest you look it up before you visit your parents, because they'll be asking you and you won't know, will you, Babs?"

"Stop calling me Babs."

"BamBam. And do you know how I know this?"

Barbara sighed.

"Because I looked it up. And do you know why I looked it up?"

Barbara pulled down her mirror to check her eyebrows.

He flipped the mirror back up. "Because I looked up Nigeria." He leaned forward into her face. "And do you know why, Babu?" He suppressed a crooked smile filled with pride. "Because I wanted to see where you were going." He sat back, satisfied. "It was important to me, that's all."

She exploded, honking at a driver. "Ah-ah! You want see pepper today-now?" Then she sat back, shaking her head in disbelief. "They're driving slow-slow," she said to Astro. "A bird that flies too slowly will drop out of the sky."

"Pardon?"

"You need speed to fly-now, my friend."

"I need some speed to get me through this trip, man." Astro ostentatiously opened his own *West Africa Magazine*. "Hey! Look at this! Three ministers have been killed in a yachting accident. Man, those yachts. Death traps."

"Just shows you where you get when you put your trust in God."

"Not church ministers, Bang-Bang. Parliamentary. In Nigeria. People close to Kolo."

"Ah-ah! Wetin? What kind of juju is on that man's head-oh?"

After driving past hills that now seemed too rich, too green and too self-satisfied, she swerved into the crescent driveway of her parents' house.

"Oh, Babu!" Astro peered through the window like a child at a fair. "Look at this place! Bra-Bra, you're always so full of surprises." He leaned over and nuzzled her nose.

He got out of the car.

She rolled down her window. "I'll be back in a couple of hours," she said in a businesslike voice.

Astro turned around, fragile, terrified, clutching his plastic bag.

"Got some important work to do. I'll meet you here in three hours."

Barbara arrived at a delightful cottage with climbing roses creeping over its windows and ivy running riot over its limestone bricks. Butterflies fluttered amid a garden of voluptuous blossoms and winking flowers in apparent haphazard design. The property smelled of lavender and spice. She parked Astro's car on the cobblestone driveway, its flowered roof a pleasant counterpoint to the grounds.

Barbara rang the bell.

A man in a pink sweater answered the door. He stared at Barbara, perplexed. He looked her up and down.

"I'm Fantasia Smythe." She held out a bangled hand.

"Sure. C'mon in, my dear." He extracted himself from his musings and led her to a front parlour. "Please sit down. Tell me, how can I help you?" His blue-grey hair fell over his eyes, whose brows had been plucked.

"I'm a missionary." She tilted her head. "We're doing important work with our flock in Nigeria." Only once she had uttered these words did it occur to her that she had forgotten to take off her Taoist yin-yang pendant. "We need some dynamite. We're building a church. Just have to get rid of the old one first." And her Black Power earrings, each sculpted into the form of a raised fist. "Can I see your catalogue?"

"Uh, sure." His lip balm glinted in the sunlight.

As she heard his steps click down the stairs, she crossed her ankles, her tight-laced shoes squeaking as she stretched her toes. She glanced around at the objects within the room: the antique chandelier, the mahogany bookcases that entirely covered one wall, two giant Chinese vases and eight etchings placed with precision in two rows of four across tasteful crimson walls. The contents of the room could probably finance a revolution in most African countries.

He reappeared with an assortment of papers and a catalogue, which he laid in front of her. "So, here's dynamite listings. We have detonators here; deflags here; RDX–that's here, but, I don't know, you're not going through steel, are you? Fuses; delays; blasters; cord. Was there anything else?"

"God will guide me." She tapped his hand, then flipped through the catalogue, creating a small breeze. Understanding nothing, she finally gave up in confusion.

"May God guide you," she said, handing the catalogue back to him. "Send the products to Fantasia Enterprises." Barbara selected a green pen, a symbolic link to the Nigerian flag and, by extension, its people. She jotted down Femi's address, her head wiggling with self-importance as she wrote.

After completing her covert activities, Barbara hopped back into the rusting Volvo and returned to the parental home in a carefree mood. Astro stood outside the gates, waiting for her, plastic bag in hand. He looked small at such a distance. She waved to him and opened the passenger door.

He got in and slammed it shut.

"Enjoy yourself?" she asked, swerving into the path of an oncoming car to avoid a pothole. She ran through the plans in her head. Although she had just bought enough dynamite for at least six months, she would need to get financing so Femi could buy explosives in Nigeria at local exchange rates and hide the expenditure from Drop of Life. She could place it under "awareness-raising" or some other such budget item.

Barbara shook herself free of her ruminations, having noticed that the car was unusually quiet. She looked at Astro to find him staring at her. "What's the matter?" she asked.

He hugged his plastic bag to his chest. "Nothing. Keep your eyes on the road."

A car honked.

"What do you mean 'nothing'?" She honked back at the car. "I can tell something's wrong."

"Oh, really? Like what?"

"I dunno."

"You don't know?" he screeched, clutching his plastic bag. "What do you mean you don't know?"

"Am I supposed to?"

"Okay. Let me get this right. I'm sitting in a car with a wannabe secret agent–"

"A what?"

"–who deliberately left her boyfriend in an open field by himself because she thinks her work is too important for the likes of him–"

"A what? An open field? It was a driveway!"

"–and lied to him about introducing him to her parents–" The bobble on his hat was jiggling again.

"I didn't lie!"

"–who, by the way, *weren't even in*!" His pink earflaps quivered with anger.

"They weren't?" She considered, perplexed by this turn of events. "But they're always in!"

"Said 'boyfriend,'" he quote-marked the air with trembling

fingers, "is now probably on some international FBI's Most Wanted list; said 'boyfriend,'" more air quotes, "has probably got his face plastered over a whole bunch of offices–"

"There's no way–"

Astro turned to stare out his window. "I'm just a microchip in your poker game–"

"A what?"

"–who was innocently misled into believing he had a bona fide relationship." His bottom lip quivered, "Call me naive." He gulped down a sob; in his averted eyes, genuine distress.

"I had something else in mind."

"Look at this!" He turned towards Barbara, pointing at his pitiable face. "You know what you're looking at?"

She huffed, having suffered a lifetime of witnessing such behaviour. "I dunno. Overacting?"

"You're looking at a pawn, a patsy, a dupe." His fingers were still pointing at his face. "The victim of a devious mind." His voice trembled. "Contact the FBI to tell them we're through, please." He bit his bottom lip and looked steadfastly out of the window. "That'll save me a lot of hassle. Particularly with the fish tank."

On the morning after her return to Ottawa, Barbara charged towards work, darting past May's blanket of tulips and the canal's bright boats. She dashed into the office, ran up to her turret two stairs at a time and picked up the phone, breathless. She dialled one of her father's former colleagues.

"Hello. Can I speak to Mr. Mortimer, please?"

"Herbert Mortimer speaking."

"Hello. It's Ernest Glass's daughter."

"Oh! How are you doing? Still at TransAqua?"

Since he had assumed it was Mary, Barbara adopted a more businesslike approach. "That's a positive. I'm . . ." she tried to remember her sister's title, " . . . Manager of Dams, of Water Dams." Sounded right. "We have a problem here. One of our people has just left. Couldn't stand the pressure." She slung an arm behind her chair. "So I fired him."

"Oh. Sorry to hear it!" Herbert replied.

"Well, as we say in the business, if you can't stand the water, get out of the bathroom." She guffawed, then trailed off. "It's an in-joke."

"I remember those," he commiserated.

"Anyway, I was wondering–could I send you a copy of some blueprints? We need an im-pact ass-ess-ment." She drew the last words out, as if he would not understand them. "You can invoice TransAqua once you're done. So sorry to disturb you. It's just that the UN's Dam Commission is flexing its muscles again."

"They ought to be disbanded."

"We're working on it."

Within a fortnight, Barbara had a rough estimate of the damage the new dam would cause. The statistics were alarming. Hundreds of thousands of people would be displaced, with no plans for compensation. The dam would submerge cities, towns, factories, crops and historical relics. She sent the analysis to Aminah, copied to her team.

After that, life at work died down to a stultifying boredom. Femi was in the thick of the action, while she pretended to file papers.

At home, she sat on her porch with her vegetarian egusi and yam, admiring the arching blue, missing her former daily companion. She yearned for a more innocent time, when she felt as if she could conquer the world, when life was something to be enjoyed, not battled, when she was able to revel in its simplicity rather than get bound up in its complexity. And the common thread running through all these times–Astro. Barbara realized she did not even know his real name, nor did it matter. He seemed to come from the heavens; to him, reality was only something to be dazzled by. He was the force who had supported her, never doubting her ability nor questioning her judgement.

Perhaps he had forgiven her.

She turned to her Wiccan charms and embarked on a small ceremony to bring her luck. Then she picked up the phone.

"Hello, Astro. It's Barbara."

"Hey, bud." His voice wobbled a bit. "What's up?"

"Nothing. Just phoning to see how you are."

Silence.

"I'm fine. So I guess you can check that off your list. Astro's fine. Tick."

He hung up.

TWENTY

Power Line

With the blueprints secreted in a generous, multicoloured handbag, Aminah visited the offices of the *Popular Star,* whose editor, Richard Nzekwu, was one of the few Nigerian journalists with ideological rather than regional leanings.

The appointment was for nine. Aminah turned up a respectable hour and fifteen minutes late. She was finally admitted to the editor's office around noon.

"Thank you for seeing me, sir," Aminah bobbed a curtsey.

"Please sit down, madam." Nzekwu was a small man, no more than five feet tall–no match for Aminah's bulk–and his legs swung under his chair as he sat.

"Thank you, sir. Oh, look at this wall! So many prizes! Ah-ah–does Nigeria have this many prizes for journalism?"

He smiled as her bellow carried through the moist air to far-flung cubicles. "Of course not." He hiccupped out a laugh. "I make them up myself!"

"Ah-ah, sir! Why are you so modest?" Aminah stood up, her large frame casting a shadow over the editor. "Look at the size of this trophy! What car could fit this trophy?"

Nzekwu's legs swung merrily under him. Arrayed behind him in order of height stood bottles of water from all over the world–Italy, France, Canada–all the great suppliers, from mountain springs to deep aquifers, keeping guard over the office's health. Outside, dotted within the vast groupings of cubicles, precious water was dispensed by large refrigerated containers. It was obvious to Aminah that, despite the prohibitive cost, the editor knew his paper could run only if his journalists had access to fresh water. Water-borne illness had bankrupted many other concerns whose proprietors had had less foresight. She looked down at him with admiration.

After the obligatory hour of chit-chat, they finally approached the subject.

"I have a story that I know your paper would be interested in."

"Oh, really?" He leaned back in his chair and crossed his legs. Not a comfortable position. He crossed his ankles instead.

Aminah had been a journalist long enough to know that a sense of drama was at the core of every good editor. So she began as she would a film. "Is that chair comfortable, sir?"

"Yes. Fairly so." He nestled into its vinyl covering.

"Is it strong?"

"Yes, pretty strong." He bounced up and down on it a couple of times.

"Can it support your full weight?"

"Yes. That's what it's doing now." He choked out another chuckle and laced his hands in his lap. "Why?"

"Because you will need it." She lowered her voice and shifted forward. "You may be in shock after what I am about to tell you."

Nzekwu scooted forward in his chair. "What are you about to tell me?"

"Something that is so incredible, even I cannot believe it."

"What? What is it?"

"It's about Kolo."

"Oh," he tutted dismissively. "That idiot! Nothing you tell me about him could shock me."

"I, too, at first thought he was just a fool. But after I heard this information, I said, 'No, Aminah, this is not an idiot. This is a madman!'" She sat back to watch Nzekwu's reaction.

He sat as still as a lizard, eyes bulging, body rigid. "And?"

"He's planning to . . ." She paused as if thinking better of it, then leaned forward in a confidential manner. "He's planning to build the biggest dam in the world at Kainji."

"Walahi!" He clapped his hands slowly, bowing his head. "The people will suffer-oh. The people will suffer!"

"There's more."

"Yes?" He became the lizard once more.

"To pay for it . . ." Aminah picked her nails, heightening the tension, " . . . he is selling the water rights to the Niger River, licences for the direct purchase of Nigerian water, and ownership of the Nigerian power supply."

Nzekwu's mouth opened. Flies entered. There was nothing that could be said.

Finally, he shook himself back to reality. "No. It's not true." He stood up and almost fell, reaching out to steady himself on the side of his desk like the greatest stage actor. "No, no, no, you're crazy."

"Here is a copy of the preliminary plans." She slapped them on his desk.

He threw them on the floor. "No, no, no, you're lying." He raised his hands to the skies. "It's not true-oh!" He turned to

Aminah, looking forlorn, lost. "Why are you lying to me? Wicked woman. Why are . . . ?" He rushed to the door and opened it. "Tunde! Monday!" he called. The two assistants rushed to his side. "Hold me back-oh! I'm going to strangle Kolo today! With my own hands, God forgive me." He lunged out the door and the two had no trouble holding him in place by the gentlest of grips at his elbows.

"Ah-ah, sir!" they yelled. "Calm down! Calm down! He will kill you-oh!" Their faces betrayed little concern that their editor would follow through on his threats.

"Tunde! Go and bring a bat!"

"Sir! But–"

"Bring a bat and hit me. Yes," he cried, "hit me! Strike me down!" He sank to the floor. He shook his head, weary. Then he perked up. "Does anyone else have this gist?" he asked Aminah.

"No, but–"

"It's our story. We'll pay you for this story."

"That's fine. But once you have published, I have to go to the other outlets."

"Just give me twenty-four hours."

As is the custom for affluent Nigerians, Kolo built a grand house in his home village far from its centre in order to name the road leading to it after himself. In the same locale, he also erected monuments celebrating its most famous son, and diverted funds from the national coffers to build a new school, a small airport, and sanitation facilities–all of which bore his name–but more was expected of him. Piles of papers lay in his in-tray. He flicked through them, disconsolate.

On a national level, vast feats of engineering, giant edifices, large-scale construction had been temporarily shelved after ministers insisted that additional financial aid be directed to flooded areas for medical assistance, food, basic shelter, kickbacks and other ephemera. Therefore, he had focused on renaming key sites: the Chief Ogbe Kolo International Airport in Lagos, the Ogbe Kolo Highway in Abuja, the Alhaji Ogbe Kolo Waste Disposal Unit in Kaduna.

Despite these small successes, he had not achieved any major goal. Most importantly, his ultimate dream of building the biggest dam in the world had been slow to come to fruition. It had grown increasingly obvious to him that the Kolo River, rather than the Niger River, should flow from Nigeria's north to its south, impeded only by the Chief Ogbe Kolo Dam at Kainji.

The intercom buzzed.

"Yes?" Kolo answered.

"Papers," the new minister of information replied.

Kolo's heart thumped. This was the worst meeting of his day.

"Bring," he ordered.

A flash of lightning whitened out the entire room as the minister arrived. Almost a minute later, a crack of thunder rocked Kolo's chair. He jumped up with a screech. It sounded like gunfire.

"Close the curtains!" he ordered, his voice many octaves higher than the majestic bass of his presidential speeches.

The minister of information strolled to the curtains, amusement etched on his aging face. "So, you are scared of a little lightning, sir?" he chuckled.

"Certainly not! I simply insist on a consistency of illumination, that is all." Kolo resolved to replace this recently appointed advisor in the shortest possible time with a much weaker, slightly dim-witted confidant.

"How are you today, sir?" The minister bore down on Kolo in paternal enquiry.

"Very well indeed. And yourself?"

"In good health, glory be to Allah, of whose favours nobody is deprived."

"Allah is most great," Kolo said distractedly as he flicked through the newspapers. He tossed aside all those owned by his staunch supporter Ikene. He checked the *Popular Star's* headlines. "Kolo's Killer Idea!" Under a graphic design that perfectly depicted plans for the new Kainji Dam, a caption read: "No barrier to a torrent of greed."

Blue fingers of panic tightened around Kolo's heart. He read on.

His plans to rebuild Kainji, as well as the deal to sell water rights to TransAqua, were laid out in explicit, florid, though not necessarily accurate, detail. Activists–or, as the paper reported, "Nigeria's true patriots"–were vowing to stop the plans "through any means necessary."

He felt a stabbing pain in his arm. "Heart attack!" he called out. "Heart attack!"

As the minister chuckled again and wandered out to call some aides, Kolo checked his chest and could not feel his heart pumping. "My heart has stopped!"

An aide ran to check his pulse. "Your pulse is fine, sir."

Kolo slapped him. "How can it be fine if I'm having a heart attack, you idiot?"

"Heart attack don finish, sir."

"Get me some aspirin! And call the doctor!" After waving away his ashen aides, Kolo scrambled to lock the door behind them. He stumbled back to his desk, his blood racing around his body so fast that his heart pounded like a talking drum and the squeezed strings of his temples ached in a frenzied summons. He no longer knew who to trust or where his enemies hid–whether they passed him in the halls, sat with him at meetings or swept his floors.

He understood more than ever how his brother had felt as the water engulfed him, choking and alone. The sound of water behind the walls, rushing too quickly through pipes too narrow, assailed him.

"Who is behind all this? It can't be happening all by itself." He wheeled a velveteen chair around to face a portrait of himself in his presidential finery. "I need to get some infiltrators–but where do I start?"

He wrote a list of ten prominent activists and circled three. He arranged for a radio broadcast that evening. He offered one million naira for the capture of these anarchists who apparently wished the nation to live without the benefits of electricity.

The next day, Kolo greeted his new confidant, the ineffective and feeble minister for the environment, with a feeling of liberation. "How are you today, minister?"

"Dangerously well, sir," the minister hee-hawed in reply. "Dangerously well."

Such bombast irked Kolo but he quickly forgave the probable plagiarist. Like a talisman, the minister's very presence presaged better times ahead as Kolo read more optimistic headlines with pleasure: "In deep water without President Power!" "Kolo: Nigerian power source!"

Some journalists, however, focused on the negative: "Activism bobs to the surface!" or, worse still, "Kolo's presidency drowning!"

Many new members had joined Femi's group in recent weeks, and most of the original members had now regained their sanity, filling the air with their usual jokes.

"Mamadou, why is your skin shining all the time? Bring my shades so I can sight you! You're a human mirror-oh! Come here. Let me check my new hairstyle."

"Allah pity you, why bother? You're still bald."

Only a few remained in a stupor. Femi's great friend Ubaldous still shuffled around the hut with his stiff gait, bundles of grasses in his ears, talking to unknown enemies. It brought tears to Femi's eyes. This man had once been one of the strongest advocates within their group, a lawyer with years of experience.

Igwe fed Ubaldous personally and, after doing so, sat at his usual spot, squeezed next to Femi. He leaned over him to grab some water, resting a hand on Femi's thigh, causing gentle friction. Femi felt a rush of pleasure. His friend sipped slowly from a gourd. Femi concentrated on the sounds, hearing each tiny gulp as Igwe swallowed the liquid, watching his friend lick his bottom lip, his tongue sliding to catch each drop.

"I have to go tomorrow," Femi whispered. "You know what I have to do."

"Be careful. I'll be waiting here for you." Igwe quickly averted his eyes, though the worry etched on his face did not escape Femi.

Without hesitation, Femi pulled Igwe closer to him, unconcerned about how the others might interpret this intimacy. He put one arm around Igwe as they gazed at Ubaldous–a man still waiting for people who would never return.

The mirrored building that rose out of the southwest desert blazed in the summer sun, burning its presence on the retinas of those who set eyes upon it. Mary walked from her car towards her office, squinting behind her sunglasses. Hot breezes wafted past her, and tumbleweed–that ever-present symbol of the desert–flitted into the distance, with each blink farther away. She disliked its disarray and its freedoms. It reminded her of Barbara. Mary's perfect bob flew in all directions. She tried to anchor it behind her ears.

After a long trek through the glass temple, Mary entered her office and sat down, a bony knee jigging up and down. TransAqua's confidence in her had waned. Disruption to the schedule through sabotage had lost them millions of dollars. She was near failure, and Cheeseman had questioned the wisdom of doing business with such a complex and unpredictable people.

A pile of newspapers lay neatly on Mary's desk. As she read each one, she threw it straight into the recycling bin in order to preserve the environment–one of TransAqua's top concerns. Kolo had assured her that the US media's sympathy for the "activists" would change. Dotted among a few reports of anarchism from comic book hyper-conservatives, the media still backed the radicals in various ways: through interviews with ordinary farmers, pictures of devastation set right next to images of rich politicians and, most damaging of all in an image-conscious country, photographs of the handsome face of the "rebel leader," Femi Jegede. Obviously, publishers had handed down specifications that editors had not quite carried out.

She felt the hollow of her stomach implode, punched with impending ruin. How had Jegede reached this level of prominence so rapidly? She had no idea how to persuade Cheeseman to keep her in on this deal. And at this rate, she thought, Kolo would want even more support from TransAqua–either a list of names for extermination or, worse still, financial assistance.

As she walked towards the boardroom, she found she could no longer camouflage herself; the transparency of the building, with its glass stairways and tensile handrails, only served to emphasize this fact. She tried to gain strength from the architecture, from its artifice: its play of power and light in a world ruled by secrets, its misrepresentation of space, the seeming fragility of its tough glass skin. All trickery. Well, she could play tricks too.

She adopted the paradigmatic garb of the non-entity. She could supply Kolo with names of her own choosing rather than bother with Sinclair's contacts. If he needed anything, she could delay or ignore his requests entirely, pretending they had been actioned. As for Femi Jegede, as usual, camouflage served as her best weapon. She could hire area boys, gangs of armed thugs, the most ruthless militia in any city–they would deal with Jegede. After all, she would only be asking them to do their day job.

She opened the boardroom door a sliver, just wide enough to slip into the room, and stole to her seat, far away from the ebullient Beano, the company charity case.

According to the blueprints, the territory to the north of the new dam construction would be flooded. So Femi worked this area, where farmers would be concerned about plans to extend Kainji Lake, their lands appropriated without compensation.

He came to some small farm holdings of circular mud houses, surrounded by towering sorghum and smaller rows of other vegetables. From a distance, the scene looked like a picture postcard of the rural beauty of a bygone era, yet any Nigerian knew that life on the farm teetered on the borderland of survival, with rats and cockroaches scurrying around in the darkness, hunting for scraps in the dust.

He heard a camera click in his mind and cursed the memory of Barbara.

The air was so thick with moisture that it was hard to gain enough oxygen. It was a demanding air whose moisture clung to his skin, creating an unseen weight that he had to carry as he pushed his way through it.

His irritation intensified with every step and Femi's jaw ached from constant clenching.

"This woman has already shaved half an inch off my teeth," he grumbled to himself. "Look at me–an action hero in a dashiki!

How is it possible that her terrorist self has thrown every last stick of dynamite in my hands when I repeatedly told her to go away?" He pondered, trying to work out a sequence of events, growing increasingly muddled, a sensation he often associated with thoughts of Barbara. "I thought I was leading this thing. But no. This grass-eating guerilla is actually leading me!"

Exhausted, he stopped to watch some women as they worked the land. They grunted out songs in time with the strokes of their hoes, though some looked sick–water in this region had been heavily contaminated. Other women, with tin cans on their heads, containers in their hands and babies on their backs, walked in haphazard lines on their endless journeys to Kainji Lake. Luckily Barbara had not seen them or she would adopt the same behaviour.

Kolo's voice crackled through the radio.

"Yaah!" the farmer said. "That Kolo na go kill all of us. He go finish this country *patapata*. Him and him Swiss bank account."

"Is his father not ashamed?" another woman asked.

"You think his family know shame?" Femi interjected, his eyebrows rigid with astonishment. He waited for a rebuttal.

The women stopped working, his dramatic outburst pinning them in place.

A farmer clapped her hands. "His father with his gold underpant, wiping his nyansh with gold toilet paper, shitting gold money?"

"I beg!" Femi roared, as if in a courtroom. "Make him do jiggy-jiggy with Swiss bank manager. Him pikin be bank account."

Some of the women in the nearby fields barked with laughter, slapping each other on the back. However, amongst all this movement, Femi noticed one girl of gaunt features, standing immobile. She did not laugh, only scrutinized him with an intense concentration. He glanced at the rows of sorghum struggling to hold on to their healthy green rather than succumb to a flaccid brown. The colours shifted in erratic patches, a chaotic pattern reflecting the unpredictability of water supply. He could try to escape, running zigzags amid their soaring leaves, but the women would know the region better. So instead, he returned the woman's gaze with a playful air. "Are you staring at me or," Femi looked around, "have I entered the exact position where you were staring prior to my arrival?" Though in many ways he welcomed death, he wished to be the agent of his own departure, not the target of a murder.

Her eyes did not blink. She continued to scrutinize him. Finally, she spoke. "Femi Jegede. You are Femi Jegede."

Femi waived this aside. "Nonsense. Jegedc is always surrounded by his militia. What would I be doing here alone if I were such an important man? Ah-ah!"

"We are poor people," she continued as if she had not heard him. "Farmer no dey get money; we be poor people. We waka half day to go get water. Now Kolo come, he say make we pay for water. Police dey charge money. Now, no money for chop food."

"We no fit even collect rainwater," another added, striking her hoe on the ground with a whack. "Or police dey come."

The emaciated loner spoke once more. "Why are you here?"

He decided to trust the girl. "Em, well I work for the power company. You see power line?" Femi pointed to the far distance. "They go for dam. Me, I go quench power line, jus' for small-small time."

The large woman grabbed his arm in alarm.

"No!" The young woman's voice stayed steady. "You no go touch power line!"

The other women thrust him to the ground, surrounding him

so that little light was visible above his head, machetes in their hands. In this tight circle of emotion, heat and rage, the girl spoke. "Show us power line. We don quench am for you. Let your mother rest in peace-now! You be Femi Jegede. I know you. We don wait for you long, long time."

One woman ran for palm wine, while another returned with gari and stew. "Ah-ah," another woman yelled, hovering over him. "Look at you. You need woman to feed your belle! Woman no go marry oga wey thin like palm leaf. Come chop food."

Femi sat like a child in the middle of this circle of human compassion, and tears softened the contours of his vision. He detected the fury he felt reflected in the eyes of others. This small act, this emotional transfer, allowed his anger to float away, taken by the heavy air and deposited in the breasts of the land's mothers–mothers, he knew, who would fight with the strength and cunning of tigers to protect what little they possessed.

And so as news of Femi's presence in the area spread, the local farmers destroyed infrastructure crucial to dam development. When questioned by the police, they adopted a mien of shock and dismay that such violence could have been perpetrated so close to their property. They screamed for husbands and sons, slapped them in front of police, furiously demanding to know if they had been involved in such wanton sabotage of public property.

Likenesses of Femi's mother and grandmother circulated in the region, even in those households struck by water blindness.

TWENTY-ONE

Face of Gold

Although the Dam Division had deployed key staff to Kainji, surrounding themselves with a preponderance of American construction crews, Beano suggested that he assume the mundane task of visiting the area, chiefly as a courtesy, in Sinclair's stead. Dam Div could be unusually sensitive when TransAqua put their lives at stake.

At Kainji, the project had fallen behind schedule as expected, but Beano's dimples managed to secure a loyalty that Sinclair's dazzling width of teeth and Glass's linear slash could never have achieved. He stood with a project manager in a Portakabin, watching an artillery of rain smash down to earth, pummelling the ground so hard that stones pinged and flipped.

"Wow! It really pours down here, huh?" Beano shouted over the rain's booming.

"No protection against it, sir," the man shouted back through the dank air. "Wish they'd invent an umbrella made out of Kevlar."

Beano released a ripple of laughter. "Project going well despite?"

"Yes, sir. We've had to build infrastructural support–roads, bridges, you name it–and fly in all the equipment." He wiped the sweat from his face and forearms. "Some shipped in, of course."

Beano flashed a bashful glance of adulation at this item of burly masculinity. The project manager might find it unsettling, Beano knew, but he would also appreciate the acknowledgement that only the tough could survive Nigeria's rigours.

"Any problems from saboteurs?"

The man's chest puffed out. "Nothing we can't handle, sir."

His fingernails shredded to non-existence with the anxiety wrought by three months of indiscriminate destruction in areas north of Kainji Dam, Kolo once more called for the newspapers. He had moved his desk behind a pillar that separated two large windows, in order to hide from potential snipers. To reinforce his authority, however, he also ordered that his portrait hang behind him, even though its frame jutted out slightly into the window casings.

The minister for the environment entered. Although the man was one of the least powerful ministers in government, Kolo enjoyed his confidant's company, if only to assure himself of his own worth–a particular humiliation inadvertently meted out to his hidden opponent.

"Good morning, Mr. President. How are you, sir?" The minister's manner seemed skittish.

"Well as can be, under the circumstances. And yourself?"

"Dangerously well, sir," he smiled at this phrase. "Dangerously well."

Kolo jerked up at the faint echo of a similar phrase, but he quickly discounted such trifles and furrowed back down into his despair.

"The news is not good. What has this country come to?" The minister bowed and handed Kolo the papers with trembling hands. "Explosions everywhere. No one knows where Jegede will strike next. We cannot find where his militia is based."

Kolo waved for the minister to sit down.

"You need to increase your protection. I can organize greater security for you," the minister said.

Kolo slumped in his chair, gave an absent-minded nod and scanned the headlines: "Opposition to the Dam Grows." Under a picture of broken power lines, the caption "Power to the people."

His heart began its erratic drumming once more, beating messages of warning. "Who can believe it?" he demanded. "In a country that has fought unification since the day Europe carved it up, suddenly all these competing mishmashed people are uniting?" His threw the papers on the table. "What the hell is going wrong?"

"I myself cannot understand," the minister responded. "It is a calamity of monstrous proportions." He drew out a long, laborious tsk.

"And who is this Jegede? What makes him so special?"

The minister had no answer.

"Here I have been trying to encourage government to work together my entire adult life and they can't agree even on one point of policy–not a single policy! Meanwhile, within a few months, this nincompoop with no effort or background whatsoever has drawn together every flotsam and jetsam of society!"

Frantic to annihilate any whiff of heroism that might attach to another human being, Kolo scrambled to deal with the situation. He waved away his minister and called Mary Glass at TransAqua. He pictured her as a beautiful woman, large, with huge breasts and an extensive backside, even though he knew she looked more like a strand of barbed wire.

"Mary Glass, TransAqua."

"Hello, Ms. Glass. President Kolo speaking. Do you have a minute?" He knew she would make one, or he would not have asked the question.

"Yes, sir. Just a moment, I'll get a pad and pen."

This was what he liked about her: efficient, ambitious, conversations pared down to their bare essentials.

"Yes, sir?"

"I am calling about the situation at Kainji." He opened his box of Quality Street and started feeling for a strawberry centre. one left–he must have finished them. He opted for hazelnut ramel. "I will be instituting a state of emergency." The caramel smoothly down his tongue, tickling his throat. "The US ssador has suggested that TransAqua deploy its own securces to protect its interests."

r own security forces? Like a private army?"

ad no idea, he thought. Of course it would be a private

inly not!" he replied with indignation. "My dear ss, that would be illegal. I'm referring to security forces mpany your personnel and protect your infrastructure. igerian Army is, of course, at your disposal. Many of them ance after their shift. You may wish to contact your oil npanies in the region for more information on structure and ing. The embassy here could arrange recruitment for you."

Yes, sir."

She really was as green as an unripe banana. And once tured, who knew? He enjoyed doing business with her. found it so easy to motivate her, unlike dealing with his untrymen.

They signed off. He took his phone off the hook for a coule of minutes of quiet reflection. Surely the experts from the

West would capture the madman at the helm of this disruption, put the entire situation to rest and allow Kolo to resume his role.

He swivelled around to look at the trees, now being blown by the wind.

Kolo's car pulled up to the American embassy, accidentally splashing the Marine guards with mud. He took an air-conditioned elevator to the ambassador's office.

"President Kolo!" The ambassador slapped Kolo on the back. Even though the ambassador dressed with increasin formality, Kolo had noticed no accompanying increase decorum. "Sure got yourself a mess here, huh? C'mon in have yourself a drink."

Kolo deeply regretted having left behind his motorca instead he made sure his agbada billowed behind him walked in, creating an even more dramatic presence.

"Please sit down, Ambassador Bates." Kolo deploye pronounced British accent to indicate to the ambass they were no longer equals.

For a moment, the ambassador seemed disoriented, b he smiled benignly and sat down. The scalp undernea crewcut, however, had turned pink.

"I'm sure you've read the reports on the difficulties w facing from the terrorists," Kolo began.

"Sure have. Can anything be done to get the situation un control?"

"I have just dispatched our security forces to the area." white lie, but Kolo had plans for three assassins, who could more damage than a whole army. "We will be penetrating t group–" He stopped short. He could not believe he had ju given the ambassador a status report! His aides could do tha

In the blink of an eye, most gently and in a most subtle manner, the ambassador had managed to gain the alpha position. Kolo changed tack.

"We need to ensure that these terrorists are not painted sympathetically by your media, or it will put your business interests in jeopardy. I'm sure you're on top of the situation." He added an inflection of enquiry to the last sentence.

"Oh, uh, yeah, of course." The ambassador smiled uncomfortably. "We've been working on that."

"Is there anything our government can do to make your work more, um . . ." Kolo paused, enjoying the ambassador's discomfort, " . . . successful?"

"We'll deal with it." The ambassador bowed his head and scratched his ear. "I'll call some people tonight."

"Do you have any project parameters? A timeline?"

The ambassador squirmed.

Kolo knew the word "no" was not part of the diplomatic vocabulary.

"I just need to get hold of six key people. They sit on all the boards. We'll get things under control by the end of the week."

"Perhaps link Jegede to more extremist groups? That always seems to work wonders." Kolo crossed his ankles. "I say," he added, "you don't have any troops we can send to the region, do you?"

"We're already overdeployed in Mexico, I'm afraid. The president's gotta consider re-election."

"That's a pity. These anarchists are making it impossible for TransAqua to operate. And, of course, the unrest is bleeding to the oil sector." Kolo sighed and looked wistfully at the ceiling.

The ambassador cleared his throat. "I'll talk to my people. We won't be able to send in regulars, but, uh, maybe a private army? As long as it can't be traced back to us."

Kolo widened his eyes. "Well, now–that's a stroke of genius! I never considered that! It might be worth talking to TransAqua. Who knows? Perhaps they'd be willing to front it." He stood, arranged his agbada and billowed away.

Kolo felt relieved. Once the American media started to shift its sympathies away from the anarchists, the Nigerian media would follow. It was obvious that he had to take extreme measures to get rid of Jegede. A terrorist could not become a national hero when a far more competent man sat right in front of everyone's eyes, already at the nation's helm.

Within a week of Kolo's call, the northern regions swarmed with a private army that guarded TransAqua and indulged in the occasional offensive foray.

Barbara had contacted him earlier for a "progress report."

Instead of admitting to his activities, he let derision get the better of him. "We're almost ready to attack. We're just trying on the balaclavas."

"You may not need them. You're black."

"This is the debate we're having. When we come to a consensus on clothing, we'll move. Then there are just turbans to discuss."

"Ah, yes. That's vital," she replied.

So Femi moved to areas south of the dam. On the banks of the Niger River, fishermen had returned, freed from humiliating employ in factories, as servants or beggars or thieves. Its sluices had prevented sediment from flushing out of the upstream reservoir, so water could not be purified by silt's natural scouring. Fish had also been trapped and the logic of plant growth, fish survival and food chain had been destroyed. Despite these hard times, the dam was now unable to withhold the bounty of the water and its fruit had been released.

The inviting odour of smoked fish wafted through all the villages Femi wound his way between shacks of women selling smoked fish, shimmering silver scales skewered in lengths across grills. He ate as much as he could, in defiance of an absent adversary who, at this very minute, probably thought he was strolling around wearing a thick black sock on his head. Usually lively and loud, the market here seemed subdued and he could hear, yet again, the distant sound of children wailing or vomiting. He squinted across the water and watched the men pulling in their nets, grunting through their labours with insistent chants. Two fishermen stood to one side, cellphones in hand, shouting commands at their small, glimmering rectangles.

Femi headed towards the logs where the older fishermen sat. He perched on the side of a boat while the fishermen sewed their nets. Many of them looked drawn and tired, afflicted by illnesses carried in the water. A picture of Kolo was nailed to a board.

On seeing it, Femi could not help but pontificate at volume. "Ah–that Kolo! He's a thief! He rob his father, he rob his village, he rob the country. One day he go rob himself too."

A fisherman spat a homemade shuttle from his lips and shouted, "Look at him and his yellow face. Him face don match colour of gold-now."

The others chuckled.

"He go build big-big dam now near Kainji," Femi continued.

The fishermen began a multi-vocal protestation. "Is he mad? He dey play with ghost-now. He dey play with angry ghost."

"Let him play," Femi replied. "Him and him juju self no wan' care. Him fat nyansh go dance with ghost. Even ghost make excuse, leave dance floor, leave bar, leave country even."

A fisherman with little remaining sight smiled to himself.

"Femi Jegede. He go come save us one day. Small time, he go come, make us better."

Femi surveyed the old man, whose eyes were covered with light blue cataracts, like a wash of detergent over brown fabric. Deep creases were etched in the skin around his mouth, yet there were no wrinkles on his forehead. His belly protruded, not as a result of age but of malnourishment. His skin, blackened by the sun, stretched over his frame, displaying taut muscles that bore witness to a hard life of labour.

"No government, no thug, no tyrant can ever intimidate you and this mass of sinews, Baba."

"Let them try," the old man chuckled. "Me, I go kill Kolo one day. Let me jus' smell him."

Now, sure of their loyalties, Femi squinted into the distance. "Dam builder need bridge. I go go blast there and there." He pointed at two supporting buttresses.

The old fisherman stared at Femi, then spoke in a soft voice. "I understand. You be the person we dey wait for. E better make I go. Me, I be old man. I don pass better life, like Kolo money."

The younger fishermen immediately protested. "Ah-ah! Why you wan' make us shame, Baba?"

"My pikin!" the old fisherman said. "If police dey come, they no go challenge old man like me." With that, he turned away to his canoe.

"Bridges now? Bridges?" Kolo yelped. "If they keep going south, they'll soon be in Lagos or . . ." the thought suddenly occurred to him, " . . . the Presidential Palace!"

He buzzed his aide.

"Yes, sir?"

"Open curtains."

The aide entered and opened the curtains. Kolo looked

outside. The skies had brightened up, but over the horizon clouds clustered together, conspiring to brew up another storm. He would have to run his errands, despite the ominous forecast.

"Car."

Unable to trust his closest friends, Kolo no longer made appointments. He preferred to surprise associates with a presidential visit. He grabbed his new Italian leather handbag and heaved himself into the back of a darkened SUV, while a body double hopped into the back of a white Mercedes-Benz. The Mercedes and an impressive motorcade turned left out of the Presidential Palace with Kolo's security detail. Kolo's bottom lip trembled. He watched the motorcade with tears in his eyes and sorrow in his heart, listening to the sirens forcing the citizenry out of the way. Ten minutes later, his Nigerian-made SUV turned right.

"Where, sir?" Innocent asked.

"Inspector General of Police." Kolo's nerves were set on edge as he stated this destination.

Nigeria's capital city, Abuja, remained in its muffle, soundproofed and sequestered, with its plush lawns, grand hotels, grassy boulevards, luxurious mansions. Very few people littered its pavements: rather like a huge mall, it had not been designed to human scale. Cleared of all distractions, bare and in order, built from scratch and rigorously controlled to conform to plan, Abuja was Kolo's favourite city. Innocent knew to avoid the areas, disagreeable to his employer, where the chaos of individual agency combated policy. Kolo wished to see no street markets, shacks or cattle on the road. So it took an extra forty minutes to reach the police headquarters. Once there, Innocent drove to a large barracks surrounded by white walls topped by broken glass and barbed wire. As they arrived, rain burst from the sky.

Kolo, who had always preferred the pomp of the army to the ignominious drabness of the police, felt heartily his lowered circumstances now that his ally Abucha was dead. Some idiots in the military had appointed Wosu P. Wosu, doubtless considering him acquiescent, little knowing that a man from a persecuted ethnic group could only have reached such heights of power through talent and guile.

He was escorted by two bedraggled police officers past walkways lined with whitewashed stones, umbrellas held aloft. Kolo hopped past puddles, handing his bag to the officers for these feats of athleticism. The officers wore rumpled shirts and walked out of step with each other in an overly languorous gait. Kolo's anxiety increased as they neared the inspector general's office.

They entered a cavernous room smelling of must, decorated with little but a large Nigerian flag and an oversized gold-framed reproduction of Kolo's face, minus the rash and multiple chins. The cement flooring had been polished red, and the hospital green paint on the walls was chipped. Hornets flew around the stationary fan.

Kolo looked at the portrait. He smiled. In this light, he looked handsome–just as handsome, in fact, as that maniac Jegede.

"President Kolo!" The inspector general saluted, his hand so rigid it quivered. He shook Kolo out of his reverie. "At your service, sir," he shouted.

"Chief," Kolo winced. "A great honour." His heart beat faster.

The two sat down on black leather armchairs. *Pffft!* As the air was expelled from the cushions, they were lowered into their seats.

"Scotch, sir?"

"Maybe just a small one."

The inspector general nervously clicked his fingers, and his aide appeared with two glasses, dirty fingers carrying them on their inside rims. Kolo smiled, wondering if this man had already mounted a conspiracy against him.

The aide poured two very small Scotches.

"This is terrible news from Kainji," the inspector general began. "Ah-ah! When are these people going to stop?"

Kolo closed his tired eyes, stroking the leatherette chair. "They are not educated."

"That is very true." The inspector general slurped back some Scotch. Kolo could hear him swishing it around his teeth like mouthwash. Once he had swallowed, he opened his mouth with a loud "Aaaah!" in appreciation.

"They do not understand complex issues." Kolo opened his eyes, putting down his own Scotch in disgust.

"It's too much for them to understand."

"They think in very simple ways."

"Very, very simple. They are very bush people, sir." The inspector general suppressed a burp but expelled the resultant rush of air in a *ffff!* through his mouth.

"I think far, far into the future. I'm an idealist."

"Of course, sir!" the inspector general proclaimed. "That is the job of the president!"

"The job of the president is to manage the country," Kolo snapped in righteous indignation, "whereas I . . ." he searched for the words, " . . . I am a visionary. It's a gift. It's a curse. I'm different. I can't help it. Neither could Gandhi." Kolo shook his head with weary resignation.

"You're a prophet, sir," the inspector general agreed.

Kolo felt himself relax in this man's company. He sipped his Scotch and lay back in his chair, looking at his portrait. The artist had added a pleasing hint of blue to his brown eyes. His skin tone had been rendered in golden hues.

"I need your help," Kolo said.

"Whatever you require, sir." The inspector general looked at his Scotch, picked up his glass and readied it for action. Then he tossed back his head, threw the glass towards his mouth and swallowed its remaining contents.

Kolo heard the liquid shooshing into foam around the inspector general's teeth again. He tried to blank out the noise. "These militants are committing treason. They must be hunted down."

"They are common criminals, sir." The inspector general swallowed more Scotch. "I will make personally sure that the police–"

"Not the police."

"Pardon, sir?"

"A policeman wants to feed his family. How much are they paid? Almost nothing. Correct?"

"Correct!" the inspector general agreed without protest. "More Scotch?"

"Just a touch."

The aide reappeared and Kolo indicated for him to continue pouring as the attendant shot worried glances at the inspector general.

"So," he continued, his eyes once again on his portrait, "since they are not paid enough to put themselves in harm's way, what incentive is there for the police to catch these people? None. They can arrest anyone and call him a terrorist. Does that make the man a terrorist?"

"Yes, of course," the inspector general replied, gaping at Kolo.

"No," Kolo replied tactfully. "You're right. It doesn't." He took a sip of Scotch and then set his glass on a side table.

"Of course not!"

"So instead of police . . ."

"Yes?" The inspector general scooted forward in anticipation.

" . . . we use criminals."

"What? Sir, what can a criminal do that a whole police officer cannot?" His face a picture of disgust, he had little understanding of the irony of his statement. Kolo had a hard time hiding his amusement.

"Nothing!" Kolo said with finality. He set his bag aside and laced his fingers across his belly. He felt like a detective explaining a crime to the perfect foil. "So why do I want to use criminals?"

"Em . . ." The inspector general looked at the ceiling, running through scenarios. After many moments, he admitted defeat. "I don't know, sir."

"Because the only motivation for a police officer is a bribe. Whereas the motivation for a criminal is . . . ?"

"Em . . ." The inspector general looked into Kolo's eyes, searching for answers. After a long pause, he again ceded victory. "I don't know, sir."

Kolo smiled. "The motivation for a criminal is life."

"Oh, I see!" The inspector general's eyes moved to the floor, as if digesting the information. A few moments later, it appeared that he had found a chink in the armour. "And what if he lies? What if he brings us an innocent man?"

"He hangs."

The inspector general smiled. Something about these words appealed to him. Perhaps because they lay in the realm of his expertise.

"Can you help me?" Kolo asked.

"Yes, sir. Of course."

"Three men–all willing to kill where necessary."

"Yes, sir."

Kolo stroked his handbag. "Bring them to me when you have selected them."

"Yes, sir. Thank you, sir." The inspector general beamed. "You are a great genius, sir. You're a man with big dreams for this country."

Kolo left, a warm glow in his heart. The skies had cleared, and he played hopscotch with the puddles. There was something about the inspector general that he liked, although he could not put his finger on exactly what it was. This had been such a refreshing experience–so different from his interviews with the police after the death of his brother.

As he lounged in the SUV–an ugly, overconfident, unsophisticated vehicle–he took his shoes off and turned on the air conditioner with his sock. He then flicked the seat cooler on. Within a minute his ample buttocks could feel the comforting chill. Next to him lay two newspapers with Jegede's smiling face on their front pages. He did not need to look at the articles–the photographs told the entire story. Nigeria had given birth to a saviour. One paper had positioned the presidential countenance as a mere inset! The other had the two "contestants" juxtaposed, featuring an unflattering close-up of Kolo's rash-ridden skin and shadows highlighting his chins.

"So, Innocent–any news of the inspector general?"

"Yes, sir," the driver answered. "Nothing."

"Pardon?" Kolo looked at his driver's neck. "Are you sure?"

"That is what the drivers told me. No visitors."

Kolo tried to lean forward, but he was stuck. He bounced against the back of the seat three times and rocked himself into an upright position just behind Innocent's ear. "Are you telling me lies?"

"No, sir."

"Better not start."

"No, sir. Yes, sir."

"For your own safety. And for your family."

The car slowed to a crawl.

"Yes, sir."

Kolo's neck snapped back as Innocent reapplied pressure to the forgotten accelerator.

The sky began to spit rain again.

Each community, regardless of its size, knew when a stranger was in its midst. Femi could hear the trails of conversation as he walked through the crowds.

"Who be this man wey jus' land yesterday? Ibrahim's cousin?"

"No, no. He left two week ago. In taxi which forget door."

"Enh! He no even stop for Usman place? He jus' waka pass. This yeye man!"

"He put leg for road by five this morning. I myself saw him. With my own eyes."

"Five? Ah-ah! Does he know who he is?"

As Femi strolled through the shantytown, he spotted a man pointing at him in the distance. Within seconds, the army and TransAqua security appeared, firing shots indiscriminately. Femi ducked behind a shack. In his haste, he slipped in the mud, tripping into a sewage ditch. He fell on his shoulder in the human waste. The stench almost blinded him. He leapt up involuntarily, in horror of the bacteria and disease the excrement must certainly contain.

A blow on his shoulder thrust him to his knees. He jerked his head up to find five men, faces covered in black cloth masks, brandishing rifles, screwdrivers and machetes. They yanked him up and away, scraping his knees raw. They all wore red strips of cloth around their right wrists. These were "area boys"–unemployed youth–the local mafia that rules every town, more ruthless than TransAqua security and less accountable than the army. He decided to put up no resistance. They shoved him into a concrete hut and forced him to the floor.

A tall man with an SMG, two belts of bullets crossing his chest and a kerchief around his mouth approached. With the slit of light offered by a tiny window, his bloodshot eyes were easily visible, even in the dust of the shelter.

"Jegede?" he snapped.

Femi did not answer.

A young area boy showing early signs of illness–thin, blistered and suffering from some respiratory distress–whipped a cloth into Femi's face.

The leader kicked the boy. "Jegede! The million-dollar man!"

Femi wanted the man to understand that the pride in those reddened eyes, a pride based on the creation of fear, was in this instance useless. What others feared, he welcomed. So he smiled. And in smiling, he began to laugh, small snickers that brought tears to his eyes. A person can consider life a tragedy or a comedy, he thought, but both were rooted in the absurd. Femi wished to greet dying–the most perverse transition of all–with the disrespect it deserved. He folded his arms to observe his own death in peace.

"Don't worry," the leader said. "The area boys are behind you. We are here to protect you."

Femi searched the faces of the young men in utter disbelief, finding no clues to their loyalty to him or to any cause except their own survival. Then, as he shifted his gaze, he noticed a small shrine, typically erected to honour ancestors, in the corner of the room. In this case, all the objects and offerings surrounded a newspaper clipping of his face.

His father's chauffeur drove Beano through the embassy gates. As he surveyed the vast compound–shipshape, sober, as symmetrical as a French garden, featuring a huge concrete edifice of severe angles–his skin prickled with pride. The unforgiving minimalism suited his father's militaristic style.

For once, the ambassador beamed on greeting his son. "Beano! Great to see you!"

"Hey, Dad! Been working out?"

"Gotta keep my sanity, son. Things fall apart over here. I don't plan to."

They entered a room of monumental proportions. "Wow!" Beano gaped around. "How many toilets in this place, Dad?" Before his father had time to blast a reply, he winked. "So, any news?"

"If I have to meet with that writhing snake Kolo one more time . . ." His face grew red, and the colour spread over his scalp. "Pompous, slippery, conceited asshole. Bottom line, I gotta call off all coverage of Jegede. At least, unless it paints him as a terrorist."

Beano studied his sneakers. Then the ceiling. "Okay. No problem. I'll get the local press in Nigeria to pump Jegede up, instead of the US press." He remembered the delicate ego. "What am I talking about? Jegede will probably get too popular for Major General Wosu to deal with when he gets into power."

Now an audible sigh. "No, son, no. Then we start the negative spin. Terrorism, killing, that kinda thing."

"Whoa. That's what I call creative, Dad. Think I should meet this guy Wosu?"

His Excellency the Ambassador of the United States of America dropped his gaze down to the tongues of his son's trainers. "Nah. It's all in the timing. Don't want to be accused of conflict of interest. Wait till he's president first."

"I wish I had your kind of, you know, like, expertise."

"Don't you worry, son. Just focus on the press for now. I'll get you some names. I know 'em all."

"You do? Jeez, Dad!" Beano took an elastic band out of his pocket.

"Don't forget radio for the rural areas."

"Radio? Really?" He tied his hair into a ponytail. He did not hear a sigh, but he saw it in his father's face. It had its effect.

"It'll–hell, let me do all this."

"You? But, Dad . . ."

"No, no. You'll just bungle it. I know what I'm doing." He scratched his crewcut. "I'll just get someone onto it. Jegede's profile'll be so high over here, the international press won't dare touch him."

"Really? You reckon it'll work?" Beano produced the dimples.

Femi returned to Jos by bus, surrounded by area boys. The air smelled of small things that inhabit the natural realm, tiny creations that nonetheless emit a powerful fragrance. He could not identify the odour, but it reminded him of peace. While searching a pocket, he found a piece of paper with Barbara's illegible rounded letters. He shuddered, remembering her in her African finery, spouting proverbs. He read the scrawl.

The rivers and seas lead the hundred streams
Because they are skillful at staying low.
Therefore, to rise above people
One must, in speaking, stay below them.
To remain in front of people,
One must put oneself behind them.

–Lao Tzu

Regardless of pressure from the foreign press, the people of Nigeria began to doubt the safety of the structures that governed the water's flow. And despite the growing epidemic of water-borne illness, despite the thousands of citizens who lay dying or blinded by it, the people came to begrudge any attempt to sell their water, even to those who pledged to purify it.

For the first time in the nation's history, the white desert sands of the north joined with the red, heavy soil of the south, the mountains of the east protected the harbours of the west. All was as one–from the nation's newest cities to its oldest kingdoms, from minarets of shining mosques to crosses on tin-topped shacks, from proud nomads on their camels to powerful chiefs on their thrones. The divisions that had wrenched the country apart throughout its tumultuous history no longer existed. The mighty Niger River and its raging waters had connected them all.

Femi's group grew bolder with each step, gathering momentum, drawing thousands of people to their cause, people of differing tongues, people whose loyalties had shifted from homeland to nation. Water knows no tongue, no village, no religion, no race, no nation group, no boundaries; it flows past these, flows through them, uniting them all.

TWENTY-TWO

Dirty Hands

More members joined Femi's group, some strong and resolute, others brought to safe harbour by friends. Those afflicted with mental illness were placed in an ever-expanding village on the outskirts of Jos, circular huts of mud, wattle and stone that opened out onto enclosed courtyards. People arrived traumatized, pilgrims in mourning, angry, defeated or crying. Relatives climbed up the plateau, bringing the ailing and unhinged, exhausted living remains of once robust spirits, looking for care and a reason for their existence.

Here, Femi hoped the rolling hillocks, tumbling to greet them, would bring them peace. Undulating breezes could caress their faces, each wave as caring as the last. In response, those lost in other worlds would mutter, or scream, or pace on bleeding feet, as if they could hear nature's song.

In addition to this great number, a greater number still: the dispossessed, the enraged, the impoverished–eager for insurrection.

For Femi's safety, Igwe ensured that he lived some distance away, concealed within a rise of boulders. Here Ubaldous also lived, spending the day circling around a blood red plane tree, arguing with unseen enemies.

The most ardent revolutionaries always managed to find Femi's hidden shelter. Among these were three newcomers, all in good health and prepared for action: Ekong, a bundle of ferocity and rage whose name, by fluke, meant War; Yussef the Ugly, whom Femi simply called "Yu"; and the charismatic Lance, with his movie star looks. Everyone knew Lance could not have been born with such a name, but they indulged him anyway.

The trio built makeshift shelters outside Femi's dwelling and offered to assist him as he prepared to visit TransAqua's construction headquarters.

All was calm. The entire arc of sky was flour-dusted with stars, on a cloudless and dazzling marine blue night. Inside his darkened hut, Femi squatted down naked and bathed, splashing water over his body with a small gourd. Drops of water tingled as they trickled down his back into a bucket. He felt Igwe's eyes on him, concealed behind dark glasses, as he dried himself and as he dressed in his ragged clothing.

Once Femi had finished, Igwe opened the newspaper and struggled to read in the flicker of the kerosene lamp. Femi tiptoed over to his friend, crouched down facing him and tenderly pulled the paper down. Igwe smiled–a sweet, accepting grin.

Softly, Femi's fingers brushed over his friend's cheekbones towards his hairline, making Igwe's nostrils quiver. The tips of Femi's fingers slipped under the arms of Igwe's glasses and, for a moment, rested there. He unhooked the glasses and began to pull them off. His companion stared directly at him with such boldness of expression, such longing, it made Femi start.

He continued to bare his friend's eyes, yearning to prolong such exposure. Igwe blinked. It seemed like pleasure.

"Thank you," Igwe whispered.

Femi cocked his head, still staring into and beyond the eyes of his most precious friend. He could hear Igwe breathing, not the soft breath of a man maintaining existence, but the shaking, violent breath of a man struggling to mask emotion. With an air of ease, Femi sat next to him, away from two kerosene lamps dancing in farther recesses of the hut. Darkness hid small movements, minor brushes, quick glances. Their arms touched.

The three new members entered. Two of them immediately froze, discomfited by the intimacy they'd interrupted. Igwe quickly put his glasses back on.

"Any instructions, Femi?" Lance, the only one blithely unaware of any tension, adjusted his new stetson.

"Yes. We leave tomorrow and we'll be gone for three days. Please get your supplies together."

Janet placed a series of newspapers on Mary's desk in a fan shape. Mary watched her assistant saunter back to her cubicle: not a good omen.

She flipped open the first paper. More tributes to the great Femi Jegede! One of the articles compared him to Ken Saro-Wiwa. In the next paper, some fawning journalist dared to draw parallels to Mandela. She chucked them aside. Two more papers had no need for the language of shadows: they portrayed him as a hero standing in his own light. Then she picked up the most putrid–a comparison to Che Guevara.

Unfortunately, she recognized the similarities. Both Jegede and Guevara exuded sexuality, incandescent beauty and a signal intensity. In the flesh, in movement, such qualities might be all one would see. But in the static images of Jegede, she discerned a person willing to die. What would others identify in a photo of her, behind that bland facade? A person willing to kill?

If she–the potential agent of Jegede's destruction–could grow so entranced by his image, how tightly would the great American public embrace him? Almost to suffocation. And that asphyxiation would paradoxically breathe life into him, while choking the life out of her.

With fumbling hands, she grabbed the phone and called Kolo.

"President Kolo? Mary Gla–"

"Have you seen the papers?" His voice fractured as his composure fled. "A bush man like Jegede wanders out of his village and blinks into the spotlight like this? A man of no substance–some inconsequential, blank-faced illiterate straying onto the world stage? He's lost! The man is disoriented! Someone should rescue him!"

"Is there a way of–"

"Don't worry!" Kolo snapped. "I'm seeing to that. Three parties have located a baffled man ambling without direction. They'll deal with him."

"Assassins?"

"Ex-convicts. Same difference. They're with him now. They appear to be taking their time, that's all. In the meantime, I need more protection."

"Yes, sir. Of course." She put down the phone, making no further effort in that direction.

Instead, she stood and looked out the window, staring down at the entrance to TransAqua. Sinclair and the boys emerged from its mirrors, heading downtown to a bar, or more likely to a strip club on the outskirts. They walked past the building's vast fountains, water crashing down mammoth blocks of rock five storeys high, some of it evaporating into the desert's arid heat. Her eyes followed as the men emerged from behind the waterfall's mist until their shimmering figures disappeared into the distance of the Acquisitions team's parking lot. From their leisurely pace, it appeared as if Sinclair had firmed up new plans, perhaps even in cahoots with Jegede to oust Kolo. She had to act decisively, on intuition–which was not her strongest point.

With a brisk search of the Internet, she researched the activities of the African Water Warriors, hard-core militia from Port Harcourt in the Niger Delta, where decades of struggle against the oil industry had produced sociopathic killers. Through a crackling mobile signal, she managed to contact the group, via an imprisoned member.

Mary cut to the chase immediately. "I have $25,000. There are three people sympathetic to your cause in Wise Water. Find one of them. Your two groups need to work in parallel. A bonus, of course, will be forthcoming."

The skies grew heavy as the humidity worsened. Throughout August, the rain fell in an endless onslaught, battering corrugated roofs like rapid gunfire, so thunderous that people had to shout to be heard. Puddles joined together into muddy streams, currents through which people had to push, planting each step firmly before taking the next. Rain abated, only to appear again accompanied by explosions of thunder and shocks of blue lightning that lit up the entire sky in cracks of neon.

President Kolo had always been nervous of the raging storms whipped up by the rainy season. He hated the constant deluge of water, loathed the unpredictable nature of lightning and the violence of thunder's boom. With widespread discontent and his presidency under constant threat, he was exhausted.

He picked his way from his residence through the long corridors and stairways to his office, sniffling at his misfortune, personally affronted that nature had seen fit to threaten his equilibrium during the time of his greatest tribulation. His besieged silhouette stood at his office window, dwarfed by the glass that towered above him. As he fingered plush burgundy curtains, he stared at the torrent. He winced in anticipation of each bolt of lightning, his fat digits clutching the velvet. They tightened as his pounding heart waited for the next crack of thunder to blast through the heavens. He waited a few seconds. No thunder. He waited a few moments more. Silence. He relaxed his grip. The crinkled velvet eased out of its tight ball, recovering in cautious stages from the imprint of his grasp.

An instant later, the heavens exploded. Kolo yelped. He ran to the curtains and rolled his body up in them, shaking. He stood there for many minutes, allowing this gentle womb to bring momentary peace to his life. He wept.

The initial euphoria of having attained the presidency was over and panic had set in. Most knew how dangerous his position was; few understood how distracting, how utterly exhausting, the preservation of life could be.

Still encased in the curtain, Kolo stroked the velvet, running his hands up and down the fabric, feeling its pile move in the direction of his hand and then flick gently back into place like tiny feathers tickling his skin. Four allies had turned against him. How many more lurked in dark corners and clubhouses? After a life spent building alliances, plotting his way into their company, bribing them into loyalty, he had now been thrust back into the position that had plagued him during the entire period of his unhappy childhood.

When the thunder stopped, Kolo crept away from the window and sat down, a shrunken figure behind a giant desk in a football stadium of an office. The bureau had been specially imported from the Congo and was made of wenge wood, a rare hardwood in dark brown with a most pleasant grain. Kolo stroked it.

Its drawers had been decorated with silver plaques depicting his rise to presidency, crafted by the famed Asiru family of Osogbo. He followed the panels. On the top left drawer, his birth in front of smiling chiefs, with his brother in the background. On the bottom left drawer, Kolo in the foreground, waving as his brother rose with the angels to the skies.

Kolo secretly scoffed at the term "identical twin." Very little about his brother had seemed a duplicate of himself. His brother's eyes were set wider apart, his nose and lips smaller, his skin lighter than Kolo's. On some level, deep in their subconscious, others must have sensed this. When people greeted them both, they shook his brother's hand first, stared into his brother's eyes and asked him questions regarding both of them.

His brother was also more affectionate. He loved to tease their mother. Kolo, on the other hand, would scurry away from such contact, hiding in cupboards with books and newspapers, more a child of his father.

The top right drawer depicted Kolo holding university degrees, with a small inset of his trip to Mecca. The next drawer showed Kolo with a sun shining above him and his arms around Nigeria's natural resources. At the bottom, on the biggest drawer, was Kolo on a throne, the Nigerian flag behind him, in an agbada so large that its ends were cut off at the sides of the panel.

Kolo shuffled papers from his in-tray to a pending folder. He listened to the ceiling, sure he could hear pipes trickling with water, about to burst over him.

The intercom buzzed. Kolo jumped.

"Police to see you, sir," his aide said.

"Bring."

The three killers selected by the inspector general walked in, dressed in shirts and ties, accompanied by seven officers. Kolo kept them standing as the aide backed out of the room.

"Worraps?" the ugliest one asked him, hitching up his trousers and lowering a baseball cap over his eyes.

The president of Nigeria's mouth froze open. Had the inspector general selected the bushest men in Nigeria? Ogbe Kolo put much stock in social codes and ritualized forms of greeting. He detested those who sank to the familiarity of "Worraps?" The insolence astounded him. Still, what could you expect from killers? Manners?

He looked them over with disgust. His eyes focused on the tallest of the trio, an attractive man with a handsome smile, perhaps too unctuous? To his left stood a small bundle of repugnance, the ugliest man Kolo had ever seen, his face riddled with poisons and exploding with pustules. To his right, a man on the verge of an eruption: hulking, taut, his red eyeballs full of rage and hate.

"News?" Kolo looked at the tallest when he spoke.

"We have penetrated the organization," the tallest man replied in a charming voice, melodious and untroubled. "The head man is Femi Jegede."

Idiots. "I am aware of that." Kolo sat more erect.

The man smiled, his eyes crinkling at the corners, perhaps in apology, perhaps insolence. "We are now within his inner sanctum."

"You mean coterie. Good." Kolo looked at his nails, selected one and started biting. "Well?" He looked at the fierce man, who had not spoken.

"We can bring you the body," the ugly one answered on his comrade's behalf. "No problem."

The fierce man kept staring at Kolo, silent.

"So?" Kolo asked. "Where is it?"

"Still alive. Body no go help, sah." The ugly one rubbed his shirt as if to warm himself up.

"Why not?"

"The people dey make trouble. Jegede just give match. Na the people who dey light the match. Understand?"

"The people?" Kolo yelped. "What people?"

"Everyone. Farmer, market woman, mechanic, palm wine tapper, even thief people." The ugly man's teeth were chattering in the air conditioning, which was working well.

Kolo's felt a pain shoot up his arm. "Heart attack!" he screamed.

The three men turned to run.

"No! Wait!" he yelled.

The trio stopped.

Kolo felt his pulse. The pain subsided. He took four aspirin, grumbling, "Three heart attacks in one month. What next?"

He snapped his fingers, ordering the trio to follow him. Accompanied by the presidential guard, they walked along long corridors and down three flights of stairs until they reached the bowels of the building. He shepherded them to a broom cupboard, where he could be certain enemies had not secreted bugging devices or cameras.

Kolo turned on a bare bulb. It served only to highlight the boils and sores on the ugly man's face. Within seconds, Kolo unlocked the door to let in a crack of air so their stinking body odour would not suffocate him.

"Kill Jegede," Kolo ordered. "But be careful-oh! It must look as if his own organization killed him. Don't bring any wahala on my head. One week. Go." He waved them away.

"E no easy." The ugly man refused to move. "The people fit kill us."

"We can kill the man, five minutes, no problem." Even in this harsh light, the tall man's face radiated a serene beauty. "But his corpse will bring more wahala if it is dead. People will want some crime scene investigation, LA-style. Latex glove will point at you. We need timing."

He had obviously watched too much American television, yet his words made sense. Kolo looked at his nails again, selected another one and began biting. "Okay. Find timing. But remember: faster service, better money."

"Okay. Like corporate bonus."

"No more than three months. Understand? Go." Kolo slammed the door and left the trio in the broom cupboard, hoping these fools did not operate on Naija time. If so, three months could mean a year.

As the presidential guard turned left, he hopped to the right, then dodged around a corner. If one of them had been paid to kill him, they would have to find a less intelligent target. He smiled as he made his way up the back stairs to his office.

He heard water dripping. His smile faded. He checked the ceiling. No leaks. He put his ear to the wall. The drip grew into a trickle, then a stream. Suddenly he heard splashing sounds, a struggle, gurgling, muffled pleas for help. His brother's voice. He put his hands to his ears and sprinted to his office, hardly able to breathe.

In the heat of Ottawa's summer, Barbara worked from home, in her garden, sitting in a deck chair, airing her feet. The flowers had thrown off their green cloaks, stepping out in exuberant style. Behind their petals, they had dabbed perfumes of differing qualities. Some, unable to contain their need for attention, had splashed on ostentatious scents. Others, wishing to maintain the elitism rampant in the world of flora, aimed for an elegant perfume. Still others, peeking shyly from behind a veil of leaves, left subtle traces of fragrance that only the most refined nasal passages could detect.

With the perfumes came the clothing. Here, subtlety was cast aside, as the flowers elbowed out the competition with increasingly brash and garish guise: large, outmoded bonnets of flamboyant pink, wide petticoats of banana yellow, ridiculous shawls of dramatic purple, all manner of unnecessary frills and flounces. It mattered little how much they clashed, only that they could attract enough attention to ensure their continued presence on earth. This extravagant rivalry seemed to mirror Barbara's universe. If Femi managed to captivate the public's interest, he could ensure his survival too.

With an officious sense of purpose, Barbara opened one of many newspapers piled up next to her chair. As a neighbour watched her studying the newsprint, she flapped the paper to straighten it. Journalists supported Femi with unswerving, undeviating veneration: "Jegede: The Gandhi of Nigeria." She smiled with pride, mixed with a pang of jealousy.

Not in the least tanned from his foray into the tropics, Beano returned in good spirits, save for a stomach bug that left him somewhat fatigued and addle-headed. He parked his bike in his office and bounced towards the weekly meeting with a slight fever.

Outside the room, Mary detained him. "How was the trip?" She peered at him through thin eyelashes.

"Rain! Storming down! I thought I'd see Noah's ark coming around the corner."

"Yeah, it's the rainy season over there."

The monotony of her voice threw Beano into a state of incomprehension. How did she manage to get up in the morning, let alone function?

"I was wondering less about the weather," she continued, "than the trip itself."

He transported his face into its dimples. "Aw, sorry. How dumb! The dam, right? That's only slightly behind schedule. It's mainly the payola, the tempo over there, the lack of industrialization, the insurgents."

"The terrorists?"

"Right. The terrorists. Other than that . . ." He shrugged. He could not read her reaction. He was not sure she had produced one.

Just then, Sinclair pushed past them.

"How'r you doin'?" Beano queried.

Two rows of white enamel sparked into life, aimed in Beano's direction. "Dangerously well. And you? How'd the trip go?"

"Dangerously wet. Had to swim to catch a taxi, with an embarrassing lapse into breaststroke."

Sinclair threw his head back and laughed, completely out of proportion to the joke. He slapped Beano on the back and stalked into the conference room without asking any further questions.

In the meeting, Sinclair spoke only of other projects, the ones keeping his job afloat in the short term.

Resembling the eagle he delighted in sporting on his bolo, Cheeseman circled like a bird of prey over another area ripe for the picking, his attention drawn by the East Africa team to the outflow of Victoria Lake in Uganda.

Silence had descended over the Niger River project; this could only mean that Sinclair and Glass had navigated through new waters to reach their personal deltas, Sinclair having apparently cut Beano adrift in the process.

TWENTY-THREE

Proving a Negative

Flimsy barbed wire fencing protected TransAqua's dam site at Kainji. Femi walked the perimeter, his eyes tracking its course. It seemed such an inconsequential barrier–it was not even as thick as a finger–yet it represented an obstacle protected by hidden forces. This insubstantial line demarcated a conversion from public and private, from outside to inside. Within its boundaries lay the vast networks of international business, shielded by the full weight of the law, government and the armed forces.

TransAqua's private army, comprised mainly of former Nigerian military personnel, guarded the enclave whose separate infrastructure cauterized the wound of living within the developing world. It cleaved to all the amenities that the West took for granted: uninterrupted power supply, clean water that flowed from taps, working telephone lines, computers, air conditioning and cable television. It housed not only the corporation's local headquarters but white houses of differing sizes for the foreign staff, surrounded by well-kempt lawns featuring all manner of ribald flora.

Having scouted the periphery of this citadel, Femi realized he could not enter the sanctum without a pass recognized by a series of high-tech electronic devices. He considered other options. He scanned the distant row of buses waiting to shuttle personnel from the site back to the closest town, twenty miles away.

A bird needs wings to fly, he thought as the sun skidded across his eyelashes, making him blink. *So why not cut off its feathers?* He contemplated for a while, considering not only methods but implications.

The three new recruits were waiting at a farmstead hut that belonged to a sympathizer. Femi returned with a plan: "We phone a bomb threat."

Uncharacteristically, Lance reacted with an explosive impatience. "So why did you make me launch new threads to come? I have a cell. I don't need to find my pulse in this city!"

Igwe pulled down his glasses and peered over them at Lance as a gesture of reprimand.

"Dat na question? Use your sense, joh!" Femi boomed. "Once job finish, we can watch you use your cell. But before, we need to show we can stroll the place at any time. So we target bus and–"

Yussef interrupted, "Why bus?"

"Bus only require pass; building require strip naked ID and consultation with forensic scientist each time you show face."

Lance settled back into a pacific composure. "Eh-heh. So we go for D & C! Detonate and celebrate."

"Yes, but we no wan' risk worker life. So we go plant firecracker."

"Are you joking?" Ekong glowered. "You wan' use toy? Are you serious? Make we bring skipping rope too?"

Unruffled by War's volatility, Femi threw his eyes to the sky with impatience and theatrically turned to Igwe. "I beg, don't let him make me spark." He then rotated back to Ekong and explained in a quiet voice, "Why use hammer if you can use pin?" He glared until Ekong finally lowered his eyes. After clearing his throat, Femi continued, "So, we use your natural assets."

The three turned to him with query in their eyes.

"Igwe, Mr. Cautious, you're ground control as always."

"Eh-heh!" he replied. "And you can cross your leg at home base too. Everyone know your eye. It's not safe for you."

"If you insist, but then you have to put your own leg for road to get their passes. People trust you."

"He's like a pet." Lance reached out to stroke Igwe.

"A pit bull is a pet!" Igwe snapped back. "Don't mess!"

"So, Lance–since you enjoy putting your hand in the mouth of pit bull, you can entertain the guards, distract them. You have a good virus for that."

"Bring photo, so they can remember you," Igwe mumbled with an unusually caustic tongue.

"Ekong," Femi flashed a look of reproach at Igwe, "you plant the firecrackers under the buses."

Ekong glared at Femi, obviously understanding the implications of his "assets."

"Yu!"

"Yes?" Yussef looked anxious.

"Drive a motorcycle just outside the gates and pretend it's broken."

"Why me?"

Lance responded before Femi could open his mouth. "Which moto will stop for an ugly guy like this? You can linger."

Before a quarrel broke out, Femi added, "Leave TransAqua on leg, enter motorcycle, and then detonate the firecrackers. There are the devices." He pointed to a box. "I go wait near bus stop make sure three commot safely. If not, I go come get you people."

"What?" Igwe cried.

"I know the exits!"

"There's only one exit-now! It's known as the entrance. Your body also want to wear cape and tights?" Igwe kissed his teeth.

"I was hoping to. Why? Do you think say I overdress?"

Around four o'clock the next afternoon, Femi arrived at an informal bus stop, marked by a concrete block. The bus carried staff from the turmoil of survival to the inner sanctum of TransAqua and the warm breast upon which so many laid their heads.

Femi sat down on the pavement next to the block. He opened a newspaper, feigning a languid interest, but inwardly too restless to digest the information. After a short period, he turned a page.

"Ah-ah!" a voice behind him shouted, making Femi jump. "Not so fast. I haven't completed my perusal."

He turned around to see a small man wearing a tattered tie and jacket and carrying an empty-looking satchel. He had an officious air, his sense of importance accentuated by his thick glasses but betrayed by the Scotch tape that held a cracked lens in place.

Frowning, Femi held the page open, struggling to contain his anger against this vermin: a man serving his own self-interest to the detriment of the greater good. After a minute, he received further instructions: "Okay. Next page."

Femi flipped the page with an irritated whack. "Don't they give you newspaper at the dam site?" he snapped.

"I hope so," the man replied. "But since I am not currently in employment in those majestic facilities, how am I supposed to apprise?"

Femi waited for the end of the man's sentence. There was none. "Why are you standing here, then? Are you selling something?"

"Can you not see my briefcase?" the man barked. "What am I carrying? Is it not a briefcase? When have you seen a vendor carry a briefcase, you idiot? I am a man of business, not a common vendor. This is why this country is in bedlam. They squander money on education. Why not just let idiots like you walk around in circles? Tie mattress around your body, let you perambulate."

Femi stared at the man. His chest was thrust out so far that his back curved in a hollow shape, leaving a large bottom to stick out in an S. His stance signalled his utter certainty that all the statements that fell from his lips could be found referenced in the world's encyclopedias as absolute truths. Something about the man set Femi on edge. He exploded. "Are you not satisfied already? You've killed over one million? You want more? Go and work at a slaughterhouse, joh. Enjoy yourself there."

He closed his newspaper.

"Who are you talking to?" The man's bald head glinted in the sun. "Who? Do you know who I am? I am an orphan of the storm. Yes, that's correct. The flood extinguished my own father. Who are you to talk? Are you someone? No! Of course not!"

Femi looked at the man closely and for the first time noticed the sadness in his eyes. Grief was the foundation upon which the rest of his emotions were now built. Looking at this man, Femi knew in an instant that he looked upon a fellow sufferer. Chastened, he calmed down.

"Sorry-oh, my friend!" Femi said, as images crowded in of his father's neck snapped back by the force of the water, his father screaming his name. "May your father rest in peace."

"Rest in peace? How can he rest in peace, you ragamuffin?" The man's voice cracked as he threw his satchel down on the road. "My mother met her own expiry date just six months after. From traumatization. My junior sister became invalidated."

Femi hung his head as tears welled in his eyes. Dozens of images flashed through his mind: his mother in the kitchen as panes of glass shattered into her eyes. He did not know how his family had died, but their terror haunted him.

The man stared at Femi, paused and dabbed his eyes with his greying sleeves. He leaned over and picked up his battered *porte-feuille*. He began to weep. "My senior sisters are at home. The crop has failed, the fish are poisoned, the corporations have polluted the land." He sobbed. It seemed as if, in voicing his wretched story, he had become aware of its overwhelming tragedy. "I have no pecuniaries. No prospect. Just suffering. What can I do?" He turned to Femi, as though he could provide an answer. The man was barely able to stand, the oppressive weight of responsibility resting heavy on his shoulders.

It was obvious to Femi that the man had never had time to grieve. As with so many other Nigerian men and women, the duties of the parents had been passed on to sons and daughters with no preparation. They had to survive with no guidance from the elders, no path, no footsteps to lead the way–this and more had all been wiped away by the flood.

"This is the only place with job-now," the man continued, drying his tears with a tattered jacket sleeve. "What does the Lord want from me? There is nothing I can do for Him! He should look somewhere else. Nobody can assist Him here."

"This is not the work of the Lord." Femi rose and put his arm around the man. "This is the work of the political machinery."

The man rolled his eyes heavenwards and muttered to himself.

Femi let go and sat down again. He flicked open his newspaper, now questioning the idea of sabotaging TransAqua. On the front page was an article about a woman who had killed her husband and children. He flipped through the pages and found more stories of family violence and local hooliganism, which had increased dramatically since the tragedy of the flood.

The man behind him shouted, "Ah-ah! These women will kill us all!"

Like so many others forced to choke back their sorrow, small irritations could set Femi off for no reason at all. This time, he did not know what he had found important in the debate, but he erupted again.

"The women?" Femi shed his earlier sympathies for the man. "Are you serious? Look, why don't you leave me alone? Go away! The bus will not come today anyway."

"Idiot!" the man exclaimed, once more inflated by his own self-importance. "Why are you lingering here if the bus is not coming? I know for a fact that the bus is coming, ergo I will continue to remain at this, the designated waiting area." He pointed to the concrete block.

Femi exploded, enraged by the man's impenetrable self-assurance. "Are you driving the bus?"

"If you probe the law," the man took off his glasses, jabbing them in Femi's face, "you will be comprehend that your dilemma is consequential because, as we all know, you can never prove a negative. That is one thing you can never prove. In law. In the courts. You can never prove a negative. Do you understand what I am now telling you?"

"Of course, but–"

"There are no buts. Your sentence cannot finish with a 'but.'"

"But, however and nevertheless, all but one person in Kainji knows that when you are standing at a bus stop, you are not in a court of law. One day, I will explain to you the difference between a bus stop and a court of law. But today, I will just tell you one thing. You cannot prove the bus will come."

They both tsked and looked into the distance for the bus. It could not have left! Surely TransAqua had taken the threat seriously?

Then a blast of ferocious intensity slammed into the air. Unseen energies flew into orbit. Detonations from the TransAqua site radiated out with convulsions that made the ground jerk up in unstable ripples of abrupt movement. The imperceptible elements that confirm the integration of existence flew off into a realm of chaotic frenzy. Severed from them, Femi entered the falling, all sounds muted, submerged in reaction to his fear.

The motorcycle carrying the three recruits careered past him, terror anchoring their bodies into rigid postures.

"What was that raucousness?" the man asked, a barely audible echo. "How can they construct the dam with such abandon, so close to the most superior building in Kainji?"

The first thought surfaced: had Ekong placed the firecrackers too near the petrol tanks? Only moments later, another thought: if so, did this bus also carry the same innocent explosive? He dearly wished for the bus to arrive intact, yet he did not want this man to witness its arrival should his suspicions prove correct.

After a minute, they heard a spluttering sound. Femi spotted the bus as a mere dot in the distance, turning a corner.

"Idiot!" the man cried. "Look! There it is! Do you need glasses to see it? Please, take my own! There it is!"

Femi stood with his mouth agape, confused, exhausted. "How could you know the bus was coming?" He asked, shaking his head back into reality. "How could you know for sure?"

"I knew because my cousin is on the bus."

"Your cousin?" Femi turned to face the man. His heart began pounding.

"Correct, my friend. He called me before he left work. He is bringing money for my sisters. He has found a job for me at the dam. That's how I knew the bus was coming." He pursed his lips in self-congratulation.

Femi looked away from the man to the bus.

"So," the man asked, turning with a broad smile towards Femi, "why did you think the bus was not going to arrive? Why were you trying to prove a negative?"

Femi stood in shock, staring at the bus. As it neared them, he could see the dam workers hanging off the sides, one or two sitting on top of the bus. These people did not look like the traitors he had imagined. In fact, they looked just like him–ordinary men and women hoping to survive the torment of everyday life.

His pulse raced.

The bus drew closer, bumping across the potholes, prayer beads and charms glinting from the rear-view mirror. Though occasionally distracted by the sound of the gears crunching and the squeal of the brakes that thrust forward the hangers-on at the sides of the bus, Femi kept his eyes on the charms, mesmerized by the irony of it all. He shifted his gaze to the driver's face. He could hardly see it at such a distance, but wondered how he had amassed such a collection, what each charm meant to him and what fears had prompted him to dangle them from his bus.

"Eh-heh!" The man with the S-shaped body thrust an index finger quivering with self-righteousness into the air. "You see? I told you the bus was in arrival. I told you so!"

Femi kept his eyes on the charms and moved a step backwards, preparing to run away.

Silence.

He saw the flash first, so bright he could not place the origin of the detonation. Then he heard a thunderous boom and felt a vibration under his feet. The sound echoed off all the tin roofs in the marketplace. Femi glanced at the man's S-shaped back. It froze in disbelief.

The guts of the bus flew into the air like shrapnel, sending Femi running for protection under a market stall. Metal shards soared high and then curved sharply downwards, increasing in velocity until they dived into buildings, embedding themselves in people's heads, chests and backs. One man was cut in half, his torso severed from his legs, his intestines sliced neatly in the middle.

Those in the bus disappeared with the force of the explosion, leaving only slabs of meat, dripping red with blood, spitting through the marketplace. A piece of flesh careened onto Femi's shoulder. It lay with the skin upwards, the colour of cocoa, soft, with small, curly hairs over it, like those on a forearm. Femi screamed. He wondered who the flesh belonged to–the driver, or the cousin of the man with the S-shaped body, or another innocent soul with family to support.

He could not touch this tiny fragment of human tissue, so he tried to shrug it off his shoulder. It stuck to him. In desperation, he flicked it away with his index finger, but the blood oozed into his clothing and under his fingernail. He vomited on the side of the road.

Femi straightened up, and something jolted him out of his stupor. He saw the man's S-shaped body twist as he began to rotate around to look at him. "Jegede?"

"Not me. It can't be." Femi turned and ran.

TWENTY-FOUR

Simulacra

In slapdash fashion, Janet fanned out the newspapers on her boss's desk. Mary had only to glance at the headlines before the unseen fingers of panic tightened around her throat. Of all the options open to them, those blundering incompetents at African Water Warriors had bombed TransAqua!

The blood in Mary's arteries struggled to make its necessary progression through her body. Her heart tried to pump it around. Her breath made brave attempts to assist in this effort. However, heart and lungs had to perform at one hundred percent capacity just to keep her fragile frame on the borderline between inert matter and living organism. So great was her anxiety that exhaustion entirely replaced it. No medically induced coma could have made her feel more fatigued.

To check whether anyone else knew of her misdemeanour–or indeed had engineered it–she staggered from behind her desk and slipped down the glass-walled corridor. Beano seemed far less buoyant than usual. In fact, he was hunched over his papers, looking intensely distressed. Impressive: she had not realized he carried "distress" in his repertoire. Jegede was now considered a terrorist–what possible interest could Beano have in Wise Water's reputation? She had no time to ponder this question in more depth, since she had to rush off to audit Sinclair's reaction.

As always on speakerphone, he lounged back in carefree manner, with his feet on the desk on top of neatly fanned newspapers, soles of his shoes immaculately shining. She lingered a moment, scrutinizing him; his demeanour spoke of ennui rather than exultation. On glimpsing her, however, his boredom concreted into malice. His self-absorption often led her to forget his formidable acuity when it came to the food chain, and he clearly recognized in this misfortune the opportunity for Kolo's renaissance, and thus Mary's rebirth. As he did not think to consider this the end of his rival's career, he obviously knew nothing of her unfortunate commission.

Just as this insight solidified into knowledge, Mary was startled back into material existence as Beano shouted after her down the hall. "It's Cheeseman!" Beano's pupils were dilated, darkening his pale eyes. "He's calling an emergency meeting now! He wants the key people from West Africa there, like five minutes ago." He tendered the same information via sign language to Sinclair through his transparent office walls.

Sinclair threw himself out of his sprawl. He caught up with Mary and Beano as they scrambled down the corridor to Cheeseman's office. They arrived to face a closed glass door, through which they could plainly see their boss reading a newspaper. Familiar with this form of control, Mary lingered with the rest of the team outside the plate glass, waiting for the storm to break, thinking Sinclair would have to dredge a bit more concern from his shallow puddle of a personality to get through this meeting.

"In!" Cheeseman finally yelled.

He stood up and turned to face the window as they arrived, so they awaited his latest performance. A skilled thespian, he rotated slowly to face them, then picked up the broadsheet from his desk, holding it like soiled toilet paper between the tips of his index finger and thumb. Bringing it to chest height, he let it fall open primly.

"What the hell is this?" He spoke with an affected calm.

Mary scuttled into transparency–a blank expression framed within a nondescript face. Sinclair feigned profound wretchedness while Beano's unusually polychromatic complexion turned not rosy, not crimson, not deep scarlet, but pale. He simply stared in horror at the photo of TransAqua's Kainji headquarters smouldering at the dam site, a wing collapsed into rubble.

"It's like an amputation!" Beano craned his neck towards the paper.

"You're damn right it's an amputation!" Cheeseman roared.

The bonehead did not seem to notice his boss's exploding anger. He just stood there, arms folded, peering at the paper, unaware of his surroundings.

In the midst of Sinclair's uncharacteristic silence, Mary took charge. The bedlam of Nigerian politics had so far allowed her to cover her tracks, yet even inside this dense jungle of duplicity, someone–anyone–might chance upon the small chink of light that shone upon her activities. And that included a man whose reflection often blinded him to anything beyond it.

"This is appalling news, sir," Mary said, in an attempt to draw out any potential discoveries.

"You think? Do you know how much this is gonna cost us?" Cheeseman slammed the newspaper on his glass desk. "We gotta get some more workers over there pronto. Get some Portakabins. Whatever we need. Just make sure you don't start yet another," he yelped the last two words, "spending spree!"

Mary's guts unclenched a little: it appeared as if no one knew of her complicity. She adjusted her stance to provide greater comfort. "It's an unmitigated disaster, sir. Bates recently visited the site and assured Sinclair that it could not be breached. It's hardly his fault, though: he's a novice in this end of the business."

Turning to his protegé, Sinclair added, as a final betrayal, "Interesting how quickly Jegede's profile escalated in the international arena. I would have thought your dad could have handled that."

"Uh, he has no, like, control over that kinda thing. At least, I don't think so, John." Beano's physiognomy streaked with ever-changing luminescent hues.

"Riiiiight. Well, maybe he can help this time 'round, Beans."

Mary gambled on the fact that Sinclair was on the wrong track. There was no reason for Ambassador Bates to support a terrorist. She continued with her exposition. "But, sir, at least we're rid of Jegede. His reputation can't recuperate from this. We'll have all the public support we need." Then she remembered to add, "Perhaps we should send condolence cards to the families, sir." Chestnut eyes swivelled to a new target, the naive dolt to her left. "Beano, could you take care of that?"

During the meeting, Sinclair had allowed his sentient stereo to be flooded with Mozart's whatever–some cultural thing Rachel had taken him to the previous evening. It had a note of ecstasy, mixed with–Requiem Mass, that was it–mixed with a slight touch of grief. Transporting himself back to the work of the self-indulgent composer, he set one of the Requiem's jingles into a repeat loop through his internal sound system and set his face to reflect its minor keys.

Sinclair noted Mary's agitation bordering on panic; not in her face, of course, simply in her unstable posture. He wondered what had caused such alarm–most probably some act by Kolo executed without prior consultation. Perhaps even a bombing? Really, very little out of the ordinary: she should be used to the president's anarchic predisposition by now.

As if enough good fortune had not breezed his way, Mary's damnation of Beano Bates induced thundering notes of conquest, his personal version of last night's paralyzingly long concert. (It needed editing, that was obvious.) Through Mary's small interaction with the child, and given the short-lived memory of a corporation, Beano had become her problem, not his, part of her history. Bad move.

The seed of privilege had tried to plant himself, confident in the fecundity of its manure, where overhanging trees had already spread thick roots. He had blithely recommended the minister for the environment–probably the weakest member of the Nigerian government–and thought he could elbow his way in! Sinclair was also certain that the trespasser had schemed to support Jegede, perhaps to destabilize Kolo. For such betrayals the boy deserved to be implicated in a future termination. So Sinclair whispered to him, just outside the range of Mary's hearing, forcing her to edge towards them. "This situation can't go on–it's spinning out of control." He waited for her to sidle even closer. "The minister for the environment is planning a coup. Kolo's days would be numbered, if he could count."

Beano strained an inferior chuckle. "The writing's on the wall, but can he read?"

Again, a mosaic of pigments irradiated Beano's complexion, all of them meeting Sinclair's expectations: he now had no doubt that the child was sponsoring another candidate. He did not bother to study Mary's expression, since she directed its various inflections. Rather, he examined her gait as she slipped back into her office. Her pace did not quicken; instead she strode away with resolution. He hoped this did not signal a change in her extermination protocols. If so, then why?

With the exception of a precautionary plan securing the minister of finance as insurance, Sinclair could now escape Nigeria's constant abrasion upon his nerves. The other two could sort it out. Sinclair eased back into his office to recommence his conversation with the president of the less powerful, poverty-stricken nation of Niger. Its new dam would staunch the flow of the Niger River's waters to Kainji, making Mary's constant renegotiations moot.

"Ah! Bonjour, monsieur le Président! Je m'excuse profondément pour l'intérruption."

"Pas de problème, mon ami. Alors, comment vas-tu?"

"Dangereusement bien, monsieur le Président, dangereusement bien."

During the bus journey back to Jos, time stretched out like an expanding rubber band. Femi felt its tension, as if his entire world verged on snapping. The bus bumped along and swerved around potholes. His skin prickled with chafing so sharp that even the touch of his clothes caused high-voltage stings of intolerable pain. He felt like screaming. In agony, Femi could let no hand touch him.

Sounds too amplified, their decibels intolerable to his ears. Usually silent, Ekong's cries for help sent jagged shards of shrill, discordant notes ripping through every nerve.

The ferocious gladiator scrambled around the bus, sniffing the air. "The smell! It's choking me!"

"What smell?" Yussef asked.

"Gasoline. Everywhere." Ekong lurched for the window and threw up over two passengers.

Yussef, usually terrified of this unpredictable and explosive character, turned his full attention to him, and whispered words of comfort. Gently, he placed Ekong in the seat next to Femi and went to clean up the vomit at the feet of the irate passengers. Lance just stared at him as he worked.

On the next leg of the journey, Yussef himself sat next to Femi, having noticed his leader's discomfort. But although Yussef's usual tangy odour was fairly weak, Femi's strained nerves could hardly cope. Its pungency engulfed him in a strangling stench as powerful as any garrotte.

As they neared Abuja, the bus backfired. Yu screamed and jumped up, then just as quickly sat down. He hunched into himself, staring at the ground. Slowly, the stench of feces reached Femi's nostrils. Yussef had defecated in his trousers.

A passenger in front whipped her head around. "Enh?" She sniffed the air. "Is that your smell?"

Femi frowned back. "Am I dead?"

"Enh?"

"Am I dead?"

"No. Of course not."

"Okay. Then it must be my own smell. Only a dead man cannot produce it." His eyelids drooped in disdain.

Highly indignant, she whipped back around.

Hardly able to move without pain, and incapable of helping Yu, Femi motioned to Igwe to assist his embarrassed comrade. His companion, sitting at the front of the bus, chose to ignore Femi's gesticulations.

At the next stop, all five of them disembarked. As soon as they found a spot to settle, Femi noticed an almost physical loosening of the knot of their friendship. He could barely move, so watched the others as he lay splayed on the grass a distance away, shocked to see Igwe grow uncharacteristically cantankerous, helping no one, the strain of recent events prompting him to resent Yu's troubles. Lance immediately trotted off to the market to buy some clothes–not for Yussef, but for himself.

As if taking care of a baby, Ekong undid Yussef's trousers and wrapped them tight in a plastic bag for later washing. The hardened warrior then laid Yussef on the grass, wiped his buttocks with leaves and cleansed him with bare hands cupping water. Afterwards, he pulled this dependent creature into some shorts. For the rest of the journey, Yussef was unable to meet anyone's eyes.

The person Femi envied most was Lance, who disengaged entirely, pretending nothing out of the ordinary had occurred. Not caring to remain in inconspicuous safety at each stop, he bought increasingly outrageous clothes and ornate jewellery, anything to spare himself from thoughts of life destroyed. All these changes stressed Femi the more: the gold too bright, Ekong too protective, Igwe too harsh.

Just when Femi could take no more, as his body grew so taut that his muscles spasmed, they reached their destination.

After disembarking, they walked for an hour to the outskirts of the city, then left the road to climb up through boulders, behind hills and past small villages.

"Finally!" Lance whooped as they spotted their compound ringed by cacti.

Yussef stopped dead, refusing to move. For some unknown reason, the sight of their home provoked a great fear in him. Tremors attacked his body and he urinated in his shorts.

Lance cackled. "I beg, Yu–remember to flip the thing out before use."

"Why don't you flip yours in before use?" Femi retorted, pointing to Lance's tongue.

Ekong flinched. Igwe merely tutted and continued walking; Femi skittered behind him, unable to deal with any new emergencies. They turned into a Z-shaped passage of cacti that served as the entrance to the compound. The other three remained behind.

To catch his breath, Femi slowed to an exhausted halt. Despite the muting effect of the cactus hedge, he heard snatches of conversation between the three newcomers.

"Kolo . . . kill Jegede." He recognized Ekong's voice.

Then another speaker's voice, very faintly, he could not hear the entire sentence, but it included the question "assassinate now?"

Femi walked towards the hedge to listen, muttering, "How can you kill a dead man, you idiot?"

The discussion was interrupted by Lance's relaxed tones. "Needs protection . . ."

"You? Protect?"

Femi could not make out who had spoken, but the surprise was evident. Who were they speaking of assassinating or protecting? Him? Kolo? He moved closer to the hedge.

"American embassy wants . . ." A carefree voice wove through the air, likely Lance's.

A question with more cautious inflection followed, the words too hushed to hear.

Lance continued in an offhand manner. "I negotiated . . . ambassador paid more. Make sure Femi is not killed. We must ensure his safety."

Femi rolled his eyes in condemnation of himself: friends, not enemies.

"We'll all be killed by Kolo." Yussef sounded nervous: a brave man or a coward? Femi could not tell. Nor could he predict what a coward might do to save himself.

"Only if he finds us." That was Ekong.

By this time, Igwe had marched far ahead, so Femi weaved through the growing compound of adobe huts, some attached to small farm holdings, circling contours of giant rocks. The improvised village had grown so much that businesses had now settled there, with butchers, mechanics and market women gathering in ad hoc marketplaces.

Many of those he passed were still ailing as a consequence of the flood, and their struggles had ravaged their bodies. Insanity touched them in strange ways: a locked gaze, odd clothing, even an arm swinging at a more acute angle than normal.

With his legs cramping spasmodically, Femi struggled up a reach of granite and then dropped down the other side into the smaller compound that he and the other insurgents occupied. The surrounding boulders strategically protected them with crevices, caves and parapets. A flame tree stood at the compound's centre, ringed by a depression where Ubaldous's incessant perambulation had compacted the earth.

Femi's mentor had grown even thinner. The number of self-selected amulets had increased, even in the few days since their departure: Ubaldous had affixed more twigs, stones, and sods of earth to his clothes and hair. His feet bled.

Femi began to weep. As he did so, his pains decreased.

He hurried down to his hut, and rushed though the compound past the other inhabitants. Once inside, he sat in a corner, trying to hide, tumbling back into the dark realm of unhappy thoughts.

"What's the matter?" Igwe crouched to touch Femi's face, stroking his cheek with a gentle hand. It reminded him of the tender caresses of his mother. Femi gazed at his friend, knowing that in his expression he would find acceptance and approval. In that face, he had found his home and the tattered remains of his destiny. Then he shut his eyes once more, ready to succumb for a few days to the safety of suspended time, struggling to forget the man at the bus stop.

But thoughts of this man pumped endlessly into his unquiet mind, until the weight of them ultimately ejected him from this internal struggle.

"Ah-ah! He's alive?" Lance observed Femi with a twinkle in his eye. "So this is how great philosophers contemplate? One day, I myself hope to learn how to use my own brain to assist me."

"Don't bother," Femi shot back. "Your brain has probably withered through lack of use."

"I doubt it," Igwe cut in. "His brain is probably better-looking than yours." He glowered at Lance. "It's working all the time, trust me."

"My brain is a work of beauty," Lance laced his hands over his head, ignoring Femi. "Since it has hardly been used, it is in mint condition. When I die, I want to have it framed."

"Since it is in mint condition, you could also sell it for chewing gum," Femi snapped.

"Hm. I'll give it a thought."

"Don't. You might ruin your work of art."

"How now, Femi?" Igwe whispered.

"Igwe!" Femi said. "The man!"

"Which man?"

"I met a man with a backyard like a shelf. He kept repeating one phrase: 'You can't prove a negative.' It is important, that phrase."

Lance flicked dirt from under his nails. "You want to listen to an idiot blowing big grammar? No, the bombing campaign has been effective."

"How?" Yussef did not dare to look up from the ground. "To turn people against Femi?"

Lance did not answer, but merely examined his nails, satisfied with their hard-won perfection.

Ekong sat down in a corner, eyes narrowed, silent, as if pacing in an imaginary enclosure. "Some people jus' like to kill. Like hobby. Kill, wipe blade, sleep."

"That stupid oyinbo woman with her Chinese proverb–she na toxic waste," Igwe muttered to himself. He then hooked Femi's arm under his to guide him outside and up the smooth surface of one of the outcrops overlooking their habitation. Once they reached the top, they lay down next to each other, the granite hard against their backs.

"How manage?" Femi asked. "No one carried bomb-now. It was a mistake."

Igwe lowered his glasses in disbelief. He had to stare at Femi for many moments before his friend noticed.

"Why you sit there like statue? Do these people have premonition, *abi*? Did they consult with witch doctor? 'I beg, kill rat to find place and time for bombing.'" Femi kissed his teeth.

"I don't want to point finger, but best to shine eye for all three."

"I heard gist. They are being paid to protect us. Anyway, no more Kainji. We move to Lagos as soon as we're ready."

"They move with us?"

"Of course. Are they not family? Lance jus' be like photocopy of Amos. Him dress jus' dey scream do-not-touch."

"Reign don' pass on that style. Yesterday call to reclaim his dress. Him and the yeye American phonetics wey he dey blow. You need to dismiss Counterfeit Amos from your mind!"

Amused, Femi nudged Igwe's ankle playfully. "He dey jealous you-now? Na wah-oh! Green-eye jealous man like you–no wonder you walk around all shaded up in your Nowhere-in-London shades!"

In pique, Igwe wrenched his leg away from Femi's, crossing his ankles and changing the subject. "And Yussef. That ugly bobo, he jus' condemn the human face."

"Poor Yu. He is like a lost boy. He jus' repeat Amos when he was small, small. When I waka with him every day to go school past the farms, he was so frightened of snake, he put his arm around my hip."

Uncrossing his ankles, Igwe flipped to his side and murmured into Femi's ear. These soft whisperings produced a violent effect, and Femi pulled his friend towards him, trembling with sadness and yearning.

With greater compassion, Igwe said, "And Ekong. You think he dey fear snake too? He advertise himself as killer. He use bomb for pillow."

"Ekong is jus' mathematical deduction. What organization does he need? He can start any war without us. Finish."

"So they stay? Why?"

"What if they are innocent? They have already lost family. Now you're wanting me to ask them to lose another!"

"No, Femi. But I have family to protect too. I don't want to lose you."

Fall's foliage made little difference, Mary thought: the dust covered the sand, which covered the scree, which covered the rubble: layers and layers of false promises, which, in the end, hid not gold but more grit.

How had the terrorists got hold of the blueprints? Mary created a mental time chart. Five months after project commencement, dozens of copies–hundreds, perhaps–had left the building, sent to engineers and project managers, funding partners and governmental ministers. Could have been a leak from Engineering. Or Sinclair. Or . . . the thought hit her hard. Barbara! An incompetent of unfathomable magnitude. She wouldn't put it past her sister to have misplaced the set she gave her.

Thus, she braced herself to face the most unsavoury move of her entire career. She decided to phone Barbara at UNEP in Kenya.

After realigning her collar, she grabbed the phone. "Hello. This is Mary Glass. May I please speak to Barbara Glass in Herman Meyer's office." She stood up and looked over the haze of fountains at TransAqua's entrance, sheets of water glinting off giant rock slabs.

"Pardon?"

"Barbara Glass, please." Maybe her sister had already been fired.

The receptionist put her on hold. After seven minutes, she came back on the line. "I'm afraid there's no Barbara Glass in Herman Meyer's office."

"Well, what about another office?" Mary squinted and spied Sinclair storeys below her, slithering behind the fountain on his way back to the office.

"There's no Barbara Glass listed at all."

"Excuse me?"

"Is there another name I could look up?"

"Can I speak to someone in Herman Meyer's department? This is very urgent. I'm calling from TransAqua."

"I'll put you through to his assistant."

Mary performed deep knee bends as she waited, her view of the entrance blocked by the air conditioner as she squatted down, the image refreshed as she stood up. Three minutes later, she spotted Janet trailing Sinclair, stop-start motions viewed through deep squats. Finally, a woman picked up the phone.

"Yes? How may I hel–"

"My name is Mary Glass from TransAqua International. I'm looking for my sister, Barbara Glass. She is apparently working with Herman Meyer."

"We have no Barbara Glass here, I'm afraid."

She stopped breathing. "Has anyone of that name recently left?"

"No. I know everyone in this department. Are you sure that's her name? There's Brenda Gibbons–"

"Of course I know her name. I'm her sister!"

"Pardon? I'd advise you to–"

"Yeah? Well, why don't you send it to committee?"

"I don't have to listen to–"

"I'd be sure to get a memo within five years!"

Panicking, Mary slammed down the phone, cracking its plastic cover. She could not figure out how Barbara had managed to get fired so quickly. Nor could she figure out why she had not told their parents of such an everyday occurrence in her life. She needed to call her sister right away: who knew where she had left the blueprints?

Mary typed "Barbara Glass" into a search engine. Within an instant, Barbara's name appeared under a website for an NGO called Drop of Life. She scrolled down, surprised that she had managed to find another job so quickly. Mary froze. Water activists! In a frenzy, she double-clicked on Barbara's name. A page blinked open.

Confronting her–an apparition of excess made flesh: her sister, Barbara. She wore a low-cut shirt out of which bulged a surplus of cleavage. The lunatic sported a massive turban under which dangled earrings the size of chandeliers. Her eyes radiating sexual desperation, a fleshy smile of self-approbation on her face, she held her head tilted to one side in her long-suffering therapeutic posture. Mary looked closer. Yes, she had a crimson dot on her forehead.

Did the brain that hid behind the dot–fully concealed, given its minute size–have any knowledge of the African Water Warriors? How much information did its sluggish neurons carry?

Mary's pared down life form almost shut down from the shock, her low pulse rate struggling for tenure. She had no idea what to do. As the minutes passed, her fear mounted: this problem presented the most serious challenge to her career yet.

From its neo-classical architecture to the National Mall to the arboretum, Kolo loved the presidential complex. It felt like home. Built as a copy of the Capitol Building, like its counterpart in Washington DC, it implied rule by the people through visual hints of Athenian democracy. It suggested a structure that had never existed, simply a frothy concept of what a classical monument might resemble, sprinkled with other assorted designs from Europe. In a final irony, the pagan monolith under which it nestled symbolized theocracy–the invincibility of the complex's anointed commander.

As president, he owned the landscape, from the immense granite outcrop of Aso Rock to the river that, by some quirk of fate, served as his greatest protection: a moat that cut off access to his villa and the three arms of government in times of danger.

This residence he intended to keep at all costs.

The minister for the environment arrived, only a little late. "How are you today, sir?"

"Surviving. And yourself?"

"Dangerously well, yes, sir, dangerously well."

Strange expression. Smiling up at him, Kolo picked his nails under his desk.

"The country seems very peaceful at the moment, sir," the minister beamed. "All due to your great guidance."

Kolo gawked at the fool. "Do you watch TV? Read newspapers?"

"Yes. I enjoy very much that form of entertainment, sir."

"Then you might have noticed the increase in riots, coalitions being formed against water privatization, violent outbursts as a result of the resettlement for the dam?"

"The misappropriations? Well, who asked them to live there?"

"Misappropriations? I think you mean resettlement."

The minister stared at Kolo, his face blank with incomprehension. "Have we resettled them?"

"It's certainly not misappropriation! It's appropriation at most. For the good of the country."

The minister frowned, trying to fathom how this new word added any value to his vocabulary. "Anyway, it's less than one million people. And they're mostly villagers. Who are these illiterates to worry about misappropriation? Where are their papers?"

"You mean, the unfortunate displacement. Good question about their papers. Not a land tenancy agreement in sight. Nothing in writing–apparently they think oral singsongs carry legal weight. All ancestral land. How convenient. We could all claim ancestral rights. I'll claim Lagos."

The minister hee-hawed. "I'll claim Nigeria. I'll start as president."

Kolo attempted a smile but it stuck before full execution.

The minister continued, oblivious. "Who has a right to land without paper? If they don't like buying property, they should be hunter-gatherers. It's not such a bad lifestyle."

"Indeed."

"In my village, of course, we do have ancestral rights, but it's well documented orally. If anyone so much as dared . . ."

"Thank you, minister." Kolo waved his confidant away, exhausted by his imbecility.

He turned to business and picked up his phone. "Inspector? This is the president."

"President of . . . ?" the inspector searched.

"The country, you idiot!"

The Inspector General of Police responded immediately to the red alert. "Ah, President Kolo. This is a great, great honour for a man of my humble position."

Fed up with flattery–to a degree–Kolo grew impatient. "What about the assassins? Where are they? It's been two months! And they let Jegede bomb TransAqua?"

"They asked me if you still want to terminate him–a ruined wreck like that."

Kolo knew the inspector general was lying. No doubt, he had lost his assassins. "Ah! I didn't realize they had been promoted."

"Pardon, sir?"

"So they are now your strategic advisors?"

"No, sir!"

"Then get them to execute Jegede!" he shouted. "Now!"

"Yes, sir."

"And if they don't, execute them!"

"Yes, sir."

"And if you don't, you can arrange your own execution!"

"Yes, sir. Immediately!" A short pause. "Pardon, sir?"

Kolo slammed down the phone.

TWENTY-FIVE

Fallen Leaf

"Hey, Barbie. I'm arranging a trip to celebrate the parents' fortieth wedding anniversary. But you don't need to come."

Barbara was loath to undergo the torture of an entire vacation with Mary and the admiring ancestors, but since her presence was not required, she obviously had to attend. "Well, when are they going? I could be in the country, who knows? Might even be free."

"I doubt it. It's all arranged for the end of September. We're off to Banff."

"Banff? In Canada?" How ironic that Mary had chosen Barbara's secret domicile!

"Yep. Initially I suggested Ottawa, but they nixed that. Nothing there."

"I'm sure you'd find–"

"I'm paying for it all, but I told them you probably wouldn't be interested."

What planets were aligning for such good fortune? A freebie, no doubt at one of those old Canadian Pacific castles! She could arrange an itinerary of spa treatments in order to spend the least time possible with the family. And more importantly, perhaps she could obtain information about the explosions. Since the tragedy, she had been unable to reach Wise Water directly, but Aminah had assured her it had been an accident. Femi's life was now in great danger, so Barbara would have to make this ultimate sacrifice to discover what guise any threat to him might take. She girded herself for the taxing assignment.

"End of September? What a coincidence! I'll be back from Kenya by then. Yep, I can come."

As Barbara had predicted, the family stayed at the Banff Springs Hotel, a magnificent bastion of human ingenuity that competed with the colossal reaches of the surrounding Rocky Mountains. In the morning, they gathered in the castle's sumptuous lounge before embarking on a survey of the surrounding area. Mary's shrink-wrapped body pranced in front of them, a smile of triumph anchoring itself to her sparse features. Barbara felt a powerful punch of envy, a sense of her pecuniary shortcomings and physical overcompensations.

After a short drive and trek, they stood at the foot of a gargantuan megalith that vaulted past the tree line into a soaring sky, a raging monomaniac that had punched its way upwards through the earth. The parents took a few pictures. Then they looked at it.

"How beautiful! Absolutely massive!" Mother exclaimed.

"Couldn't build on it if you tried," Father added.

The parents' necks craned upwards for a few moments and then, simultaneously, tilted down again to the horizontal and panned over to Mary for the next exhibit.

With this small action, it occurred to Barbara that her sister had made a critical error of judgement. The repetitiveness of the natural world, its overpowering immensity, the bald insolence of a back turned away from human hand, would eventually strike her parents as both menacing and monotonous. They craved Culture.

Barbara took full advantage of Mary's predicament. "There's a famous lake near here, right, Mary?"

"A lake? How interesting!" A fat paw pushed an errant piece of hair behind Mother's ear and patted it back gently.

With Mary pinioned into silent fury, they drove to Lake Louise, a glacier-fed vessel bearing waters of phosphorescent turquoise.

"Just like a postcard!" The parents sighed in appreciation, taking a long breath. Then they looked back at Mary for the next attraction.

She hesitated. "There's a path along it. We can walk the length of the lake."

"Wonderful idea!" Father braced himself for an excursion. "Fresh air. Exercise. Good girl."

"And what's at the end?" Barbara asked innocently.

Mother tilted an ear towards Mary.

Faltering, Mary hesitated. "Uh, well, nothing. We, um, we walk back."

Both parents' eyebrows raised at the same time to the same height.

"Or," Mary ventured, "we could see Emerald Lake."

"Sounds fascinating," Mother beamed. "What's that?"

"It's a lake," Barbara interrupted. "It's a different colour." She leaned in towards them to further elucidate. "It's emerald."

The parents looked at each other, the horror of the holiday suddenly dawning on them.

"Any antique shops?" Mother enquired.

"Interesting architecture? Bridges?" Father added.

"It's the antiquity, architecture and engineering miracle of Mother Nature herself." Barbara swept a balletic arm around the panorama of Lake Louise.

As the tips of Barbara's fingers deliberately entered her sister's field of vision, rage curdled within Mary. Nevertheless, she quickly improvised. "We can see how the rental car's nav system compares to yours. I believe it shows footage of surrounding attractions."

The parents perked up, walked at a clip to the car and adjusted the nav system's settings. "Oooh! Well, look at that. Stunning architecture!" They watched the lambent images of the Chateau Lake Louise, the hotel in whose car park they sat.

"What would you say that is? Limestone? Granite? Some local rock?" Mother opined.

"They certainly knew how to build in those days. No expense spared." Father stared at the miracle of architecture on the rectangular screen.

"Well, off we go," Mother backed out of the parking lot, reluctantly removing her eyes from the nav system. "Heads down, girls!"

"Mary . . ." Barbara's low crouch muffled her speech. "I heard some group bombed your thingy in Nigeria. Water Wipes, Why Water, some name like that. Know them? Must be quite a hit, huh? What'r' you planning to do?"

Mary's innards grew taut. Did she mean Water Warriors or Wise Water? "Probably kill them. How should I know? Nothing to do with us. What's it to you?"

"Nothing. Just making conversation, that's all."

"Is the Dam Commission interested? What do they think, Barbie?"

"Well, obviously, they think that Fem–uh, Jegede just made a mistake. They've told him off. He says he won't do it again. So maybe TransAqua should, you know, let it go."

Mary's clenched guts relaxed now that she knew Barbara had no information about the AWW debacle. "By the way," she said, straightening from her duck, "it's intriguing how much you know about the Dam Commission's advice. I saw Meyer the other day."

"Who?" Barbara queried, straightening her Vietnamese tunic.

"Your boss."

Barbara thought she recognized the name. She fished around for it. "Oh, Herm!"

Mother looked over a precipitous drop as she drove. "You call your boss by his first name?" A small smile played on her lips. "Well, I never."

"That's the modern way, my dear," Father said, leaning back to help his wife negotiate the narrow road. "First names and T-shirts."

Mary continued, "Strangest thing. He'd never heard of Barbara. No idea who she was." Her little grey teeth clenched in a thin smile. Barbara imagined wrapping her strand of pearls around Mary's thin neck and choking her. Then selling the pearls.

"So, Barbara," Father said, "are we or are we not allowed to tell our friends about your job?"

"Isn't there some way to change to a less secretive post?" Mother asked in a plaintive wail. "This puts us in a very awkward position, you know, dear."

"Well, it puts Barbara in an awkward position too," Mary piped up. "You see, she doesn't work for UNEP at all!"

"CIA?" Father asked, eyebrow visor raised.

"UNICEF?" Mother asked, her eyes glittering with hope.

"No, Barbie works for Drop of Life, a left-wing, fringe organization–"

"Mary, I . . ." Barbara tried to interrupt her sister, but then the word hit her. "*Fringe?* Did you say fringe?"

"What?" Mother repeated.

"–aimed at stopping all corporate activities."

"A fringe organization?" Barbara exploded. "What the hell is that supposed to mean?"

"She has no benefits to speak of."

Mother stepped on the brake, mid-ascent. Father grabbed his heart.

Barbara's mind raced to salvage the situation, but a small "f" word–"fringe"–held her hostage.

"And she has no diplomatic immunity," Mary continued.

Father looked as if he were in the first stages of stroke. Stage stroke.

"And," the final stab, "she works in Ottawa."

"Ottawa? That backwater?" Father spluttered, miraculously recovering from his heart attack. "Canada is a socialist country for Gods' sake with, as you can see, a total absence of population!"

Did he say *backwater*? "They're not socialists; they're liberals!"

A split second later, Barbara realized the implications of such an admission.

"Same difference, miss," Father replied.

Barbara felt crushed. She lived in a backwater doing fringe work.

Mother accelerated; she tended to drive in tempo with her heart rate.

"Yes," Father said, surveying the landscape with the scrutiny of an engineer, "a communist terrorist. I see it all now. Once you piece together the puzzle, it all makes sense. Vegetarian. Environmentalist. African music . . ."

As their bodies swayed to counteract the car's violent movements, Mary snapped a smile. "I need the blueprints back, Barbara, or we'll sue."

"You'll do no such thing!" Mother interrupted. "We've had quite enough trouble for one day. And Barbie, you give those blueprints to your sister right now."

"I don't have them on me, Mom! Anyway, they've been copied hundreds of times."

Mary clutched her spindles into tight fists, making an unexpected cracking sound. "If you don't leave your tin-pot mob within a week, TransAqua will sue you right down to the crimson dot on your forehead."

Barbara snorted. "Yeah, right. And where would your career go after that?"

Unexpectedly ambushed, Mary hesitated, but then pulled her seat belt forward so she could lean towards the front seat. "Dad, do you know what Drop of Life is planning to do next? They're investigating the Inga Dams in the Congo to stop Inga III from being built."

"That's a lie!" Barbara gasped.

"They say the project was a white elephant. They're looking at cost overruns and corruption."

"How dare they!" Father exploded. "That was one of my finest pieces of engineering. They have no right to . . . I'd like to see them survive those conditions."

"They're planning to prosecute, Dad." Mary continued.

Father's visor eyebrows stiffened into horror.

Outflanked yet again, Barbara felt sick: Mary had planned this, and she had fallen for it. "Dad, you can check on our website. We have no intention–"

"Intention or not, you will most definitely leave Drip of Life." Father pinched out the words, unable even to look at his daughter. "Bloody heretics."

"Dad, I can't do that. People's lives depend on me."

Mother swerved into an unexpected U-turn, whispering "Airport" to her husband in explanation. "I know disowning your daughter is a bit old-fashioned, but since a group of terrorists is more important to you than us, you are no longer welcome in this family."

Barbara took the next flight out, hoping to stave off an ever-encroaching panic, just hours before her parents aborted their own foray into the tedium of the natural world. If they could dispose of her with such surgical precision, how little must she mean to them!

"Name?" The check-in attendant reached for her ticket.

"Barbara."

"Alrighty! Awesome!" Great dental work: his teeth in perfect rows. "Well, hey, Barbara, just call me Darrell. Would you mind sharing your last name?"

"I've been disowned by my family. I have no last name."

"Think positive, hon. DNA, move outta my way! Now, sweetie, would you mind sharing your previous surname with me?"

She slammed herself down on his counter. "All those years," she blubbered, "those millions upon millions of seconds, swept away like dust."

He patted her. "There, there, sweets. They'll come around. Meanwhile, you-just-live-your-life!" He gave the air a small punch of encouragement.

"I guess so. Just commit myself to work. One hundred percent."

"One hundred-exactly! Now, hon, about that former surname."

She rooted in her bag for various documents and handed them all to him. As he checked through ("Immunization? No, don't need that." "That ticket's old. Plucky girl. Lagos, Nigeria? You-are-a-lucky-young-lady!" "Oh hey! You go to yoga, huh?" "Here we go: passport and ticket. Now that didn't take long, did it?"), she continued musing. "Perhaps they wanted to see a reflection of their perfection in me and they could never find it. And maybe," she lifted her tear-stained head from the counter while he quickly verified her passport photo, "they saw only their most unspeakable flaws."

"You look great to me, hon. You've got great skin. Don't let them tell you any different." He handed her a tissue. "Gate four. To your left. You go for it, girl!"

As she plodded towards the plane, she wondered whether to feel elated or abandoned. Unlike the clans and families in Nigeria, which stuck so tightly together, whose ancestors were as real to them as the living, she felt as disposable as the wrappers on the food court counters. She needed no flood, no calamity, no great wretchedness to wipe out the memory of her existence. If her family could erase an entire shared history so quickly and with so little emotion, she could disappear entirely and no one would even care. Like a leaf falling from a tree.

Her spirit shattered, Barbara returned to Ottawa.

Harsh commands filled the grounds of the recuperation facility within which Femi lived–a voice of authority exclusive to the army. The military had fanned out within Jos, and now it had moved on to the villages.

Feeling the electricity of fear surge into their compound, Femi grabbed Igwe's hand and pulled him until they reached the crevice of a boulder high above their settlement, as the other insurgents scrambled to get away. With the sudden realization that, in their haste, they had left gourds of water in their hut, along with papers and provisions, Femi slid over the top of a rock slab to peek at the movement below. Ubaldous continued walking around the flame tree, dragging his bandages behind him. A soldier bludgeoned him until he fell.

"No!" Femi gasped.

A soldier turned his head. Femi ducked, a frantic pulse pummelling his temples. It seemed strange. Recently, he had felt entirely indifferent about his fate. Hearing Igwe's uneasy breath next to him, he realized that though he still welcomed the peace of oblivion, he did not wish to leave his companion behind alone.

The sound of boots grew louder. Femi pushed Igwe's head down. "I beg, Igwe, stay there! These your gold logos could them." He peeped around the rock. Two soldiers immediately beneath them stormed into their hut, tipping over pots, pans and gourds. One looked directly at their boulder, indeed straight into Femi's eyes, yet appeared not to see him.

"Am I a lizard?" Femi muttered to himself. "Can the man not point and at least give me some dignity?"

The soldier turned away with a frown, a sharp nod of his head indicating that Femi should duck back down.

A sudden howl–high-pitched, eerie. Ubaldous had struggled to his feet and, roaring, charged at the soldiers, his arms held up as if controlled by magical forces. Flinching to avoid his touch, the soldiers left the compound at a trot, obviously fearful of spending any great time with its lunatics.

Immediately, Femi descended to comfort Ubaldous, while Igwe rushed for water, cloths and disinfectant.

"Ubaldous!" He used his sleeve to wipe up the blood on his friend's forehead. "It's Femi. Don't worry. E don' finish."

"Who don' finish?" a policeman snorted with an arrogant drawl of near-authority. He came up to Femi's face. "Nothing don' finish yet. That was army. This be police. No be same thing."

"Thanks be to Allah! I was worried. They jus' ran through the place. What kind of job is that?"

With a fearful expression, Igwe pointed to a spot behind the policeman with a trembling hand. "Na evil spirit enter you-oh! Enter your head. From behind you!"

"Where?" The policeman swivelled around, weaving and ducking.

Igwe did not reply: he slackened his jaw and began dribbling.

This disturbance affected Ubaldous outside, who started chattering loudly to himself.

Panicking, the policeman ran away, fearing the evil spirits that had invaded the unfortunate occupants of the village.

Igwe immediately got up, wiped the spittle from his mouth and appealed to Femi. "We'll be hunted like bush rat if we stay here. What am I saying? Even bush rat know how to run."

Despite his concern over Igwe's alarm, Femi grew intransigent, refusing to compromise on this obvious practicality, yet not quite knowing why.

"What's your problem, Femi? You hear the snap of my finger? This sound should have made echo in Lagos, not Jos. Twenty-five million people to hide among. Instead, you choose some small half-million, who-are-these-new-people town. I beg, Femi. Why you dey risk all these lives?"

These insistent questions immediately prompted the answer he had been too confused to discover himself. "First, most important reason, Lagos too crowded to hear your finger. Second, minor point, Ubaldous. He's too fragile."

His companion immediately understood. Ubaldous, an early mentor, one of the earth's most generous gifts, had shared almost all he possessed with Femi when he had moved to Abuja, sometimes going without food to support him. His faith in Femi's legal talents had been so great, he had tutored him through the small hours, declining work to do so. But now this great man struggled through unknown topographies, the horror of which neither Femi nor Igwe could imagine. Ubaldous plugged his ears with leaves to fight the enemy voices jeering at him. And beaten though he was, once again he was pacing around the flame tree with jerky, uneven steps, his feet bleeding through his bandages.

Wincing at the sight of the bloodied feet, Igwe walked over to the distraught man, to pace beside him on his circuit around the tree. Alighting on an idea, he called to Femi to join them on the circuit. "Let me construct a bier. We can carry Ubaldous to Lagos."

"The man can move, Igwe. It's hard to stop him. In fact, he could carry his own bier, my friend. That's not the problem. His mind cannot survive the journey. He needs peace, not Lagos. Let the others go there."

The day after this conversation, Ubaldous's condition improved dramatically. He made it clear to them all that he wished to stay in Jos permanently.

A long wail, swooping down like a bird of prey, summoned Femi and Igwe from their hut.

Igwe yelped.

Fixated by the sight of bleeding feet, dangling legs and the bodily wastes that ran down them, Igwe sobbed. "He heard me, Femi. He must have heard."

Ubaldous had hanged himself from the branches of the flame tree.

Once again, a great numbness settled within Femi, like that felt by those strange children born without a sense of pain, who cannot feel the heat of a flame. It found room among the other erasures of his life. "He didn't hear you, Ig. He just knew."

The immense sorrow of losing their once fierce fighter plunged the compound into mourning. Even the unbalanced grew quiet. Occasionally, mumbled stories about Ubaldous's many victories laced through the stillness. To honour his memory, Femi named the village after him. Ekong erected a signpost outside the village. Lance laid flowers upon it. Yussef did not emerge from his hut.

After burying Ubaldous under the flame tree that had been his counsellor and his friend, they prepared to move to Lagos. Only the ailing stayed in Jos, muttering angry words to the skies, protected by friends and sheltered by huts on the hills.

Among the followers, Hassan secreted a stone from his village within his belongings, his expression overlaid with distrust, certain that no one could prevent themselves from stealing a treasure so precious. Zainab folded three pages of recipes her mother had written for her, using only the tips of her nails to touch the paper, as if it were made of onion skin and its surface contained the first known script. Her friend Azuka carried two stringed instruments, though she could barely remember the songs her grandmother had taught her. Nevertheless, she knew her humming would be the last record of an entire clan.

The final descendents of now extinct peoples slowly made their way to the country's former capital and largest city, Lagos.

After a week of recuperation, Barbara reluctantly slipped on a flowered Lurex shirt, stretching its purple blooms across her chest, almost flattening her breasts. She matched this with a pair of orange pantaloons, jammed her feet into a pair of Turkish shoes with turned-up toes, then grabbed her Peruvian poncho and bundled off into the chaos of an autumn day.

Crimson and gold leaves spun like whirling dervishes intent on draining the last gasps of energy from life before they bid the world a dizzy goodbye. In two weeks, three, four perhaps, she knew the winds would come–wild gales, furious that these brash and buxom colours had raised a challenge, thrashing and whipping them until they fell, carpeting the land in soft, submissive layers. There they would lie, muted browns, beiges–ripped, tattered, exhausted.

Gums greeted her. "Hey, Barbara, did you enjoy your holiday? How are your parents?"

"Awful." She watched as Gums' smile faded into concern. "They found out I was working for Drop of Life and had simultaneous strokes. Now they have to be fed Jell-O through a straw. My dad gets green, my mom red. That's how we know whose is whose."

Gums' eyes widened. "Oh, I'm so sorry."

Barbara shook her head in frustration. "Just kidding."

"Well, I guess you're glad to be back here, then?" Gums ended on an optimistic note.

"Nope," Barbara sighed, unwilling to be drawn into the warped reality that bred Gums' relentless cheer.

Gums looked around furtively, smiled a "till later" and made a hasty escape.

Barbara climbed up to her turret hideaway. At her computer, she checked to see how the situation in Nigeria had progressed. Riots had broken out and farmers were attacking infrastructure in broad daylight.

Gums poked her head around the corner and darted a note in her direction.

Hey Barbie!!! Great weather, huh? Another wonderful day in paradise ☺ Jane has asked for an emergency meeting with you asap. ✡ Krystal

Barbara crept off to Jane's office, her Turkish shoes squeaking as she tiptoed, avoiding the other staff who might be lurking in the wings to assault her with the ritual of the morning greeting.

The antiquity had parked herself behind her desk, life's manuscript carved into her leathery skin. She wore a sari of oranges and golds, across which she had draped a veil of screaming red. And though the colours told of passion and violence, the overall effect hinted of acceptance and peace.

"Where have you been?" Jane's tree bark skin settled into stern disapproval.

Barbara was stunned by the relic's expression. She had expected praise for her hard work. After all, they had come so close to toppling Kolo's regime. Then she realized there might be a simpler explanation. "Oh my gosh! Have I missed something here? Some kind of do? A birthday, perhaps?"

The antique tossed four newspapers at her. "They're reporting that Drop of Life is backing insurgency in Nigeria. Is this true?" Her voice could barely control an underlying tremor. Parkinson's, perhaps? Or anger?

"Absolutely not. Well, technically no." Fiddling with a bangle, Barbara reasoned that Drop of Life had not backed insurgency, it had been at its forefront.

"I also understand that Jegede's group may be involved in recent terrorist acts."

"No, no, that's factually incorrect." It was one act, and not that recent–a whole month had passed.

Jane sat silent and Barbara was forced to continue. "We were involved in PR activities."

"Not according to accounting! What's this bill from Fantasia Enterprises?" Jane slammed it on the desk, oblivious to any dangers from osteoporosis.

"Construction of a recuperation facility in Jos."

"With Drop of Life financing?"

"Can't remember. It was a while ago."

"Who the hell gave you permission to do that?" Jane shouted, her features as lively as any sixty-year-old's. "You've jeopardized the work of the entire organization! Thanks to you, Life Blood is threatening to cut our funding off. We need you out of here immediately, and, of course, we're severing all financial links to Jegede's group."

Barbara screwed up her eyes in order to better understand these ancient murmurings. "You're firing me?"

"Yes. That's exactly what I'm doing. Well observed!"

Barbara shrank into her poncho. This marked the end of her most fertile period: an era of almosts. She had almost fallen in love. She had almost defeated TransAqua. She had almost toppled a regime. She had almost kept a job. Reaching over Jane's desk, she gathered up the newspapers, planning to paste the articles into a scrapbook.

Seeing in print how much she had already achieved, she could not help but protest. "If you fire me, that's as much as an admission of guilt. So far, your funding partners are only making spurious–and, I might add, libellous–connections between Drop of Life and insurgency, simply because of our very active PR campaign in the region. Surely you wouldn't want me to imply anything different?"

The wreck glared at her through a belt of wrinkles, a disconcerting gaze. Age only served to increase their authority, like monuments once gaudy that had now decayed into grandeur. But a buried stream of indignation spurred Barbara on, dictated by her need to protect Femi. "You can't be so reckless as to give the media any hint . . . I mean, you can trust me. I'm a loyal employee. Besides, we've got nothing to hide, right?"

Jane studied her. "How much do you want?"

"Just my wages. I'm asking for time to secure Femi's safety. I'll do it from home, if necessary."

"We will continue to pay you," the obelisk pronounced, "but only until the end of the financial year. Now get out!"

Barbara swirled out of Jane's office, her poncho enhancing the effect.

Crestfallen, she tramped up to her office turret. The sounds of Siberian throat singing escorted her through her disappointment. It did not occur to her that an immediate departure equated to one without delay. But her relaxation was soon interrupted by the human resources manager, a woman called DeeDee with a voice that dripped with aspartame. "You're supposed to leave, dear," she whispered.

"I am quite underwhelmed by my treatment here so far." Barbara kissed her teeth as her eyes travelled down DeeDee in disdain.

The woman sighed into her paperwork, then escorted Barbara off the premises.

Homebound, Barbara's drooping deportment limited her gaze to the dead leaves at her feet, the battered, pulped, macerated muck that despoiled the cityscape, cleaving to the treads of shoes, slipping people up. The manure of trees: like her, life's excrescence.

Drained of her remaining energy, she slogged home at a funereal pace, finally making it to her front door. There, in a leaden stupor, she searched her Hausa handbag for keys, swaying slightly. Unable to find them, she retraced darkened interior routes with her fingers, feeling through all the crevices of the bag in a state of narcosis, prodding for holes. No keys. She shook her bag. No jangling. She looked at her porch door and began to sob, little coughing sounds that evacuated tears of frustration and inadequacy. The skin on her forehead tightened.

She reached inside her pantaloons pocket for her tissues and touched the cold, hard surface of keys, as always aloof and unmoved in their feudal reign over chaotic minds. She pulled the set out with trembling hands and jabbed one into the slot, succeeding at this simple act only after a number of attempts. The moment she entered, she threw her bag on the floor and stumbled to her bed.

Days later, Barbara awoke, her mind enshrouded in a gauze of abandonment and failure. Simple routines, habits and events–cleaning teeth, making free-trade coffee, pouring oat milk–took enormous time and concentration. Different liquids spilled over the kitchen counter. Her hands would not stop trembling.

She thumped herself down in an armchair, adjusted a picture of Femi on her shrine and wondered how to help him stay alive. Weary and lacking concentration, she punched in the new number in Lagos to see if she could get through to him, and after four attempts at this basic task, finally managed to order the numbers in the correct sequence.

For the first time since the explosions at TransAqua, someone answered.

"Hello. It's Barbara. How now?"

Silence on the other end.

She injected greater modulation into her monotone. "Femi? How body-oh?"

"It's Igwe," the voice snapped. "Which body? Ubaldous body dead. Femi body hunted. My body fear everything. Maybe one body be virus, and kill all of us. So which body you and your New York-Paris-London international dynamite self dey interested in? Please gist me! But wait first. Make I settle down for best comfort. Just a minute."

He cut off the phone.

She managed to punch in the numbers one more time.

He had turned the phone off completely.

This last call wounded her the most, stabs that pushed out from within her body, piercing the very wall of her skin. Igwe's frenetic solicitude, hovering over Femi, protecting him, indicated to Barbara that he knew the worth of a person. And it was suddenly clear that he, like all others, held her responsible for Ubaldous's death–indeed, even the bomb fatalities; worse still, this bleak harvest would continue until each member of Femi's group had been massacred, buried too deeply to hint of their misfortunes, their hands leaving no trace of their tragedy.

She kept thinking of Femi: the beauty of his face, a face that told of the splendour and majesty of Nigeria's past, a breathtaking beauty that described the country's dreams. She had hoped to enact her future through the fecundity and lushness of his habitus. Instead, her hand had pulled him through her own sterile landscape and, in doing so, had led him to his almost inevitable end.

And so she cried, grieving for a man who had not yet died.

Once again, days passed. Barbara did not clean her teeth; she had no energy. Her tongue felt around the inside of her mouth, wondering how much longer she could bear to rest in her own filth. She sweated at night. The sheets smelled. Her body itched. She could hardly move.

Dozens of hazy thoughts circled in her mind. Those that terrorized her, she tried to banish. They flitted in and out, despite her constant vigilance.

With a listless hopelessness, Barbara wondered if Astro could help, whether his world of growth could save her from a propensity towards destruction. Gentle memories of fish swimming underneath Astro's apartment floor calmed her. These small creatures provided him with an insight into a vanishing realm of innocence. Perhaps the belief in the existence of that innocence gave Astro his special energy, whereas the absence of the same belief gave Barbara hers.

Tired, worn and weak, she picked up the phone. "Hey, Astro!"

"Who is this?"

"It's Barbara."

"Oh." He sounded disappointed.

Silence.

"Oh, hey, Barbara." He had used her entire name. "How are you doing?"

"Fine. I thought I'd come and visit. D'you mind?"

"No, I'm busy."

"Busy? What kind of busy?" She wondered if he had a girlfriend.

"Busy busy." He did. He slammed down the phone.

She went straight to bed.

The next day she awoke, her chest constricted by panic. Dressing completely for the first time in days, she tore out of her apartment. As she staggered around Ottawa, trying to pull herself together, small things brought her to tears: a particular colour of Astroturf green, children wearing caps with earflaps, bobbles jiggling as they ran.

She spotted the haven of a gardening centre and ran to it. On entering, she was immediately enwrapped in the familiar smells, the tender fragrances of Astro's fellow travellers–the leaves, the dew, the plants. Her body crunched forward, retching out almost endless tears.

Ailing, she collapsed onto a bench to watch a man tending seedlings. His hands immediately attracted her attention, fingers putting a seed to bed, pulling its blanket around it, protecting it. Seeing her, the gardener approached.

"Need any help with gardening? It may initially seem daunting, but you'll get the hang of it."

She shook her head, recalling those other midwife hands, those of her lost companion, which delivered small seedlings to the light of day, nurturing them with the milk of fresh water. She used to wonder what events had shaped them, those long fingers, those strong veins. Never again would she sit in the company of someone who dreamed, not of glory, power or triumph, but of flowers and grasses.

Barbara walked home through the leaves, watching herself from above, not quite connected to her physical being. She entered her apartment and found herself lying in bed days later, not knowing how she came to be there. She sat up, her heart beating as if she were being attacked. She thought she might be insane.

She existed on very little sleep, dozing only in the early morning when teeny stars struggled for display, elbowing past night's shadows. Though she made a concerted effort to remember the activity of her waking hours, she found that she continued to lose time. She could not even concentrate on the small routines of daily life. It took hours just to open her eyes, days for her to gather enough energy to stand up. While her life had always been lived in vivid colour, now she saw only greys. Her heart beat with greater insistence and intensity, as if it were a separate being within her, trying to escape. It felt like her body were trying to kill her. The erratic pulsing often woke her up. She would gasp for air and felt like screaming.

As days passed, the crack between being and feeling opened up ever wider. The more she pondered her failings, the more she spiralled into the darker reaches of her mind, that area whose currents pulled her down into its oblivion. Her waking life now alternated between sudden surges of violent, choking panic and long stretches of stultifying stupor.

Sometimes Barbara sat, holding vigil over time, fighting the daze, willing herself to remember each moment. During these occasions, she waited for a call from Astro. She waited to hear Femi's voice. Her desperation even drove her to wait for her parents to ring. Nothing.

Barbara wanted only rest, only peace, only acceptance. All else was gone. Debilitated by clouded thoughts, with a body barely able to cope, she continued to sink into despair. Hope had always been her constant companion, urging her on through the torment and folly of life. She did not know how to sustain life now that all hope had gone.

She could hear the howl of autumn outside.

Barbara finally responded to a call to action. In movements that appeared mechanical and effortless, she filled up her bathtub with hot water. She then walked into the kitchen, took a knife from a drawer, lay in the bath and cut her wrists.

TWENTY-SIX

Absolute Zero

A duvet of rich burgundy silk draped over the edges of Kolo's bed. Underneath its plump embrace, within its tender custody, lay an ailing president. His carved ebony bedside table, on which a small crystal table lamp cast its benevolent light, overflowed with medications, liniments and vitamins. A portrait of a healthier and more confident Kolo rested above the head of his bed, separately illuminated. All the curtains were closed.

Kolo lay back on fleshy pillows, picking at the Chinese ties on his pink satin pyjamas. He smiled in weary fashion. Today TransAqua would start to move in the mighty turbines. More people would need to be displaced. And now they would see what they had only heard of. Trouble loomed like a black cloud.

If he succumbed at this early stage, the Kolo name would not live on. He wondered what had happened to his three assassins. Three months had passed. They had not succeeded in killing

Jegede nor even reported on the TransAqua bus bombing. He had never expected them to stick to schedule, but neither had he imagined that they would disappear altogether. Against a background of orchestral soft rock, he wondered whether Jegede's group had killed them first.

Easing himself up, he leaned over for the phone, intending to call the Inspector General of Police, a man whose life grew ever shorter with each blunder. Suddenly, his hand stiffened, hovering over the handset. Water. He heard it spurting somewhere above him, trickling down the walls.

Noises to his left made him jump: jets and sprays of water on the other side of the door threatening to blow it apart. He pulled the covers over his face so that only his eyes were visible. Gathering his courage, he staggered to the window, lurching in a zigzag pattern so that enemies would be unable to follow the motion. Cautiously, he peered out from behind heavy brocade curtains and squinted at the ground. He could not jump from such a height.

As he scanned the perimeters of the governmental complex, the splashing noises abated. It was unusual weather: the sun shone with a white intensity. The temperatures soared to push human endurance to its upward limit. The sky grew increasingly fanatical, in a capricious shift from the humid season's blazing merriment of yellow and blue to the dry season's white glint and back again, like the flash of a gunshot. Its explosion of radiance attacked the eyes, making it difficult for a man to hit a target at any distance.

The walls looked secure. The guards seemed calm. Still, enemies might have paid off the sentries.

He turned back to his room and froze. He heard a noise. A gushing sound. He looked at the ceiling. They must be trying to flood him out. He called his guard.

"Caretaker. Now."

The guard left and within five minutes opened the door to an old man in blue overalls. Kolo waved the guard away.

"Yes, sir?" The caretaker bowed.

"You see that?" Kolo pointed to the soundproofed ceiling.

"Yes, sir."

"Take it out tomorrow. I want cement. And no water pipes anywhere."

"Cement?" The old man looked up at the ceiling. "Yes, sir." He scratched under his arm.

"And call the guard."

The old man hobbled off and soon the guard returned, his ornamental epaulettes flashing with golden arabesques, his eyes hidden behind sunglasses.

"Bring." Kolo pointed to a few prized possessions, including his medications. He wrapped himself up in his duvet and waddled out of the room.

Kolo led the guard through corridors and down stairs. The thunderous cadences grew fainter, until they could no longer be heard. They finally came to the garage, where Innocent was polishing the Mercedes. The guard lowered his sunglasses on his nose so he could see better.

"Bring sheets!" Kolo ordered. The guard flinched, betraying his surprise. Kolo clicked his fingers. "Now!"

The guard, assuming his sunglasses hid his disbelief, put the medications down on the Mercedes' hood. Innocent opened the trunk as the guard left to retrieve the bed linen from the presidential bedroom. When the guard returned, Kolo instructed him to place the bedding inside the trunk, as taut as possible. He had already commissioned a specialist to adapt the bulletproof trunk for flotation, with at least three days' supply of oxygen.

"That'll fool them," Kolo said to himself with a giggle.

Mary sat in great pain, her irritable bowel syndrome radiating out from her abdomen. Despite the discomfort, she descended into deep thought. She clicked back on to Drop of Life's website, but could endure only a few moments of Barbara's lecherous leer. After all that Mary had engineered in Banff, Barbara had obstinately maintained her tenure with this makeshift crew. Mary could think of no threat great enough to budge her. She had to deal with the situation before Sinclair stumbled, or rather slipped, onto the information.

Death always worked.

Perhaps a bit radical. Still, the promise of death might prise Barbara away.

She picked up the phone, stood up and looked out over TransAqua's fountains to the thirsty desert.

"Hello, Daddy. How are you?"

"On the mend, my dear. Still recovering. Watching the old tick . . . It's Mary!" he screamed. "No, your daughter. No, Mary, dear." He turned back to the phone. "Mother sends her regards. Heard from you-know-who?"

"Nope. She's still at Drop of Life." She felt sick just thinking of it. "Daddy, can't you persuade her to leave Ottawa? Please?"

"Far be it for me to interfere in her life," he sighed in a singsong voice. "I'm only her father, after all. That carries very little weight with some people. What can I do? An apparently corrupt engineer like me, too incompetent, by the way, to build one of Africa's most famous dams."

"But, Dad, I've just talked to the Nigerian president. They have a contract out on her life."

"No more mention of her name, please. It'll upset your mother."

"Dad! She may be killed." Mary twirled a rubber band around her index finger.

"Well, she got herself into this mess; she can get herself out of it. Your mother's health is very fragile."

The phone clicked. "What about my health?" her mother shouted.

"It's very fragile, dear."

"What?" Mother's voice cracked with alarm. "What is it? Cancer? Is it cancer?"

"He's sending out his hit men," Mary continued, flicking the rubber band off one index finger and onto the other. "She needs to get back to the US."

"Who's sending hit men? Who needs to get back to the States?"

"The Nigerian president. Barbara."

"No more mention of her name in this house. It'll upset your father. She's *persona non grata,*" Mother said, the tail end of her sentence wobbling with emotion.

"But her life's in danger." Mary flicked the rubber band even higher.

"She's made her bed. She'll have to lie in it," Mother said in her most clipped tones. "We have to think of your father's health. He may not have long to live."

"What?" he yelled. "I don't?"

"If," Mother continued, "we continue to harbour terrorists, as Mary is proposing."

"What's the doctor told you?" Father shouted. "I demand to know! It's my life, after–"

"But, Mom," Mary whined, "I might lose my job if she keeps working with terrorists."

"What? Oh my God! They've fired you?"

"No. I was just saying they will when they hear Barbara is with Drop of Life."

"Not both of you!" Mother sounded as if she were about to faint.

"Mom, I haven't been fired. Is there any way you can persuade Barbara to leave Ottawa?"

"When has she ever listened to us?" Mother asked, a sob breaking through her fainting spell. "She hardly knows we're alive."

"You can tell her she's been disinherited," Father veered off topic, "and that includes any monies from the Inga Dam work. Since it's so ethically offensive to her."

Mary suddenly hit on a solution. "Tell her you're dying, Dad. That'll work!"

Silence.

"I'm not saying you *are* dying," Mary explained. "You're both in good health."

"I wish that were the case," Father said, a plaintive note in his voice.

"Her antics have almost killed us," Mother whispered.

"Call her up, Dad. Tell her you're dying. She'll come home. Please!"

"But, Mary–"

"She'll get them to stop the Inga Dam investigation if she thinks it's caused you health problems. Anyway, I need to keep my job. Do you want the neighbours to hear you have two unemployed daughters?"

"Ernie." Mother's firm tone suggested she had now recovered. "Do as she tells you." Yelling. "Mary needs her job back."

"Okay, love. Anything for our Mary. Give us the number to Life Drop."

After they got off the phone, Father tried Barbara's numbers in Ottawa, only to receive no answer.

There was a smell of indifference, of competence, of formality, and it was this scent that first pierced Barbara's consciousness. She opened her eyes. Through the fog of her bleary vision, she could see insipid green all around her. She looked down. As she concentrated, bandages slowly came into focus. Her wrists. Bandages on her wrists. Around her, a grubby white curtain set on a rusting aluminum rod. She began to weep, weary, defeated. She had survived.

She would have to try again.

Someone dabbed her eyes with a handkerchief. She turned her head to the side, her neck stiff. Behind the sedating daze, there was Astro, with a crooked, encouraging smile.

"Hey!" she said in a croak. Her throat was sore, her eyes puffed.

"Hey, Babu!" He leaned over and kissed her softly on the forehead. "Finally, you're awake!" Two teardrops landed on her nose. "At last, man. What have you done to yourself?"

"What am I doing here?"

"The people at work found you. A woman called Krystal phoned. You'd put me . . ." He sniffed bravely. "You'd put me as next of kin." He squeezed her hand, his bottom lip trembling. "Babu–don't ever do this again, okay?" He began to weep.

"So don't leave me, okay?" Tears fell to each side of her face. She did not know why he would stay–she had betrayed his immeasurable faith in her. But if he stayed, here was the branch she could hold on to through the current of her despair.

As Barbara succumbed to sleep, she heard a match being struck. The comforting scent of Astro's ylang-ylang incense accompanied her into slumber.

"Could you turn that announcement down, please?" Astro frowned. "My patient here is in a very fragile condition."

"I'm afraid we can't. It's the safety instructions," the flight attendant whispered as she demonstrated the inflation of a life jacket, miming these actions as softly as she could.

Following Astro's grave prognosis, the airline had upgraded Barbara and her stern, tawny-haired attendant to first class, so great was their concern over her health. As per Astro's proscription, all noise in the cabin was stifled. Few of their cabinmates dared to tinkle the ice in their drinks in the face of Astro's disapproval.

In Washington DC, on entering his apartment, Astro led Barbara to a deck chair. "Just sit down here, Babble," he said, helping her into the chair as if she had an ambulatory disability. "There you go. Now," he squatted beside her, speaking softly and clearly, but with the authority of a medical professional, "I'm just going to get a blankie, okay, bud?" He searched her eyes for signs of comprehension.

She blinked.

Satisfied, he hurried off and returned a moment later. "Here we go. One blanket coming up. Now, I'm just gonna put it around you, okay, bud? That's right, just lean forward a bit. Good work! Now, lean back." He wrapped her like a hot dog. "Great. Now, would you like some tea?" He hovered over her with concern.

She looked up at him through her bundle of blankets, feeling like an idiot. "Astro, I'm . . ."

"Yes?" He crouched forward a bit, turning an expectant ear towards her mouth.

She looked at his ear, annoyed. Realizing her attendant had no clue as to the difference between depression and a deep coma, she huffed out, "Sure, thanks."

"Okey-dokey. I'll go to the kitchen," he pointed to the kitchen as if she had no idea of its location, "which is just around that corner." He enunciated his words clearly, taking time over each vowel, each consonant, as if she had also forgotten the rudiments of the English language. "I won't be long. If there's anything you want, just holler. So . . ." he looked down, " . . . where am I going?"

"To the kitchen."

"That's right. And I'll be back . . . ?"

"In a moment."

"Good job!" He tucked a wayward edge of blanket under Barbara's legs. He stood back and surveyed his work. Satisfied, he widened his eyes to speak to her again. "Okay, if you want something . . . ?"

"Just holler."

He looked down at her, pride fanning across his face. "Atta girl!" he whispered, suppressing a crooked smile of congratulation. He hesitated, then made a decisive swivel kitchenwards.

Barbara heard him take the mugs out of the kitchen cabinet and fill the kettle with water, explaining every move, as if hosting a cookery program. She knew he thought it would help her: constant chatter is considered beneficial to comatose patients. "Okay, first warm the pot with hot water . . ."

Barbara unravelled herself from her winding sheet and tiptoed through his apartment, looking for signs of his girlfriend. She entered his bedroom, embraced by walls of crimson and scarlet, feeling that she had ventured back to the origin of all mystery. She neared the scattered cushions that represented his bed and gasped. A furry massage glove was wedged between his pillows–not a sexual toy she remembered having purchased. She stared at it, trying to extract its meaning. She wondered what his new girlfriend looked like. She imagined a tall woman with long fingernails, meowing through Astro's intercom. She pictured her purring in ecstasy, back arching as Astro stroked her with the fur glove.

She burst into tears and flung herself onto the bed, burying her head under a cushion to cover her sobbing.

She sneezed. The sex toy moved. Barbara sprang back. A cat! Barbara sucked in a breath. This was worse than expected–the woman had moved in her pet, despite the fact that Astro was tending to an invalid severely reactive to dander.

She heard Astro rattling the teapot, so she rushed back to her postpartum position on the beach chair.

Astro came back, carrying a tray.

"You've got a cat?" Barbara asked, tears streaming down her face, choking back the sobs.

"You saw the cat?" He crouched down in front of her. "Don't go near it, Babu. You have 'allergies.'" He quote-marked the air. "Do you understand?"

She blinked back tears and nodded.

"Good." He hunted around for a handkerchief. "Aw, man, I didn't know your allergies were so bad." He wiped her tears and held the handkerchief as she blew her nose.

Once he had settled her down, he squared the edges of the tray so they lay parallel to the table, looked at the tray again and realigned it. It overflowed with leaves, mosses and flowers, at the centre of which lay her tea and cookies.

"Whose cat is it?" she asked, tears springing to her eyes again.

"My neighbour's. You know–the guy downstairs. Remember when he took care of my apartment? Well, believe it or not, he stole my sax."

"So you stole his cat?"

"No. To 'steal,'" air quotes, "means to take property. A cat is a living being, not property." He knelt to fuss again with her blanket.

So he had kidnapped a cat. How could she have doubted him? He had only taunted a neighbour, not replaced her with a new girlfriend. She sighed. What a mystical spirit of nature!

"I'm so sorry about the way I treated you, Astro. I saw such horrific things in Nigeria, and you were the only piece of innocence I had." She stroked his hand with the back of her fingers.

He kissed her fingers, pressing his lips against them. "I'm not as innocent as you think, Bobble," he said into her fingers, "and you're not that tough, either."

That night, having evicted the cat from the room, they lay in the enveloping warmth of his bed, Barbara listening contentedly to his breath: a wisp of an inhale, a hush of an exhale. These small sounds, which she had taken for granted, filled her with a sense of renewal. These sounds would provide her with the strength to finish what she had started. She turned to rest her head on his chest, so she could hear his heartbeat and return once again to the amnesia of the womb.

Within a month, Kolo's garage decor had changed radically, with deep-pile carpets, pleasing ochre walls and fancy cornicing. An interior designer had selected the best antique furniture, above which hung giant paintings, honorary doctorates and photographs of Kolo with foreign dignitaries. In the middle of this grandeur, underneath a heavy chandelier, sat the white Mercedes-Benz. This bedroom had no windows, a bulletproof door through which the car entered, and numerous oxygen cylinders. Kolo had also installed a bathroom.

The sound of dripping had increased slightly since he had moved to the garage, but nothing as loud as the unexpected surges of gushing water in his former bedroom. He felt safer. But if, by some terrible fate, his enemies sought to flood the garage in order to drown him, he only had to open its mighty door to reach the safety of open ground.

"One of my best ideas. Apart from the security benefits, no one would think of finding me here," he murmured to himself.

From his pyjama pocket, he took out a key and opened the trunk, then hopped inside and nestled into the bedding for an afternoon nap. The Benz had been his own private joke. The former president, semi-illiterate as far as Kolo was concerned, had been interviewed during his short presidential campaign by a newscaster whose British accent struggled to integrate Nigerian inflections.

"So, Minister, what motto will provide the direction for your presidency?"

"Enh?" The candidate responded. "White Mercedes-Benz!"

The studio went silent.

While President Mu'azu had never been able to purchase his prized motor, Kolo paraded the fact that he would never have made such a basic error.

He sniggered.

Suddenly, the garage door opened.

Kolo yelped and, with fumbling fingers, tried to close the trunk's lid. The guard entered, flung off his sunglasses and cocked his revolver.

"It's okay, sir. Just Mechanic." The guard kissed his teeth and addressed himself to the intruder. "Why can't you come through my own door? You can't just open garage door like personal toilet. Look at your miscreant self causing confusion. Ah-ah!"

"I have to attend to car. Where am I supposed to enter-now?"

"This my own door. Right here. Come first around servant entrance. Then at least you can go through security like proper minion."

"Okay. Next time. But I need map."

The guard kissed his teeth long and hard. "Get at security gate. Not from Presidential Guard himself." He flipped his sunglasses back on and slammed the door.

Kolo peeked out of the trunk. His heart beat faster. "How did you get in here?"

"Some people outside. I just dashed them some money." He began to take off his mechanic's clothes.

"How dare you enter the presidential bedroom! How did you even know you'd find me here?"

"The whole of Nigeria knows you sleep in garage, sir. Me, I thought you were jus' crazy, but now I can appreciate. A presidential garage is not like a garage at all." The man's eyes travelled around the room, steeped in admiration.

"People know?" Greater panic clutched at Kolo's chest and squeezed it tight.

No answer from a man still under the spell of opulence. Still in his trance, he chucked away his overalls to reveal a garish cowboy shirt, with multiple gold chains around his neck. His trousers appeared to be made from snakeskin, and his boots most definitely crocodile.

Kolo quickly scribbled notes and a quick diagram indicating new security measures to protect the garage, muttering to himself. "Typical Nigeria. Everyone has to know everyone's business." When he finished, he turned to the man. "I wanted Jegede dead. Where is he?"

"Still alive, sir," Lance answered.

Kolo lowered his eyelids in a contemptuous gaze. "Is that so? And when are you planning to do your job, Mr Omeke?"

"Jus' Lance is fine."

"It's been four months. I should have had you executed by now."

"How can you execute a man you can't find?" The man chuckled as he eased himself into an antique chair. He sat straight-legged with feet wide apart, as if parading his groin. "Anyway, I have had a few problems. Some one person paid me to ruin Jegede. This I did immediately. I'm sure you know of my work."

Kolo contemplated, then his heart almost stopped. "The TransAqua bombing?"

The man could scarcely hide his pride. Under these lighting conditions, despite his obvious beauty, Lance possessed the insanity of detachment. "Then some other one person paid me even more to protect Jegede. This I did immediately."

"What?"

"Enh-heh. Now you can see my problem. I cannot please both. This is dilemma for Solomon. And you never offer me anything. How can I work for free?"

"I offered you your life, you idiot! You wouldn't be here without my authority!"

"What do you think I am? Some yeye mercenary? Some beggar, blue-collar killer? Take time, my friend. I don't offer my class-one skills for small change."

Kolo could hardly believe the subject of this conversation. It felt dreamlike, conjured up by a playful sorcerer. "What about the other two?"

"They work for me."

"Christ help us. He's set up a business. Alright, how much are you asking?"

"Two hundred thousand dollars. Just a bit more than the others, for quick service."

Finally coming to his senses, Kolo exploded. "Are you out of your mind?"

"Probably. But those are my terms. Take or leave. If I protect Jegede, no other assassin will be able to kill him. I can smell killers." Lance fastened an eerie gaze on Kolo, one that told of his own death should he decline this offer.

"Okay. Two hundred. But I want him dead this Thursday evening."

"Fine. Do you have business card?"

"Why?"

"So I can put on body." The man laughed, gold fillings sparkling in the light of the chandeliers. Once he had kicked out the tail end of his titters, he resumed. "If you want the job done well-well . . . time."

"Your *client*?" Perhaps the garage air had created this hallucination. "What kind of time?"

"Three months."

"Again? Three more months?"

"Well," the man fiddled with the fringes on his shirt, "I had too many clients in the first three. Now I can devote time to you exclusively."

Promising himself to personally attend this man's execution once he had performed this one-minute task, Kolo offered 50 percent up front, the rest of the payment on delivery. "But," he added, "if I need quicker delivery, it's essential that I have access to immediate service. So, how can I get a message to you regarding that?"

Lance Omeke stared at the chandelier, pondering, tutting as he dismissed each new thought. Finally he murmured, "Client contact must be kept to a minimum. Wait-oh. I have an idea. Go through African Water Warriors. They have a contact for me."

By mid-December, Barbara had recovered. The pines and firs had finally come into their own, outlasting the cocksure folly of spring blossoms, the brazen dazzle of the summer's floral displays and the presumptuous pirouettes of autumn leaves. Now perennials stuck out like mere twigs, defiling the landscape with their nudity, while their seasonal gimmickry lay in brown tatters on the ground. In contrast, across the accepting boughs of evergreens lay a kaleidoscope of Christmas lights, strands of jewels winking at passersby. Huddled close to them, fat men in red suits marked the time of generosity and overdrafts, joy and disappointment, acceptance and rejection.

After a stroll through the winter streets, Barbara and Astro returned to the apartment. Astro creaked open his mailbox in the lobby and a card fell out onto the floor. He picked it up and passed it to Barbara. She recognized her mother's handwriting. Inside, a Christmas invitation.

She crumpled it up and threw it in the garbage.

"What's up, Babs?"

"My parents want me to come for dinner to celebrate the winter solstice."

"You gotta go, man." He picked the card out of the garbage and flattened it out. "They're your parents. They're trying to build bridges."

"No way. They're toxic." Barbara emphasized the last word. She had read many books on the subject. "I've had enough of their verbal and emotional abuse." She had also seen a therapist.

"You don't have to go alone, Bibble. I'll come with. If your sister is there, maybe you can get some info. Might help you with your other problems."

She clutched her breast, lanced by An Insight. As usual, Astro had found the key, a talent with which she had rarely credited him. She felt the euphoria of coming victory. "We can work as a team, but . . ."

Astro whipped around, holding on to an excited inhale.

"We won't tell them I went to hospital. Just feeling drained, okay? All they know is I took a few days off work because of fatigue. If they hear I went to hospital, they'd try and get me committed to a psych ward in DC. Believe me, Mary would stop at nothing. Now, the quickest way to get anything from my sister is to belittle her, or praise me, which is actually the same thing. We could strategize together–"

"Together? Strategize together? Me and you? Wow! You and your corporate-speak." A crooked smile of reverence rifled across Astro's delicate features. "Tell you what–I'll bring some smokes." He adjusted his Alice band. "That should calm us all down, man."

"Your ideas just get better and better." The look on her mother's face would be worth the trauma of a visit, as would her father's chest seizure. "Perhaps you could wear your dress while you're at it."

"Aw, I don't want to shock them, Bing. They seem a tad conservative."

"A 'tad'? Do you know how huge a tad can be?"

Astro planted hardier winter flowers on the roof of his Volvo and plugged in some twinkling Christmas lights. With almost two hours to spare, he ushered Barbara into the passenger seat and took off at a crawl, pulsing the accelerator as he drove. He insisted on total silence so he could concentrate.

He had spent a lot of time preparing for this meeting, assuming a more formal mien. He scraped his hair back into a tight bun and shaved the light stubble on his chin. He donned an orange tie, then wrapped himself in several layers of mismatched clothing, topping it with a powder pink hat with earflaps and a bobble. In solidarity, Barbara had matched her clothing to his, employing an array of items from the highest reaches of Tibet to the barest regions of the Sahara. Noting the severity of his coiffure, she had also swept her hair from her shoulders, rolling it in a French twist held, to some extent, by two chopsticks.

They pulled into the driveway fifteen minutes early. Barbara noticed that her parents had not had their windows cleaned. They must be feeling the pinch of the new water rates.

The front door opened, her father behind it holding a pan of roast potatoes and wearing a frilly apron. He stood at its threshold in an uncomfortable silence and scrutinized them both. "Well-well-well-well-well. Our terrorist seems to have lost weight." His oven mitts needed cleaning. "Ah–and who is this? I thought you were bringing a boyfriend."

Astro threw himself at Barbara's father and drew him into a deep embrace. "Hey, Dad. Great to meet you!" There were tears in his eyes.

Father's eyes popped out of his skull. "This is your boyfriend?" Trapped within Astro's clinch, the pan of potatoes forced Father into a posture of crucifixion. "This is a . . . Where's your mother? Catherine!"

Barbara's mother steered her square features to the front path, barging in front of Father to block any unwelcome visitors. "Barbara–what the hell are you wearing? Take those clothes off immediately!"

"Hey, Mom!" Astro threw himself at her boxy frame. "It's so great to meet you, man." His bottom lip trembled with emotion.

"What's this?" Mother, hands pinned to her sides, rolled her eyes towards Barbara.

"Astroturf." Barbara's eyes sparkled with pride. "My boyfriend."

Two pairs of eyes bulged with incomprehension. They glanced down at the creature's trousers for confirmation.

"Hey, Mom, Dad! Great place." Astro wiped his eyes. He walked into the house and placed his sandals neatly next to each other. As he bent down, Barbara noticed a tear in the thin fabric of his Middle Eastern pants, through which his gender could be clearly identified.

Mother stiffened. She had obviously seen the evidence too. "Dinner will be ready in approximately twenty minutes."

They entered the drawing room to find Mary standing by the

drinks cabinet, her stick frame thinner than usual. "Astro, this is my sister. Mary, this is Astro–my boyfriend."

"Your what?"

"Hey, Sis!" Astro smothered her in an earnest hug. "Great to finally meet you."

"Get it off me!" Mary yelled, backing towards the sitting room, her globe eyes bulging out, putting her on par with any nocturnal creature.

"Hey!" Astro put his arms around both sisters, creating a small huddle. He looked down at both of them. "C'mon now, guys. You're sisters! We're family."

Mary squirmed out of his arms, shuddering. "Don't you even think of touching me again or I'll call the police."

"Could someone turn the heating up, please?" Astro asked the curtains, yellow eyes enquiring under his pink cap flaps. "Bit chilly in here."

"Astro?" Barbara moved into the living room. "This is Grandma."

A tiny, innocent face looked up at them.

"Awesome. Hey, Granny!" He tickled her as if she were a small child. "How [poke] are [poke] things [poke] with [poke] you [poke]? I bet you could tell me all kinds of secrets about this family."

Grandma giggled. No one in the family paid this much attention to her. "I sure could, young lady. I sure could."

Barbara's family froze at -273°C–absolute zero, the freezing point of all liquids–their deeply hidden secrets rendering them glacial for the briefest of moments, glaring at Grandma, each pair of eyes holding different threats and entreaties. Barbara was the only family member who remained at room temperature.

Astroturf broke the spell. "Well," he said, looking around at his guests, "I'll light one up before lunch." He took his bong and a bag of marijuana out of a voluminous pocket. "Hey, Ern," he turned to Father, "care to join? Sis? You look like you could do with some. Gran?"

"We can only smoke outside, Miss Turf," said Grandma, levering herself out of her chair.

Mother's mouth hung open, mercury fillings reflecting the flashing colours of the Christmas tree lights.

"Drugs?" Father gasped. "Certainly not." Then, returning to his role as host, "Drink, Astro?"

In the dining room, each place setting was arranged with prickly attention to detail. The crystal glasses shot off sharp, disapproving glints; the silverware yawned with superiority. Although the candlesticks and vase of flowers framing the centre of the table initially appeared welcoming, once the guests sat down they loomed, obscuring the view.

Lying in the table's epicentre, the carcass of a turkey sat as a glorious centrepiece on a platter of sculpted silver. And, as a tribute to the magnificence of this kill, no vegetable, no starch or sauce shared this triumphant staging, save for some sprigs of parsley to underscore the bird's vast dimensions.

After pulling a firecracker which lay by his place setting, Astro excused himself and returned with a picnic basket. Following British tradition, he put on his paper hat with the rest of the family, and, against tradition, began to unload the basket.

"Oh, doesn't she look adorable with her hat on?" Grandma smiled in Astro's direction.

"She sure does," Mary murmured.

Barbara shot a look at Mary. She felt like stapling the paper hat to Mary's head.

"What have you got there?" Mother asked, confusion clouding features that otherwise questioned very little in life.

"I've brought our dinner, Mom," Astro replied, laying out buttermilk curd, tabbouleh salad and unleavened flatbreads from Ethiopia. "As you know, Babs and I are 'vegetarian.'" He enunciated clearly as he quote-marked the air. "That means we don't eat meat." He looked at her to see if she had understood.

Blood collected around Mother's multiple chins as gunpowder grey eyes stared at him, unblinking.

Dissatisfied with her response, he continued. "That means we don't eat turkey," he pointed at the bird lying on the side table, legs akimbo, "which is what you have sitting there. A turkey." He checked her again for signs of comprehension. She blinked. Now satisfied, he forged ahead. "Don't worry, though. I've brought enough for all of us." He placed some sprouted moong dal salad on the table.

As Father carved and placed body parts on plates, Astro served fufu from West Africa, okra and dishes made from pungent unripened cheese. Before Father could offer his guests red wine, Astro topped up their glasses with boza–a drink of fermented millet.

The rest of the Glass family looked at their plates as if dead rats lay upon them. Sifting through the vegetarian fare, they picked at their turkey. Only Grandma, her olfactory senses severely dulled by age, tucked in with pleasure.

"How are you doing, hun?" Grandma looked at Barbara with concern.

"She's doing fine, thanks," Astro replied, still exercising authority over his ward.

"You still feeling a bit down?" Gran asked, glancing from Barbara to Astro and back again, unsure as to whom this query should be addressed.

"She's getting stronger every day," Astro replied.

"Walking should do the trick." Grandma now looked directly at Astro for all matters concerning Barbara's welfare.

"Don't worry. I've got that covered." Astro flicked his serviette open with self-assurance. "We're on a programme. A structured programme."

"Oh!" Grandma seemed impressed.

"So," Father turned to Astro and commenced the interrogation, "what do you do?"

"I work with plants, Dad," said Astro. "I can see that someone here works with them too!" Mother flushed with pride, then stiffened back into disapproval.

"So, you're a gardener?" Father continued.

"No, I work with plants, Ern."

A note of bafflement. "And where do you live?"

"Just outside DC, Earl." Astro's paper hat quivered as he spoke. "Babu and I met in the same yoga class."

"Really? Well, you must be very flexible, then."

"Sure am, Ed."

"That must come in handy." Father took a loud gulp of his wine.

"Sure does. Barbara can be quite demanding, despite her age."

Father almost spilled his wine. He cleared his throat. Mother actually stopped eating.

"You ever tried yoga, Millie?" Astro turned to face Mary. "You should. You'd really get a kick out of it. Loosen you up a bit." He reached over and ruffled her hair. "I say that with all due respect there, Sis."

Mary sat stupefied, not knowing what to do now that her perfect bob was in utter disarray. Barbara closed her eyes, thanking the universe for the great joy that had descended upon her.

"Dad," Mary stared at her father through the mess of bangs that stuck into her eyes, "why don't you tell Barbara about your heart?" She emphasized the last two words, prompting her father.

"Oh, uh, yes, Barbara," Father replied, sucking on a bone. "I've seen a doctor recently."

"Really?" Barbara munched her kale. "Dad, could you please stop snarfling? So, what did the doctor say?"

"Barbie," Mother put down her fork for a microsecond, "your father is in very poor health. You've caused us a great deal of worry."

Astro stared at Mother, yellow eyes burning with query. "Is that why you didn't phone Babu for so long?" he asked. "Aw, I see it all now, man." He turned to Barbara. "I knew they couldn't be that heartless."

Mother fired off a look of buckshot grey in Astro's direction. "The doctor says he may not have much longer. We know how much your job means to you, but he needs you here."

Barbara almost dropped her kamut bread. "Dad!" she gasped. "What is it? Is it diabetes? Your liver? Cirrhosis?"

"What? How dare you! Certainly not!" He thundered, placing his wineglass back down on the table. "It's the old ticker." He placed his hand over his right lung, looking frail. "It could go any day now."

"Really?" Grandma butted in. "You didn't tell me–"

"We haven't wanted to worry you," Mary intervened, patting her grandmother's hand with her consoling spindles.

"Sorry, E." Astro spoke up with some authority–the authority of a near paramedic. "Babs has been pretty worn out herself. She's under my care. What's this?" He pointed both index fingers at his face. "This is where the buck stops. And this here isn't planning to let her down." Yellow eyes looked around the table with autocratic command. "Meanwhile, perhaps Marnie can help you out."

"Mary?" Father yelled. "Absolutely not! She's working!"

"Well, I'm sure they'll let her take a few months off whatever it is she does, right, Millie?" Astro spread some baba ghanouj over a kelp cracker and handed it to Barbara.

"My name's Mary," her lips tightened, disappearing altogether, "and I'm Associate Director of Acquisitions–"

Astro pointed a finger gun at her. "Middle management, right? I could tell. You know how?" He leaned forward. "The longer the title, the less important someone is. As you get higher up, the titles get shorter, till you get to one word–'president'–or just letters–'CEO.' " Think about it, man!"

"How dare you!" Mary detonated.

"You'll be able to get someone to cover for you. Piece of cake." Astro reached for his glass and held the boza to the light of the chandelier. "I'd like to propose a toast."

Father gulped back the last dregs of his wine and refilled his glass. Mother curled her fat paws around the delicate crystal, sniffing the boza within. Mary sat, arms crossed. Grandma smiled, waiting for Astro's pronouncement.

"I don't know if you guys are aware," Astro began, "but we've got a VIP among us."

Grandma gasped. "Really? Who?"

Astro turned to beam at Barbara, suffused with admiration. "Someone we all know as Barbara Glass, the woman who has pretty much brought an evil regime to its knees!" A tear escaped. "Her name'll be in the history books. Guaranteed."

"Barbie?" Father's body perked up a bit. "History books? How?" His eyebrows shot up in an admiring query, eyes fixed with blurry pride on Barbara as he sipped his wine.

"History books?" Mary interrupted. "You must be joking! This brain-on-a-budget? She doesn't even know she didn't organize a bombing!"

"Right now, Molly, is not the best time to depress her!" Lips rigid with disapproval, Astro discharged his sternest look.

"Femi Jegede," Mary turned to Barbara, "wasn't involved in the killings, you imbecile."

"Not involved?" Barbara choked on her boza. "You mean . . . ?"

Again Astro intervened: he catapulted another look of fierce censure at Mary, then returned his attention to Barbara. "I'm really sorry, Bang-Bang." Astro dabbed at her mouth with gentle solicitude. "No one likes failure, but it's part of life. Accept it."

"Failure?" Barbara announced gustily. "Not on my watch!"

Astro gazed at her again in adulation. "I've seen a big change in her since she came back. She sat next to chimpanzees on the bus and everything. They get to go half-price as they don't share one hundred percent of human DNA."

"I didn't know chimps roamed free like that," said Father, layering more turnips on top of his forkful of turkey mammary and potatoes.

With this last exchange goading her past discretion, Mary snapped. "Chimpanzees don't ride on buses! Is this what she's told you? How gullible can you get?" She pushed her elbows into the cutlery on either side of her, leaning towards Barbara. "Since you don't know, Barbara, it wasn't Wise Water, it was the African Water Warriors."

Barbara appeared flustered. "The AWW? No way! But I only sent them a handful of explosives. Who would have guessed?"

"Pardon?" Mary cackled. "You did what? Can you even spell their name? Get the address right?"

"Do I detect some jealousy? ''Tis the green-eyed monster that doth mock the beef it feeds on.' Dante. *Paradise Lost.* Well worth a read."

"I didn't know Shakespeare was such a plagiarist." Mary tittered again and leaned even farther forward. "Guess who does know their address." She dabbed her slit mouth with a starched serviette.

Outwardly oblivious, Barbara countered, "Just because a snake has scales doesn't mean it can play music."

"Barbara," Mother said, "could you stop citing those annoying little proverbs, please? You're no longer in Africa."

Mary squeezed out a smile. "Yeah, well, Barbie, I think you'll find this snake did just that. You couldn't fund a deal like that with your pocket change!"

Barbara now leaned towards Mary, her cleavage bunching up just below her neck. "No, you're right. I couldn't. But does TransAqua know you could?" She tilted her head.

Mary's mouth slotted open, her eyes filled with terror as she finally realized the imprudence of her disclosure.

This tiny morsel of information would save Femi's life, shifting blame for the bombing away from Wise Water and towards the genuine terrorists, the AWW. Barbara glanced at her accomplice, Astro, proud that their joint efforts had pushed Mary to the point of such a damning revelation. Astro's lips crunched into an admiring smile, his eyes glazed with tears of pride.

Barbara's parents' eyes, meanwhile, also gleamed with tears, but these appeared much more bountiful, plumper and of greater weight–plus they were accompanied by the sound of wailing.

TWENTY-SEVEN

Unnecessary Details

Now aware of the depths of TransAqua's involvement in the massacre of their own staff, Barbara returned to Drop of Life. She wrote Jane a note in her most florid prose, guided by Astro's near-legal linguistic abilities.

> I am deeply honoured by your gracious invitation to continue my humble contribution to the struggle to bring to book those invested in the unutterable devastation inflicted on the Nigerian peoples. To this end, I wish to bestow on your august presence recently acquired information that proves beyond any legal doubt that Wise Water, Nigeria, Inc., bears no responsibility for the heretofore antecedently abovementioned calamity, for which new information I beg an audience.

"That'll work," said Astro.

"Gotta figure out a way not to get Mary into too much trouble, though."

"Wanna protect a mass murderer, huh? P'raps you need some more downtime, Bibby." He looped a scarf around her neck, placed his hat on her head and tied the earflaps down, knotting the string underneath her chin. She stepped into the lavender moon boots he held for her, although he had bundled her up so well she could not see them so she felt her way, following his instructions.

He put the cat in a crate and handed it to Barbara. Then he picked up an assortment of plastic bags full of his clothes, and the giant suitcase that held Barbara's. He ushered out both of the creatures in his custody, and all three made their way to Ronald Reagan International Airport.

They got out their passports, boarding cards and the cat's vaccination certificates, and made their way through the security checkpoint. As they approached, Astro froze in panic.

"What's the matter?" Barbara asked.

"Oh, man!" Astro looked around for an escape route. "I don't have the cat's passport. We'll be caught!"

Barbara tutted. "Astro," she huffed. "Don't be ridiculous. Just tell them you forgot it. I'm sure they'll understand."

The officer beckoned them over. Barbara dragged Astro up to the counter. Astro's trembling hand aligned two passports to a neat edge on the officer's desk.

The officer flicked through the cat's vaccination certificates. "Cat, please."

Astro nervously raised the crate. The cat crawled to the back of it. "He's real scared of uniforms," Astro clarified. "Not that he's carrying. He's clean. He doesn't even like catnip."

"He? It says on this paper the cat's female."

"Uh . . ." Astro's voice wobbled with uncertainty. "Well, it used to be. But we had her–you know–done. So now," he glanced at Barbara for confirmation, "she's male."

"She prefers," Barbara announced at some volume, "not to be confined within the gender roles that patriarchal hegemony has so narrowly constructed." She looked around at other passengers for support.

The officer grabbed Barbara's passport. "Name, please."

"Her name's Barbara," Astro replied, still operating as her trusted guardian, "but her friends call her Barbie." He put his arm around her as a protective gesture.

"No, they don't!" Barbara protested.

"Yes, Barbie," Astro looked at her as if her name had been wiped from her memory, "they do. She's pretty ill," he informed the officer with a sigh. "Some days she remembers. Some days . . ." He shook his head in pity. A chopstick fell out of his hair. "Well, you can see for yourself, right, bud?" He hugged Barbara closer to him.

The officer looked from one to the other.

"By the way," Astro leaned forward in a confidential whisper as he picked up the chopstick, "I forgot the cat's passport."

The officer gave him a strange look, his stamp hovering.

Barbara stared at him with all the innocence she could muster.

Shaking his head, the officer stamped their boarding cards and waved them through.

"Hey! Thanks, man." Astro pointed a finger gun at the officer. "Much appreciated." He cocked the finger gun and made a clicking sound. "You guys are awesome."

They landed in a February snowstorm and slipped their way across Ottawa's snowy pavements, making tracks quickly erased by the snow. The icy wind froze the hair in their nostrils, the cold air making them feel light-headed.

Every moment the landscape changed as more snowflakes floated to earth, distinctive as fingerprints–millions upon millions of fingerprints under their feet as they trod. All around them it lay, water in all its forms. At its coldest, it could crush the hardest rock, yet at its warmest it disappeared altogether. They trudged to a taxi rank.

After they entered the cluttered shrine of Barbara's apartment, they released the cat, which took off on a tour of the premises. Astro unpacked his plastic bags and laid his clothes out in neat geometric piles. Barbara lobbed the clothes from her suitcase onto the floor, grew bored and wandered off to fling herself onto the sofa.

Once he had put the bedroom in order, Astro marched into the kitchen to make dinner and afterwards cleared the plates from the table, tidied up the front room, made some hot goat's milk and settled down with Barbara in front of the fire.

After a while, he poked his head above a horticultural magazine. "What's up, Babs? Something wrong?" He turned a corner of the page to mark it and placed it on top of a pile of her papers, books and tarot cards.

She was struggling with a realization. "What am I doing here? I have no real evidence to present to Drop of Life. I can't quote what some emaciated mass murderer told me at a family dinner!"

Astro looked at his ward with the concern of a camp counsellor. "Calm down now, Skippy. Let's not get excited."

Barbara thanked Parent Nature that Astro did not wear half-moon glasses, or he would be peering over them at her as he spoke. "Astro, TransAqua owns Nigeria's water, not just the rights. If you want to put your toe in a puddle, you have to get permission. You can't even collect rainwater in buckets because it's seen as undue competition. In this scenario, how exactly am I not supposed to get excited?"

"What's this, Babu?" He pointed to his face with both index fingers.

"Dunno." she huffed. "Improv?"

"No, it's a guy who's concerned about the rights of puddles, just like you."

She sighed. "So?"

"Just be logical. It's in Drop of Life's interest to help you, right? Plus, it helps them fire you. Win-win for them." He patted her on the head.

"Their mouths move when they read! They're not interested in information."

"Well, if that's the case, what do they do? What do they specialize in, Bibble?"

There was little she found more annoying than Astro's obsession with the unnecessary details of life.

"Who knows?" she exploded. "Look, could you stay on topic, Astro? I'm stuck. I need help here."

He picked up his horticultural magazine and unfolded the page corner, another habit that annoyed her greatly. "Details matter. Find out what each person does. Stop trying to do everything on your own, Bee. You're not that tough, remember." He licked his finger and turned the page.

She had few other options open to her, so she wrote down in her curly handwriting "Find out what D of L do." Then she ticked the item. The tail end of the tick ran off the edge of the page.

Barbara was left to fume by the fire, pondering their relationship. Astro, doling out snippets of wisdom for her benefit, represented the locus of oppression: he the patriarch with the soft brown bedroom slippers, she the deferential and submissive wife figure. Astro put down the magazine to adjust the cushions behind Barbara's back. *Yes,* she thought as she leaned forward, *patriarchal hegemony has had a deleterious effect.*

The doorbell rang. "I'll get it," Barbara said and marched downstairs. Behind the splintered transparencies of her frosted porch windows, she saw the fragmented image of a gummy smile.

"Hey, Barbie!" Krystal waved.

Barbara frowned and opened the door. She had been unable to set boundaries with Gums on the "Barbie" issue, despite the assistance of her bungling therapist. If she did not put a stop to this, soon Gums would be calling her "Bar."

"My name's Barbara." With the temperature down to -10°F, Barbara could see her breath as she spoke. "Can you hear that last syllable? Let me pronounce it for you again. Ra. That's Barbara. Not Barbie. Barbie is a doll. Though I have many doll-like qualities, I am not a toy. C'mon in."

"Sorry. Barb'ra. How'r'ya doin'?"

Barbara wondered why Krystal's lips had not frozen onto her gums.

"Terrible. Great. I'm bipolar. I never know."

"Oh." Gums seemed unsure of how to construct a response that did not include the word "awesome." "Well, I have some awesome news for you."

Barbara vowed never to underestimate the resourcefulness of this woman.

"We followed that piece of paper you told us to–from prose to poetry? The prose is that TransAqua plans to charge for access to water at all levels–shipping, fishing, drinking, everything."

"You're kidding!"

"And their proposed fee structure for fresh water is astronomical. It's incredible, Bar! TransAqua is changing the name of the Niger River to the Kolo River."

Had Gums said "Bar"? She replayed the words, editing out their chirpy tone. As Barbara neared the end of her review, the impact of Gums' findings hit her. "You've got the TransAqua contract? They're changing the name of the river? Well, we'd better send the news off to Aminah, pronto!" She clapped her hands.

"Yes, I've done . . ."

While Gums continued her monologue, Barbara recalculated. Through information, rather than violent uprising, they could bring the regime to its knees. Femi should have paid more attention to her in the first place. Men, she thought–their problem is they never listen.

The next day, Barbara prepared to meet the ancient effigy again, but she still had no plan. Stalling by her front door, she squinted at the porch windows, trying to make out the hidden worlds drawn by the frost. A memory popped into her mind of her family frozen for a moment, of pleading eyes. The images revealed by the deceptive frost, evanescent and changing, appeared to be carved into the glass, the ephemeral masking as permanent. This fraud possessed promise. Language could easily perform the same function.

Barbara wrapped herself up in her Mongolian coat for the winter trek to the office, adding her balaclava for greater warmth, glad that it had finally come in handy. Pink mukluks helped her grip the icy pavement as she bundled out the door to work. Barbara's footsteps, the sound that heralded her passage through the world, were now silenced to a mere whisper. She strode past skaters opting to remain outdoors in sub-zero temperatures on the Rideau Canal.

"It's the only world they know," she sighed, forgetting the three other seasons she had already encountered in Ottawa. "I expect they have developed an extra layer of blubber to cope." Some Canadians of Somalian heritage skated past, oblivious to their contribution to the flaws in her theory. Meanwhile those of Chinese origin she placed as Inuit. "They must feel quite hot down here," she thought. "Probably like summer to them."

On entering Drop of Life, Barbara hooked her cloak on top of Brad's grey overcoat and marched upstairs, past an abstract Indian tapestry of a waterfall in blues, turquoise and royal purple. As she looked at it, a tremendous calm overcame her. She examined the intricate stitching and the haphazard materials that had been woven into the fabric–beads, mirrors, glass. Underneath, the title: *See the Bigger Picture.*

She stood before it, transfixed. Something within the image reminded her of her own life: haphazard, chaotic, seemingly irrational. What would emerge when this scatter was put together? What was her bigger picture?

And then the answer came. She had one quality above all: energy. She did not wear away hard rocks with soft water. No, she smashed into them and destroyed them. She was the waterfall. She represented not so much the flow of the universe as its rush, its force, its urgency. This must have been what Femi had seen in her on their first meeting, what her parents had never seen and what Mary must have always suspected.

She marched upstairs to Brad's office, intent on using her prodigious energy, and found him hunched over some papers.

"Top of the mornin' to ye," she said in her best Irish accent, then a dramatic pause for the punchline, "and the rest of the day to meself." She guffawed at her own joke.

Brad shot up and offered her a chair, his bland expression overlaid with–Barbara squinted to distinguish the emotion–yes, it seemed like excitement. She docked her body into the seat's berth.

" . . . followed . . . accounts . . . found shares . . ."

"Pardon?" Barbara forced herself to focus.

"Kolo bought TransAqua shares before he arranged to sell the company the water rights."

"Ah, now that's interesting." Barbara lounged back in the chair, interlaced her fingers and looked at the ceiling. "Very, very interesting . . ." Brad's logic made no sense to her. "By the way, Brad, what's the problem with Kolo buying TransAqua shares before the water sale?"

Only the greatest detective would have noticed the change in Brad's features from excitement to shock. "It's illegal!" Even when immersed in such a powerful emotion, his voice hardly carried. "It's insider trading! Bad PR for TransAqua." He would most definitely benefit from stage training of some sort, Barbara thought, and vowed to mention it to him at some juncture.

"But there can't be anything wrong with that. My father used to do it all the time."

"Yes, but it's highly illegal. And there's an issue of scale here. The number of shares Kolo bought clearly distinguishes the transaction as unethical and illegal. It's in the millions of dollars."

"Ah–I understand. Why didn't you say so? You must realize, Brad, I'm an information junkie. I need details, facts, data."

He waved an index finger above the numbers, not daring to touch them, as if they might pollute him. "Well, there's also clear evidence of bribery–"

Barbara gazed at an army of figures laid out in confrontational columns and rows. "I am inductive rather than deductive."

"–at all levels of government."

"According to Jung's categorization, I am sensing rather than intuitive–"

Brad's dry fingernail traced a line down a column of numbers. "There's evidence of financial mismanagement at the World Bank."

"–which is probably why we have so little in common." Once again, she attempted to reinforce the deeper significance of her words, but he seemed quite literal-minded. A touch of Asperger's?

"In *toto,* approximately 30 percent of funds have been siphoned off."

She slouched in his chair. "I don't really understand a word of what you've just said, Brad."

"It's bad, Barb."

She perked up. "Why didn't you say? We'd better send these off to Aminah!"

"Yes, I've already done–"

"Good work, Brad." Barbara lay back, focused again on the ceiling and crossed her arms in contemplation. This new strategy of hers had taken less than a year to bear fruit. How ironic! But something still niggled. "I don't understand–how did you do all this?"

Brad mumbled a few words that floated off to the vast space in the ether where all unimportant speech lodges.

"Pardon?"

"Well, for example, I'm a forensic accountant–"

"You're in forensics?"

"No, no, no!" He uttered a nasal bleat that Barbara deduced was a laugh. " . . . forensic *accountant* . . . look for financial irregularities . . ."

She found it hard to concentrate on each word, so his conversation came to her in waves.

"And Krystal . . . retrieve information from any computer system . . . world."

"She's a hacker?"

"Oh, no, no, no!" More bleats from his nasal passages. "Well . . . yes, but she's highly skilled." The last two words did not emanate from the back of the throat, as is their usual provenance, but rather from the upper reaches of the nasal cavity.

"And Mimi?" Barbara picked up Brad's stapler, remembering that she needed one.

"She's, well . . . can secure confidential information from corporations . . ."

"An industrial spy?" Barbara yelped. She imagined Mimi acquiring information in tanning salons around the world, offering a peeling cleavage as enticement.

"No, no, no." Brad peeped outside his office. "Well . . . yes, but we call it corporate liaison."

Barbara could only guess what covert role the ancient effigy played, with her unmoving, tree bark face. "What about Jane?"

"She, uh, well, I guess she distributes information. Her contacts are unrivalled."

"Contacts?" Barbara imagined a jewel-encrusted black book, locked within a bank vault. "I see." Barbara stapled into thin air, the staples flicking onto Brad's desk with little ticking sounds. "So, once we get the information, she makes sure it goes public, right?"

" . . . ight."

Barbara turned Brad's lamp off to prevent glare and adjusted the chair to a lounging position. She lay back and digested the new information, as Brad hovered at her side. She remembered the hand in the mud, its desperate signal to all who went past. She felt that somehow she was answering its call.

When she emerged from her meditations, Brad had disappeared. She double-checked the room. Yes, he had definitely disappeared.

With so much to do, she grabbed Brad's stapler and sailed up to her office.

Priming herself to phone Femi, Barbara anticipated the venom he would spit at her. She gazed at the clock, queasy with trepidation, urging herself to face his loathing. After all, she only had to survive for maybe ten minutes. She picked up the receiver gingerly, as if it were already infected with his hate.

"Femi, my friend!" A slight Nigerian twang crept into her voice. "And?"

The voice sounded tired. "Barbara. Long time. Worraps?"

"I have body." Unaware of her mismanagement of Nigerian dictum, she continued. "And your own?"

"I have my own body too."

She heard giggling in the background.

"But I was planning to lease it," Femi continued.

"Lease your body? You need money?"

"For the body I occupy? Yes. It needs water and water is so expensive, we can barely afford to drink. I think TransAqua is considering charging dogs for drinking from puddles."

"Well, we're here to protect those puddles," Barbara replied with some self-importance.

"But if you can't, the dogs will have to deal with the militias in control of the illegal supply, just like us."

The fact that he had not slammed down the phone gave her more confidence. She rushed on in a gust of enthusiasm. "I have it from a very reliable but dangerous source at TransAqua that someone hired the African Water Warriors to do the bombing."

"What? Why?"

"To discredit you."

"They'd kill their own people for that?"

"They'd kill for much less-oh! Drop of Life will get this information out. But you can also help yourself. I have a new plan."

"Oh no." Femi sighed.

"Not sabotage." She cleared her throat, leaving a dramatic pause. "As a Taoist, I have always said, the man who throws shit–will his own hands not be dirty?"

She heard a groan over the line–perhaps a sufferer remembering the past, the good times. With a hand on her chest, she attempted to hold back her emotions. "You remember the chief we met? The one with the incredible aura?"

"You mean the one whose aura you noticed only when you were told he was a chief?" His antidepressants had obviously worked. "You mean that chief?" Barbara mentally noted to send a lower dosage next time.

"He knew something about Kolo's past. Could you get it out of him?"

"You'll just cause more wahala. It can't be corroborated."

"Neither was the bombing. Rumour is more powerful than truth. Kolo can be whispered off his throne."

"Now I understand!" Femi exclaimed, as if stumbling out of a dream. "So that's what he meant. You can't prove a negative!" His words threw her into confusion. "I can see you're now a proper Naija woman! Okay–later!"

"Later. By the way," she added, "remember me to the chief."

She could hear Femi breathing, so she knew he was still on the line, but she did not hear a response.

"Femi? Did you hear me?"

After a moment, the line went dead.

Strange, she thought. *The connection to Nigeria is so erratic.*

Barbara had sewn herself harem pants for winter. Unfortunately, the thick yellow tweed selected for its warmth also added volume to gathers that should have draped downwards. She looked like a balloon whose only countervailing effect was the balloon on her head–a turban in light blue she had made from sheets. A turban, she felt, would identify their group for generations to come, much like Che Guevara's beret. She still awaited the swaths of authentic indigo ordered from a Nigerian wholesaler on the Internet with her credit card.

She walked into the boardroom, the fabric around her thighs creating a swishing sound, her Black Power pendant rattling against two Celtic necklaces and a brooch in the form of a Nigerian flag. As she entered, she bowed a Namaste to all and sat down, her harem pants puffing up around her waist.

Krystal gummed a smile that glistened with encouragement.

The ancient monument was shrouded in a sari of light cerulean blue and a veil of moon white. "Welcome back."

"Thanks." Barbara closed one eye, picturing the tree bark in an indigo turban. The turban would work. She must be a winter. "I think I can get Nigeria sorted out now."

The crimson dot on Jane's forehead moved as an expression fought through its wrinkles and crevices. "This has been disastrous for us."

"Disastrous for *you*? You sit here like colonial masters telling Nigerians how to become effective activists, yet you know nothing about us!"

"The sun and moon don't orbit around you, hon," said Mimi, her tanned breasts peeling. "Galileo proved that."

Gums cut in, troubled by conflict. "Oh, Barbie, you've got so much energy and confidence . . ."

Barbara mentally converted from Canadian to American. Rough translation: *you're arrogant.*

" . . . but this is a real challenge for us."

. . . *entirely unacceptable.*

"The internal audit . . ." Brad began, his voice carried away in trebles off the vocal register.

Barbara raised an admonitory hand. "Wise Water did not plant the bomb." At the collective gasp, Barbara leaned back, placing an arm on the back of Brad's chair, her breasts distorting the flowers on her shirt so they looked like coloured sausages. "It was the African Water Warriors, funded by . . ." for some reason, she continued to protect her sister, " . . . corporate interests."

"How do you know this?"

"I have managed to secure an informant at the highest level at TransAqua."

Jane did not seem convinced. "So what exactly is your strategy?"

Brad uncharacteristically interrupted. "Easy. I'll follow the financial trail, Krystal can access the electronic data–"

"No!" Barbara fairly jumped. "We don't have that kind of time. Femi's life is hanging by a thread. Just find out where AWW got their explosives from, how they planned the bombing. We've got no need to trace further back."

Jane stirred again. "How do we do this?"

"You! No one else can do it. You know people in the right quarters. Maybe contact NGOs who'll know local arms dealers and we can work back from there."

The Easter Island effigy nodded assent. "Anything else?"

Barbara got up and went to the white board, where she listed their successes. "So we know–thanks to Brad–that Kolo has been involved in insider trading, the World Bank is mixed up in illicit practices, and there is corruption at all levels of government. Three points so far. From Krystal we've learned that TransAqua plans to push up fresh water prices, ban all collection of water, effectively own all water supply in the West through rights and licences. And rename the Niger River as a favour to Kolo. There we have four more points." She excluded Mimi from all congratulations.

"Jane, we need your jewel-encrusted black book. After publicizing information about the AWW bombing, we'll need to release these other reports in stages, rather than all at once.

We're up against formidable enemies, so we'll need a continuous battery of intelligence."

Wrinkles plummeted over her boss's eyes, implying strong consent.

"We have to think like journalists and, more importantly, like Nigerians." Barbara flicked through her book until she located Astro's notes. "We can use something much more subtle than sabotage. Just words. Whisperings, even. Something that floats through the air, so gentle, so delicate, is still strong enough to bring a government down. Now, Femi is getting a critical piece of information regarding a hidden event in Kolo's past that could spell the end of his presidency." She turned to Mimi. "However, there's one last job we need done to tie this up. Could you infiltrate TransAqua and find out what they're up to? My sister heads up the bid for Kainji."

There was a collective gasp.

"Your sister?" Mimi almost dislodged her contacts.

"You won't get any information from her, but she has a rival there–John Sinclair."

"Sure, hon. No problem."

Barbara mirrored Mimi. "Thanks, sweetie." Then she sailed out of the conference room, despite her balloon trousers' aerodynamic resistance to such a movement.

TWENTY-EIGHT

Loose Lips

As Barbara's need for action peaked, her brain became increasingly addled–she did not know what item of business to focus on next. Mimi had not called for a month, so Barbara presumed she had taken the opportunity to sneak off to a sweat lodge or rebirthing ceremony.

Then the phone rang.

"Hiya, hon."

Barbara recognized Mimi's singsong, baby-girl tones. "Hey, Mimi." Barbara turned on the lamp she had taken from Mimi's desk. "Any news?"

"I've spoken to someone called Janet, your sister's assistant. Do you know her?"

"Nope." Barbara moved Mimi's former lamp closer to Mimi's former corkboard.

"She had an affair with Sinclair, but it didn't work out. She says he's crap in bed, and insisted on smearing blancmange all over her. She can't face mousse-like desserts anymore."

"Really? Well, tell her to try Tantric Sexperience in Arizona. They have some passable masturbation workshops–"

"Look, hon, these people have enough money to pay for someone to do it for them." Mimi sounded almost jealous. "You're not going to believe this, but Kolo himself was behind the deaths of Abucha and his other allies. Guess why."

"I don't see how a workshop can hurt."

Mimi continued, undaunted. "This is how it works: Sinclair mentions in their regular meetings that he has a rival bid for Kainji. Mary gives Kolo the name of Sinclair's contact. Then Kolo gets rid of him."

"What do you mean by 'gets rid of'?"

"Assassinates."

Barbara flicked open her notebook to write down the details. Her purple pen hovered over the paper. She realized she had nothing to write.

"Mimi, sugar, do you have any data? Names, dates, etcetera."

"No. Only General Abucha. Janet was too drunk to provide details."

Barbara wrote down "Janet–drunk–no details."

"But I do know Sinclair's next victim is the minister for the environment. If he goes down, then you'll know I'm right."

"Great!" Barbara wrote this down, her head wiggling with assurance. "I'll get Jane onto it. Awesome work, hon."

"No problem, sweetie." Mimi actually sounded like she was enjoying herself. "I've met Sinclair briefly, and my God, he's an absolute dreambo–"

Barbara slammed the phone down, unscrewed the fire alarm and lit some incense on her shrine. She visualized her sister's downfall: the headlines, Mary's disgrace, her parents' humiliation and the neighbours' shock.

Her sense of triumph was both fleeting and faint, soon replaced by unaccustomed anxiety for her sister. She tried to concentrate on her conquest, meditating on a vision of scales seesawing to a new position. The image vanished, supplanted by an image of Mary's spindles reaching out of a clay tomb. Why was she involved in such a desperate game? In the face of her sister's potential annihilation, Barbara doubted whether she could continue their rivalry with the same grim resolve. It seemed odd that such a transition should occur, but when she thought back, she could easily pinpoint the occasion of the shift: the moment she spotted the hand in the mud, beckoning change, bidding farewell to unimportant things.

A warm tingling spread through her body as she pictured the smile on Femi's melancholy face and the pride on Aminah's. So she chanted for the Nigerian people, for fresh water and for the safety of her friends.

New Age music floated over the sound of waves crashing and seagulls calling to each other, while Tibetan monks chanted an endless "ohhmm."

She heard a bang on the wall.

Doubtless someone hanging a wall chart.

The winds began to blow–wild, gusting storms bringing with them the fine powders of the desert. Harmattan had enveloped Nigeria, sweeping over every surface, snaking into each hidden corner of life, curling into every crevice. Dust crept over tables and under sheets, immune to any degree of vigilance against its incursion. As far south as Lagos, sand drew across luminous skies and wrapped them in a brown haze. It dried people's skin into scales and whipped into eyes, making them itchy and sore. Even those with the thickest eyelashes blinked their way through the season.

Despite the fact that pilots had no ground vision and airports lacked radar, Femi flew from Lagos to Jebba on Onada Airlines. It operated in any weather, as the company paid its pilots per flight. He met Aminah in the airport at Jebba, having no trouble spotting her since she wore a wrapper of unbridled patterning inspired by the full range of colours of the known spectrum, and above this a voluminous buba that exploited an infinite number of dyes to excite the farthest observer. Neither skirt nor blouse could hide her excessive curves. Her headdress had been starched and tied into a structure that any builder could only admire.

"My friend!" she yelled at the top of her voice, obliterating the announcements over the PA system. "Here I am!"

"Make I see," he boomed back. "So–you have body, as Barbara says."

Aminah threw her head back and screeched. Within moments, the sound destabilized into a violent wobble that Femi knew heralded the onset of riotous laughter. Though no one turned to face her, she was a pre-eminent artist in this arena–with spectrum, innovation and diapason unmatched by any other–and, like his fellow countrymen, he could only listen in awe. As always, attracting maximum attention served as their most efficient camouflage, as Jegede the legend was rumoured to hide in shadows.

Once she had reached his side, Aminah whispered, "So, who bombed the bus?"

Images of bloodied bodies arcing through the air bombarded Femi's thoughts. "We think it was the African Water Warriors, but we have no proof. Igwe suspects a virus within. Most of us think that crazy white woman and her gunpowder goddess self organized something. Who knows?"

"Barbara Glass? She was the first one I considered. I was shattered by the thought."

They snickered.

"And yet she sounded so upset, talking about the losses suffered by 'we Nigerians.'"

"Hmm." She raised her eyebrows well into her headwrap. "Well, at least TransAqua's business is suffering."

"Why did they think they could do business in Nigeria? Which person did they think would collect their money for them and then, like an idiot, hand it over? Are they mad?"

They both shook their heads, mystified.

It took a day to reach the village that sheltered the woman who knew too much about Kolo's past. The air still bore a mild, uneasy tang. The thatch on some of the huts had blown away; their mud walls had cracked. The village seemed to be entirely deserted. There was only a haunted silence, broken by tiny sounds like lizards tickling across the sands.

Skinny chickens pecked at the grain that had fallen at the entrance to the village granary. Femi approached it, conscious of a rustling sound within–maybe a child hiding. He rose up on the balls of his feet to peek over its threshold, then screamed. The granary was teeming with rats, four or five deep, fighting for the remaining kernels.

Aminah stood with her hands on her vast hips, staring at a dead dog. "Water sickness," she said.

Femi looked around for the ancient vendor. His stall still stood at the village entrance, but there was no trace of him.

In shock, they headed for the chief's lodgings, Femi scolding himself for not coming sooner to talk to him about Kolo. "With all this death," he said, "who knows if Kolo's nanny will be alive? And if she is, will she able to talk?"

"Everyone is able to talk, although sometimes in silence, sometimes in screams."

They entered the low concrete building where the chief had held his audience, and took off their shoes.

The chief, thin and bedraggled, sat on his chair, a few remaining retainers by his side. He had shrunk to almost half his size, so the skin hung tight to his bones. He seemed close to death. Femi and Aminah prostrated themselves before him, but he continued to stare into the middle distance. Femi wondered if the chief had lost his memory–or his mind.

Then a retainer whispered into the chief's ear, and the old man broke out in a smile, the skin tightening over his bones. "Ah! Femi Jegede!" The chief continued to look past Femi to the other end of the room. "You have returned! I greet you!"

The chief held out his hand. An aide beckoned to Femi, who approached the dais. As the chief grasped Femi's hand, with a warm smile still playing on his lips, Femi realized the man was blind, ravaged by the diseases carried by infected waters.

"Sir," Femi said, "I'm so sorry to see you in poor health."

"Enh, well," the chief replied, "we all have to go sometime. No man can argue with death, so no point causing wahala when it arrive."

Tears blurred Femi's vision and he felt embarrassed by his reaction. Weeping would only prove to the chief that death lay close to him now, and he was glad for a moment that the man could not see. Femi tried hard to control himself, but the more he tried, the more the tears fell.

The chief gripped Femi's hand more tightly. "Tell me, my son, how can I help you?"

Aminah moved forward and pressed an enormous starched handkerchief into Femi's hands. He wiped his eyes. "Well, oga, when we last met you, long time ten months, you mentioned a woman in your village who worked for Kolo's family. Is she still alive?"

"Yes. Of course." The chief murmured something to an aide, who left the hut, then he turned back to Femi. "Kolo! I will be happy to see that crook back in the gutter where he belongs, if the rats will let him in."

"No. The rats won't let him in. They're too smart." Femi smiled. "But probably the Swiss will, along with his bank account."

The chief cackled a dry laugh.

A few minutes later, an old woman entered. She looked like a gecko–thin, with huge, bulbous eyes and greying, translucent skin, on which dust had settled. Though she must have been almost eighty years old, she appeared lithe and intelligent, her movements executed in tight, aggressive jerks.

"Victoria," the chief said, "these people have come to ask you about Kolo. Please tell them all you know."

She twitched around, flicking her stare from Aminah to Femi and back. Her eyes came to rest on Femi, her features settling into distrust.

Taking an immediate dislike to her, he asked a short question, phrased as a statement. "Apparently you know a secret about Kolo."

"I know nothing!"

"Nothing that makes him fear you?"

The woman paused before replying, much like any reptile waits in rigid silence before pouncing on its prey. "No!"

One last terse query. "You have no idea? Money? Drugs?"

He waited for her to uncoil her answer, killing all further probing. She did not disappoint. "No!"

Relieved to be rid of the woman, Femi glanced at Aminah, indicating that it was time to give up, but she sat down, firmly beaching her extensive buttocks on a small stool, obscuring it entirely.

"How is your family, ma?" she asked, her mighty voice ringing round the hut.

The woman jerked her head towards her. "Them all don quench."

"Water sickness?"

The old woman did not reply, but her eyes lost focus, one drifting off to the ceiling while the other remained on Aminah.

Aminah gestured to the woman to sit down. She hesitated, then perched on the edge of a stool, no flesh to spare for that activity, in a position of imminent escape.

"I'm sorry, ma. No parent should bury her own pickin." Aminah unfastened the sturdy clasp of her mammoth handbag and offered another starched handkerchief to the woman, then slipped out a pen and notepad.

"But there is only one person who can stop this happening again. One person." She held an index finger up in front of her to reinforce the number. "And that person . . . is you!" Aminah's powerful hands snapped her handbag closed.

The woman's errant eye returned from the ceiling to Aminah's face. She stiffened into curiosity.

"Tell me, ma–are you surprised that Kolo became president?"

"Sometimes. No one talked to him as a boy. Now everyone wants to talk to him."

"Why did they not talk to him?" Aminah's voice obliterated the sounds of nature from outside the hut.

"He was cursed. His twin brother died."

"How did his brother die?"

The old woman hesitated, her body inflicted with nervous tics. "Nobody knows."

"But you do."

"I was only a servant."

"Servants know many things."

The woman hesitated once more, then spoke in jagged phrases. "Kolo killed him. He pushed him in pool."

"He killed his own brother?" Aminah shrieked, making Femi and the chief jump.

"Yes. He never saw me, but I saw him." Again, she threw a strange look at Femi that he could not decipher–only that it contained discomfort.

Undeterred, Aminah barked, "Why would Kolo kill his own brother?"

"He jealous. The brother very fine, well, well. Very handsome boy. The brother look like angel."

Femi ran through Kolo's history in his mind. "I thought Kolo was an identical twin," he said.

"Yes, but Kolo was ugly. Very, very ugly. Killer then. Killer now."

"So, is Kolo crazy?" Aminah's excitement lifted her voice to stadium level. "Crazy like his mother?"

"Kolo na craze-craze." The woman twisted her index finger on her forehead. "He dey craze like politician."

Femi found it hard to trust the old woman's account. She had either hidden the unbelievable truth for decades to protect Kolo or she had erected a formidable armour to protect herself against guilt. Why had she never told this story to anyone? Had her neglect of the boys compelled her to shift the blame onto an innocent Kolo? Had her mind, twisted by some hidden resentment, turned an innocent accident into a calculated murder? Had her attachment to his brother nurtured a hatred of Kolo for all these years after his death, a hatred that had finally led to betrayal?

"Thank you, ma." Femi bowed low so that Aminah could not prolong her interrogation and the chief gave her permission to leave.

"Such a story!" the chief exclaimed.

"It's hard to know what the truth is," Femi ventured.

With few qualms about veracity, Aminah, a hardened journalist, reminded him of their purpose. "I beg, our job is not to worry about Kolo's nightmares–we have our own. If she tells us this is fact, enh, well, it's a fact."

Rumour has its purposes, and in this case, its objective was to topple an autocrat. In this forgotten village, on the periphery of the flood's thunderous rampage, they had found their instrument.

Back in Lagos, Femi hunted for the photograph of Kolo kneeling before the village chief. While sifting through papers, he came across a picture of his family and paused to breathe in the scent of the fading image: the fragrance took him home. He wiped his fingerprints off it, flattened its edges and, as he did so, noticed Kolo's photograph underneath the pile. Reluctant to leave behind such an enveloping memory, he handed over the evidence of Kolo's humiliation to Aminah, barely able to speak. "I thought this might be useful one day."

"I'll set it next to the article. I don't need to mention there's no link between the two." Aminah smiled, cheered by the hidden perks of her profession. Readers always assume the worst when the powder keg of words and ostensibly related images are combined.

Mimi's prediction came to pass. She found a note in Mary's waste bin: Sinclair had dumped the minister for the environment. Within the month, the man was killed in a skiing accident in the Swiss Alps.

In the bitter cold of March, Barbara sat in her turret office in Ottawa, reading Mimi's report with disbelief. Forlorn, she went to see Jane, perhaps the most formidable member of Drop of Life, but within wisdom's close custody. Forgetting to knock, Barbara clumped into Jane's office, near tears, plopped herself into an armchair and crossed her legs. Her sarong fell fully open, displaying large purple underpants.

With little option, Jane cut short her phone conversation.

Unable to look her boss in the eye, Barbara talked into her lap. "Mimi has now found proof of a chain of extermination from Sinclair to my sister to Kolo. It has just culminated in the death of the minister for the environment."

Fossilized for many moments, Jane locked Barbara into an evaluating gaze. "Your strategy was to expose complicity at all levels of the organization, regardless of rank. Give me the full details–I'll get the media on it."

Barbara hesitated. "Do we have to mention my sister? I mean, she may be a murderer, but she's very fragile. I can't even conceive of her life outside the corporation."

"And what did you think people like that would be like? Look at the armature they construct in order to feel important."

"I don't think it's just a hunger for importance, Jane." Barbara tilted her head. "Killing helps her fit in. It makes her feel part of a unit."

Vortices of wrinkles reformed into a gentle expression of concern as Jane at last warmed to her. "Barbara, she's disposable. The unit operates on instability. And it's also unaccountable for its actions. That combination promotes lawlessness."

Barbara tipped her head in the opposite direction, listening to this ancient wisdom.

"All your sister has done is move from the confines of the family to its larger version, the corporation. And in the same way, she has no doubt battled for position, never questioning the underlying values, ethics or benefits of the institution. Am I right?"

Barbara sniffed in response.

The phone rang and Jane ignored it, opting instead to hold Barbara's hand. "She's just a serial killer," Barbara pleaded. "Maybe we can overlook that."

Jane squeezed Barbara's hand. "The problem is she's also a mass murderer, my dear. Brad has been able to track who was involved in the AWW and how they got financing for their armaments."

"Yeah." Barbara slumped into her Nigerian buba blouse. "She's always trying to impress. She's a Capricorn. She can't help it."

With a last pat of the hand, Jane offered words of encouragement. "You've done everything you can. Femi will be much safer from now on."

At home, Barbara recounted her triumphs to a companion in brown slippers who waggled his foot in approval. Although he appeared outwardly calm, she was nevertheless conscious of Astro's guilt at abandoning those other living things that depended on him–his fish, his plants, his seedlings. Having regained her stability, she suggested that he return to DC to make sure his dependents were safe. With much exhortation, he packed his plastic bags and left with the cat, realizing the time had now come to exchange it for his saxophone.

Once he had gone, Barbara forced herself to rifle through her photographs, each one prompting fresh recollections and deeper sorrows, trying to find the most flattering picture of Mary. At least she would go down in a blaze of glamour.

TWENTY-NINE

Hat with Curtain

A single photograph pushed Kolo to near nervous collapse. It depicted him kneeling in front of a village chief, begging him, according to the article, not to reveal that he had killed his own twin brother.

Emitting a short yelp, he tore through the other papers, then raced to his office in blind abandon, frenzied and beyond all comfort. Kolo peeked through the curtains to assess public reaction. In the far distance, he saw the army trying to hold back masses of screaming people, lashing them with whips.

He retreated to the garage, zigzagging through corridors so that the water could not engulf him, and pulled the trunk door closed, as if re-entering the womb. There he shot home several bolts.

Kolo wept, wailing into his Thai silk pillows, screaming for a saviour. Stubby fingers clutched the duvet, holding on as if it could embrace and console him, as if its warmth came from his brother's arms.

The article triggered a host of recollections that became superimposed on all his other thoughts. He remembered a time when he had been loved, accepted and cherished, not only by his brother, but by his family and his clan. His brother's love had felt as close as his skin, as warm as the blood in his body, as constant as his own heartbeat. He might have detached from his brother in the womb, but during the eight years of their shared childhood, and into his adult life, he had never felt unconnected to him. His love for himself and his love for his brother were as one.

For nine months, he had allowed the Inspector General of Police to evade his responsibilities and the killers to dawdle, no doubt in awe of the great Jegede. And, of course, picking up "clients" right, left and centre. Whether or not the time was propitious, Jegede now had to go. Only such an act could divert the public's attention from Kolo's humiliation. He would find someone else to pin the murder on, even if it had to be another of Lance Omeke's clients.

One thing he knew: a rumour cannot be stopped. It requires no proof, has its own momentum and allows others to behave with unchecked malevolence. The village had considered him a murderer, had vilified and exiled him, as the whole country now would.

Hardly able to breathe, he put on his mask with its umbilical link to the oxygen tank, prey to the whims of both gasoline and pure oxygen, at the mercy of the tiniest spark.

The sprawling slum of Ajegunle sheltered Femi and his group. Crammed with workers from the world's third-largest city, heaving with its detritus and fermenting toxic pollutants, it steamed with activity day and night. The stench from open drains and the asphyxiating fumes of burning tires settled within their pores.

They had no electricity, water or sanitation, and found no place to perform ablutions in private. Initially, Femi had rented space for a mat under an overpass, but eventually he and Igwe managed to hire a shack, sleeping in shifts with his followers.

With information from Barbara and assistance from Jane Singh's black book, the vigorous efforts of Aminah and fellow journalists soon redirected responsibility for the bombing towards the AWW, and the public hesitated, then their opinion lurched towards a rapid resuscitation of Femi's reputation. Photographs and heroic likenesses of him reappeared throughout the country. Though none had set eyes on him, barbers offered their clients the Femi Fusion, clothiers advertised Jegede Jeans and partiers danced to the Femi Funk. In market stalls around the country, T-shirts depicting Kolo bowing before Femi sold in the tens of thousands.

Six months after arriving in Lagos, a bearded Femi was finally able to wander through the streets to open a bank account–unusual in a cash economy but necessary should Barbara wish to transmit funds. Yussef offered to accompany him on this thankless task. They struggled onto a bus and pushed through the door, jamming themselves between other passengers, squeezing their flesh until it settled into the interstices of the heaving mass of flesh. Femi had to twist one leg around a man's body until it rested on the man's crotch, while his buttocks settled in the hollow of another man's back. Another man's torso was flattened against Femi's stomach. Yussef was similarly confined, though, as a smaller man, he was more at the mercy of the swaying crush of blubber. Femi, towering over the crowd, breathed freely. Yussef appeared to be suffocating, his nose jammed into the armpit of a particularly feisty journeyman ostentatiously carrying a briefcase. Few on the bus could afford to bathe.

"Ah-ah!" the journeyman shouted to no one in particular. "This Kolo! What a rogue! What a ruffian!"

"He's a termite!" another yelled. "That Femi Jegede will crush him like the insect he is!"

"He's worried-oh!" someone else responded. "He's shitting in his gold underpants. Femi will grind him up. This morning, Kolo's driver came to pick me up in his white Mercedes-Benz. 'What is that on the seat?' I asked the guy. 'What is that smell?' My eyes were watering-oh. I could hardly see, the smell was so bad. 'Enh,' he said, 'it's shit. Kolo shit in his white Mercedes-Benz.' 'Joh–let me take the bus today,' I said."

The passengers erupted into furious laughter, heating up the air.

"Did his driver come with you?" came a bellow.

"Yes," Femi squawked. "I came with him."

The passengers once again exploded into loud guffaws.

Yussef motioned helplessly to Femi as they approached their stop. They managed to dislodge themselves from the steaming bodies and made their way to the chaos of the bank. There, a vast mass of people stood in haphazard lines, cursing at each other, small scuffles breaking out as some people from the back successfully bribed the cashiers for service.

"Femi," Yussef confided as they stood in line. "Stay away from War and Lance."

"Why?" Femi replied, looking over the heads to find a better spot. "They're your friends, Yu."

"We don't know each other well, *sha,*" Yussef replied.

"Ah, yes–yours is a northern name. Did you come from the far north?"

"Yes. My brothers and sisters died there. The water was not clean. Even when we found clean water, our containers were dirty. Look at me–every disease has landed on my face."

He laughed, his transparent, grey teeth a testament to his lack of nutrition.

"Nigeria is a very rich country-oh." Femi shook his head. "Where does the money go?"

The woman in front of them turned around. "To the politicians, of course," she barked, her hands on her vast hips. She scrutinized Yussef. "Ah, it's true-oh. You're very ugly. Look at that." She made as if to confer with Femi.

"And you?" Femi snapped. "Are you a movie star? Look at your ugly mouth! Why don't you close it so we can see daylight again?"

A small commotion broke out as the three argued and others jumped into the fray.

Once everything calmed down, Yussef spoke low to Femi behind a cupped hand, angry eyes focused on the back of the woman's head. "Your life is in danger, brother. I am here to protect you. Kolo has sent killers to find you."

"How do you know this?"

Yussef hesitated. "I met them in prison."

"You were in prison?"

"Three years. A policeman murdered my father for protesting when Kolo took all the water from our well." He picked furiously at a pimple. "So I killed him."

Femi felt for this young man, who had had no chance to live a life that others take for granted. Even Yussef's face, bursting with all manner of sores, could once have been handsome.

The woman in front turned around in horror. "Who? You killed who?"

"And since then," Yussef added nonchalantly, "I find it quite easy to kill people who annoy me. Even people with big lips—they take longer to choke, but if you take time, you can get the job done."

The woman pushed past them, out of the bank.

They edged forward a good two feet.

As the days wore on, the three friends became more agitated, which aroused Femi's curiosity.

He took two jerry cans to buy water from a local trader, and Ekong volunteered to take two more, suggesting they stroll through the makeshift walkways of the shantytown for greater privacy. They meandered through the narrow passageways, trying to avoid the waste strewn across their path. Ekong's wild eyes shone in the flicker of kerosene lamps. Femi could see him stealing sideways glances at him, his eyes never at rest, checking pathways and shacks.

Ekong indicated that he wished to walk in a less crowded area, on the outskirts of the shantytown to a cheaper water vendor. Femi felt ill at ease but followed him nonetheless. They neared a garbage dump. The stench was unbearable: death was all around them.

Femi listened to the sounds of the shantytown, the cries of the dying, their bodies expelling any small nourishment they consumed. He accidentally stepped on a stray dog chewing on scraps, its fur riddled with scabies, ribs protruding from an emaciated body. The dog let out a pathetic yelp. Ekong's hands flew to his pockets, as if reaching for a weapon. Femi jumped back.

Then, just as unexpectedly, Ekong kicked the dog. They heard its ribs crack. The dog screeched out some faint yowls, struggling for breath.

Enraged, Femi snapped, "Ekong, why not go back home?" He reached down to help the dog, which cowered away from him. Ekong remained silent. Femi studied the young man for a moment. "I beg, forgive me, my friend. Because your name is from the east, I keep forgetting your family could also have died in the flood."

"Not in–after. Kolo's company took our water downstream from the Benue River, and my family could not afford to buy it. So we drank contaminated water."

"Ah! I'm sorry-oh!"

Ekong's eyes darted around; the man was apprehensive, edgy. "I haven't told you everything. I came from prison. I killed an official who wanted to take water we had already purchased. I had to protect my younger brothers and sisters. Two had already died. I was senior brother."

"Who can blame you?" Femi asked. "Who would do otherwise?"

Ekong's expression relaxed, and he hesitated before speaking again. "Listen to me carefully, I beg. Your life is in danger. Kolo's spies are living with you already. Someone else arranged that bombing, to put blame on your head. Do not trust anyone. I am trying to protect you, but I have to sleep sometime."

Femi thought back to those anxious eyes in the middle of the night, to Ekong's constant agitation, to the nerves that could set a man against an innocent dog. Ekong stayed awake each night to watch over him.

"You must get some sleep," Femi replied. "Everyone has to go sometime–even the finest orator in the world can't talk his way out of death."

When they arrived at the water vendor's, they found that the tap had run dry.

The next day, Femi went to the market for supplies. Lance, donning his tan cowboy hat with the white fringe, asked to accompany him. His personable nature and affable manner made him easy company.

As they rounded Jankara Square, Femi noticed a man with a ferocious face–a huge, stinking mass with wild dreadlocks snaking from his head, colour of rust, pumpkins and sand. They were matted with all manner of life's waste: mud, clay and anything this monster might have accidentally laid his head in. He wore no shirt, only a pair of oily shorts slung low on his naked hips, while his trousers lay twisted over his hair. His fatty face screamed at passersby.

A young lady strode past him in a flamboyant nylon shirt with flounces and frills cascading down the front.

"Hey, bitch!" the man yelled. "Yes, that's right! You! Birthday cake! Look at you! Why you wear icing on your shirt? Come, let me lick icing for you."

She tutted at him and walked on.

"You prefer make boss eat icing? Okay, go-now! He go eat icing for you–yam and scram. Yam and scram. He no go leave him wife for you-oh." She hurried her steps, visibly flustered.

The man then spotted Lance. "Hey-hey! Look at you!" He pointed at Lance's fringed cowboy hat.

"Look at me? What about you?" Lance laughed. "Where your trouser, my friend?"

"Why you wear curtain on hat? Are you Elvis? Who you dey hide from?" The man jerked his head back and cackled. "You no go open curtain? Let me see your face. Watch out, my friend." He turned to Femi. "Watch out for man wey hide behind curtain. He see you. You no see him."

Lance chuckled easily. "Crazy, crazy man. These Nigerians!"

Femi shook his head, smiling. "This country! Ah-ah!"

They turned into the market's twisting paths, weaving through the endless mud, hopping over open drains and ducking under corrugated roofs. Thousands of people milled about, haggling for each item–cloth, car parts, curry–producing the raucous confusion that so efficiently cloaked Femi's movements in the big city. Even the odours appeared to comply, coiling and mingling with the clamour, so that the haze of fish stew, perfumes and raw sewage shrouded them.

Lance put an arm around Femi's shoulder as they walked. "So, you talked to War and Yu?"

"Yes."

"Did they tell you how we met?"

"No, as a matter of fact, they didn't."

"We met in Kolo's office." Lance paused, grinning pleasantly.

"What?" Femi tried to stop, but Lance indicated that he needed to urinate and drew him down a small alley.

"In Kolo's office. He hired us to kill you." Lance unzipped his fly, pulled out his penis and peed onto the side of a shelter.

"Eh? Kolo hired you?"

"No. To be exact," he chuckled, "the Inspector General of Police hired us: three men who wan' slaughter Kolo, jus' to pound him greasy, yellow brain, dry it, add sugar for make puff-puff. Yu, for having killed his father; War, for having stolen his family's water; and me." He laughed. "Ah, Nigerians! What a country. Where your friends are your enemies and your enemies are your enemies."

Femi looked at this charming man, laughing as pleasantly as if he were telling a joke in a bar.

"Instead of choosing assassins to kill *you,* the inspector general chose three people who wanted to kill Kolo."

"And why would he want Kolo dead?"

Lance zipped up. "I think so the minister of finance can become president. He's the inspector general's brother-in-law."

"Are you in government too? This your cowboy hat looks very official. Why you?"

Lance stopped behind some debris and piles of garbage.

"Why me? Because I killed three men." He tenderly patted a passing child on the head.

"Why?"

"I tried to join the ministry of natural resources and they rejected me, although I was highly qualified. I wrote to everyone, even Kolo. No answer. Nothing. Can you imagine? Corrupt bureaucrats!"

"And?"

"And so I threatened to kill Kolo. I killed the interviewer first." He shrugged.

Femi sought the mystifying depths he had not so far encountered in this man. "Why?"

"I was angry."

"What? Why?" Femi asked.

Lance's eyes creased as he smiled, squinting in the shaft of sunlight piercing the alleyway. "I was angry. That's all." He had a mischievous look in his eyes as he played with the fringe of his cowboy hat.

"So why did you kill the other two men? Were they Kolo's?"

"Oh, no." Lance laughed. "I can't even remember why."

The puzzle finally came together. War had suspected Lance all along, and Yussef too, though he was too timid to point the finger of blame before he knew for sure. "Aaah. So it was you who organized the bombing."

"'Organize' is a strong word. It implies something complicated." He scored under his nails to rid them of any dirt. "I just contacted another group–got paid. That's all."

It was at that moment that Femi realized that these attractive, equable features, this charismatic and intelligent face, now radiating an intense excitement, would be the last he would ever see. He thought of his beloved grandmother singing songs of their ancestors as she stroked his forehead, his dear grandfather and his tales of magical spirits, the delighted arms of his mother and father opening wide to accept him. He prepared himself to rush into them, to throw himself back to those who had been lost to him.

There was no use, he knew, in arguing with death.

"Please tell Igwe that I–"

Lance waited with a leer, and Femi realized that Igwe would already know everything he wanted to tell him.

He saw a silver glint and then felt a sharp pain in his neck, as Lance's hat tumbled, in silent submission, to the ground. Femi wrapped his hands around Lance's to hold the blade as it plunged deep inside him, for he could feel sensations now. He succumbed to an intense, blissful elation. Their hands met at the hilt of the knife as blood oozed out over them. He could feel the warmth of Lance's flesh and the hot discharge of blood spurting over them. Lance smiled, an ecstatic, joyous expression. The emotion amplified as it transferred to Femi and spread through his entire body. Femi beamed back at Lance, a gaze that acknowledged the power of their union and the flow of their twin destinies.

Lance pulled the knife away, and the flash of metal struck Femi's stomach, entering hard and deep. Femi felt the pain of entry, a powerful punch, a twisting, searing pain that sent a flash of heat through his abdomen. Lance, his eyes wild with desire, withdrew the knife, and Femi began to fall. Lance drew Femi closer to him, wrapping his arm around the hollow of his back, the tips of his fingers caressing his buttocks. He struck again, two more stabs to Femi's chest. Femi heard his ribs crack. He watched Lance twist the knife, making small circling motions above the soft and giving flesh, watched as blood shot out to drench Lance's shirt, soaking them both, dripping, gushing. Femi rushed into his parents' arms, jumping into the village river with his brother, his body surging into a euphoric rapture, his groin hard, racing home, running through landscapes of light. As Lance pushed out a scream of exultation, a burning sensation rippled through Femi's body.

It was the last sensation he ever felt.

A woman with a baby on her back and a large bag on her head picked her way through the treacherous waste at the back of Jankara Market, garbage as high as hills, avoiding the used needles, broken glass and jagged tins in her path. She hoped to find some discarded food or clothing, some small crumbs for her baby, some scraps to keep them both alive. She saw a shirt lying in a pile of rubbish next to a muddy cowboy hat and rushed to claim them. She threw off the bags and food covering them and lifted the hat's fringe. Her hand touched flesh. And then she saw the splendour of the man for whom her people so fervently prayed, who adorned their shrines. She screamed, dropping her bag and waking her child, a high-pitched shriek of horror, of fear, of the misery of her entire life.

News of Femi's death spread–first as small drops: tears that fell behind a flash of logos, in the eyes of his companion, waiting for a man who would never return. It continued as a small trickle, filtered out in the sweat of those who toiled the fields, drops of suspicion held in the breasts of those who fished the waters. It grew in waves as news streamed through villages and shantytowns, farms and homesteads. Fury against Kolo rose, no longer angry whispering and repressed complaint, but a turbulent and raging current of confrontation against the forces of authority. Accounts rushed forth from these strongholds, spewed out in towns and marketplaces, a violent torrent of hatred mounting against a deluged president.

That tide wound its way to the great cities and the capital, a mighty, roaring force smashing through the indifference of its inhabitants–a thunderous surge that threatened to wash away the dirt of Kolo's regime.

And along with the facts, the data, the information, came its Nigerian chaperone: rumour. A great man in life, Femi was to attain immortality in death. More and more shrines built in his honour sprouted in villages deep in the countryside, while pictures of him spread to city households, where anger hammered nails into concrete walls. Stories of his valiant efforts multiplied–of the time when he had made Kolo kneel before him in a small village hut, to the thousands he had saved from the flood, to news of sightings in the hills of the east or the jungles of the Congo. In some areas, he had even been known to turn palm wine into clean, fresh water.

With his death, Femi finally secured the bliss that had eluded him in the final chapters of his life; divested of emotions almost too painful to bear, and unattached to a physical body, his spirit became inviolable. No hand could touch it; it seeped into the mind, that area that has no seat within the body. In doing so, it described a nation and its mourning, its aspirations and its despair, not for the span of a regime, or an era, but for centuries.

Here was a man who flowed past clan, past language, past boundaries. The Gandhi of Nigeria had been born, his gentle face ready forever to grace the walls of Nigerian embassies, its already handsome aspect rendered more beatific with each successive generation.

And sitting in Abuja, at the geographical centre of all this tumult, sat a robust woman whose tears would change the course of Nigerian history, whose sorrow caused her voice to grow even mightier, a voice that would soon disturb the eardrums of millions.

THIRTY

Departure

The computer's jingle informed Barbara that it was ready for use, already open at the *Nigeria Today* website. Hoping to gauge the political temperature, she meandered over to scan the articles and peek at its welcoming images.

There, in a photo just bigger than a stamp, lay Femi's lifeless body.

A chill shot up her spine. She screamed and swivelled around, feeling death's icy breath behind her ear, as if it stood behind her. The sensation lingered, yet she could not find its source. Petrified, she sat rigid for a moment, then swiftly turned back to the computer and enlarged the image with a double-click, thinking that perhaps she had made an error. But the greater detail only offered more proof.

Barbara had never seen Femi asleep. She had had no idea of how that beautiful face might look with closed eyes. And now she saw an infinite lingering. It looked like sleep, but his sockets were too deep, as if death had stamped a seal upon his eyes.

That final sleep had not erased the expression from his face. He appeared to have died in a state of elation.

She touched the screen, as if doing so might animate those features.

A tear pricked her eye. She felt it sting.

Had it been a good day that day? Had he been frightened?

She felt paralyzed, as if her own life had stumbled.

Had the sun shone that morning? Had he smiled then?

His features intimated that he had embraced the final intelligence with senses heightened, as if ready to transform into the highest abstraction.

Had he seen the knife? Had he felt it? Did it hurt?

Tears fell down Barbara's cheeks, warm tears that heated up her face. Sobs jagged her body.

Had it been a good day? Had the sun been in his eyes?

Her mind raced with myriad thoughts that condensed to produce an intense focus. She grabbed her bag and charged to the front door–and kept running, sprinting down the road, rushing past the landscape of an early spring. The boastful buds that thrust their way past the snow sickened her with their mocking ignorance of the soundless night of life's cycle.

She had left everything too long. She could no longer even try to protect her sister, whose active hours were spent in the pursuit of murder–she realized how much harder she would have to push to wash the evil away.

THIRTY-ONE

Haven and Hell

Kolo woke up disoriented and on edge. He lay back on his iridescent silk sheets, checking the skin around his miniature nail beds, breathing through an oxygen mask to combat the effects of the gasoline fumes that permeated the garage. He flicked open his new embroidered Spanish fan and began to air himself.

Although the international press had not condemned him for an alleged childhood incident, they took exception to assassination; whereas in Nigeria, the opposite held true. Unlike most paradoxes harboured by Nigeria, this one did not work in his favour.

He set down his fan in order to stroke his brother's photo: in doing so, he felt his own body being caressed. Their former nanny had been arrested and imprisoned, accused of the dereliction of duty that had led to his dear brother's death. The thought of her created a sensation of implosion, so that Kolo's breath sped inwards, choking him.

Despite her conviction, the stench of fratricide still clung to him. Discussions would be taking place within the molue buses, taxis and marketplaces. He had no doubt that contracts on his life were being negotiated, some for as little as a crate of beer, though he reckoned he had few months' grace: Nigerians were not known for punctuality.

According to his calculations, if Lance Omeke had performed his task promptly, it would erase the collective memory of that childhood incident for enough time for public revulsion to abate. Kolo predicted that today could make or break his presidency, a handy euphemism for the difference between life and death. He had a plan to shift blame to another for Jegede's murder. At that point, he hoped this irritating domino effect would come to a halt.

Picking up a book of poetry, Kolo considered his fate. Alone, rejected, politically isolated, he needed to focus most of his remaining presidential efforts on the building of the dam and the renaming of the river that would allow his name to flow through history. Only then, he thought, would he be happy to cede his presidency to a less able candidate.

He whistled for his security guard.

"Yes, sir." As the guard entered, he saluted, almost slicing out his eye.

"Toothpick!"

"Sir." The guard spat out the offending object.

About to slam the book closed, Kolo noticed one particularly irksome poem. "Listen to this man: 'If you can meet with triumph and disaster and treat those two impostors just the same, you'll be a man, my son.' Rudyard. What a name! Serves him right."

"Ah-ah! Has this idiot never been to Nigeria?"

Kolo tossed the book aside. "Apparently not. From now on, I'll stick to John Pepper Clark." He closed his eyes in reverie.

"'Fear him his footfall soft light as a cat's, his shadow far darker than forest gloom or night–'"

"J.P.?" the guard interrupted harshly, knocking Kolo out of his trance. "We did him at school. Why can't the man just say what he means?" He kissed his teeth in protracted disdain.

Affronted by such disrespect, Kolo thought he would leave the man with a lasting legacy inspired by Kipling: lessons culled from his own experience, infused with dread for the coming day. "Words of wisdom: if you have talent, hide it; if you have a brain, deprive it of oxygen to downgrade; if you're a great man, best to leave the country."

"You speak of Jegede, sir?"

Kolo paused long enough for the man to suspect his error.

The guard accompanied him in silence to the office.

Following ever more labyrinthine routes, it took Kolo an hour longer to make his way to the office. The sounds that had once appeared to be minor trickles, endless drippings and echoes of faraway streams now overwhelmed him with their violence. Giant surges of water, torrential floods and booming explosions engulfed him.

Today, the waves of noise outside offered an added backdrop of suffocating anxiety. He already knew the source of the additional unruliness.

He buzzed his new confidant, the minister of finance. "Bring!"

A few minutes later, the minister entered with a pile of papers from all media sources. "How are you doing today, sir?"

"Well. And yourself?"

"Dangerously well, sir, dangerously well."

Before he had time to reprimand the man for such casual interchange, words ricocheted off newsprint, trailing a smell of gunpowder: "Kolo! Killer!"

Each headline fired off the same message: a sociopathic lunatic sat at the helm of the most unfortunate of nations. Despite his repeated threats of incarceration, journalists' reportage had grown rampant, their claims vying for implausibility.

Kolo grabbed the carved gold armrests of his chair. "Look at these fools. Where's their evidence? And how can they put 'killer' and 'murderer' in the same article? What do they mean by 'murder'? They don't seem to understand that this term possesses great cultural diversity."

He'd touched on the minister's bête noir–journalism–and the man responded with heat. "How can a killer be a murderer at the same time? Everyone knows killing is sanctioned. Murder is a completely different matter. No one likes a murderer. These people can't even define their terms."

"Would you call a soldier a murderer?"

"Exactly!" the minister thundered in unequivocal support. "You may be a killer, Excellency, but how could anyone call you a murderer?"

A spasm caught Kolo's big toe. He spoke in a severe, low tone. "How can I be a killer if I have never killed anyone?"

Wrapped up in his condemnation of journalism, the minister of finance swept past this distinction. "Who trains these people? They can't get anything right. They're just journalists. Read this–they call you a demon in human form and expensive agbadas. As if they have ever seen a demon!"

Wishing the minister had selected his words more carefully, Kolo sniffed back a sob. "This is ridiculous! Women are saying Jegede straightened their hair or yellowed their complexions by a mere touch of his never-manicured farmer's hand. Oh, here, listen to this. Men are crediting this donkey, who has simply wandered from his stall in some yeye nowhere corner of Nigeria, who cannot even wipe his own buttocks, flicking his tail for all to see, with the propitious deaths of their enemies."

Far down in the mall, past the river moat whose drawbridge protected the governmental complex, voices had risen to drown out all other sounds, threatening to entomb Kolo in their clamour. Surely the water pipes would soon burst, flooding his office and smothering him.

The minister of finance closed the curtains. "Is this job worth it? Why waste your talents on such an unworthy country, sir? Please. You must calm down. Your heart is fragile. Do you want me to get the doctor?"

Kolo massaged his breast. "Yes, please." A sight added to the pressure on his chest. He collapsed back in his chair. "Christ on the cross! The international press has actually retouched Jegede's photos! Is this what they call journalism?"

The minister of finance kissed his teeth at the mention of his pet peeve.

The phone rang. "Yes?"

"Mary Glass, sir. I've just read–"

"A moment." Kolo waved the expectant minister away. "Continue."

"–these articles on Jegede."

A very unusual call–he could hear panic in her machine-gun delivery.

She continued without waiting for his reaction. "We have informants within water activist groups here who have linked the bombings to the African Water Warriors, not Wise Water. That means only one thing, sir."

Was she too about to indict him? Et tu, TransAquus? "Please go on, Ms. Glass."

"Pardon? Uh, well, I think it's obvious, sir. It seems to me that whoever killed Jegede did it on instructions from the AWW."

Smart woman–one step ahead of him this time. He felt uneasy trailing, and did not believe in sudden reversals. One small test, just to check how deeply she had been involved. "Okay. I'll get the Inspector General of Police to bring in . . . well, probably Ekong."

"Pardon?"

"Ekong. He is our assassin."

"That's not compatible with the name I heard. Lance Omeke, sir, is the rumour."

She had proved his conjecture: only two people knew Ekong's first name and Lance's last name–the president and the inspector general. "I never believe in rumour, Ms. Glass. Omeke would be too worried about soiling his clothes. No. I'll get Ekong."

He put the phone down–let her stew, since she had tried to act independently of him–and then he called the inspector general, ordering him to the presidential complex. With one phone call, he would set the wheels in motion to place the blame on another member of Jegede's organization. A certain Igwe. No first name, apparently. He would commission one of the other two assassins in Omeke's "business" to implicate the man.

In anticipation of the inspector general's visit, Kolo opened the curtains, careful not to lift his eyes past the moat.

To while away the time, he opened the bottom right-hand drawer to extract all the clippings about his brother's professed murder. He sat with his hands over his eyes, as if shading them from the sun, ready to lower his hand further should anyone enter unexpectedly and see his tears. He could not stop them falling.

A rap on the door jolted Kolo out of his thoughts. He stuffed the clippings back into the drawer, slammed it closed and wiped his eyes on his agbada. "In!"

The inspector general marched to the sound of his own private military band, head high, body rigid. He stopped in front of

Kolo's desk with two stamps of his feet that made the chocolate trays rattle, then saluted with a quivering arrow of a hand that found its target. "Sir!" he yelled from the very depths of his belly.

"Bring Lance Omeke."

"Sir?"

"One of the assassins you hired."

"*I* hired, sir?"

"Yes, inspector. You." At least this would hurry him up for once.

A slow dawn illuminated the intellectual vistas of the inspector general's mind. "Omeke? You mean Lance Omeke did it?" Did the man not have faith in his own choices?

"Yes, done. Bring. Contact the African Water Warriors–they will find him. Then get rid."

"Yes, sir." There was relief in the inspector general's voice. "No problem."

That must be it, thought Kolo. *He wants to tie up loose ends.* A strange reaction from a man who had expressed such faith in the talents of his convicts; he did not expect to hear the inspector general sounding so ruffled.

The inspector general launched another quivering arrow to his forehead, slapped it back down to his thigh, then executed an intricate 180-degree swivel.

I must contact Wosu P. Wosu, Kolo thought, *and see if the military can train the police in basic practices such as marching, saluting and turning. After two years, they can perhaps progress to more complex protocols, such as proper attire and decorum.*

Members of Kolo's publicity team now rushed in to fuss over him. Unlike most other departments, he had ensured that Public Relations was staffed principally with Westerners who had mastered the art of spin. A few Nigerians tagged along for training purposes.

A woman took charge, her hair scraped back into a ponytail so tight she looked almost bald. "Mr. President, it is imperative we deal with this situation at once. And I'm afraid, sir, there's only one way out. You need to speak of your admiration for Jegede."

She flipped the first draft of a public announcement in front of him. He read it rapidly.

"I'll do no such thing." Kolo's voice echoed off a high ceiling.

"You need to keep your presidency safe."

The last word hit home–on the left side of his chest, to be precise. He started scratching out phrases with his pen. "Well, we can take out 'national hero' right now. 'Self-made man' will do."

"Certainly."

"'A human colossus'? You have to be kidding. Replace with 'very human.'"

"Yes, sir."

"'Provided direction and unity for the country?'" Kolo simply stared at the head of PR.

As these negotiations took place, she beckoned to an intern, who arrived with a large rectangular object wrapped in brown paper.

"What's that?"

"A portrait of Jegede. You'll need to replace your picture with his, just for a short period of time."

As they unwrapped a magnificent depiction of the man standing in a god-like pose with a preternaturally angelic face, Kolo's restraint took flight. "In oils? You've done it in oils? Have you gone insane? Take it away right now. And who commissioned it, pray tell?"

"I did." She brooked no opposition.

He tried to stare her down, but she stood firm.

"Crayon, then. And you don't need to find Nigeria's greatest artist–best to support a student."

"No crayons, sir."

Eviscerated by this new humiliation, Kolo ensured that a small portrait of the terrorist was executed in acrylic paint with crude mounting. In order to accomplish this, they delayed two days. The press officer removed the resplendent oil painting of a majestic, light-skinned president that hung behind the presidential chair and replaced it with that of the regrettably sublime features of Jegede, then summoned the media. Kolo read out a statement clarifying his deep respect for Nigeria's greatest icon. While the press took their snapshots of an imperious Kolo underneath Jegede's painting, his aides hauled their president's now redundant image to the basement, accidentally damaging some of the rococo flourishes to its frame.

When they were all gone, Kolo sat down behind his desk, a shattered man, hardly able to speak, knowing that someone–or something–was trying to drive him to the brink of insanity. Riots had broken out in every major city, with thousands massacred by supporters of the same idol. Each time he thought of Jegede, visions of his brother's face became more bloated, blue in colour, his eyes wide, as he sank downwards.

He needed to move on the Igwe scheme, but so far he had been unable to contact the assassins. He considered phoning the inspector general again. As this thought lodged in his to-do list, his assistant buzzed him.

"Yes?"

"Lance Omeke, sir."

"Finally! Bring."

Lance strode in, wearing a black Stetson with a butterfly logo on the front. "Worraps?" He smiled with a row of strong, intelligent teeth. "Jegede is gone."

Kolo's spirits rose. "Did you bring body?"

The man surveyed the rich textures of the room, with its Italianate chairs, embossed velvets, rich patterned carpeting and ivory inlaid tables. Kolo had taste: this he knew. Lance seemed particularly struck by the three chandeliers that hung over their discussions, and gazed up at their many rainbows like a child mesmerized by a toy.

"Did you bring body?" Kolo repeated, not irritated, simply happy that at least one person appreciated the splendour that accrued to a presidency.

"No. No transportation."

"Ah, I see." Kolo sat back and laced his fingers over his shrinking belly. His body ached. "What took so long?"

"Enh, well, you said three months, *sha*."

He closed his eyes and sighed. "Since when has three months lasted four months?" He kissed his teeth. "How do I know he's gone?"

"Don't you read newspaper? They've written about my work. It's even on the television. Ah-ah! You're president. Why can't you follow these things? It's your job. Anyway, at least I myself am a professional. I took photo."

"Aaah. Good, good. Bring." Kolo laid a hand on his desk: he could hardly raise it to beckon to the man.

Lance placed a stash of photos near Kolo's hand. Kolo gasped. The man had taken thirty photos–twenty-nine more than necessary. They appeared to serve as trophies, as a form of murderous pornography. Wincing with revulsion, Kolo sorted through them, placing them in piles of full body injuries, head, chest, lower body and so on. Jegede looked as if he had been stabbed over a hundred times. An unexpected boon.

"Good work. Good work." Kolo pushed the photos aside. "So, you need your release papers? And payment, of course."

"Yes, sir."

"Before you go, I would be interested to find out who paid you to protect Jegede."

"My clients rely on being anon."

" . . . ymous is the full word. But they know you're operating a bona fide business, so they understand you're paid for a range of services. Paid ten thousand, for example. Diversification is key. Your clients would be aware of that. A man has to live, after all."

"Confidentiality and diversification. It's my motto."

Kolo wrote a cheque. "So?"

"American ambassador."

Kolo's pen stopped mid-figure, blotting ink over the cheque. The crewcut had actually dared to attempt a plot in Nigeria. Was he mad? "Look at the man. If I thought he could read . . . No, it must be books on tape. He listened to *Conspiracy for Dummies,* then thought he could vault into the top league. Idiot!" He tried to brush aside the very idea, although it niggled him slightly when he considered it.

Kolo shook himself free of these inner irritations and finished writing a cheque that would never get cashed. "Go and see the inspector general. He will provide your papers for you. I will tell him you're coming." Kolo piled the photographs together with weary gestures and threw them into his desk drawer.

"Okay, sir." Lance made as if to reclaim the photos but obviously thought better of it. He hesitated before leaving. "Thank you, sir," he finally said.

"No, thank *you.*" Kolo shivered. Was this the kind of killer they would send for him? "Nice doing business with you."

Lance bid him a respectful "Later" and left.

For a moment, Kolo settled into the high back of his scaled-down throne. How could he have been so short-sighted? With Omeke, he could implicate at least two others, as well as incriminate him in an internal struggle for power at Wise Water. He had no need of this Igwe character.

A great calm overcame Kolo as he picked up the phone. "Inspector general? Omeke is coming for his release papers."

Since the day his people had hung the portrait of Jegede above the presidential chair, Kolo kept a strict separation of his life into two spheres–his haven and his hell. His haven was his garage, increasingly decorated with personal items: his portrait, various medications and creams, Napoleonic furniture, cupboards for his agbadas. Here, he could relax in his Chinese silk pyjamas, sink his toes into the lush cream carpet and stroke the grain of the curtains that covered the garage door. They were made of heavy velvet and fringed, like those in the presidential offices, but he had chosen royal blue to grace this personal paradise, a colour that did not adorn the windows in the floors above.

In his haven, Kolo allowed no daily distractions, no newspapers, radio or television–merely the staples of a tranquil life: classical music minus any gloomy Germanic influence, Quality Street chocolates, biographies of great men.

As he zigzagged his way to his hell–his office–past broom cupboards, storage lockers, food stores, and upwards to purgatory along windows that gave a view of Aso Rock, he encountered the cubicles of small fry, then climbed past the offices of potential presidential rivals. As he progressed, his safety grew increasingly precarious, his step more erratic. By the time he reached his office, his pace had escalated into a hesitant sprint.

Every day, same routine: slam door, check window, curse Jegede's portrait, flop into seat, take Aspirin, consider relocating portrait, ring for minister of finance, grab newspapers, greeting, response, detailed examination of Jegede's ascent to glory, wave aide away.

Today, he had a meeting that he hoped would raise his spirits somewhat. After dismissing the minister of finance, he opened his briefcase and took out some new footwear. He then grabbed his parasol and headed for the nature reserve behind the governmental complex.

"Good morning, Ambassador Bates!" A more rugged habitat provided a fitting backdrop for such a meeting. Kolo wore trainers under his agbada. "I'm not sure I've shown you the national arboretum. It's a wilderness, absolutely untouched by human hand."

Side by side, the president and the American ambassador strode past a series of gates manned by military sentries and into an area landscaped with varieties of local trees, flowers and undulating pathways.

"Beautiful, isn't it? We copied the DC model, of course."

The path wound around trees with leaves too stiff for the wind to rustle. The ambassador peered at Kolo, leery.

"I wanted to talk to you about this Jegede business," Kolo continued. "We have the culprit. The man wanted to wrest control of Wise Water. A handsome man–he thought his face would better suit the T-shirts. I find it hard to disagree."

"Uh-huh." The ambassador did not look reassured by this amiable chit-chat.

"He's a sociopath, of course. I was surprised to find he considered you an ally. You'd apparently paid him quite a sum."

"What? Me?" Rays of pink leapt to the surface of the ambassador's face.

Two paths diverged in an unkempt wood, one more travelled. Kolo took it. "Yes, a certain Lance Omeke–hope I'm pronouncing that right. We'll have to display the body, of course. We've become a very visual culture, like yours. I just wanted to ensure you wouldn't be tied up in any kafuffle."

The ambassador's response took a long time to come. No doubt he was mentally replaying his tapes of *Scheming for Simpletons.* "I had nothing to do with Jegede's death."

"Of course you didn't. The very idea! No, Omeke must have acted on his own. Lovely tree, that." Kolo's admiring gaze travelled up the length of a basic palm.

"Yeah, 'course the guy did."

"Well, then, I'm sure you'll be willing to confirm that at the press conference this afternoon."

Posing in front of a large American flag, the ambassador attended the identification ceremonies–which lasted many days. He constantly reaffirmed the inspector general's account of a play for dominance within a chaotic organization–an act that unwittingly implied a CIA conspiracy to eliminate Jegede.

Kolo stood in the background, by Omeke's body, framed by yet another portrait of Jegede, his face a vision of despair. This time, he had no need to perform: the oil painting behind him aroused an overwhelming depth of emotion.

The papers featured pictures of Lance Omeke's corpse, dressed in his most garish clothing to convey an implied message of greed. Omeke's photographs of the multiple stab wounds to Jegede's body confirmed the attack. Despite their macabre content, these too hit the front pages in colour, looped through news channels and introduced the day's events on most websites.

But regardless of the grisly, uncontrolled nature of the attack on Jegede, the pungent odour of suspicion still lurked around Kolo–Nigerians were no dupes and had little respect for the presidency.

Therefore, his office continued to circulate pictures of Jegede's butchered corpse, along with the bloodied Stetson.

"If I had asked for an assassination," Kolo's official press release stated, "one bullet would have sufficed"–a fact that made sense.

THIRTY-TWO

Glass Tank

In March, Kolo hosted a Canadian delegation. These people Kolo could not abide: whenever they visited they insisted on talking about the environment (his, not theirs), poverty (Nigeria's, not aboriginal people's) and, most vexing of all, embarking on some form of physical activity.

The prime minister wished to climb Aso Rock to get a panoramic view of Abuja. Apparently, a postcard would not suffice. The man's lack of sophistication astounded Kolo. What European head of state would soil his handmade shoes to pursue such a folly? The female politicos were even more sensible, with their stilettos fiercely protected.

The prime minister was most amiable, which made the experience even more unbearable. "Great day for a hike, huh? What an awesome country!"

"It's like many others, I can assure you. I hope I don't sound immodest when I say it's our culture that differs."

Photographers gathered at the base of the rock, clicking their cameras as Kolo shook hands with the PM. Then the torture began. They ascended.

After ten minutes, Kolo could no longer hold back the sound of his puffing. Thankfully, the Canadian prime minister had climbed on ahead. Surreptitiously, Kolo sat down on a small rock to regain his breath.

One of the prime minister's entourage attempted to take a photograph. A stern military sentry impounded the camera and almost arrested the culprit. The incident allowed Kolo a few extra minutes of rest.

Just as he recommenced climbing, a wheezing and aggrieved minister of finance caught up with him.

"Hey!" the Canadian prime minister shouted from his position higher up the rock. "Glad you could join us."

The minister shot him a look of profound disdain.

"News is bad today, Excellency," he said.

"What this time?"

"Em . . . Something to do with purchase of shares, insider trading, tapping of funds," the minister rolled his eyes heavenward in disbelief that these issues should cause any untoward coverage, "and other details of the contract with TransAqua."

"Details? Of the contract?" Kolo's heartbeat, already pounding and erratic, doubled in speed. He searched his minister's face to see if he could spot any mention of the renaming of the Niger River, but the minister's emotions were still roiling with condemnation of the media.

"Follow them up the rock," Kolo commanded. "I'll go back to the office and join all of you later. Apparently, they'd like a game of golf." He slipped down the precipitous granite back to the level corridors of the governmental complex.

Once he had slammed the door to his office, Kolo loped to

his desk. A letter lay there, and he recognized its logo. In exquisite language, the World Bank informed him of their intent to pull out of the Kainji deal. Kolo had to act quickly before the World Bank's intentions made their way to TransAqua.

He turned on the television news with trembling fingers. Corruption, water pricing, trading irregularities: he could explain all these concerns away. In countries like Nigeria, these were everyday offences that plagued every regime, whether military or democratic. Only one item could bury him–the most damaging discovery of all: the renaming of the Niger River. He would get Glass to deal with it. He reread the article. She would definitely need his help–another game of tit for tat.

As Mary scrolled through the website, she mentally ticked off the problems. The World Bank could deal with its issues regarding privatization and stipulations on the use of American contractors. Price, ownership of water and cost of doing business in Nigeria–the newspapers' word for which was "corruption"–these terms and conditions differed little from other water contracts, save for their excess and audacity. PR would handle that.

The most damaging allegations, from which it was unlikely TransAqua could recover concerned Kolo's purchase of shares–insider trading. For this, TransAqua staff could technically go to prison, lose their jobs or even relinquish their bonuses.

She braced for another phone call. "President Kolo?"

"Yes?" he whispered. The phone crackled.

"Insider trading? You purchased shares prior to the signing of the contract?"

"It is almost impossible, Ms. Glass, beyond the bounds of any game theory matrix," his voice grew louder, "that anyone could have traced such shares back to my enterprises! It's insulting!"

"A forensic–"

"Even the greatest forensic accountant, assisted by Hercules Poirot himself, would have to spend years . . . This is Nigeria, Ms. Glass. Our systems are not crude!"

Mary grew defensive. "I can assure you, with all due respect, Mr. President, that American companies also have intricate systems to conceal–"

"Not in the elaborate, complex manner that . . . Let me explain, Ms. Glass. In Nigeria, we have perfected this to an art form. It bewitches us. It gives us aesthetic pleasure. To us, this is the ultimate in hedonistic gratification. Talk to a mathematician. He will explain to you the crystalline beauty of a theoretical proposition of pure abstraction."

"We're in the realm of applied maths now, I think," Mary said flatly. "The theoretical construct has been verified."

"Who could have done this?" Kolo sounded awed. "He'd be worth hiring."

"We don't have time to find out. We need a way out of this problem. It could sink us."

"I have my own little quandary, Ms. Glass, which could get me killed. If you state publicly that you needed to change the name of–"

"Done. I'll give the job to Beano Bates. The ambassador will be forced to back him on it."

"Bates?"

"Yeah, he's the US ambassador's son. Might have to train him to read first. He hasn't got beyond comic books."

"Hereditary affliction, then."

Speaking of such afflictions, Mary wondered how the papers had got hold of her photograph, which she remembered Barbara taking during some adult education course in photography. She shook herself free of these musings. "And the other problem, sir?"

"None of the shares are in my name. The purchase must have been an initiative by some overzealous executive here. I'll publicly fire him, with appropriate compensation, of course. By a strange quirk of fate, all my VPs are from small villages, so payoffs aren't astronomical."

"You'll make a statement?"

"Both written and verbal, with the VP responsible for such an atrocity by my side."

"Thank you, President Kolo."

Mary cut off the call before he had the chance to sign off and trotted to Beano's office. She swung his door open, catching him on the phone. He immediately slammed it down. His blush did not start from his neck and rise upwards, nor fan out from his cheeks, but most bizarrely dropped downwards from his forehead, like blinds. It deepened into a pleasing scarlet as she delegated Kolo's task to him.

Only moments after Mary got back to her desk, Janet entered–new hairstyle, blonder, skirt tighter. "Cheeseman wants to see you."

The eyes of the office were on Mary as she descended from her exhibit and made her way to Cheeseman's office. Although she looked directly at her boss as he threw the contents of his desk at her, her concentration flew to the periphery, to the faces outside the glass walls, witnessing the mime of her disgrace. Later, she could not even recall what he had screamed at her. Only when she walked out of his office did her full senses return to her. Her colleagues' eyes followed her back to her glass case, her footsteps echoing in the hushed silence, her head high, jagged face set in rigid despair.

Cheeseman expected her to sort out the insider trading fiasco before the end of the week. Worse still, he posted security outside her door. In effect, he had fired her, references contingent on her completing a public relations reversal. She wanted to collapse into tears, to crawl under her desk in a ball. Instead, she turned her unproductive shame into a more productive emotion–an explosive rage that wished to vent its power.

"Janet! In. Now."

Janet scurried in, concern in her eyes but pleasure in her body language. "Hey, Mary!"

"Hey, Janet!" Mary mocked her assistant's merry tones. "How are you doing?" She kicked the door shut with her foot.

"Uh . . ." Janet appeared to ponder, then made the fatal mistake. She aimed for a therapy-soft voice. "I dunno. How's it going for you, Mary?"

"Fine." Mary smiled a barracuda smile. "You're fired. I want you out by the end of the day."

"What? Why?"

Mary brought out a file, her tight knot of biceps bulging. "Here's a dossier I have completed, dating back one year. It details the confidential information you have passed on to third parties." Always precise, Mary had listed all of Janet's known exchanges with Sinclair.

"Oh God! You knew?"

"Of course I knew, you idiot!" Mary threw the file at Janet, who was able to dodge it as a result of her work on core strength.

"Please, Mary," Janet begged. "I didn't know she was a spy. She just kept buying me drinks. I didn't know it would be published."

As if a bolt of electricity had been applied to her dying body, Mary surged back to life. Janet had passed on company information to someone outside the company? This small fact would save her hide. This involved more than just the slug Sinclair.

"You signed a confidentiality agreement before you were hired." Mary licked the skin around her thin lips. "Which I'm sure you remember. I would suggest that you provide us with full disclosure before you leave. Or you'll be prosecuted."

Janet began to cry.

"And we'll need full details of your affair with Sinclair–both work-related and personal."

"Personal? But–"

"Everything."

News of Janet's betrayal of information to the media spread immediately, while details concerning Sinclair's disastrous sex life circulated even more rapidly. Relieved, Mary found that the debacle granted her the kiss of life within TransAqua, now that others knew how the vultures had acquired such dangerous facts–a terrifying occurrence, as such transactions were not exactly atypical of corporate life. The condemnation about to attach to her instead transferred to Janet. A pariah in the industry, Janet left without references, severance or a goodbye party, escorted off the premises by armed security guards.

Mary kept a wary eye on Kolo, trusting little in their pact, but he acquitted himself magnificently. The virtuosity of his performance captivated a contrite Western press corps.

"We are a Third World, developing, backward nation, with little knowledge of the minute intricacies hidden within the financial small print inflicted on us by the great institutions of the Western world." Kolo grabbed a battered and makeshift lectern to contain his emotion. "This poor man," pointing to the unfortunate VP, "does not even have an MBA! He is barely literate. Yet he wanted to advance his career in the water business. Is that such a crime?"

In return, Beano Bates's dimples explained that the renaming of the Niger River was a mere "contractual technicality" (secured his hair behind his ears at this point) to distinguish it from the

Niger River in Niger for internal purposes only. This in no way betokened (who taught him that word?) an actual change to the name of the great Niger River. TransAqua certainly had too great a respect for the great cultural wealth of the great nation of Nigeria to entertain such an idea! Four "great"s in two sentences, Mary noted–the most you could expect from Beano's vocabulary.

Wow! magazine requested a lifestyle interview with Bates, while Kolo appeared in voluminous agbadas in numerous television and Internet interviews. After a further week of press sniffing, the trail grew cold, public interest waned. Mary's intestines relaxed and her job was reinstated. All augured well for April.

In a glass office within TransAqua's desert palace, one of the regular readers of the *International Post* issued a smile that stretched into a slash. The front page of its business section bore a rather becoming photograph of the Associate Director of Acquisitions for the Sub-Sahara at TransAqua. Mary Glass flushed with pride, hoping that her parents, Barbara and Sinclair had already come across the article. If a picture tells a thousand words, she could not wait to read the words themselves. Flattery, adulation, tales of masterful machinations–even the font promised as much. Goosebumps shot up her arm, raised hairs attached to high, conical peaks. What a wonderful surprise! The publicity department had not mentioned that they were running a feature on her.

Finally, she could put all the nonsense about insider trading, corruption and so forth behind her. She readied herself for promotion and gulped down some water.

The headline was even more flattering: "The Reign of Bloody Mary." She settled back to find out why she had been selected for such a prominent and comprehensive article.

Mary froze. There, in black and white, every minute detail concerning the elimination of Kolo's adversaries. The article oozed contempt: assassination never played well in the Western press. Perhaps more damaging, however, she had been characterized as brainless, an easy foil for an African's scheming.

Using her peripheral vision, she scanned the office through thin slits. A slow reader, Beano had not finished skimming through the article, but he had lowered the paper sufficiently to reveal the shock that had released the muscles around his jaw, leaving his mouth hanging open. Sinclair unclipped his headset and gazed dreamily at Cheeseman's south-facing office, no doubt considering how to adjust its lighting to ensure a less vivid environment for his reflection should Mary's mess pull the boss down with her.

The phone rang. Mary jumped. Her nerves, often frayed, were now in tatters. A number of red lights blinked. She wanted to avoid the calls, but did not know whether any were important–one of them might be Kolo, or Cheeseman. On the other hand, perhaps the calls were just from the press or the police.

Mary phoned reception and instructed them to forward calls from the media straight to Publicity. A moment later she redialled. "I forgot," she said. "Forward all calls from the police to Publicity as well."

The minute she put down the receiver, the phone rang again.

She exploded. Reception had not understood these basic instructions. Morons.

"Mary Glass," she screamed. "What the fuck is it?"

"How *dare* you speak to your parents like that!" her mother shouted. "Well, I never." She turned away from the phone. "It's Mary! I've finally got through! Pick up the other phone!" She turned back to Mary. "Well, I've got to say, young lady, that you've got . . ." The other phone clicked. " . . . a real cheek."

"What is it?" Father asked.

"She answered the phone 'Mary Glass,'" her mother spoke in a shocked hush, "with the 'F' word in the same sentence!"

"How dare you use our name!" Father yelled. "It's time you got married. Use someone else's name for once."

"As if it isn't bad enough to have a terrorist in our midst, now we have a killer." Mother started blubbering. Her sobs caught, and she struggled for breath.

"But, Mom–"

"How *dare* you refer to your mother as your mother!" Father screamed. "You've lost that right."

The sobbing amazingly stopped. A hard resolve took its place. "You will never again refer to me as your mother."

"Dad, I–"

"Who?"

"I–"

"Who?"

"Mr. Glass . . ."

"That's better."

"It's all lies. All of it."

"It's in the newspaper, dear," Mother said. "Are you trying to tell us that newspapers lie?"

"No, Mom, I–"

"What?" both parents screamed.

"I mean, Mr. and Mrs. Glass, it's just that I–"

"Ernie, we're lucky we escaped with our lives," Mother whispered–an aside that Mary heard clearly.

"But, Mr. and Mrs. Glass . . ." Mary whined.

"Don't you dare threaten us, young lady," Father snapped. "We are your parents, after all!"

The line went dead. Mary slowly put down the receiver, everything smashing into shards around her. A mirror can only reflect that which stands in front of it.

She swivelled around to survey the desert. The sand seemed endless. It struggled on its hands and knees towards an unforgiving horizon. The landscape's shroud of rubble and dull hues subjugated everything of beauty in sight. Even the pink flowers of the cacti housed its oppressive dust. She did not resent the desert's dominance. Water meant everything. Mary worked with water, in a partnership of mutual cooperation and understanding. Therefore, to her, the desert was a friend–a financial cohort. Its existence ensured hers, and hers ensured its expansion. They were, as Al-Anon would put it, codependent.

However, at this moment, she would have preferred to work in a lush country where she could walk among trees and behind bushes, unseen.

Red lights were still flashing. To keep herself together, she decided to pick up another line and face whatever the day had to offer.

"Hey, Mary!" Beano had adopted Sinclair's drawl. "If you need help transferring to Sewage–it's not glamorous, but it pays well. If anything goes wrong in Acquisitions, that is."

"You mean if I'm in big shit, you'd like to really pile it on, right?"

"Oh, no, I–"

"Fuck you!" She slammed down the phone.

She had to do something, but no plan came to mind. The phone rang again. Though exhausted, Mary answered it. Perhaps better news would greet her.

"Hey, Mary."

The worst that could happen.

Barbara.

"What the hell do you want?" Mary growled.

"Just wanna make sure you're okay." This was the most unbearable, the most agonizing, the most refined torture in Mary's universe: Barbara addressing her in her consoling voice. "Do you want me to come and stay with you for a while?"

"Fuck you!"

"Mary, you'll be fine, believe me. You're talented, smart. You'll be picked up in no time."

"Picked up? You think I've been fired?" Mary yelled, caring little whether the rest of the office saw or heard. "I don't believe it!"

"What? No, I . . . You've been fired?" Barbara asked. "Oh no! Well, think on the positives, Mary."

"What?" The glass around Mary's office vibrated.

"Just remember," Barbara perked up, "miracles happen."

What *Chicken Shit for the Soul* crap had Barbara been poring over? Mary threw the phone back on the hook.

Mary could feel herself breaking. The image she had been so careful to perfect had shattered. Even Barbara had profited from the opportunities her arrogance had offered. How many others had also exploited this shortcoming, a fallibility that had not been clear to her before now?

Pale blue trousers bedecked the haunches of the man who sat perched on the very edge of the meeting table, his stabilizing right leg jigging from pure nervous energy. It made the entire table rattle. The same nervous motion afflicted most of the limbs sheltering underneath it.

Sinclair battled hard not to sprawl in his seat, but for once he felt eminently relaxed. Coverage of TransAqua's activities had grown relentless. Now that the scent of insider trading had grown cold, the media had turned their attention to the "accidents" that had befallen Kolo's ministers. After numerous false starts, Mary's career at TransAqua would at last be terminated. She could not–under any circumstances known to him–survive this latest round of scandal-mongering.

Some movement at the end of the table caught his attention: Beano flicking his hair, staring directly at him with query in his eyes. Caring little that Mary could see, Sinclair put up an index finger and mouthed "one week," an indication of Cheeseman's usual tactic of allowing a week for "succession planning." Then Mary would have to hand over all her files to Beano–an interregnum, of course, denied to Janet.

Cheeseman had his back turned to the assembled team, arms crossed, a point on the far wall having secured his attention. In a barely audible growl, he announced, "I want each and every one of you here to pack yer things and leave within the hour. The division is no longer open fer business."

Sinclair absorbed these dramatics impassively, given that Cheeseman was still sponsoring his deal with Niger, as well as the backup plan for the minister of finance, but the ever-ignorant Beano pinged off his chair, his face as horrified as if the Patriots had lost the Super Bowl.

"Sir," Beano gasped, "after all we've invested–"

"Down the toilet, son."

Son? A cloud crossed Sinclair's horizon.

Beano reluctantly sat down and leaned forward, elbows on the table.

"Down the toilet," Cheeseman sighed. "We backed a serial killer. No biggie. Anyone could have made the same mistake. Gather yer things."

Silently, Sinclair slid his chair away from the table, waiting for the unhinged maniac to find his target in Mary. Just needed a trigger.

“Strange guy, huh?” Beano proffered.

As Mary plastered herself against her chair, blue veins accentuating her pallor, Sinclair dispatched a flossed smile of condolence in her direction.

Cheeseman turned around slowly, the volcanic outburst an inevitability.

THIRTY-THREE

Saline Solution

Everything teetered on the edge of oblivion, but somehow Kolo managed to maintain a modicum of authority in government. Fresh riots had broken out in every major city, the miserable squabbling with the desolate, resulting in tens of thousands of deaths.

Daily, Kolo followed the same drill, ricocheting down corridors in tortuous patterns to his office. However, for hunted men nothing can be more dangerous than routine. Knowing this, Kolo launched a surprise visit on his aide.

As Kolo entered, the minister of finance punched out of his chair and slammed down the phone. "President, sir. A great honour."

Kolo hauled himself onto the minister's desk and perched on its edge, settling less flesh there than comfort dictated. "Can you believe this coverage? You would think I'd committed a major crime. These people were plotting to kill me!"

Baffled, the minister shook his head. "In most courts, it would be considered self-defence, Ogbe. No court in the world could prosecute you on that basis."

Hardly believing that the man had dared to use his first name, Kolo immediately considered leaving. The minister obviously correlated a personal visit with deep friendship. Nevertheless, Kolo was desperate to be consoled. He edged his buttocks farther onto the desk. "Self-defence doesn't even begin to describe the constant plots to kill any man brave enough to lead this barbarous country. I'm suffering from battered wife syndrome. It's the only way to describe it. The fear is constant."

"Is this thing worth it? Why not hand over to some other unfortunate?"

"One word. Bedlam." Kolo sniffed in self-importance.

"In that case, Ogbe, you had no option but to eliminate your rivals."

"Would anyone have done any different? I was pushed against my will." Kolo took a bottle of Aspirin out of his pocket and popped four pills. "Want one?"

"No. Thank you, Ogbe."

Again, Kolo balked at the use of his first name. He shook his head, considering the dearth of talent around him. "Can you hear water?"

"No. I can hear an air conditioner."

"I can hear running water. It's relentless. I suppose it's a form of tinnitus. Anyway, how are you today?"

"Dangerously well, sir."

Kolo's neck jerked up, his heart racing. He studied the comforting face in front of him, executing some internal calculations. "Well, I have a country to run, such as it is." After hoisting himself off the desk, he sped away.

In his office, Kolo made a quick call to a computer engineer and then read the papers. Liberal groups had at last unwittingly come to his assistance. What had taken them so long? "Glad they found some time for me, after planting their organic this-thats," he muttered.

The papers' coverage had turned to indignation, incensed that a multinational corporation, the IMF, the World Bank and assorted international financial institutions could squeeze dry a crippled, desperate country, to such a level of exploitation that a corporation would own its water, control pricing and, worst of all, force that country, against its will, to surrender the name of its river, a sacred heritage. Any leader would crumble under such pressure.

A knock on the door.

"Who?"

"Engineer, oga, Mr. President, Your Highness."

"In!"

"All files duplicated to your system, sir, Excellency, President."

Kolo's eyebrows rose. "Very good! Very fast! I'm impressed!"

The IT engineer almost collapsed in gratitude, and threw himself down in full prostration. Kolo waved him up and away with a grand sweep of his hand.

Once he had locked his door, Kolo sat down to investigate the files of the minister of finance. The screen lured the president of the Federal Republic of Nigeria to its flickering beacons with the direct evidence of his speculations scrolling gently into the ether. So, he had been right. Behind the apparent chaos hid an underlying causal pattern.

Sinclair, the architect of the death of his closest allies, had projected a consistent personality: a critical error. Only the deceased minister for the environment had liberally deployed the phrase "dangerously well," which meant only one thing:

Sinclair had not been scheming with the other ministers whose deaths Kolo had ordered.

A cold anger rose in Kolo's breast, stoked by piqued vanity. Sinclair had considered him a mere marionette! He did not like to be outmanoeuvred, particularly by a simple supplier of services with a lexicon of a hundred or so words, contained in a dozen or so meaningless catchphrases strung together in an arbitrary manner.

He would have to play a vigilant game with the minister of finance, a more astute strategist than the minister for the environment and certainly a bolder contender. But first, he had to get rid of the minister's sponsor. About to call Glass, he hesitated. Even a man of his abject humility had a small modicum of ego to protect.

He waited until 6 a.m. TransAqua time before he dialled the company.

"John Sinclair, please," Kolo reached for a box of Quality Street while on speakerphone.

"Just a moment, please." The receptionist sang out the last word.

"John Sinclair speaking."

"Pardon, I asked for Mr. Cheeseman! Who is this?" Kolo's stubby fingers dived into his box of chocolates, searching for a strawberry centre.

"Unfortunately, you've been put through to John Sinclair, sir."

"John Sinclair?" Kolo sounded nonplussed. "This is President Kolo." Miraculously, he found a strawberry delight on his first attempt. "I had hoped to speak to Mr. Cheeseman."

"Mr. Cheeseman is away at the moment. Anything I can help with, President Kolo?" The voice dripped with concern.

Kolo popped the chocolate into his mouth. He sucked loudly

on it, rubbing his tongue up and down its surface, lost in thoughts of revenge.

"Can I be of any help, President Kolo?" the catchphrase repeated, unable to widen out to new expressive horizons.

"I apologize for the interruption," Kolo said. "State business, I'm afraid. Where were we? Ah, yes. I'm having some difficulty with Ms. Glass's handling of the account."

"In what way can I be of help, President Kolo?"

If this man repeats my name just one more time, Kolo thought, *I'll . . . well, that's moot.*

"Ms. Glass doesn't seem to understand the uh . . ." Kolo leaned forward into the speakerphone, " . . . the Nigerian way, shall we call it? I've just opened the newspapers and . . ."

"Ah, yes." Kolo could hear the smile in Sinclair's voice. "Not good."

"Not good?" Kolo screamed. "Utterly unacceptable, Mr. Sinclair! This isn't the way we do business here! Who is the source of these leaks? It must be someone at TransAqua."

"We haven't yet identified–"

"You don't know? What do you mean you don't know? That's not good enough, Mr. Sinclair. I need to speak to Mr. Cheeseman immediately!"

"Tell you what, President Kolo . . ." Kolo cringed at the repeated mention of his name: he knew these basic sales techniques and felt insulted that Sinclair cared to use them on him, " . . . I'll come over personally. How about that?"

"How will that help, Mr. Sinclair? You can't stop your employees from blabbing to anyone with a pad and pencil."

"I'll look into it personally."

"Thank you. I would be very grateful."

"Don't mention it, President Kolo."

"I won't, Mr. Sinclair," he replied. "I won't if you don't."

Sinclair offered up a conspiratorial laugh. "Touché, President Kolo. Touché."

"So . . ." Kolo waited for the tail end of Sinclair's laughter to glide out, " . . . will Mr. Cheeseman be coming too?"

"Uh, no. No, no. I, uh, I can handle it. How about this Thursday, President Kolo? I think I can get things off my plate by then."

"Thursday?" Kolo sounded surprised, pleasantly surprised, honoured. "Are you sure? That would be wonderful. I am busy all day, but we can meet for dinner." Kolo closed his eyes, trying to focus on the conversation rather than on the symphony of water in his head.

"Thursday it is, President Kolo."

Kolo slammed down the phone. He rifled through his memory, contemplating the various qualities of the innumerable doctors who had attended him over the years. Finally, he selected one highly competent physician of limited imagination and almost pathological introversion. His nickname had become more popular than his real name. "Get helicopter ready. Bring Dr. Sikily."

Once Dr. Sikily arrived, Kolo issued instructions. "You are the only man I can trust to complete this task without hiccups. There are few competent people left in this country."

The man's chest pumped out at this news, but no word slipped past his lips.

"Go to Jebba Dam area. Collect water from the most poisoned sites–places where bodies are still floating or diarrhea is there. You're a doctor, so you'll know. Some Western scientists want samples to test to find purification methods. The helicopter is waiting for you. Be back by tomorrow."

The man opened and closed his mouth as if this signified actual speech. He then bowed and departed, his white coat flapping behind him.

Moments later, Kolo's aide rushed in. "Pilot say helicopter don quench for petrol."

Kolo stared in disbelief. "Well, get petrol from civilian aircraft, you idiot!" he barked.

The aide scuttled out again.

The next day, despite a minor mishap, with the helicopter crash-landing a few miles short of its destination, the doctor arrived back at the presidential complex, wearing a neck brace, a plaster cast and bandages. He placed the samples gingerly in Kolo's reception area.

When he was gone, Kolo called Cook. "I need this water filtered, but do not boil it. Please repeat back these instructions."

"Filter water, but no boil."

"Correct. Return bottles as soon as you have finished. Throw filter away. What do you do with the filter?"

"Throw away."

"Correct. The water is too dirty to use filter again. It is for presidential monitoring purposes only."

"Aah." The cook's mouth drooped with disappointment; he could not pilfer the filter for his own use. *Amazing how ungrateful people are, even when you're trying to save their families,* Kolo thought.

A few hours later, Cook returned with the filtered water.

"I need Sparklex to purify the water. Please bring Uzonna from Sparklex."

"Sir."

Uzonna arrived panting, his forehead dripping with sweat. Suffused with veneration, he hardly dared look at the president.

"I don't know if you are aware, but Sparklex has sent me this water with a special request for bottling." Kolo fluffed up his agbada to impress Uzonna further.

Trembling with awe, Uzonna could not answer.

"They are trying to target the Nigerian palate. Please bottle and send it back to me, but mark it on the bottom with a blue dot. It is for monitoring purposes only."

By the next day, Kolo had two crates full of infected water. His steward would serve them to his guest. There was no way Sinclair could survive ordinary tap water in Nigeria, let alone infected water. And with six people involved in this transaction, not even the greatest detective could trace the polluted water back to him.

Ironic, Kolo thought. *The peddler will be flushed away by his own goods.*

Kolo then buzzed his assistant.

"Cook."

"Yes, sir."

He issued specific instructions. Salty, peppered snacks should stoke Sinclair's thirst. Salt to kill a slug. He needed to make him thirsty enough to drink at least five glasses of water–just to be sure. If he could keep Sinclair in Nigeria for one week, the water would riddle the poor man with all kinds of diseases that no manner of Western medicine could cure.

Kolo stood up and crept to a window. He peeked from behind the curtains. He had neither dealt with the minister of finance, a violently intelligent man, nor found out why the American ambassador had supported Jegede. Yet all now seemed quiet. He looked out over the compound walls and wondered how many on the other side of its embattled heights were plotting to shorten his life. The gushing noise exploded again in his ears, this time drowning out the radio and all other surrounding sounds.

He took sharp, shallow breaths to try to control his breathing.

After a close inspection of his golden agbada for hidden snakes and scorpions, Kolo dressed in meticulous fashion for his meeting with John Sinclair. Everything had been prepared, down to the last . . . well, Kolo thought, as far as any Nigerian could plan. And, he mused, it had been a while since he had felt truly stretched, intellectually or dramatically.

Sinclair arrived punctually at 8 p.m.

"Welcome, Mr. Sinclair," Kolo beamed, squeezing his weak hand. "How are you doing?"

The man seemed handsome, but was dressed and coiffed in such a self-conscious fashion that it erased any beauty he might have had. He had an easy smile that appeared to be looking at a mirror no one else could see–its reflection pleased him greatly.

"Nnnnot bad, President Kolo," Sinclair replied. "Dangerously well."

Still, Kolo could see that Nigeria had already beaten some of the life out of the man. His moussed hair glistened, and some of the gel had slipped down the sides of his face to the tip of his ear. His entire face gave off a greasy glint. Even his aftershave had a slightly punchy edge to it.

"Something to drink?" Kolo's agbada billowed out behind him as he walked, a confident stride leading to the reception area. "Water? Sparklex? Snack?" Kolo snapped his fingers and his steward disappeared.

"That would be wonderful, Mr. President." Sinclair sat on the plump crème brûlée armchair offered to him. "Wonderful country, Nigeria. Delightful." His tired eyes betrayed other sentiments.

"Some people find it a bit trying," Kolo said, "but I'm partial to it." He smiled for a brief moment, until the pain from his rash caused him to disengage the muscles.

"Absolutely." Catchphrase number seven. "Oh, absolutely."

Kolo's steward opened two bottles of water, poured them into two glasses and left snacks on their side tables. *I'll give him a week,* Kolo thought. *A week at max.*

Sinclair reached for his glass. He sat back with the water in his hand, its condensation dripping into his palms.

Kolo shifted forward, muscles taut. He smiled. "Well . . ." Kolo lifted his glass and tinkled the ice cubes. "Cheers!"

Sinclair tinkled back, smiled, allowed the glass to hover near his mouth and discreetly replaced it on the side table.

Kolo froze. He hoped Sinclair did not suspect anything.

"How refreshing!" Kolo took a long gulp and smacked his lips. "Nothing like a long, cold drink of water in this climate."

"Oh, absolutely, President Kolo." Sinclair lifted the glass to his cheek to cool it down, closing his eyes for a brief moment and sighing. Then he replaced the glass on its coaster.

Unable to believe his eyes, a desperate Kolo motioned to the steward. "Turn air conditioning off," he whispered.

The steward's eyebrows rose, but he followed the president's orders.

"Oh no! Not again!" Kolo tutted. "Bloody power supply. Can't be relied upon. Steward! Open windows!"

A searing gust of burning air whooshed into the room.

"Best to keep hydrated," Kolo advised his guest, raising his glass again. "A toast to our partnership."

"A toast, President Kolo!" They clinked glasses.

Sinclair allowed his lips to touch the rim of the glass, pretended to sip the water and then set the crystal back down.

Kolo's brain shifted into high gear. Who, in this chain of events, could have tipped Sinclair off? Only six people were involved: his aide, the doctor, the pilot, the cook, the bottler and the steward. Kolo considered the bottler: a Sparklex employee.

As he ruminated, he caught Sinclair glancing at the glass. Not at the water, he realized, but at the ice cubes. Kolo cursed. The steward had not followed his instructions. Next time, he would have to write them down.

"Ah, the ice cubes," he exclaimed, as sweat trickled down his face. "I was wondering. Steward!"

"Yes, sir."

"Sparklex. No ice. Only Sparklex, okay?"

Steward set down another glass and opened a new bottle of water. Sinclair settled back with an expression of relief and took a sip of water.

"Do help yourself." Kolo indicated the snacks.

"I would love to, President Kolo. Unfortunately, I'm allergic to peanuts."

"Someone from your team mentioned that. We made sure to eliminate them from the kitchen."

"Very thoughtful, sir." Sinclair tossed back some salted snacks.

Kolo breathed a sigh of relief.

Within a minute, Sinclair was gasping for air.

"What's the matter?" Kolo ran to his side, terrified that they had both been poisoned by the cook. "Get doctor! Get doctor!" he screamed to his steward, as he loosened Sinclair's tie.

Sinclair pointed to his throat. "Pea-nut! Pea-nut!" Then he pointed to his briefcase, mouthing "medicine"–an action Kolo ignored.

"What? But . . . Get cook!" Kolo shrieked. "Hurry!" He could hardly believe this turn of events. If he had known the extent of Sinclair's peanut allergy, he would not have spent so much energy getting the water.

The cook ran in.

"Did his assistant not tell you he could not eat peanuts?" Kolo yelped. "Did you put peanut into this snack?" He grew increasingly angry: Sinclair was outsmarting him again by dying in this manner.

"No peanut, sir," the cook replied, terrified. "Only groundnut oil."

"You idiot!" Kolo slapped the cook on the face. "Don't you know groundnut is peanut? It's the same thing! Where is my aide? And get American ambassador! Now!"

Kolo could not afford another murder laid at his door. He had to ensure that this would be witnessed as an accident. Sinclair had really thrown a wrench in the works this time.

Hubris, I know, Kolo thought, *yet my plan was so perfect, so watertight, so symbolic.*

"Ep-in-eph-rine!" Sinclair rasped through an ever-swelling throat, pointing at his briefcase. His face was turning blue.

"You have medication?" Kolo asked, his expression of concern peppered with shock. "Aha! Ms. Glass mentioned something . . . or was it Mr. Bates? I simply can't remember." At the mention of these names, Sinclair's pupils dilated.

Kolo rifled through Sinclair's briefcase and found the medication, which he hid in his pocket. *If I hadn't been a politician,* Kolo thought, *I would have made a great actor. Same skills required. Perhaps after I leave politics, I could try the stage.*

"Mr. Sinclair, I'm afraid you might have forgotten to bring it."

Sinclair stared at his briefcase, his throat increasingly inflamed, forcing him to wheeze–a tremendous effort–for precious air. His face turned purple. Small beads of sweat appeared on his forehead. Kolo rushed to cradle him. The air filled with the racket of Sinclair desperately trying to take in oxygen, air travelling past his vocal chords, a rasp that could be heard in the kitchen and at the gates of the presidential compound, a loud, passionate clinging to life.

"The doctor will be here soon." Kolo patted him on his breast pocket in a consoling manner. He cursed himself for not putting more emphasis on the end of the sentence, wrench more passion from it, more gravitas perhaps.

Sinclair opened his eyes. Kolo looked down on him, a wide grin alighting on his face. It calmed him to think that he had, after all, made some small contribution to Sinclair's death.

And that Sinclair now knew this fact.

After a few minutes, the rasping deadened into short croaks. The life ebbed out of the man just as the American ambassador rushed in. Three hours later, an ambulance arrived, a veritable miracle of emergency attention by Nigerian standards.

Although Kolo had enjoyed watching Sinclair suck in his last breaths, it had also reminded him, in the end, of his own mortality, of his brother struggling for air as his lungs filled with water. He realized with violent clarity that he was now in an untenable position, a position he would be unable to quit in any manner that would entail his survival. Here he sat, the most persecuted president in Nigerian history, a victim, unable to resign without provoking prosecution and on his heels, his aide, a man too intelligent to ski in the Alps, go yachting, or crash in a military plane. Even though Kolo knew Glass would continue to support him, any dog could back the minister of finance. And the American ambassador fit the spec. His feeble attempts to joust in Nigeria now began to unnerve Kolo. Here was a mongrel with whom the minister could do business, yet as a result of all these regrettable deaths, Kolo could not even consider the minister's extermination for at least a year, maybe two.

So he would have to remain the country's leader, looking constantly over his shoulder, knowing that his enemies, and even his closest friends, would at any moment be plotting his downfall in a bloody coup d'état.

And his most cherished of dreams–the miracle of engineering in honour of his presidency–would crumble to dust, smashed like Kainji Dam by the deluge of support for Femi Jegede, a torrent that he had managed to hold at bay only for a brief moment of time, a small blink of history.

He hung his head and wept. He had not wanted much from life. Why, he wailed, had a man of his abilities been burdened with presiding over the most wayward of nations?

Kolo retired to his haven to await the abatement of the storm this event would doubtless generate. Exhausted, he wove his way back to the garage, with its adjoining bathroom. He dragged himself into its tiled majesty to turn on golden taps.

He sniffed the air and wheeled about, struck with terror. No one in sight. Yet that smell . . . rank, unwashed, asphyxiating. What memory?

"Guard!" he shouted.

"Sir!"

"In!"

The guard entered the garage, his aviator sunglasses still perched on his nose.

"Did someone come into this room?"

The guard considered for some moments, checking every minute of the day. "Yes, sir."

"Enh? What is your problem? Have I not told you never–*never*–to let enter? Did I not say?"

"Yes, sir."

"And?"

"Em, it was Innocent. He go for get car clean."

"Ah. Why didn't you say? I said 'someone,' not 'Innocent'! Anyone else?"

Another long deliberation, then a memory alert. "Ah, yes, sir.

He had no weapons. He came from Inspector General of Police. Same man you talk to in supply store. So garage same-same."

Quaking with rage, Kolo came within an inch of the guard's face and flicked his sunglasses to the floor. Unfortunately, the man was very tall, so he still held the advantage. "First of all, broom cupboard is not supply store. We met in broom cupboard. Why would we meet in supply store? What kind of madman do you think I am?"

"Sir, not . . . no, not mad at all. Never. No, sir."

"Second of all, in what way is my bedroom, regardless of its former function, like a supply-store-broom-cupboard-what-have-you?"

"Sir, not . . . no, not same at all. Never. No, sir."

Kolo opened the Mercedes' trunk, to double-check for intruders. "No more visitors to my bedroom, only cleaners. If you see this man again . . . which one was it?"

"Crazy one, sir."

Kolo breathed a sigh of relief. At least they had not let the ugly one in, with all his sores and pustules. "If you see him again, accompany him to the broom cupboard as before. I can meet him there."

"But he waited long, long time, sir."

"Yes, well, there was an unfortunate death to attend to." Kolo's index finger sailed forward, pointing towards the other side of the door.

Another intricate turn, just as inelegant as the police's, and the guard marched out.

After running his bath, Kolo beached himself within it and lapped the water against his body, wondering what Ekong wanted him for.

He submerged himself farther into its cleansing embrace, mouthing the words of John Pepper Clark's soothing poetry:

"Fear him his footfall soft light as a cat's, his shadow far darker than forest gloom or night–"

He sank farther down into the tub until the water reached his neck.

THIRTY-FOUR

Mary's Garden Grows

After packing her few personal items, Mary sat back, put her feet on her desk for the last time and flipped to *TV Afrique.*

She yawned. She had run out of adrenaline. She rocked her chair as news flashed by of floods in Mozambique, death squads wreaking havoc in Congo as more emerald deposits were found, a Senegalese filmmaker receiving the Nobel Prize for Literature and then a surprise item–Kolo and the American ambassador giving a joint news conference.

Sinclair. Dead.

The chair stopped rocking.

This could mean only one thing.

Promotion.

Within hours, Corporate Communications had laid out a strategy to ensure that all blame rested squarely on Sinclair's gelled head, isolating it on that slippery spot so that it could not besmirch any other reputation. Cheeseman, with an eye to his own tenure, protected Mary. She managed to scramble back into the corporation under the radar, to turn away from the harsh glare of publicity and to hide from all scrutiny. She recognized that it would take years for her reputation to recover outside TransAqua, but at least she would be able to keep her job.

Cheeseman called an emergency meeting the next day. Mary had donned her best blue suit and pulled her hair back to display the acute and obtuse angles of her face. As she entered the meeting room, all eyes turned to her.

Co-workers marvelled at her ability to maintain composure–serenity, even–as she presided alone and in all secrecy over matters of life and death. Mary could feel the change as her peers began to crave a similar power. Beano pointed a finger gun greeting at her. The associate directors looked at her with pride in their eyes, as if she were an extension of their own egos.

She heard heels clacking in the distance, a hurried, irregular pace. *He must be under considerable stress,* Mary thought. *He's probably had to take over all of the Slug's files–both pages of them.* Her mouth stretched into a wry slash.

Cheeseman bounded in and slammed the door, sniffing.

Cocaine.

He sat down, resting his ankle on his opposite knee in alpha-male position.

"Well, y'all've heard of Mr. Sinclair's unfortunate demise . . ." he began.

"Tragedy," Beano said. "Terrible tragedy."

"Great pity," Cheeseman acknowledged the sentiment. "We've sent flowers. The bigger tragedy is lack of succession planning. It's impossible to make head nor tail of his files. We need to appoint someone to his spot immediately."

Butterflies struggled for space in Mary's meagre stomach.

"Glass," Cheeseman pronounced, sending Mary's heart knocking against her ribs, "I've decided to give you the position. You seem tough enough for the job. Let's congratulate Ms. Glass for a reward long overdue."

The room erupted into cheers and loud applause.

The feeling of acceptance was momentary. Mary only had to scan the table to return to her state of heightened anxiety. There were no friends here, only competitors.

Within two days, after positive media reports began to emerge expressing shock at the actions of a rogue operator, Mary moved to a bigger fish tank and Beano moved into hers, without even a slight delay for convention's sake. His boxes had been packed even before the emergency meeting. She then realized who else had known about Sinclair's visit to Nigeria, a child perhaps persuaded by the president to divulge lethal information about his colleague–a ploy Kolo had not been reticent to use with Mary.

More vulnerable than her peers could imagine, Mary spent the next few days recovering from the shock of near dismissal. She developed a sore on her lip as she bit the skin off it constantly.

After another restless night, Mary returned to the Acquisitions floor at 6 a.m. exhausted, passing her former office, now occupied by a man with hair flopping over his blue eyes and a plastic smile as irksome as Sinclair's. She hated Beano as much as his mentor. Worse still, she knew that, lacking Sinclair's oversized ego, he was twice as dangerous, charming people with his carefree, laid-back manner. While Sinclair swam around like a parading shark, Beano lurked in camouflaged silence like the venomous and deadly stonefish.

In preparation for the team meeting, Mary phoned Kolo to negotiate further rights to the Niger River. It took over an hour to get through, as different levels of security vetted her call.

"Ms. Glass?" Kolo answered at last, his voice quivering with emotion. "I'm sure you've heard the tragic news."

"Yes, sir," Mary yawned silently. "Terrible news."

"Are you taping this conversation, Ms. Glass?" Kolo's voice had changed to a steelier tone.

"No."

"Well, I can hear a tape."

"I'm not taping. I have an interest, as you do, in keeping our conversations private. And since I didn't know Sinclair was coming to visit you, I'd hardly have the time to–"

"Mr. Sinclair dropped in of his own accord, Ms. Glass. Apparently, he had an allergy to peanuts." His voice reverted again, carrying more pathos and sorrow. "Ms. Glass–it's a mainstay of Nigerian food!"

"Well, you weren't to know, sir."

"But the cook knew, Ms. Glass. He just didn't know groundnuts and peanuts were the same thing." He blew his nose so loudly, Mary almost dropped the phone.

"You sound devastated," Mary said in a monotone.

"I am," Kolo whimpered. "I am. So," he revived, "how can I help you?"

"To meet our original targets of servicing all your fresh water needs, we'll need to acquire rights to the Benue River as well. It's cleaner water and flows into the Niger, so it's basically," she thought of a term to minimize the damage, "an offshoot."

"An offshoot? The Benue? That's like saying the Atlantic is an offshoot of the Pacific! Impossible! You'd have the whole country in a stranglehold! You'd have, well, effectively you'd have our entire water supply."

"Well, sir, the Benue is technically a tributary. And it would be wonderful to name a river after your brother, President Kolo. Twinned rivers nourishing your great country."

Silence.

"You drive a hard bargain, Ms. Glass." Kolo sounded weary. "Okay. Let's go ahead."

Since she now had the upper hand, Mary felt she could broach a subject of even greater importance. "We also need to discuss embezzlement, fraud, water rackets. It seems a lot of our revenue is disappearing."

"That's not fraud, Ms Glass. Our people are working with an American company, so it's simply the local way of achieving wage parity. There's little I can do about that. Unfortunately, you have laws on minimum wage. Local officials are merely ensuring compliance."

Mary had a hunch that more questions would only suck her further into Nigeria's deviant ethos. "And our water is also disappearing. Our pipes are being cut."

"Certainly not! Not in Nigeria! It's a hot country, Ms. Glass. You must expect some evaporation."

"And your bureaucracy seems unable to deal with pilfering on either issue." Defeated, she waited for another warped rationalization.

"Pilfering! In Nigeria? This is not something we tolerate, Ms. Glass. And as soon as we can afford to pay our police force, it will be dealt with. Meanwhile, we rely on these individual water collection agents and other such entrepreneurs."

"President Kolo, we cannot–"

"Did you hear that?" Kolo sounded anxious.

"No. What was it?"

"Dripping. I think something's leaking. They're trying to flood this place."

"They? Who is they?"

"You know. *They,*" he whispered. "Don't worry, Ms. Glass, I only sleep an hour at a time, so there's absolutely no way they can get me. Absolutely no way."

It took several weeks for Mary to read through all the emails in Sinclair's inbox: he had little method and didn't seem to know the function of the delete key. The slime had made deals with multiple territories in Niger that would divert a sizeable portion of the Niger River before it flowed onto Nigerian soil. She as yet had no specific idea how to revoke these contracts, so she sent them off to a language specialist. Knowing Sinclair, there would be loopholes created in the interstices between English and French.

Sinclair's emails and chats with the minister of finance were of particular interest; this name she would not forward to Kolo. She would deal with him herself, as a separate, perhaps more resilient, candidate. A few emails mentioned a connection between the minister of finance and the Inspector General of Police. The latter had personally selected Lance Omeke to assassinate Jegede. Mary, unable to eat for days, grew dizzy. Sinclair had been within a tentacle's width of discovering her collusion with the African Water Warriors and the explosions at TransAqua's dam site.

She clicked back into her own email inbox and scrolled down until she alighted on another item of interest. The private investigator she had hired had written back. She opened the email.

He had unearthed the mystery of the woman at the bar to whom Janet had divulged so much confidential and damaging information. Her name was Mimi Minto, and she was not a journalist–she worked for Drop of Life.

In a fit of anger, Mary's small muscles and thin bones tried to overturn her desk. Even in her fury, she noticed her new secretary observing her with the eyes of a birdwatcher, and she surreptitiously let her desk drop back into place.

An invoice from a friend of her father's slipped to the ground. She snatched it up. Her company had been billed over $10,000 for a report interpreting the blueprints for the dam–no doubt for Drop of Life.

How could someone as mercurial as that imbecilic mess of a sister have organized anything, let alone seen it through? Not one cell in her entire overfleshed body contained any element of predictability, reliability or focus.

Then three words from her MBA popped into her mind: flexible, fast, futured. They described the advantages of small companies over behemoths such as TransAqua–a motorboat versus an ocean liner.

Mary focused on the only avenue available to her: retribution. Surely she could find a way to get back at Barbara.

An idea surfaced. A great idea.

Mary called her sister on computer phone–she wanted to see her face.

"Barbie! It's Mary. I'm on camera."

"Ooh! Just a minute." After an incessant wait, the half-witted lunatic figured out how to work this basic technology. One day she might even be able to flush the toilet without any assistance. "Hey, Mary! Can you see me?"

What the hell was that material satelliting out from her head? Did the toddlers' shop not carry her size of shirt? How many bangles, mathematically speaking, could be fitted onto the human arm? "Yeah. I can see you."

"What's up? Find a new job?"

This embodiment of ineptitude dared to condescend to her! Rage lashed through Mary's body. "No, actually. I just got promoted to–"

"Well done! Congratulations! Miracles happen, huh?"

Mary grabbed the edge of her desk, the only anchor for a rage that threatened to grow violent, caring little for telltale fingerprints. "I don't know why, but you've been out to get me. I've never done anything to deserve that, but hey, water under the bridge. And anyway, you messed that up, as expected. But you know what? You've inspired me. It'll be my new hobby to annihilate every last thing that means anything to you. And I mean from your work–"

"I'm leaving."

"–to your house–"

"I'm moving!"

"–to every element of your lifestyle–"

"It's changing!"

Each utterance seemed to cheer Barbara, as if these neutralizations merely conjured up new adventures.

"–to your relationship."

"I've tried that myself–didn't work. Astro's pretty needy."

Barbara stared at the screen eagerly, awaiting more suggestions. Mary decided to drop the big one. "I'll hold you responsible for Jegede's death. You, Barbie. Apparently Lance Omeke's work with the AWW was financed by a Ms. Glass–probably someone like yourself with a preference for armed insurrection."

Barbara's smile collapsed. "I wouldn't try that, Mary. It's cruel, it's wrong, and I simply won't let you."

"You won't let me?" Mary snickered. "Someone tells you to get the blueprints. Woohoo! Mission accomplished. So now you actually believe you're heading up the FBI or something?"

"But, Mary–"

Mary cut the call dead, even more enraged. She seethed, wishing to smash her body against the glass panels, just to see them shatter. She could smash them, because they didn't move.

Debris like Barbara, too immature to invest in those things precious to others–status, wealth, power–would be harder to obliterate. How do you trash garbage?

Realizing the degree to which this calamity had distracted her, she raced to a team meeting seven minutes early, where she found Cheeseman already seated. He seemed under an inordinate amount of stress.

"Ms. Glass," he said in his most sarcastic tone. "Thanks for dropping by."

"Mr. Cheeseman. Sorry I'm late."

"Siddown. Update."

A muscle on Mary's neck bulged with apprehension. "Well, uh, as you know, I uh, I've uh–"

"What the hell do you think this is?" Cheeseman yelled. "A support group? I'm not interested in sharing an emotional experience with you, Glass. I want facts." A stalactite of spit stuck stubbornly to the centre of his mouth as he spoke. "So spill."

Beano and two other members of the team entered the room.

"Kolo has agreed to the sale of rights to the Benue River in the east. It's a huge acquisition. The details will be on your desk tomorrow."

Cheeseman stared at her, threw his head back and laughed. "Whoa!" He issued another volley of spitty laughter, wiping non-existent tears from his eyes as more team members entered the room and scuttled to their chairs. "Promoted a few weeks and . . ." he leaned forward, screaming, " . . . you've only made *one* goddam phone call! What the hell do you think we're paying you for? Get your act together, sister, or you're outta here."

"Yes, sir."

"Nigeria isn't the only country in Africa and the Middle East. Buy a map."

"Yes, sir."

"We've handed you the deserts of the world on a silver platter, and this is all you can do?"

"I'll get right on it, sir."

"You bet yer skinny ass you will. By Friday next week."

Beano smirked.

Mary could see only one solution to her predicament: oust Cheeseman. His position was evidently exposed, isolated, precarious.

On returning to her office, Mary closed her eyes, trying to quell her fury. Barbara invaded every thought, distracting her. She had to deal with her sister first. She opened her eyes, clicked on to Drop of Life's website and picked up the phone, determined to execute Barbara's downfall. "Hey, Krystal! It's Barbie."

"Oh, hi there! I didn't know you weren't using your full name anymore."

"Only to close, close friends, Krystal. I'm trying to wrap up here on TransAqua, but I can't remember how to log on."

"Oh, Barbie!" Krystal tinkled into accepting laughter. "You're at home, right? Okay, here're your passwords. And you'll also need remote access, so you'll need this information . . ."

Mary wrote down a long string of codes. "Thanks. Could you put me on to Brad?"

"Sure, hon."

Barbara could never have obtained all that information on the deal–secured within a password-protected environment–and she certainly had nothing to do with forensic accounting; the muttonhead could not even do her own taxes! Responsibility rested with someone higher up in her organization, perhaps that sari woman.

After a microsecond, a man picked up the call. "Brad Chambers speaking." An efficient, intelligent voice saturated with discretion flowed through her earpiece. Her arms prickled with goosebumps. His website picture made him look like quite a catch.

"Hey, Brad. It's Barbara."

Cheeseman clopped past her office in his cowboy boots, their spurs ringing a persistent message of menace. This would have to wait, in case he spotted any incriminating information. She would give the whole thing a week–tops. "Will call later," she said and hung up. He would be used to this unpredictability from her sister.

Mary wondered if she could engineer a meeting with Brad after Drop of Life's crash.

Beano sniffed his new office, realizing that Mary had not even left behind her scent! He watched the silent film in her new office with interest, giggling when she was unable to turn over her desk, wondering what conversation could have provoked such a facial expression, pinched with increasing vexation as she spoke into her camera phone. He particularly admired the impassivity with which she received the blistering attacks that turned Cheeseman's countenance towards the blue end of the spectrum. Studying Mary was more intellectually stimulating than watching Sinclair, whose emotions he had had no difficulty reading.

At the end of Act I, Beano picked up his phone. "Hey, Dad!"

"Beano." His father sounded weary, absolutely spent. "It's chaos. Anarchy. The apocalypse."

"So, nothing new, huh?" Beano snorted a "gotcha" laugh before his father could detonate. "Time for Major General Wosu P. Wosu? I've got this feeling I'll be promoted again very soon." He thought of little else but the corner office, with its great view of the mountains. Perhaps in unconscious anticipation, he had worn his mountain boots to work.

"Kolo's so weak, we no longer need a military man from the east to placate him. Besides which, we miscalculated. That Wosu is already having clandestine meetings. I reckon we've got another Kolo on our hands, kid."

"Dad–you gotta be kidding, right?" Alarmed, Beano mentally logged out of the corner office. Without his own candidate in power, Mary might ultimately connect Jegede's positive press coverage to him.

"Should have figured that out–that's how someone with his undesirable ethnic background got so high in the army in the first place: slimy, sly, calculating."

"Who has Wosu been visiting?"

"The usuals. The paramount leaders, politicos, embassies, you name it. So in answer to your next question, no, we can't get any religious mileage out of this. He's done too much groundwork. No one you can trust over here, son. And I mean no one."

"Jeez, Dad. That must be tough." All his work, flushed down the toilet. But what might be salvaged if he pulled the lever first? His day brightened and he gazed once again at the corner office. "I've heard–it's just a rumour now, sir–that Wosu will try to get his Igbo cronies into power and secure oil from the Delta for the east. To me–and I'm no, like, politician–that seems potentially divisive. Is that right?"

His father pondered. After some time, he replied, "Yep, I'll work on it."

"So the country probably needs firm leadership from the Middle Belt."

"Military?"

"It'll wash the stench of Kolo away."

"I don't even think your Sewage pals could do that." The ambassador choked at his own joke.

From his bottom drawer, Beano pulled out a binder entitled "Wastewater: Pathogenic Organisms." Within it, a list of contenders for presidency. "Okey-dokey. Here we go. Ever heard of Brigadier Jamal Abdullah?"

"Never."

"Very pleasant guy, apparently. He failed Sandhurst twice."

"Perfect."

"The British High Commissioner's son failed with him."

"Even better!"

"Plus, he's got a daughter trying to get into Harvard."

"Any hope?"

"Not a chance."

"Guess he'll need a bit of help with that."

"Well, education is important, Dad, as you've always said."

When Mary crept into the office the next day, all was silent. Faces ashen. Expressions hollow. Cheeseman anchored motionless. She scrambled into her tank, catching a quick view of Beano, head in hands, she supposed, since all she could see was hair.

She clicked on to a news website. TransAqua had once more made the front page. She could only hope that some other dupe in the company had taken the heat off her. But she noticed yet another of Barbara's photographic masterpieces of her, alongside images of Cheeseman, the CEO, Sinclair and even a short-haired Beano, circa Sewage era.

It was not the usual reportage–they had unveiled a new narrative style so engrossing that even Mary could not wait until the denouement. Beautifully designed graphics described how Sinclair had tricked Nigeria's president into assassinating rivals to protect those his team at TransAqua supported. And, the kicker: an entire paragraph outlining Sinclair's manipulation of her.

With enormous effort, Mary raised her eyes and saw the entire office staring at her–some eyes reflecting Kolo's demon, others Sinclair's dupe. Mary felt violated. That slug, may he dance in the flames of an everlasting hell, had stripped her of all dignity, watching all her naked intrigues with a lecherous grin of expectation. She hated Sinclair, loathed him, wished he were still alive so she could watch him die again. More than that, she abhorred the person who had unveiled her humiliation for the world to see. Barbara. How much more ammunition did her sister have stored up, ready to detonate just as Mary recuperated from each successive blow?

Her door still open, Mary waited for a sound but heard only the rustling of a newspaper or the clicking of a computer mouse as the staff read the narrative of their own downfall. She rose, shut herself in and, regardless of this defining catastrophe, renewed her onslaught on Barbara. Her sister must have purchased explosives. That would ruin her career.

Mary picked up the phone. "Brad Chambers, please."

"Okay, hon, just a minute," an anonymous voice sparkled.

"Brad Chambers speaking."

"Oh, hi there, Brad. It's Barbara. Just trying to wind up this Nigeria thing. Congratulations on the forensic thing, by the way. I saw some diagrams in a magazine. Those Nigerian systems and things. Pretty inventive, huh?"

"Ms. Glass, they exhibited a degree of perfection that is hard to imagine as the creation of a human mind. To describe its sublime formations would lie outside the narrow confines of language."

She almost swooned. "And yet predatory–you can feel the carnal nature of its invention, Mr. Chambers."

"There is a saying that tells of the inexpressible beauty of Nigerian financial structures: 'Whereof one cannot speak, thereof one must pass over in silence.' Are you familiar with the aphorism?"

She put her hand to her chest. "Wittgenstein. *Tractatus.* Proposition 7. So, are Nigerian accounting systems of such exquisite design?"

He passed over this question in silence.

"You must be highly talented, Mr. Chambers."

"I am a seeker of beauty only, Ms. Glass. The builders are the talented ones. Like your sister."

"Who? Mary?" she sneered.

"No, Ms. Glass. Barbara."

Mary's inhalation caught: outwitted again. The magic of the last few moments dissipated into the polluted air that sustained Barbara's breathing. "Where is she? Standing next to you? Let me speak to her."

"I think she's at home." Brad sounded discomfited. "She, um, believes in the energizing qualities of the afternoon siesta."

"I do apologize for that unwarranted outburst, Mr. Chambers. How did you know I wasn't Barbara?"

"She knows nothing about accounting, Ms. Glass. None of its mystery and awe."

"And yet you call her talented. You should know better, Mr. Chambers. She's completely harebrained."

"Her thinking is . . ." long pause, " . . . non-linear, like many . . ." another ponderous pause, " . . . creative people. But she alone had the faith that we could challenge a corporation or topple a government. And her speeches . . . very powerful, Ms. Glass."

"*She* organized all this?"

"Oh yes. None of us would have dared."

Such counterintuitive information chipped away at the solidity of her knowledge, and the concretion began to disintegrate under the pressure until only the rubble of confusion remained. Had the tilt-headed buffoon been capable of all this? Mary's mind sped back to their childhood, shuttled back and forth in frenetic recall, desperately trying to reconstruct that which now lay in ruins. Nothing made sense.

At last Mary spoke. "All that energy devoted to one cause. And do you know what that cause was, Mr. Chambers?"

"Water, Ms. Glass. The welfare of the Nigerian people."

"No, there you would be wrong. One reason only. She did this to wreck my life." Mary said it simply, but the fact of it hurt her greatly, as if the vessel of her identity had suddenly emptied.

"With all due respect, Ms. Glass, I believe in this matter you may be mistaken. She refused to let us divulge two critical pieces of information until yesterday, to the great . . ." long pause, " . . . chagrin of our executive director. The first concerned your financing of the TransAqua bombing."

"I had no idea that the AWW would do that!" she protested. "I only asked them to discredit Jegede."

"A great pity. Perhaps you should have told her."

Mary remembered slamming down the phone on her sister. *But, Mary* . . . What had Barbara been about to say? She pictured the turban, the expression of concern, the tilting of her head while displaying cleavage, wanton and depraved. Mary grew physically repulsed at the imaginary sight.

Brad Chambers continued. "The second fact: that you *knowingly* supplied names to President Kolo. That you, in effect, served as executioner by proxy."

When Brad described it that way, her actions almost seemed unethical!

"None of the other information could be traced back to you solely or directly," he continued.

"And Barbara managed to curb herself? Why?"

"Because she has a great deal of respect for you. At least, she always spoke about you with the greatest reverence, Ms. Glass."

Mary despised her sister more than ever. Since childhood, that buffoon had dared to look down on her. This most recent act–protecting her–only demeaned Mary further. Barbara's actions would destroy a very valuable corporation, at least, in its present manifestation. This was typical of Barbara's condescending, holier-than-thou, head-tilting, therapy-dispensing, botched job of a personality.

"I'm ruined," Mary said. "Everything I ever worked for."

"Ms. Glass, ask Barbara for help. She's very creative, extremely bold. She'll find a way out."

"There is no way out!" Mary whispered.

"Ms. Glass, whereof one must not be silent, thereof one must speak. This is Barbara's credo." His last words sounded prophetic.

Unable for once to contain her emotions, Mary burst into tears, wished a hurried goodbye to Brad and slammed down the phone.

As Brad's words chiselled away at her convictions, Mary studied the reflective panes of TransAqua's glass building. The transparent walls sent a clear message that the people within had nothing to hide, yet if that were so, the company would have no need for the walls at all. In fact, she realized, the glass served quite the opposite function: to dupe people into thinking that sight equated to sound. But what could be observed offered no clue as to words spoken, or actions taken, within its cells.

Even if she divulged all she knew of the corporation's activities, she could not shatter these walls. In fact, they would not even crack. Far from fragile, they were solid, built to withstand earthquakes. Not like glass at all. Another deception.

She heard Cheeseman's spurs ringing down the corridor, their clinking directed at her office, the sound of a hunted man searching for prey.

In frustration, she picked up her keys and tossed them at a pane. She wondered how far they would bounce. They clacked against the wall and then dropped straight down. The glass had very little give. She sighed–it could not even play games. As she went to fetch her keys, an anomaly caught her attention.

The impact had left a spiderweb crack in the glass. The action did not shatter it and the fracture was no larger than the size of a hand. But the notion that she could chip this adamantine material came as a total surprise.

The door opened and, for once, she allowed an emotion to reveal itself. She smiled.

She had the option of destroying Cheeseman from within TransAqua, as quarry, or from without, by cracking the glass. Either she could maintain the system or she could make a small contribution to changing it. And for once she refused to be rushed into making a decision.

THIRTY-FIVE

Blue Skying

Barbara settled back in her new waterbed, flipped open the British left-wing journal *The Internationalist,* and scanned a report on the sale of water rights.

After an hour, she turned off her bedside light and turned on a lava lamp. She watched as the globules of wax flowed over each other, slipping, slithering, arching, flexing. Next to her bed, she had laid out an assortment of aids and devices in order of sequence. She closed her eyes, thinking of the wax, considering its shapes, dreaming of a life spent sliding over other shapes, lathered in hot oil, behind a glass encasement for all to see.

At 10:15 p.m., there was a knock on the door. She raised herself with difficulty from her waterbed and went down to answer the door, breasts hanging low in a diaphanous nightdress.

A man stood outside in dark blue overalls and a baseball hat, carrying a toolbox.

"Oh, excuse me, madam," he exclaimed. "I didn't mean to disturb you. I didn't know anyone'd be in. The landlord sent me."

"The landlord? He hasn't notified me."

"I can wait here while you call him, ma'am." He looked at his watch. A testy note entered his voice. "Or I can come back later." He leaned in the doorway.

"Who the hell are you, anyway?" Barbara stood blocking his entry, hands on hips.

"I'm from the water commission." The man's eyes scouted the room.

"Really?" Barbara waited for more information.

"Apparently there's illegal use of water in here. I have to scan the property."

"At this time of night?"

"Well," light eyes shot her a look of utter indifference, "either I come in or you go to jail. Now–what will it be?" He elbowed past her and slammed his toolbox on the floor. "Do you know where the meter is?"

"No, I don't. You'll have to look for it yourself."

"Got pink buttons? Two large pink buttons? You've never seen it?"

"No," she replied. "The only pink buttons I've seen recently are these." She opened her nightgown. "Now, I don't think–"

"You don't think?" Giant yellow eyes looked at Barbara in contempt. "I'm the engineer here, ma'am. I'll do the thinking." His baseball visor jiggled as he spoke. "As it happens, those are exactly what I was looking for. Now, I just have to get the radar out." He undid the last two buttons of his overalls and flipped out his instrument.

"Okay," he said, "let's see what we have here." He put his fingers on Barbara's nipples and twiddled them gently like dials. "Uh-huh," he said. "Interesting. Very interesting."

"Look, I–"

"Please, ma'am," yellow eyes closed in concentration, "don't disturb me while I'm working." His penis hardened, activating a quasi-pneumatic mechanism.

"Okay," he said, looking down at his apparatus, "looks like we've got something here." He turned slightly. "Now, where's it pointing? What's in there, ma'am?"

"My bedroom."

Following his erect dowser, Astro picked up his toolbox and moved officiously to the bedroom. Barbara followed him.

"Uh-huh." Astro stopped by the bed and flipped open a sheet to display the waterbed. "And what do you call this, ma'am?"

"This? Oh, uh," Barbara twirled a strand of hair, head tilted, "I didn't know waterbeds were covered by–"

"Well, they are." Astro pulled a pen and notebook out of his pockets. "You'll have to get this licensed–"

Barbara sidled over to him and stroked his earlobe. "Sir," she breathed, "are you sure there's nothing I could do . . . ?"

"It's more than my job's worth, I'm afraid, ma'am." He handed her a piece of paper.

She ignored it and reached out to touch his penis.

"Please, ma'am," Astro said, "don't play with the equipment."

Barbara let her nightie fall to the ground.

"Ma'am," he warned, "you're not making this any easier."

"Look," she whispered, "why don't you stay for a drink? Show me how your equipment works. My boyfriend's in DC. He won't be back for a couple of weeks."

He looked her up and down. "That's against regulations. Anyhow, I'm sure your boyfriend wouldn't be very happy about it."

"Aw, he'll never find out. He works with plants. Believes everything I tell him."

"I've met some pretty intelligent people who work with plants, you know."

"Then you haven't met my boyfriend," she winked. "Tell you what, I'll oil your equipment for free."

Astro thought about it. He put his toolbox down. "Fair enough."

She grabbed his equipment and rubbed it against herself a few times.

"That's strange," she said. "I can't find the oil button. You're an engineer. Could you find it for me?"

"I'll try my best," he shrugged. "No guarantees, though."

The next day, refreshed and serene, Barbara donned her brightest purple wrapper for her last trip to the office, leaving a snoring Astro in bed.

Perhaps, she thought, *I'll experiment with some bright pink lipstick.* She applied it. She smiled. Then she relaxed the smile and frowned. She mouthed a few words to herself and then giggled. She guffawed and, just as suddenly, gasped. Yes, the lipstick seemed to do its job–a fine accompaniment for the spectrum of emotions she might have to deploy.

Although she only had one more day left at Drop of Life, her heart felt light and open. She sauntered into the office, banging the door behind her.

Gums poked her head around the corner. "Hey, Bar! Awesome day, eh?"

"Not bad," Barbara replied, using one of her father's most irritating sayings. "Not bad at all." She flung her Norwegian cloak on the hook, on top of Brad's grey scarf. "Could be worse."

She wondered how her parents were faring with the neighbours, with one terrorist and one executioner in the family. She pictured them answering the questions with numbers.

"How's Mary?"

"Seven dead, by last count."

"And Barbara?"

"Over forty. Very determined young lady, our Barbara. Very determined, indeed."

She marched up to the second floor, where she barked a greeting to Brad. He jumped out of his chair. As far as she remembered.

She bowed a Namaste to Jane.

As she rounded the staircase to the third floor, she sang out a "Hiya, hon!" to Mimi before Mimi had a chance to do it first.

Then she entered her office turret. She began packing her belongings. As she looked at her stapler, she realized how much she would miss Brad, remembering how much his help had allowed her to achieve, recalling his devotion to her. A small note from him requested her sister's number. Such an obsessive man–probably planning to audit Mary. She sat back and reminisced over their days of victory. Yes, she would certainly miss him.

Even lions must live in a pride.

She decided to give him the stapler as a gift, and to sign him up for a drama class.

She set the stapler aside, wrapped up her pots of aromatic oils, a tennis ball–shaped figurine of a fertility goddess and Mimi's halogen lamp. An image of Mimi under a tanning bed flashed into her mind. *Without this woman's dogged determination,* Barbara thought. *Without her* . . . She set aside a ticket to a sweat lodge for Mimi. Perhaps the moisture would help the peeling somewhat.

She then hunted around for presents for Gums and Jane. She had no trouble finding a gift for Gums: a chit for five unused sessions with her therapist. In that time, the therapist would be able to enlighten Gums as to the unfortunate reality of existence, a realm far removed from the fog of her pathological optimism.

Barbara could not think of anything to give Jane, yet she did not want the effigy's dementia to erase her from memory. She hunted in her handbag for a photograph of herself. Perhaps it would come in useful in the future. She found a particularly flattering one of her wearing her winter harem pants and a turban. She set it aside.

Trying to stave off an increasingly gloomy mood, Barbara turned on her computer to check the latest headlines.

She read about Kolo giving TransAqua the rights to the Benue River. The country was in turmoil, with the army and police force under siege. There was a picture of the minister of finance shaking hands with the sultan of Sokoto, and another of Brigadier Jamal Abdullah, the newly appointed head of the armed forces, meeting with the American ambassador. Kolo was as good as dead. Sadly, she realized that whoever ascended to power might continue the work Kolo had started, pleasing the superpowers while pocketing the profits.

Barbara sighed. She had failed to protect the one person who could have brought permanent change to Nigeria.

Even though TransAqua's shares had crashed, it had laid off most of its staff and it had been subjected to audit and public ridicule, it would simply re-incorporate under another name, and its stock prices would rise again.

Barbara sat still, imagining Femi's disappointment in her. She once thought herself equal to the waterfall, yet all her might had produced nothing. She had propelled nothing forward; she had pushed nothing aside. She could not help anyone, even while working at maximum capacity.

She took an amaranth flour muffin from her bag and nibbled it while she stared aimlessly at her computer screen. But then something caught her eye.

It was a photograph of Aminah, with hundreds of thousands

of people behind her, some carrying palm tree branches, others with their fists in the air. Even the soldiers surrounding the crowds gazed at her, smiling. She wore a giant wrapper with Femi's face stamped all over it. *Well,* Barbara thought, *maybe I'm just a cascade. Because this.*

This is the waterfall.

Barbara felt the joy of accomplishment, even if by proxy.

Finally, like the leaf, Barbara sensed it was time to let go.

She clicked on to another website. Not this time, about Nigeria, but about water.

And there it sat–an assault to logic, a scandal to propriety. In ferocious, resplendent colour, a large ship pulled a bright white iceberg out of the Arctic's sapphire blue waters. Once melted, the water was destined for TransAqua's new incarnation, Globo-Elixir.

Having been violated for its oil and mineral wealth, the Canadian Arctic was now being dismantled for its water, piece by piece–an iceberg here, a snowbank there–with little thought as to the long-term consequence of this project.

Barbara thought of the Inuit of Canada's north. She pictured herself in moose hide, chanting songs in an igloo as they stroked polar bears by their fire and penguins sniffed through the garbage. She thought of her waterbed and wondered if they would mind her building a rectangular igloo.

It would prove to be interesting legal ground–whether ice could be considered part of international waters, as Globo-Elixir claimed, or a piece of land, a territory or region, as Canada proposed.

On a whim, Barbara searched for organizations involved in iceberg preservation.

She wanted to stay on in Canada. It had elected its first openly gay prime minister, it had initiated some bold environmental protocols, and, of course, cannabis was legal. How could she return to the prehistoric posturing of the United States?

She unearthed, with difficulty, three small groups: one based in Stockholm, one in Russia and one in Washington DC. She checked the name of the DC group's director. She gasped, almost losing her balance on her kneeling chair. Norm Blacksmith–the ousted vegan director of the Association of Rare Heritage Stock and Poultry!

With this helpless, fragile entity at the helm, there was no doubt in Barbara's mind that the organization would need all the assistance she could offer. They would certainly need a satellite office in Ottawa, given that the Canadian Arctic was in the greatest danger.

She hiked up her wrapper with confidence and dialled Norm's number.

Acknowledgements

For entertainment, my father liked to hop in the car, drive to some area of Nigeria that illustrated the follies of "modernization," laugh to the point of needing supplementary oxygen, and then drive back home. As a result of these forays, our little family saw the white elephants for which the World Bank has become so justly famous.

One day, however, he took us somewhere that made him smile with delight: Kainji Dam, an eerie monster that loomed out of the landscape, a towering crucible that made me wonder if the man even slightly cared about his young family's safety.

Many years later, having little else to do but meet an urgent deadline, I wandered lonely through the Internet. Knowing that big dam projects usually produce more harm than benefit, I sought out information on Kainji. Unexpectedly, I came across an article describing its state of disrepair, sadly similar to most large dams in poorer countries. It was predicted that it would soon collapse and the rupture would kill one million people.

Given that few politicians seemed interested, I considered what to do that involved least effort. Having decided to write, I phoned in a plausible excuse to delay my deadline. ("My car won't start." "Just send an attachment then." "My computer's down." "Okay, so send a fax from the corner store." "My leg's broken.")

I had three long-suffering friends who helped thrash out ideas. Despite the fact they all complained about my neediness ("she's aged me ten years"), they were too naive to realize the benefits of caller ID. Moreover, I had the great fortune to live with the Himbeault family for five years, being fed and entertained by them–a rare generosity.

Julie Donovan offered unrivalled patience in a friendship that has lasted over two decades and provided dazzling philosophical insight, which I have claimed as my own; Kathy Himbeault, a friend of great compassion and imagination, sautéed neurons in her efforts to rework entrenched plot problems; and Bunmi Oyinsan has worried and fussed over me, while maintaining an extremely strict ITK (I Too Know) Pidgin fundamentalism, and thus will need resuscitation when she sees the changes made to her red pen scribblings.

I have never understood why writers get to rattle out their acknowledgements but anyone else, computer technicians, for example, do not get to thank God, their parents, their manicurist or cat when they've sorted out computer meltdowns. For this reason, this section is the hardest to write: a bit pompous and of necessity it excludes so many collaborators.

I'm very grateful to Critical Ms, a writing/editorial group with outstanding critiquing skills–particular mention to Kathy Himbeault, Ruth Walker, Gwynn Scheltema, Fred Ford and Sue Malarkey; as well as Dean Cooke at the Cooke Agency and

Anne Collins of Random House Canada. And all of those who inspired, amused or supported me, including Darrell MacInnis, stern critic who insisted on absolute silence, John Picton, professor emeritus at the famed School of Oriental and African Studies–an early and cherished intellectual mentor, Dr. Connie Ojiegbe, Adaoma Wosu, Ogbe Guobadia, Pier Wilkie, Margo Timm, James Esson's "any dog can do that" father, the Writers' Circle of Durham Region (WCDR), a necessary hub for writers, my parents and sister, Vivi, whose humour infuses the pages, and most particularly my brother, Nick, who has lived in Nigeria all his life and thus helped me refresh my knowledge of it, after finishing his usual "this place will kill me" diatribe.

Peter Enahoro, a journalist and satirist whose work has inspired me, proved long ago that only the strong have the capacity to laugh at themselves, and Nigerians with their incomparable sense of humour are living proof of this. No less influential is Anthony Enahoro, an elder statesman and pro-democracy activist who, even in his eighties, continues to campaign for justice regardless of personal risk.

Most importantly, I express deep gratitude to those many activists who devote their energy, hours and lives to protect the rights of the rest of us. In Nigeria, environmental campaigners, water access advocates and dam activists; in Canada, the Council of Canadians, a unique organization advocating for progressive policies on water rights, among other issues; and finally, along with many other groups, the Blue Planet Project, a global initiative securing the right to water as a public trust.

Carole Enahoro was born in London of a Nigerian father and an English mother, and grew up in Nigeria, Britain and Canada, and still shares her time among the three. With a background in art history and film, she has worked as a filmmaker, journalist and lecturer, while pursuing an abiding interest in political and social issues. She is currently pursuing doctoral studies in the UK, researching spatial practice, power and satire in Nigeria's capital. This is her first novel.